The Outcast Blade

And the world ignited behind him.

Stained-glass windows blew out. Doors blew open.

As the explosion split ancient brick walls, a thousand slates tipped from the roof. And in the after-second of silence, fire whooshed through shattered windows, carrying a scream that filled the air, followed by another, and another. Until the night echoed with a choir of pain.

Lady Giulietta crossed herself.

The dining hall stood for another second, and then one end sank through the ground into the fiery fury of wine cellars below. Flames billowed skywards as Tycho drew his sword and pushed Lady Giulietta behind him. His first thought was to protect her from attack, his second to get her and her child out of there. There was an arch with a locked door next to the grain store. He needed to find _____ a key.

"That was _____

"How did _____ Giulietta asked, looking at Tyc _____ as somehow tied to a quilt that _____ in the first place. It wa _____

I s _____

By Jon Courtenay Grimwood

The Assassini
The Fallen Blade
The Outcast Blade
The Exiled Blade

The Outcast Blade

Act Two of THE ASSASSINI

Jon Courtenay
GRIMWOOD

www.orbitbooks.net

ORBIT

First published in Great Britain in 2012 by Orbit

Copyright © 2012 by JonCGLimited

Excerpt from *The Folly of the World* by Jesse Bullington
Copyright © 2012 by Jesse Bullington

The moral right of the author has been asserted.

Map copyright © Viv Mullett

*All characters and events in this publication, other than
those clearly in the public domain, are fictitious
and any resemblance to real persons,
living or dead, is purely coincidental.*

All rights reserved.
No part of this publication may be reproduced,
stored in a retrieval system, or transmitted, in any
form or by any means, without the prior
permission in writing of the publisher, nor be
otherwise circulated in any form of binding or
cover other than that in which it is published and
without a similar condition including this
condition being imposed on the subsequent purchaser.

A CIP catalogue record for this book
is available from the British Library.

ISBN 978-1-84149-848-5

Typeset in Adobe Garamond by Palimpsest Book Production Limited,
Falkirk, Stirlingshire
Printed and bound by CPI Group (UK) Ltd, Croydon, CR0 4YY

Papers used by Orbit are from well-managed forests
and other responsible sources

MIX
Paper from
responsible sources
FSC
www.fsc.org FSC® C104740

Orbit
An imprint of
Little, Brown Book Group
100 Victoria Embankment
London EC4Y 0DY

An Hachette UK Company
www.hachette.co.uk

www.orbitbooks.net

For Jams, who got lost in the Venetian backstreets for four hours and passed the same building five times because the city kept remaking itself around him; and Eun-jeong, who took me round a palace in Seoul. Thank you . . .

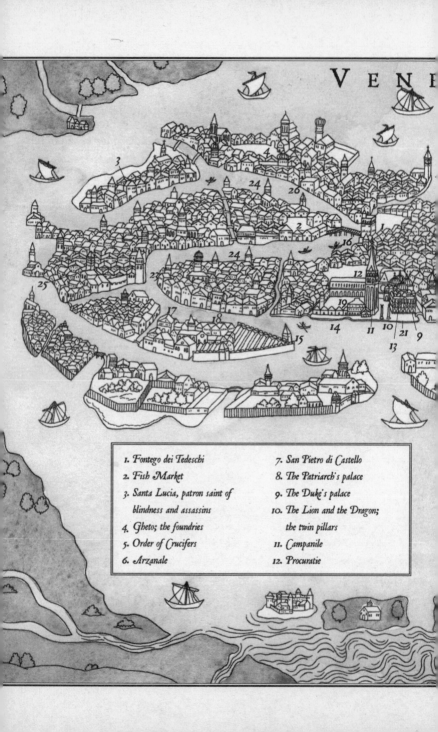

VENE

1. Fontego dei Tedeschi
2. Fish Market
3. Santa Lucia, patron saint of
   blindness and assassins
4. Gheto; the foundries
5. Order of Crucifers
6. Arzanale

7. San Pietro di Castello
8. The Patriarch's palace
9. The Duke's palace
10. The Lion and the Dragon;
    the twin pillars
11. Campanile
12. Procuratie

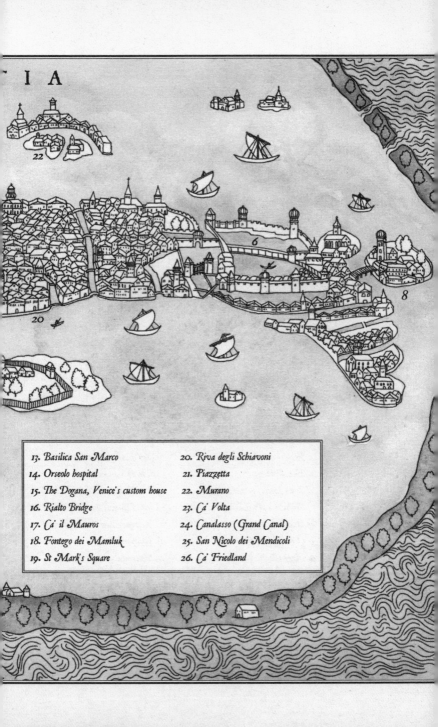

I A

22

6

8

20

13. Basilica San Marco

14. Orseolo hospital

15. The Dogana, Venice's custom house

16. Rialto Bridge

17. Ca' il Mauros

18. Fontego dei Mamluk

19. St Mark's Square

20. Riva degli Schiavoni

21. Piazzetta

22. Murano

23. Ca' Volta

24. Canalasso (Grand Canal)

25. San Nicolo dei Mendicoli

26. Ca' Friedland

The Millioni family tree

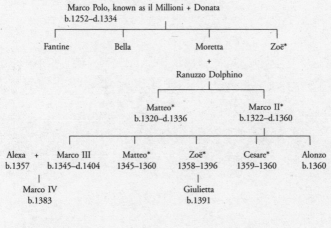

Marco Polo, known as il Millioni + Donata
b.1252–d.1334

Fantine   Bella   Moretta   Zoë*

+

Ranuzzo Dolphino

Matteo*
b.1320–d.1336

Marco II*
b.1322–d.1360

Alexa + Marco III   Matteo*   Zoë*   Cesare*   Alonzo
b.1357   b.1345–d.1404   1345–1360   1358–1396   1359–1360   b.1360

Marco IV
b.1383

Giulietta
b.1391

* Murdered

First Republic
1336–1348

Second Republic
1360–1362

Dramatis Personae

Tycho, a seventeen-year-old boy with strange hungers

The Millioni

Marco IV, known as Marco the Simpleton, duke of Venice and Prince of Serenissima

Lady Giulietta di Millioni, his seventeen-year-old cousin, widow of Prince Leopold, mother of Leo. Ran away from Venice and is now returning

Duchess Alexa, the late duke's widow, mother to Marco IV. A Mongol princess in her own right. She hates . . .

Prince Alonzo, Regent of Venice, who wants the throne

Lady Eleanor, Giulietta's young cousin and lady-in-waiting

Marco III, known as Marco the Just. The late lamented duke of Venice, elder brother of Alonzo, godfather of Lady Giulietta and the ghost at every feast

Members of the Venetian court

Atilo il Mauros, once adviser to the late Marco III, and head of Venice's secret assassins. Alexa's lover and long-term supporter. Engaged to Lady Desdaio, daughter of . . .

Lord Bribanzo, member of the Council of Ten, the inner council that rules Venice. One of the richest men in the city, Bribanzo sides with Alonzo

Prince Leopold zum Bas Friedland. Now dead. Until lately leader of the *krieghund*, Emperor Sigismund's werewolf shock troops. (His brother Frederick is the German emperor's only remaining son)

Dr Hightown Crow, alchemist, astrologer and anatomist to the duke. Using a goose quill he inseminated Giulietta with Alonzo's seed, leaving her with child

A'rial, the Duchess Alexa's *stregoi* (her pet witch)

Atilo's household

Iacopo, Atilo's servant and member of the Assassini

Amelia, a Nubian slave and member of the Assassini

Pietro, an ex-street child, Assassini apprentice and sister to Rosalyn (now dead and buried on Pauper Island)

The customs office

Lord Roderigo, Captain of the Dogana, Alonzo's ally

Temujin, his half-Mongol sergeant

The Three Emperors

Sigismund, Holy Roman Emperor, King of Germany, Hungary and Croatia. Wants to add Lombardy and Venice to that list

John V Palaiologos, the Basilius, ruler of the Byzantine Empire (known as the Eastern Roman Empire), also wants Venice. He barely admits Sigismund is an emperor at all

Tamburlaine, Khan of Khans, ruler of the Mongols and newly created emperor of China. The most powerful man in the world and a distant cousin to Duchess Alexa. He regards Europe as a minor irritation

PART 1

"These violent delights have violent ends . . ."

Romeo and Juliet, William Shakespeare

Prologue
Constantinople 1408

Incense filled the air inside Hagia Sophia, the largest and most famous cathedral in the world. Beneath its huge dome, small boys scattered rose petals on thousand-year-old marble mosaics, which would need scrubbing before nightfall to remove the stain.

Ahead of the shambling figure of John V Palaiologos – God's ruler on Earth, Basilius of the Byzantine Empire – walked his cross bearer, carrying a huge crucifix with an icon of Christ in its centre. Had the crucifix been solid it would have been impossible to lift. But it was made from beaten silver, chased and fretted and hammered into shape over a light wooden frame.

Under the icon was a piece of the True Cross. There were a thousand such relics but the patriarch of Constantinople had judged this one real.

As the emperor approached, his courtiers fell to their knees.

The mind of the Basilius was old and as tired as his body; and his body ached on waking and hurt worse in the approach to sleep. He might claim his growing hatred of his empire came from a simple wish to find himself in the company of God. In his heart the Basilius knew he was tired of life.

He'd inherited the throne at nine, his German mother having pawned the imperial crown for 300,000 Venetian ducats two years before he was born. It was a miracle he survived his childhood. That only happened because he was more valuable alive than dead. At the age of seventeen – exhausted by uncertainty – he ordered the slaughter of both Regents, their staff and households. The coup was quick, brutal and performed by a tiny group of the imperial guard who'd grown disgusted by the empire's chaos.

A revolt by the cousin of a Regent ended brutally. The army was purged of untrustworthy generals and the civil service reordered. Wealth found in the strongrooms of the Regents and the treasury master was returned to the treasury and taxes lowered. An action that brought John V Palaiologos the loyalty of Constantinople's merchants. It was the first time taxes had been lowered in fifty years.

The new emperor watched and learnt. He identified his friends and his enemies, and those who pretended for whatever reason to be one when they were really the other. At the age of twenty-two, he slaughtered the son of the Seljuk king at Cinbi, after Prince Suleyman and thirty-nine of his father's knights crossed the Hellespont in boats hired from Genoese merchants.

Having ordered the massacre of every family from Genoa in Constantinople, the Basilius led an attack on Sulyman's father. The loss of lands, his sons and most of his army rendered King Orthan so desolate he sued for peace.

In the years that followed, the Byzantine emperor reconquered provinces thought lost for ever. Of course, if the Mamluks had not hated the Seljuks the outcome might have been different. Those were thoughts wise historians kept to themselves.

And so courtiers wearing armour whose design was a thousand years old knelt on mosaics even older and averted their eyes.

"Andronikos . . ."

The emperor's mage stepped forward.

4

He was tall and thin, wearing simple robes that managed to look more striking than the gold-embroidered tunics of the governors, independent princes and courtiers around him. Many men in the East claimed to be mages. A few were charlatans, most could do simple magic, produce fire, read minds, rid houses of troublesome spirits. A handful could see the future as it would happen. Andronikos could see all futures, weigh them and make fate's dice fall one way rather than another. The man had ridden at the emperor's right hand the night they killed Suleyman Pasha and changed the tides of history.

"Majesty." Bowing low, Andronikos adjusted his robe and struggled to stand. His bones were old and enough of them had been broken in battle to carry their ache into later life.

"What have you learnt?"

The mage ran through the city's rumours, the assassinations and assignations, secret raptures and rapines. The Mithraic cult was gaining in strength. A slaughtered white bull had been found by the river. A Seljuk princeling had arrived in the city planning the Basilius's death. There was always a Seljuk princeling planning the emperor's death and the emperor suspected the Seljuk king used it as a cynical way to rid himself of troublesome younger sons.

"And Venice?"

Andronikos drew together his fingers.

"No need for masking spells. No one will hear us." The emperor was right, of course. The chanting of plainsong and rustle of robes, the squeak of fans swinging overhead and the gasps of the slaves who dragged the ropes that worked the fans created their own masking spell.

"Good news and bad news . . ."

The emperor waited. He was used to men starting sentences and then hesitating to check if he wished to listen to the rest. Andronikos should be above such behaviour; but the emperor had once jailed him for speaking out of turn. Jailed him, confiscated his estates, co-opted his eldest son into the army and sent the boy south to die. The mage had been more cautious in his opinions since.

After a life of simplifying politics and hardening his empire's boundaries, increasing trade, securing alliances and forging treaties that would last – all the while pretending to be interested only in God – John V Palaiologos had let the Mamluks transport a caged demon through his lands a year ago in return for the renewal of a minor treaty.

Wolf-grey-haired and white-skinned, the demon was kept captive in a cage with silver bars. That it could travel only at night should have warned him this was a bad idea. And though the emperor wouldn't dream of admitting it, Andronikos had been right to advise against the Mamluk plan.

Only the fear of standing before the recording angel and being called to account for his sins stopped the Basilius from having the sycophants who'd agreed it was a good idea slaughtered.

Sacred checks and balances, his confessor said. They kept the scales almost level. If the world lost those it would be unbearable.

"Lady Giulietta . . ." Andronikos's voice was carefully neutral.

These days the emperor called his granddaughters by their mothers' names and his great-grandsons by the names of their fathers. Occasionally he called his librarian by the name of a slave who'd filled the post thirty years before. That was one advantage of surrounding himself with old men like Andronikos. The Basilius knew who they were. His mind would never decide they were someone else. He fought to remember the girl and failed.

"Well?" he said crossly.

"The late duke of Venice's niece."

"Zoë's daughter? How is Zoë?"

"She was murdered by Republicans, majesty."

"Ahh . . ." The emperor considered this. Decided he probably remembered that. And remembered something else. "Zoë married one of my nephews? Is that right?"

"Not a happy marriage."

"Ahh . . . What about this daughter?"

"Her husband died in the recent battle off Cyprus."

"We've discussed this, haven't we?"

The mage nodded and kept his face impassive. "There's a child," he added. "And rumours about its parentage. We've touched on that, too."

"The husband recognised it?"

"Yes, majesty. He named it his heir."

"That's all that matters." Enough noble families had used natural sons or adopted children to continue their lines; it was an ancient Roman tradition, and since the Basilius was in a direct line from the Caesars, why would Andronikos expect him to be troubled by that? "Cut to the core."

The emperor's mage took a deep breath.

"Her husband was Sigismund's favourite bastard . . ."

Sigismund was the German emperor . . . Well, technically he was the Holy Roman Emperor, King of Germany, Hungary and half a dozen other places of equal unimportance.

"And this matters why?"

"Majesty. The new duke of Venice shows no interest in women. We already know his mother's threatened to have her co-Regent poisoned if he marries and produces an heir. So, all Prince Alonzo can have is bastards, and those can't inherit the throne."

"Why have we not discussed this?"

"We've touched on it," said Andronikos, hurriedly adding, "but not in any depth. All this only matters now because Sigismund will offer Venice another of his bastards for Giulietta to marry."

"Sigismund wants Venice?"

"Majesty, he's always wanted it."

"You know what I mean. I mean, he intends to have it? By

marrying his natural son to Zoë's daughter, then claiming Venice in the name of Leopold's legitimate son when the time comes?"

"Yes, majesty."

The emperor sighed.

"Shall I order the child killed?"

"Checks and balances, Andronikos. I'm too close to meeting God to want another infant on my conscience. And killing its mother won't work either. We need a counter-proposal. A husband more suited to our needs."

"Indeed, majesty."

The emperor thought about it while plainsong halted and restarted, and fans swirled warm air down from the domed ceiling to be cooled by huge unglazed jars that wept bead-like tears. Around him, his entourage talked quietly, having fought hard for positions that required only their ability to show reverence. The emperor knew how ridiculous that was, and suspected Lord Andronikos knew how ridiculous that was, and imagined his courtiers knew also. They still fought for the positions, though. The empire had been like this for hundreds of years.

"Where's Nikolaos?"

"On his estate, majesty. Under guard."

"He is as he was?"

Born of a freed Varangian slave, Nikolaos was the handsomest of his sons, with blond hair and broad shoulders that might have come from a statue of Hercules. The youth was virile and charming, beautifully mannered to his women in public but savage in private. It was a woman who saw him exiled. A duke's daughter, she'd been beautiful, talented, intelligent and obstinate in the face of his wooing.

A perfect target for his rage.

"Majesty, this might not be wise."

"Giulietta's the daughter of a Byzantine prince, her mother is the granddaughter of another, our blood flows in her veins, not Sigismund's. We'll send them Nikolaos. If Venice's spies are any good they'll know what they're getting. Tell Duke Tiersius we're exiling Nikolaos after all."

"He wanted Nikolaos dead."

"Death. Venice. It's all the same."

1

Venice

On the first of May, in the same hour of the night that the Basilius spoke to Lord Andronikos about the situation in Venice, the flagship of the Venetian fleet put into its home lagoon, its rails smashed by storms and its sides scarred by battle.

The *San Marco* was the fleet's only survivor.

On board was the *demon* the Basilius regretted letting pass through his empire. Called Tycho, he hated being on board for three reasons: 1) being over deep water made him feel weak and sick, 2) he could not shake his nightmares from the battle, 3) the girl he loved had locked herself in her cabin and refused to come out. Not what he'd intended when he revealed his true nature to her.

"By yourself again, Sir Tycho?"

The *demon* scowled.

Arno Dolphini was one of the few crew members unimpressed by Tycho's part in their recent victory. Mind you, even those who *were* impressed believed him recklessly ambitious. Why else would he risk courting a Millioni princess so soon after the death of her husband?

Except I loved her first, he thought bitterly.

And she'd been the one to seek him out on the night deck of the *San Marco*, dressed as no newly widowed woman should be in a thin undergown made clingy with sweat. The mere memory made Tycho's throat tighten. "My lady is upset."

"Screaming baby and dead husband? I'm not surprised. Still, no doubt her family will choose her another prince soon enough."

Curling his hands into fists, Tycho stared at lights on the shore, willing himself not to hit Dolphini. The young man was a bully and an idiot, the spoilt heir to a massive fortune. The real reason he wanted to rip out Dolphini's throat, however, was that he spoke the truth.

"Come on. You're missing the fun."

On arrival, the *San Marco* had been ordered to join the quarantine line like any other newly arrived ship. Lord Atilo, its captain, was not the kind of man who felt he should be made to wait.

"You dare tell me what to do?"

Don't show panic, Tycho thought.

But the messenger was already measuring his drop to the dark lagoon behind. If he reached the rails he might be able to jump before Atilo struck. Only then the Regent would have him hung for cowardice. The look on the messenger's face said he knew he was doomed either way.

"Those are the Council's orders, my lord."

"Damn the Council. I'm coming ashore."

"You'll be arrested."

Even Lord Atilo looked shocked at that.

"I've just sunk the Mamluk fleet. Saved Cyprus from capture and protected our trade routes. Do you really think anyone would dare?"

"My lord. Your orders . . ."

Atilo il Mauros wanted to say that no one gave him orders. Except that wasn't true: Duchess Alexa did; her son would have done had he not been simple. And Prince Alonzo, the Regent of Venice, also had the right.

"I've fought storms for three days. My ship is battered. My crew are exhausted. I did this to bring you news of our victory."

"We have the news already, my lord."

"How could you possibly . . . ?"

"It was announced last Sunday."

So cross was the old Moorish admiral that he growled in fury. It would have been funny if he hadn't also fallen into a fighter's stance the messenger was too ignorant to recognise. Atilo's temper was about to boil over. When it did he would strike for the man's heart.

The night air would fill with the stink of blood, and Tycho would have to fight his hungers. He was exhausted, sick from days at sea, and uncertain he could stop himself from becoming the beast he was on the night of the battle.

"Let it go," he said.

Atilo swung round, seeking his one-time slave. *"You dare question my authority?"* The messenger was forgotten and all Atilo's attention on the perceived insult. When Atilo gripped the handle of his sword, Tycho wondered how far the old man would take this . . .

"There will be no fighting."

The voice from behind Tycho sounded less confident than its command suggested. And the red-headed girl who pushed past as if he didn't exist was shaking with anger, nerves or tiredness. At Lady Giulietta's breast was an infant, half covered by a Maltese shawl.

"Tell the mainland I accept quarantine. I do not, however, accept being confined to this ship with idiots. The Council of Ten will find another solution. You may use my name when you send this."

The messenger bowed low.

And Giulietta di Millioni, Prince Leopold's widow and mother to his heir, turned for her cabin secure in the knowledge she would be obeyed. The Millioni were good at that. Assuming others would carry out their wishes without question.

So good, that they always were.

Tycho slept through the next day in the darkened hold of the *San Marco* on earth he'd brought aboard at Ragusa, a port on the Adriatic coast. The sun hurt him, being above water made him sick, daylight blinded him. His illness was well known.

The sailors avoided him. Everyone avoided him.

Atilo's officers were careful to give him the courtesy his recent knighthood demanded. And his friendship with Lady Giulietta, complex as it was, made them more uneasy still. Only Lord Atilo's betrothed, Lady Desdaio Bribanzo, came and went as if nothing had changed.

"Tycho . . ."

Rolling to his feet, Tycho only realised a dagger was in his hand when Desdaio said, "Is that really necessary?"

"My apologies, lady."

She looked doubtfully round the hold.

His walls were crates, his floor space made by pushing those crates apart. A square of old canvas over the top kept out any sunlight that might filter through a hatch above. His thin mattress rested on red earth.

"It makes me feel less sick."

"You always know what I'm thinking."

"Some days I know what everyone thinks. Your thoughts are usually more pleasant." He watched her blush in the gloom, turning aside to hide her embarrassment at his words.

"I came to say Lady Giulietta's message has been answered."

"My lord Atilo sent you?"

Desdaio almost lied out of loyalty to the man she was to marry, then shook her head because honesty was in her nature. "I thought you'd want . . ."

A snort above made them both look up.

Giulietta stood at the top of the steps, with Leo asleep in her arms and a starlit sky behind her. She wore a scowl, and a black gown bought in Ragusa. Both scowl and gown had become armour in recent days.

Tycho only just caught up with her.

"What did you come to tell me?" he asked.

"That Lord Roderigo is here."

"Captain Roderigo?"

"He's a baron now. My uncle's doing. I'm surprised your little heiress didn't tell you that. You seemed to be having a friendly chat."

"It's not . . ."

"Like that? Isn't it? What is it like then?"

"My lady, we need to talk."

"We have nothing to talk about. You should know I plan to leave Venice the moment I get the Council's permission."

"Where will you go?"

"What business is that of yours?"

"I simply wondered, my lady."

"To my mother's estate at Alta Mofacon. Leo will be happy there and I'll be away from this sewer of a city."

And from you. Tycho knew what she was saying.

Across his shoulder Lord Roderigo wore a sash with the lion of St Mark, signifying he was here in his capacity of head of the Venetian customs service.

"My lord," Lady Giulietta said.

Roderigo bowed. Looking beyond her, he let his jaw drop at the richness of Tycho's doublet. Although what stunned him was the half-sword at Tycho's hip.

"He's been knighted." Atilo's tone was disapproving.

"For his part in the battle?"

"Before that."

"He was a *slave*."

"Indeed," Atilo said.

"I was knighted for what I *would* do." Tycho's smile was bland. "King Janus believed I might be of some small help."

"And were you?"

"He won the battle for us," Giulietta said flatly.

"How did he do that, my lady?"

"No idea. We were sent below."

Lord Roderigo believed he saw a boy pretending to be a man. An ex-slave pretending to be a knight. Tycho was happy to let him think this since Roderigo was Prince Alonzo's man and it was Alonzo who had Tycho sold into slavery.

"When do we go ashore?"

"Who said anything about going ashore?"

"You're here. I doubt you'd come in person if we had to remain aboard. So, since you're here, we're going ashore."

Roderigo's stare was thoughtful. "Food has been landed at San Lazar," he admitted. "Also wine, ale and new clothes. Because of Lord Atilo's great victory the Council have shortened quarantine to ten days."

That was an impressive concession.

"But it's a leper island," Desdaio protested.

"My lady, no leper has been there in fifty years. Nowadays, the White Crucifers treat those wounded in battle. Since there have been no battles in Venice for twenty years," Roderigo shrugged, "they have time enough for prayer. My lady Giulietta, if you'll take the first boat . . .?"

She smiled graciously.

"And, Sir Tycho, if you'll travel with her?"

Lady Giulietta's smile turned to a scowl.

Stone steps disappearing under dark waves were a common occurrence in Venice, where such runs helped adjust for tidal differences. Most of the water steps in the island city were algae-green and slippery underfoot. The steps up to the *fondamenta*, the stone-lined embankment at San Lazar, had been scrubbed so clean on the Prior's orders that the chisel marks of the original masons could be seen.

"My lady." The Prior bowed.

"Lord Prior."

His knights wore mail under their cloaks and carried swords. Their mail looked unscrubbed and almost rusty, but the recently sharpened edges of their blades glittered in the torchlight.

"This is an unusual honour, my lady."

Giulietta's mouth twisted and she was about to say something rude when Tycho stepped forward. "I'm Sir Tycho."

The Prior stared doubtfully.

"Lord Atilo will be here soon." Tycho still found it hard not to say *my master*. Although that relationship was done and its ashes sour in both their mouths. "He presents his compliments, and thanks you for your hospitality. In particular, the hospitality you extend to Lady Giulietta and Lady Desdaio. He knows . . ."

"It's true, Desdaio Bribanzo is with him?"

"Yes," Tycho said.

The Prior pursed his lips. "They will be given separate quarters."

"I doubt she'd have it any other way," Giulietta said tartly. "And if she did I doubt my lord Atilo would allow it."

The Prior kept his disapproval to himself after that.

2

White Crucifers dedicated themselves to poverty, chastity and protecting pilgrims on the journey to Jerusalem. They avoided the company of women whenever possible, and it had been over a century since the last one set foot on St Lazar. It being well known that the female sex carried the taint of sin. And so, five hundred young monks prayed, worked their gardens, practised their weapons and did their best to ignore Lady Giulietta's presence on their island.

Sitting in her room, Giulietta twisted the ring Leopold had put on her finger until her finger was raw enough to hurt. She'd like to be able to ignore herself too. And how could she disagree with the Crucifers' opinion?

She wasn't sure which disgusted her more.

What she'd let Tycho do on the deck of the *San Marco*. Or that she'd sought him out so soon after Leopold's death. She loved her husband. Leopold was a good man.

Had been a good man.

When she was at her most desolate, scared of being recaptured and already pregnant, Leopold zum Friedland found her on the

18

quayside after she'd been turned away from the patriarch's palace. He reduced her to tears with kindness.

Something she didn't expect from men.

It was a strange love; but no one had a fiercer friend, and he married her for all he never tried to take her to his bed. He stood father to her child. He died so she could live. Tears backed up in Giulietta's eyes.

Leopold made her feel safe

And Tycho . . . ?

She swallowed hard.

If she felt guilty it was Tycho's fault.

On the deck of the *San Marco* he'd taken advantage of her sadness, and then told her terrible lies. He'd used what happened eighteen months before, when they first met in the cathedral, when he took the blade from her hands . . . He should have let her kill herself; before she met Leopold, before she had Leo, before she met him.

She hated him for it.

Lady Giulietta repeated that to herself.

He was nothing. Merely an ex-slave for all he had the face of an angel and a fear of God's light more suited to a creature from hell. Her nurse had warned her about men like him.

Staring across the lagoon to Venice beyond, Giulietta came to a decision and made herself a promise. It didn't matter that he made her feel . . . Lady Giulietta refused to put how Tycho made her feel into words. She would ignore him from now on. And she would behave like the Millioni princess she was.

Leopold's widow.

She had responsibilities, a child and a reputation to protect. How dare he assume there was room in her life for him?

Princes ruled countries according to the rule of God. So Lady Giulietta had been taught. Within these countries their word was the law, quite literally. But there were several Orders of Knighthood where the Grand Prior's word was law within the Order, wherever the knights might be. She should have realised the Prior would want a chance to impress the princess he'd taken in so unwillingly.

"Must I . . .?"

Lord Atilo smiled. "My lady. It would be rude not to."

"God forbid . . ."

Trestle tables were laid in the monastery hall.

The Prior sat himself in the middle of the top table with her to his right, her baby in a basket at her feet. Atilo sat to the Prior's left. Next to Atilo sat Desdaio, with Tycho on her far side.

The Under Prior took Atilo's place on Giulietta's side of the table, meaning Lord Roderigo had the seat beyond. In placing his deputy above the captain of the Venetian customs, the Prior was stressing his Order's independence.

But for all the Prior's manners were questionable his feast was magnificent. Barolo wine darker than velvet. Whites from Germany made sweet by letting their grapes rot on the vine. The Order brewed its own ale and provided barrels of it. The food was equally impressive. Fresh bread from the kitchens, pickles and salted vegetables from the gardens, dried mutton soaked until it was salt free, and skimmed until the fat was gone. Carp from the pond, fried anchovies from the lagoon and grilled eel with fennel.

Everyone ate on huge rounds of stale bread.

Those at the high table left theirs to be cleared away. Those on the lower tables ate their rounds softened with the juices from the meat. After the pies came puddings, mounds of sweetmeats and candied fruit, fresh dates and plums. Wine and ale flowed so freely a glass only had to be a little empty to be filled.

"You don't like wine?"

Tycho shook his head at Desdaio's question. He'd grown sick

of wine that Easter, when he had to drink his way from tavern to tavern on a trail that led him to Alexa and Alonzo. He failed the task they set.

The memory of being ordered to kill Prince Leopold made Tycho glance along the table towards Lady Giulietta. So he caught the moment a man appeared in a doorway beyond. Temujin was Roderigo's sergeant, and the blood between the sergeant and Tycho bad enough for each to want the other dead.

Since Temujin had not arrived with Roderigo he had to be newly landed. A supposition strengthened when Lord Roderigo pushed back his chair, muttered some excuse to the Under Prior, finished his wine in a single gulp and headed for the exit. At the doorway, Roderigo turned back and saw Tycho watching. His expression was unreadable.

Returning his attention to Desdaio, Tycho froze.

"You're staring," she protested.

How could he not? Her face had become translucent, and, beneath it, bone glistened yellow. Her eyes, famous for their beauty, were empty hollows. *The skull beneath the skin . . .*

Death stared at him from her face.

"Tycho . . . What's wrong?"

For a second he felt like a man drowning. Without asking, he downed her wine and stared around him, shocked by the skulls staring back. Not just the high table but row upon row of Crucifer knights with skeleton faces. Their flesh was there. But death showed beneath. "Leave here," he told Desdaio. She would have replied but he was already gone. Giulietta blinked, finding Tycho beside her.

"How did you . . . ?"

"No time." Jerking Leo from his cradle, Tycho grabbed Giulietta's wrist and dragged her upright, sending her chair tumbling backwards. The clatter halted conversation around them. "Move."

"Give me Leo . . ."

21

"You have to come with me."

"*Tycho, give me my son.*"

"You want him to die?"

A few of the more observant Crucifers on the lower tables had their bodies angled to show they knew something was wrong without knowing what.

"Is there a problem?" the Prior demanded.

"Yes," Tycho said.

"I was talking to Lady Giulietta."

"I wasn't." Tycho sped Giulietta towards the door, then hurried her into a wide courtyard, only stopping when he reached a grain store on the other side. When he handed Leo back, the baby's face was rosy, its laugh gurgling.

"Stay here . . ."

"Tycho, you can't . . ."

"Or die." He left the choice to her.

A few seconds later, he reappeared with Atilo and Lady Desdaio, dragging the young woman and elderly Moor at blurring speed across the courtyard. Only releasing their wrists when they reached Giulietta.

"What the hell . . .?" Atilo demanded.

And the world ignited behind him.

Stained-glass windows blew out. Doors blew open.

As the explosion split ancient brick walls, a thousand slates tipped from the roof. And in the after-second of silence, fire whooshed through shattered windows, carrying a scream that filled the air, followed by another, and another. Until the night echoed with a choir of pain.

Lady Giulietta crossed herself.

The dining hall stood for another second, and then one end sank through the ground into the fiery fury of wine cellars below. Flames billowed skywards as Tycho drew his sword and pushed Lady Giulietta behind him. His first thought was to protect her from attack, his second to get her and her child out of there.

There was an arch with a locked door next to the grain store. He needed to find someone still alive who had a key.

"That was gunpowder," Atilo growled.

"How did you know we were in danger?" Giulietta asked, looking at him strangely. As if his saving her was somehow tied to a guilt that involved trying to blow her up in the first place. It was obvious she trusted him even less than she had.

I saw death in your face.

Roderigo's sergeant appeared in the doorway and I saw death in your face and in the face of your child and all those sitting around you.

"I just did," Tycho said.

His answer did nothing to reassure her.

Tycho looked for wounded survivors from the hall and realised smoke would kill any who survived the fire and explosion. Oily billows filled the air around them with the stink of charring meat and burning brick dust.

"Dead gods, my lady . . ." The voice from the arch that had been locked was loud. Lord Roderigo bowed to Giulietta, nodded to Atilo il Mauros and Desdaio, and ignored Tycho altogether. "Are you safe?"

Giulietta nodded.

"Then we must get you away from here."

"She goes nowhere with you."

Roderigo's eyes narrowed. Although Tycho was the only one with night sight to see it happen. The man's blade was half out of its scabbard before Atilo stepped in front of him. "Put back your sword."

Lord Roderigo shook his head.

"If you don't," Atilo said flatly, "Tycho will kill you."

"I'll take my chances."

"You will not," Lady Giulietta said. "At least, not until the Regent and my aunt have asked how you knew to leave the banquet at that point. And how Sir Tycho knew the hall was about to explode. After that you're free to kill each other at will."

3

The palace of the Millioni was the grandest in Europe.

A confection of cream and pink supported on an elegant
colonnade of marble, and positioned alongside the open expanse
of lagoon, Ca' Ducale was built from bits of other buildings
stolen from all over the Mediterranean. In that fact could be read
the entire history of Duchess Alexa's adopted city.

Her bedchamber looked out from the second floor in a suite
of family rooms that housed her son Marco, the Regent Alonzo,
and Lady Eleanor, who'd been Giulietta's lady-in-waiting until
Giulietta went missing.

The room Alexa liked most was a floor above.

The blue study was where she retired to think or work the
quiet magic her son's subjects whispered she practised without
really knowing whether they believed it or not. They were right
to whisper it. Saying it aloud would have brought the Council
of Ten down on them.

Scowling at what she'd just seen, Alexa brushed her fingers
across the water filling a jade bowl and fractured the picture of
the still-burning monastery into a swirl of colour that faded like
endlessly diluted ink.

She'd seen enough.

Her scrying bowl was mutton-fat jade. It was older than the celestial empire of China itself and had arrived from Timur the Great – whom some called Tamburlaine – a few months earlier in reply to one of her reports. That the khan of khans sent such a present showed unusual, indeed worrying, respect on his part. Either that or an acute understanding of how difficult her position as Duke Marco's mother was.

The Khan's other present lay curled around her feet.

The lizard's tongue was purple and its eyes bright yellow, with black pupils that narrowed against the light. Its scales were tiny and iridescent. The frill around its neck expanded if the creature grew cross. The frill felt softly spiky to the touch, as if held up by boiled fish bones. Alexa had been shocked when the creature first unfolded fragile wings. *They're common in my country* . . .

Her lie had been instinctive.

I couldn't believe you didn't have them here.

How could she tell her ladies-in-waiting she'd thought Chinese winged lizards a myth? The dragonet was unhappy to be woken before dawn, and its yellow gaze baleful enough to make her smile. Half an hour later, she'd just enticed it on to her lap when guards came to attention outside her door and someone knocked. News of the explosion at St Lazar presumably.

She was surprised it took that long.

The eleventh of May in the fourth year of his reign was not one of her son's better days. Duke Marco sprawled on his throne like an ungainly spider, his legs over the arms on one side, his head tipped back over the other, one hand scratching his groin. Marco IV had seen ghosts.

Specifically, his father's ghost.

The Council of Ten had to wait while he explained this.

His stammer making it m-m-m-minutes before they could get to the matter of real importance. The explosion at San Lazar and the close escape from death of returning runaway Lady Giulietta di Millioni, second in line to the Venetian throne.

Since the death of Marco's father, known to Venetians as Marco the Just, a label Alexa chose for him, her primary goal was to keep their idiot son alive. Her secondary one was to keep the city out of the hands of the Byzantine emperor, the German emperor, and her own brother-in-law. One of whom was undoubtedly behind this outrage. Alexa's third goal was to protect Giulietta. It came lower on her list, but she still took her niece's safety seriously.

In front of the thrones stood Lords Atilo and Roderigo. Sir Tycho stood one pace behind them. Roderigo's Mongol sergeant had been made to wait outside.

"Is G-g-giulietta safe . . .?"

"She's gone to the basilica to give thanks for her safety and to pray for the soul of her dead husband." A demand, Alexa thought sourly, impossible for the rest of them to refuse without looking impious.

Alonzo snorted.

Her brother-in-law was everything her son was not.

As much at ease among the shipbuilders of the Arzanale as among the city's merchants and nobles. In early maturity he'd been handsome, even beautiful. Now his face was soft with good living, his voice rough with wine as he ordered guards to admit the Mamluk ambassador.

"Your highness . . ."

Having bowed to the throne, and touched his fingers to his heart, his lips and his forehead in ceremonial greeting, the Mamluk avoided looking at Duke Marco again. Since his pride was notorious and his sense of the respect owed a servant of his master unbreakable, the fact he'd waited an hour in a deserted audience chamber stressed how seriously he took news of the explosions on San Lazar.

He might be presenting himself to the duke, but he was

speaking to Alonzo and Alexa first, the Council of Ten second, and those gathered at their orders third. The pretence that he addressed the twitching fool on the throne was simply that. Pretence. "My master is not responsible for this outrage."

"Do you know that for certain?" Alonzo's voice was cutting. "Does your master tell you everything he does?"

"Yes, my lord." The ambassador held Alonzo's gaze. "Everything."

The Regent of Venice considered that for a moment. When he spoke again his face was calmer and his voice mild. A stranger wouldn't have guessed he was the man who burnt the Fontego dei Mamluk only a few months earlier, nailing the chief merchant's daughter to a tree and ordering her flayed alive. Though the Mamluk ambassador was unlikely to forget it.

"We have your word on this?"

The Mamluk ambassador nodded stiffly, then added, "You have my word. The sultan did not order the explosion that destroyed the Crucifer hospital."

"It was not destroyed," Atilo said.

"Damaged then . . ." The Mamluk's curtness revealed how much he hated acknowledging Atilo, a man he despised as a turncoat to his own race and a traitor to his religion. "Any help we can offer solving this crime is willingly offered. Should we receive information we will share it. We would not wish you to believe we are breaking the truce we have just signed."

The almost total loss of the Venetian and Mamluk fleets in battle off Cyprus had left both sides shocked. And the sultan's offer of a year's truce had been accepted with little reluctance. Venetians were pragmatists. The more enemies you had the fewer people you could trade with.

"My lord ambassador," Alexa leant forward, "do you plan to remain in our city?" Her question was almost gentle. Its weight in what she avoided mentioning. That the ambassador's brother was among those who died in the recent battle.

"W-w-webs," Duke Marco suddenly said.

His mother stared at him. His uncle, the Regent, simply looked disgusted.

"S-see?" Marco pointed at the ceiling.

"They shall be cleaned away this very morning," Duchess Alexa promised. "Every single last one of them. Next time you're here they'll be gone."

"W-where will the p-poor spiders live? Everyone has to l-live somewhere." Her son sounded sorrowful. "Even s-spiders with nowhere to live." Having exhausted that day's supply of words, Marco kicked his heels against the legs of his throne, curled into a ball and began to suck his thumb.

The duchess looked thoughtful.

"I think," said Prince Alonzo . . . Then stopped as Duchess Alexa abandoned her chair to kneel in front of her son. Gently she pulled his thumb from his mouth and nodded towards the ambassador.

"Is he a spider?"

"He l-looks like a s-spider to m-me."

It was true the Mamluk ambassador was tall and thin, and dressed in a robe that made him look thinner still. The fat turban he wore could have looked like a spider's head with a little imagination.

Well, maybe a lot of imagination.

"Is the Fontego dei Mamluk yet sold?"

Count Corte, whom Alexa asked, blinked furiously at finding himself the unexpected centre of attention. "We've had offers," he said carefully. "Good offers. From the Moors and the Seljuks."

"Has it been sold?"

"No, my lady."

"Then it is returned to its original owners."

She smiled at the ambassador, who was so shocked he forgot to keep his face impassive. "My lady, that is unexpected."

The balance of power in Venice had changed and Alexa intended to provide proof. In removing Lady Desdaio without permission,

Atilo had risked disgrace. He'd also made it impossible for Alexa's brother-in-law to seduce the richest heiress in the city. In winning a battle against the Mamluks, Atilo had put himself beyond punishment. Since he was her man – as surely as Roderigo was Alonzo's – her hand was strengthened.

Bowing lower than usual, the Mamluk bid farewell and left the room, walking backwards as his customs required. He left so speedily everyone suspected he feared she'd change her mind.

"Now," Alexa said. "Tycho will tell me why he thinks Lord Roderigo is involved in this." When Roderigo opened his mouth, Alexa scowled. "You'll have your turn later."

"My lady. Roderigo was on the island with us."

"*Lord* Roderigo," the duchess corrected. "These things matter."

"I'm sorry," Tycho said. "*His lordship* was with us. But when I looked up at the banquet and saw his sergeant, who was not, I knew . . ." Those watching probably imagined Tycho gathered his thoughts. But he was wondering how to word what he needed to say. "I *knew* something was wrong."

"You knew this how?"

"My lady. Please. I just *knew*."

"This knowledge gave you proof Lord Roderigo was involved?"

"No, my lady. I simply thought . . ."

Tycho saw the duchess look at a fat little man at the far end of the row of chairs arranged in front of the thrones, who shook his head. Quietly dressed and seedy in appearance, Dr Crow was reputedly the greatest alchemist alive. He'd questioned Tycho already on how he knew death was coming. He took for granted that Tycho did; his only interest was how.

I just did had probably disappointed him.

"You were right about the danger," Alexa said. "Wrong about Lord Roderigo's involvement. Prince Alonzo tells me he sent Roderigo's sergeant to confirm no disease had developed. If it had, quarantine was to be extended. Lord Roderigo locked the door to the courtyard because that was what regulations demanded."

"My lady . . ."

"This was a Republican conspiracy. Arrests are already being made. We have dangers enough outside not to tolerate traitors within. Lord Roderigo is a loyal servant to the throne and was not involved."

"No, my lady. Of course not."

The duchess was waiting for something. After a moment, Tycho realised what. Although she was too subtle to make it an order. Turning to the Captain of the Dogana, he offered apologies for his insult.

Roderigo grunted.

"And now," Alexa said lightly, "to other matters. Who was the last armiger executed?"

"Sir Tomas Felezzo, my lady. An hour ago."

"His house now belongs to Sir Tycho as reward for his part in the battle. Its contents, however, belong to the city. Have the building emptied. I take it no family exists to contest this order?"

"All executed, my lady."

"Republicans?"

"Every one of them. The worst kind."

That would be clever ones. Or those with influence.

30

4

Tyrol

The wolf pack streamed through the high alpine meadow, leaving mountain grass waving behind it. The wolves moved so lightly that the tiny blue flowers flattened beneath their paws sprang up unbroken. Seen from above through the eyes of a hawk they formed an arrow, a dozen racing beasts spread in a vee from their leader who ran ahead as if challenging the outriders to catch him.

And there was – indeed – a hawk.

High and cold in the Tyrol sky it wheeled and gyred above them as it considered what it saw, before rising through the winds to navigate a high pass from this valley to the one beyond. The hawk was tired and hung on the very edge of exhaustion, but its task was done and food and petting waited as reward for its return.

"Master Casper . . ."

"Seen it, majesty."

The falconer, who was Emperor Sigismund's magician and came from the far north of his empire, and had the cheekbones and sallow skin to prove it, threw up his hand to let the exhausted hawk sink its talons into his gauntlet. Then he bent his head close to the hawk's own until they touched.

31

Hunger and tiredness. And an arrow's head of lupine smoke streaming across waving grass far below.

"They are found, majesty. The next valley across."

Sigismund, who styled himself Holy Roman Emperor for all his enemies called him emperor of the Germans, stared towards the point where valley floors joined. He knew these mountains well, having hunted the area as a child. "Follow me," he ordered.

The wolf pack had begun its day chasing down a stag and killing it with brutal efficiency, then kept running for the sheer joy of it. Humans knew to avoid their valley. It had belonged to the ancestors of the wolves long before all humans now living had been born.

They ran into a sharp wind that streamed their own scent behind them and brought them warnings of dangers on the wind ahead. Because of this, they knew horses were close long before Sigismund's lead huntsman sighted their pack.

When he did, the man raised his horn and blew a note that echoed off the valley walls and deafened those around him. Still in their vee formation, the wolves kept coming, and when a foreigner riding with Sigismund grabbed his crossbow, Sigismund himself shook his head.

"Wait," he ordered.

The emperor was old, still broad-shouldered but with grey in his beard and his eyes were weaker than when young. He wanted to see the pack in formation for himself, marvel at what it must be to be one of those creatures.

Looking up, the lead wolf grinned.

"Hold," Sigismund ordered. "Everyone will hold."

Gripping the reins of his stallion, Sigismund forced the terrified horse to stay steady as the wolves split at the last second and streamed like smoke around the riders. A man was thrown, another's ride bolted, but most managed to obey the emperor's order to remain where they were. Tumbling with the speed of their stop, the wolves scrambled upright and turned to charge the riders.

"Enough," Sigismund shouted. He was laughing.

The lead wolf, who was neither the biggest nor the most fearsome, bowed its head in acknowledgement. Its body began to change, the fur along its spine splitting to reveal flesh and human skin as its pelt somehow turned inside out.

The young man who stood naked before the emperor bowed again, while behind him the rest of the pack underwent the same transformation.

"It hurts?" Sigismund asked.

"Not as much as becoming *krieghund*."

The pack could inhabit one of three states: human, wolf or a human/wolf hybrid. The last of those required a truly brutal transformation. But then *krieghund* bore no resemblance to anything natural.

"Majesty . . ." A huge bearded man came to stand beside Prince Frederick. He too was as naked as the day he was born, with a gut proud as a jutting chin and sword scars on his chest. The wolf master and the emperor were old friends for all Sigismund was human and unable to run with the pack.

"My son's training is finished?"

The wolf master stared at the young man beside him. He seemed to be considering. "If needs be, majesty. Of course, there is always something else to learn."

"Even at our age," Sigismund agreed. He lowered his voice. "And what I'm learning is that I should have made my move on Venice earlier."

"The Basilius?"

"Andronikos is pushing him into making a move."

"How, majesty?"

"By saying I'm making one." The emperor shrugged. "Which means I have no choice but prove him right." The men around Sigismund took the emperor sliding from his horse as permission to dismount. Although they stayed back when he put his arm around his son's shoulders, steering him away from the rest.

"They say next winter will be hard."

When Sigismund said nothing else, Frederick looked at his father, wondering. The emperor sometimes spoke in riddles or expected his silences to be read for words. This time it seemed he simply meant it. Next winter would be hard.

"I'm sorry," he added.

"For the winter?"

The emperor chuckled. "So like your mother." It was rare for him to mention the mistress he'd loved but not married; being already married to Queen Mary of Hungary. Frederick's mother had brought her looks and her laughter. Queen Mary had brought him a kingdom to add to his others.

Frederick understood.

"I have a task for you. Not one you will enjoy."

"I am yours to command."

Sigismund nodded. "It's been three years . . ."

The emperor halted for Frederick to compose his expression.

It was three years since Frederick's own wife and child died of plague. Three years in which he'd fought his way out of sadness and found peace and even happiness in his hunts with the wolf pack. He knew he was not Leopold, who had been the elder and their father's favourite. And, at seventeen, Frederick understood he still looked like a boy while his elder brother had been a man.

But he had married at thirteen, which was more than Leopold had done, and he had sired a child. His body might have been even slighter back then, hair more faded blond, his moustache vestigial, where now it was simply token. But he had loved and bedded his wife, who'd been older, stronger willed and cleverer, and who loved him back for reasons he still didn't understand. For a year they had been blissfully happy.

"As I said. I'm yours to command."

Sigismund sighed. "You are to marry Lady Giulietta di Millioni and bring Venice into the empire."

"Leopold's widow?"

"I'm sorry. But if you don't marry her a Byzantine prince will. The Basilius will acquire a base in Italy. We can't risk that."

5

When Lady Desdaio had taught Tycho his letters the previous year she had done so because she had been impressed by his keenness to learn and the effort he put into his studies. That was what she told him anyway. How was she to know that he'd learnt to read for one reason only?

He'd learnt to read so he could study a manuscript stolen from a book maker in the days immediately after his arrival in Venice. A manuscript he'd now read so many times he could recite the words by heart; although reciting them brought him no closer to understanding how what the words said was true could be.

Tycho had kept the script hidden in the floor of the cellar at Ca' il Mauros, Lord Atilo's house, to which he'd insisted on returning while his new house in San Aponal was cleared at the duchess's orders.

Sometimes Tycho felt he recognised enough of the story in the manuscript for it to be his story. And other times he decided what he thought he recognised was so impossible it must be the story of someone else.

Slowly – because Tycho still read slowly, although he no longer needed to use his finger to follow the lines – he read the words aloud and listened to them echo off the walls of the little cellar that had once been his slave quarters.

In a year when the world turned colder, and canals froze in Venice, blizzards smothered a town beyond a huge ocean no longship had crossed for more than a hundred years. The blizzard almost buried the woman approaching the gates of the last Viking settlement in Vineland. She had walked an ice bridge from Asia. Not this winter. Not even the one before.

She was at Bjornvin's walls before the gate slave saw her. His orders were to admit no one. He would have obeyed, too. But she raised an angelic face framed by black hair. Even at that distance, he could see she had amber-flecked eyes.

Without intending, he descended the ladder from the walls, removed the crossbar from the gate and opened it . . .

The scribe was Sir John Mandeville's squire who'd travelled with his master across the whole known world. The story of Bjornvin's fall came from a bitter-faced crone with a withered arm far beyond Muscovy, who told it to a Franciscan envoy to the Khan, who had his own scribe record it.

The Franciscan later told a Benedictine friar who told Sir John, who remembered it well enough to dictate it to his squire. The events in the manuscript happened over a hundred years before.

Food became rare in the year the stranger arrived. The snows melted later and arrived earlier, fell for longer and lay deep. Lord Eric and his warriors grew used to making do with less food. His slaves starved. And the oldest, Withered Arm, was weak before her contractions began.

It was a bad birth. Any birth was bad in winter, in the slave quarters, with no light, when the mother was cold and hungry, but this one was worse. The child had turned inside her. Mothers died of such injuries. Babies died too.

"Let me look. I have skill . . ."

"Lady. It's not right."

Had anybody heard, Withered Arm would have been whipped for her politeness. They were slaves. But she'd shown the stranger a respect she'd never shown anyone else. Also pregnant, but not so close to term, the stranger lifted Withered Arm's smock with casual disregard for what the older woman wanted. As they thought, the cord was round the infant's neck. "Your child's dead," the stranger said.

"I can feel it kicking."

"As good as dead. You have a knife?"

"Under the straw."

"Keep steady," she ordered. Casually, she edged the blade down her wrist to where her fingers ended. "It's done."

Withered Arm sobbed. She knew.

The stranger hid the butchered scraps under straw, having tied off the cord, and waited for the afterbirth. "Now my turn."

"Lady?"

Although Lord Eric had a wife, mistresses and slaves to bed no woman had given him a child. He'd claimed the stranger as his slave and took her pregnancy so badly he flogged her himself. She hadn't changed her story. She was pregnant when she arrived. Her kind simply took longer.

"For my child to become yours we need my baby now."

"You'll die."

"I welcome it."

"And when Lord Eric asks why I didn't stop you?"

Denied the pleasure of killing the stranger's child, Lord Eric would slaughter Withered Arm without thought.

"Come here," the stranger ordered.

She punched Withered Arm without warning. Hard enough to blacken her eye and start it swelling. Before Withered Arm could retreat, she did it again. "I had that knife. We fought. You couldn't stop me." She nodded towards the blood-soaked scraps under the straw. "That was my baby. This is yours. Understand?"

Without waiting for a reply she began to cut open her belly.

It couldn't possibly be him. Yet how could it not? Tycho's memories of Bjornvin were too vivid, his hatred of a woman with a withered arm who'd allow him to believe she was his mother too fierce.

Folding the parchment, Tycho wrapped it in oilcloth and added it to his small pile of possessions. He suspected he'd learnt all he could from its words. If he wanted to find out who he was – although he suspected the real question was *what* he was – he'd have to find other ways to do it. Tomorrow, or the day after, he would leave Atilo's house for ever and the parchment would go with him, a talisman of sorts. But first there was the Victory feast.

6

The tables set to celebrate the defeat of the Mamluks filled Ca'
Ducale's new banqueting hall; a room so new it stank of turpentine,
brick dust and plaster, and so vast it was said to be the largest in
Europe.

Pity it's not finished, Tycho thought sourly.

Scaffolding still covered one wall. The ceiling beams were held
up at one end with props. The ceiling itself, which would be carved
and painted, and hung below the beams had yet to be made.

Everyone in Venice was finding their places.

Well, everyone who mattered to the Millioni. Tycho imagined
they came for the lavish food, for the half-naked jugglers and
acrobats, for the right to say they'd attended, or because their
absence might be used against them.

To judge from those at the reception a large number had come
to gawp at him.

Tycho understood why. How many men in Venice had been
shipped south and sold in the slave markets of Cyprus, only to
be bought and freed for ten times their price by Lady Desdaio?
That he was now a knight only made him more intriguing.
Understanding didn't mean he liked it.

The richer of the men around him wore velvet cloaks shaved in intricate patterns and embroidered doublets in the latest style. The young ones wore prominent codpieces, older ones hip-length jackets. Breasts overflowed from their wives' low-cut gowns, gold circled perfect necks and pulses throbbed like tiny butterflies.

Lord Roderigo stood with the Regent. When Tycho caught Roderigo's gaze the man scowled and Tycho glared back. He *knew* Roderigo had something to do with that explosion. He didn't care what Alexa said.

"Sir Tycho . . .?"

An usher stood next to him, dressed in the gold and scarlet of the Millioni livery. "Lady Giulietta is waiting."

"For what?"

The young man blinked. "You're going in together, sir."

"*This is not my idea* . . ." Giulietta looked close to tears. The usher might as well have been invisible. And, with a hurried bow, that was how he made himself, retreating through the crowd to leave Lady Giulietta soothing her baby, and glaring at her partner for the evening.

"My aunt says I must sit with you." Her scowl made Giulietta look younger than her sixteen years. "I owe you my life. Apparently."

Tycho resisted saying she owed it twice. Of course, the first time the person he'd saved her from was himself. Instead he shrugged to say it was nothing.

Giulietta flushed. "Marco's idea."

This translated as *Only a madman would make me sit next to you*. Turning to see what made her scowl deepen, Tycho saw Arno Dolphini, who'd been aboard the *San Marco* with them. "The man's a fool, my lady."

"And a liar."

Tycho wondered what he'd been saying.

Lady Giulietta wore her hair up as befitted a once-married woman, its flaming red contrasting with her widow's gown, which was cut from black silk that shimmered as she fidgeted. Around her neck were rubies the size of pigeons' eggs. Prince Leopold's ring circled her finger. The only unusual thing was the baby in her arms.

"You're taking Leo in with you?"

"I'd like to see them stop me."

In a world where noble women rarely breast-fed, and fathers sent sons away at an early age to learn warfare or trading – as happened to Marco Polo himself – Giulietta's concern for her child was close to open rebellion.

"Leo looks . . ."

"Miserable."

Tycho suspected that was her.

Courtiers read their fortunes in where they sat. Fresh alliances were formed as families realised previously ignored neighbours had become more powerful; old alliances broken as those once favoured found themselves spurned. A feud to last generations began when one noble decided another had his place.

The top table was laid with circles of stale bread and two-pronged silver forks, a Byzantine affectation adopted by the Venetians long before it reached mainland Italy. Tycho only knew this because Lady Desdaio, Atilo's betrothed, had told him their history.

Did Giulietta realise silver burnt him?

Duchess Alexa did. So did Roderigo and Atilo who once captured him in a silver net . . . "I can't use this, my lady."

"Spear food with your dagger. Scoop gravy with the bread . . . You were a slave. Why should my aunt expect you to have manners?"

Tycho held his temper.

How was she to know that their sitting together troubled him as much as it obviously troubled her? A heavy stink of smoke might rise from torches on the walls, and the stench of the crowd and the savour of meat roasting in the kitchens might fill the hall, but all he could smell was the orange water she used as scent, and beneath it the musk of her body, addictive as opium.

He should say something.

Anything would do. He could ask how she'd been, or say something about Leo, apologise for . . . Tycho picked up his wine glass and put it down again. If he started apologising where would he stop?

Yet what did he have to apologise for?

She'd be dead by her own hand if he hadn't stopped her in the basilica. He'd never have found her again if Alexa hadn't sent him to kill Prince Leopold and Tycho ended up saving the prince instead. The creature Tycho became the night of the battle he became to protect her. Did she expect him to apologise for telling the truth?

He *had* been sent to kill her Aunt Alexa.

And he'd been sent on her Uncle Alonzo's orders, or so he'd been told by a Mamluk prince whose life he spared. The boy had no reason to lie and no lie had shown in his eyes.

Tycho went back to pushing his food around the table.

Talk ebbed and flowed around him. Most was boring, several conversations close to outright rude, a few intended to be private. It was one of these that hooked his interest. Largely because Giulietta had turned away to calm Leo, and Tycho refused to let himself look to see if she fed the child.

So he noticed when the Regent summoned Dr Crow with an imperious click of his fingers. Everyone noticed that. Only Tycho had the sharpness of hearing to make out Alonzo's words to the little alchemist.

"You're certain the secret's safe?"

"My lord, we've been through this."

"*Answer my question.*" Alonzo spoke so loudly Lady Giulietta tensed. Dropping his voice, Alonzo added, "You'd better be certain."

"I stake my life on it, my lord."

43

"You've done that already."

A wave dismissed the man, who left, head down and face troubled. Perhaps Tycho only imagined the man glanced at him as he went.

"My lady," Tycho said.

"I'm going to feed Leo," she said tightly.

A servant stopped her before she reached the door. He did so politely, with embarrassment and a low bow, his nod towards the Regent showing where the order for her return originated. Glancing towards the exit, she seemed to consider leaving anyway. Although she returned to her place.

"Apparently I can't leave until the banquet is over."

Since Prince Alonzo had already used the privies twice he was obviously making a point about Leo. "You fed him at your wedding. Remember Leopold removing the lace shawl to reveal . . . ?"

Giulietta flushed.

"Not that," Tycho said hurriedly.

The flash of breast had been unintentional. Leopold meant to show the scar on Leo's chest. Proof his adopted son was Leopold's heir *in all things*. Since Leopold was *krieghund* his son would be, too. A werebeast, tied to the changes of the moon. The child would be dead if Alonzo or Alexa knew.

Turning his chair, Tycho said, "I'll look away."

"Make sure you do."

Saliva flooded Tycho's mouth as she undid her gown, his dog teeth ached furiously. He could smell sweat and feel heat rise from her flesh. Turning further away he found Duchess Alexa staring.

"My lady," Tycho said to Giulietta.

"*What?*"

Leo wailed, Tycho caught a glimpse of nipple, people tensed and he lost Giulietta's attention as she returned the baby to her breast, covering both with Leo's Maltese shawl. The next time Tycho checked Alexa was talking to Alonzo.

44

"My lady, when you were abducted . . ."

Giulietta froze.

"You said men dressed as Mamluks took you and were attacked in their turn, and your new captors held you on an island in the lagoon?"

"I think so."

"You don't know?"

"I was blindfold, wrapped in a carpet and carried through streets, locked in a deserted room." Her voice was rising and Tycho wondered how much she'd drunk. His own body adjusted for wine. Giulietta's didn't.

"And the *krieghund* killed your new captors?"

"*Yes,*" Giulietta said. "*He . . .*"

Her voice died away and she swallowed. The beast that killed her captors became the man who loved her, without ever bedding her. The complex, charming, deadly and now dead Prince Leopold zum Bas Friedland.

"Sorry," Tycho said. "I didn't mean to upset you."

"*Everything upsets me.* Look at what I'm wearing . . . My husband is dead. I'm not allowed to feed my child in private. And worst of all . . ." She waved her hand to where Alonzo and Alexa sat; one drunk and the other watchful. "I'm back here. In the bosom of my loving family."

"*Giulietta.*"

But he'd left it too late.

Her chair was scraping back.

This time no guard tried to stop her leaving.

"May I join you . . .?"

Looking up from his cup, Tycho found the Regent standing over him, while half a hundred courtiers pretended not to watch. Alonzo tapped Lady Giulietta's abandoned chair as if he might need permission to sit.

"I'd be honoured, my lord."

"What's wrong with her?"

"She's tired."

"We're all tired." Prince Alonzo caught his irritation, reaching for a honeyed almond and sucking it slowly while he let his scowl dissolve. "These have been difficult times for all of us."

Tycho waited.

One almond followed another.

When the Regent reached for a glass it was Tycho's own, which Alonzo then emptied in a single gulp, waving away a servant who hurried forward with her jug. "Don't want women listening when men talk, do we?" Alonzo shrugged. "I know we've had our differences . . ."

One way of describing his order that Tycho be sent south to be sold in the slave markets of Cyprus.

Tycho had more sense than to say this and simply nodded, wondering what Alonzo wanted. Because he wanted something. The way the Regent was forcing himself to be polite said he wanted it badly.

"You and my niece? You've become close?"

"My lord?"

The Regent sighed. "Enough fencing. I'm a simple man. A soldier. I like those who speak plainly and tell the truth. Did you befriend Lady Giulietta on the return trip?"

"She needed to talk, my lord."

"Of course she did. Women always do. What about?"

"Her husband's death."

Prince Alonzo stiffened at the words. "You were at this wedding? It was done properly? With a real priest and legitimate witnesses?"

"Prior Ignacio took the service. King Janus witnessed it. The entire Cypriot court was there. I acted as groom's man . . ."

"You?"

"I was his choice."

Bending closer, Alonzo said, "You knew what he was?"

"A *krieghund*, my lord. A werebeast from the Teutenbourg forests. You told me the night I was given my instructions. But he fought hard and died well, and Lady Giulietta wouldn't be here without him. My lord Atilo can bear witness."

"Do you know how my niece and he met?"

"No, my lord," Tycho said firmly. "I know nothing of that."

"And the brat . . ." Prince Alonzo's voice had a studied neutrality. "To whom Leopold passed his lands and titles. Do you believe it is his? I've been told zum Friedland's interests ran in other directions."

"Leopold claimed him."

"So I'm told. Does Giulietta claim it's his?"

Sweat beaded the Regent's forehead where greying hair swept back in the old style. It was hot for mid-May and the man was drunk, but not enough to explain his scarlet face.

"My lord . . ."

"Answer me, damn it."

"You would need to ask her, my lord."

Outrage flooded the Regent's features and he stood, whether to draw a dagger, stamp away or shout was unclear. But the truth was, Giulietta hadn't named the father of her child. *I went to Leopold's bed a maid.*

She'd sworn those words in a chapel full of White Crucifers in Cyprus. And yet Leopold had asked Tycho if the child was his. And Giulietta claimed she was untouched still, the child cut from her by a Jewish surgeon. A riddle Tycho couldn't begin to unravel. Since the child must have a father.

"My lord, some things are best left unspoken."

Prince Alonzo sat down again. He sat, pulled his chair close to Tycho and draped one arm heavily around his shoulder. "So," he said. "We get closer to the truth. She's told you the child is not his?"

"Prince Leopold told me."

The Regent froze. "He knew?"

47

"We spoke of it only once. But Leopold knew."

"And my niece has never told you who the father . . .?"

"As I said, my lord. Some things are best left unspoken."

Sitting back, the Regent clicked his fingers for the servant he'd dismissed earlier. She was young and full-figured, exactly the kind to attract Prince Alonzo's attention, and for that Tycho was glad. Although, seeing the tightness in her eyes when the Regent wrapped his arm round her hips he felt sorry for the girl.

"Perhaps I've misjudged you."

Alonzo was talking to Tycho obviously.

Words had little to do with what he had planned for the girl.

Understanding he was dismissed from his own seat, Tycho stood, bowed to the Regent and left. When he glanced back, the girl sat in Alonzo's lap and everyone was pretending not to notice. Apart from Alexa, who looked rigid with fury.

Her gaze nailed Tycho as he headed for the privies and fresh air outside. Apparently she held him responsible.

7

When the servant girl reappeared next morning it was with the bowlegged gait usually found in Venetian boys newly introduced to the saddle. "Drink this," a liveried messenger said.

She stared at the liquid doubtfully.

"Duchess's orders."

From her vantage point Alexa discovered this did little to assuage the girl's misery. Even three rooms away from her brother-in-law's chambers Alexa had heard the yelps, whimpers and cries.

She had a right to be miserable.

Her messenger also gave the girl two gold ducats and told her to keep them hidden, five pieces of silver so people would know she'd been rewarded, and a handful of copper to buy passage to the mainland.

There would be no child from Alonzo's sport. With Marco, Alexa had a different problem altogether. It was not that Marco had to be restrained from bedding anything female.

He could not be started.

Sighing, Alexa watched the girl pocket the coins, unaware her action was observed through a spyhole. And then, that problem solved, the duchess headed for her son's chambers, already knowing what she'd find.

Another girl untouched.

No one had bothered to learn the name of last night's offering. Infinite care had been taken, however, to ensure she was in sound enough mind to know what would happen if she upset Marco.

She'd done as ordered. Smiled prettily, leant forward so her full breasts swayed inside her gown, leant back, so they jutted skywards. Duke Marco had shown not the slightest interest.

"My lady, we must accept facts."

Duchess Alexa glared at the alchemist.

So confident was Dr Crow in his position he barely bothered to look contrite. Instead he brushed dirt from his rotting gown. The man could afford new clothes but rarely bothered to buy them. He cared little about appearance. So he said . . .

"She is unbedded?"

"Was and is," he said brightly. "You could strip her naked, tie her down, leave her here for the rest of the year and she'd remain so."

"Then what's he been doing for the last eight hours?"

The duchess was happy to arrange bedfellows for her son but drew the line at watching what happened. A surprising delicacy in a woman rumoured to have made the late duke her willing servant with unspeakable bed skills. The rumour was untrue. Theirs had been a love match, surprisingly enough.

"Well?" Alexa demanded.

"What his highness always does, my lady. Hums to them, offers them sweetmeats, tells them little stories, brushes their hair."

Marco looked over from where he sat up in his bed and smiled. He held a book in his hands. It was upside down.

"What do you read, my lord?"

"W-w-words, w-words, words."

Dr Crow smiled in return.

The Jewish girl beside him had her head turned away. Her

face was drawn and her lips tight. She knew she'd failed, but was too scared to realise how many others had failed before her.

"Get the girl up. Get rid of her."

Duke Marco's lips trembled and his eyes brimmed. Opening his mouth, he shut it again and chewed his lip. After a second, he took the young woman's hand and gripped it tightly. When he squeezed, she locked her fingers into his.

"Her f-father is a r-rabbit."

Alexa sighed.

"But s-she's another s-spider."

"Give her father money," Alexa told Dr Crow. "I'll find her a post in the palace tomorrow."

Marco nodded.

"You should sleep," Alexa said. "Desdaio is coming later."

"D-desdaio," the duke said happily.

Alexa had once hoped Desdaio and Marco might marry, making the Millioni, already one of the richest families in Europe, even richer. Unfortunately, her son was an idiot and Desdaio had fallen for Atilo. And anyway, her son showed as little interest in Desdaio in that way as he did in any other girl.

How could Alexa preserve her husband's inheritance if Marco wouldn't produce an heir?

"Be k-kind to Elizavet," Marco said suddenly.

"Elizavet?" His mother was shocked he'd bothered to learn her name . . . "You like this one?"

March nodded slyly. "Send her to T-t-tycho. Tell him he's not to h-hurt her. They can be spiders t-together."

Alexa sometimes wondered if he understood more than she thought. And then, as if to prove her thought ridiculous, he'd begin eating the pages of a book to taste the words, or stand naked in a rose bed because he wanted to know how it felt to have thorns, and the doubts would leave her. Her son was the fifth Millioni duke of Venice. A worrying number of Venetians were beginning to say he might be the last.

8

"We have spies out asking questions."

"But no answers?"

Duchess Alexa flushed. "*Giulietta . . .*"

"I could have been killed. You realise that?"

"Many people were killed."

Monks, and they didn't like me anyway. Giulietta caught herself in time. It was bad enough even to think of it. "I know," she said. "I'm sorry."

"It's not just about keeping you safe. You belong here."

"I'm Leopold's widow and I belong at Ca' Friedland." Lady Giulietta hoped her voice sounded firm. Truth was, she wasn't really sure how she felt about living at Leopold's ramshackle palace on the Grand Canal. She simply knew she didn't want to live with her aunt and uncle.

"I'll talk to Alonzo and we'll decide."

"There's nothing to decide. And I'm done with that."

"Done with what?"

"W-what, w-what, w-what, w-what . . ."

Her cousin was kicking his heels in a window seat as he watched seagulls fighting for scraps over the Molo. He seemed fascinated by the way they hung static above the water steps, riding the wind with tiny flicks of knife-blade wings. The afternoon was hot, the lagoon beginning to warm. The canal behind Ca' Ducale had started to smell and by next month would stink.

Having looked defiant and decided that was childish, Giulietta tried for grown-up and determined instead. Her previous methods of arguing had involved shouting, slamming doors and bursting into tears. Whatever the argument she invariably lost.

One thing *had* changed though.

She was sixteen, widowed and had a child. In all the days she'd been back neither her aunt nor uncle had threatened her with the whip. So maybe they'd adjusted how they thought of her without realising. Surely that should make it easier for them to adjust to her living elsewhere?

"I said, done with what?"

"Getting everyone's permission for everything."

"I'm the duchess," Alexa said stiffly.

Giulietta sucked her teeth.

"Gods, I *understand* how Venice works. I need the Ten's permission to leave the city or trade in rare goods, buy new estates or build a palace. Even remarry, although why I'd want . . . I *know* you and Uncle Alonzo rule Venice."

Duchess Alexa's shoulders stiffened.

"Because Marco is bored by such things," Giulietta added hastily. Hearing his name Marco grinned happily.

"This has to do with that boy."

"Which boy?"

"You know perfectly well which boy."

"I have no idea what you're talking about," Giulietta said. She closed her eyes and took a deep breath before allowing herself to continue. "Really, I have no idea at all."

"Then why are you so cross?"

"Because you won't leave me alone."

There, now she was crying. Standing, Giulietta felt a hand on her shoulder and turned to find Marco wide-eyed and offering her a purple scarf. Having wiped her nose, she hesitated about handing it back.

"K-k-keep it."

"You arranged my marriage to Janus. And don't you dare say I had to marry someone. You arranged my marriage to a Black Crucifer because he ruled Cyprus, and Cyprus controlled the trade routes out of Egypt."

"He was Black only briefly."

"So everyone says. Black Crucifers torture people."

"For the remission of their sins."

"*I don't care.*" Her voice cracked. "You arranged the marriage. And then . . ." She stopped and glanced sidelong at Marco, wondering how to word what came next. She'd been told to murder Janus, but slowly using the poisons her aunt provided. Every kiss would harm him a little more.

"You know what I was expected to do."

Duke Marco stopped swinging his feet. Though he didn't leave the window seat to which he'd returned, nor take his gaze from a fresh flock of gulls. Both women knew he was now listening.

"I'm sorry," Alexa said.

You are? That was what Lady Giulietta wanted to say. "It's too late," was what came out of her mouth. Giulietta paled, appalled by what she'd just said.

"Too late for what?" demanded a voice.

Uncle Alonzo, obviously. He stood in the doorway dressed – as ever – in his breastplate with a doublet beneath. A dagger of the finest Toledo steel hung from his hip and he carried his helmet casually.

"To stop me moving into Ca' Friedland."

"Why would we want to stop you? I think it's an excellent idea. You get to live in a shabby, unfashionable ruin. The rest of us are spared the sight of your miserable face." He looked from the scarf to her red eyes. "As if there isn't enough bawling from that brat of yours."

"Leo's not a brat."

"No. Of course not. He's a zum Friedland prince and you were his father's virgin bride."

Lady Giulietta opened her mouth and discovered no words would come. So she swung away and saw Marco watching. When he patted the bench beside him, she ran to where he sat and let him wrap his arms around her. He was eight years her senior, although it looked less.

Up close he smelt like a stevedore.

It's the sun, she thought. And then realised she was wrong. His lavender doublet was dark with sweat, his throat slick with perspiration. Tiny bubbles of white froth edged his mouth.

"Aunt Alexa. Come here. Quick."

The duchess scowled, only to realise Giulietta was serious and what she took for insolence was shock. Grabbing Marco's face, Alexa turned it towards her. "Tell me," she demanded. "What have you eaten?"

Marco tried to look away.

"*Marco.*"

"A plum."

"You know what I've said. You mustn't eat *anything* that hasn't been tasted first."

"It was purple."

"Fetch my poisons box," Duchess Alexa snapped.

God knows what the guards in the corridor thought, if they dared think at all, as Lady Giulietta hammered her way upstairs and slid to a halt outside her aunt's office, slamming the door as she hurried inside.

Half a dozen Millioni portraits glared down at her.

Servants whispered that the surface of the chest was poisoned. That simply to touch it and lick your fingers afterwards was to die.

Giulietta hesitated on the edge of picking it up.

And then the thought of Marco's unhappy face made her grab it anyway, knowing she loved her cousin, idiot or not. She almost tripped she ran so fast downstairs with Alexa's box held to her chest. At the entrance to Marco's chamber, the guards opened the door without bothering to come to attention first.

Dumping the chest, Giulietta turned.

"Where are you going . . .?"

"To wash my hands."

"No need," Duchess Alexa said. "I started that rumour myself years ago. It's been keeping this box safe since." Taking a parcel from the chest she ripped it open and pulled out dry leaves.

Putting a leaf to Marco's lips, she scowled.

Opening a second parcel, she touched grass to the froth edging his mouth. A fern frond finally turned pink at its edges. So she took a glass bottle, eased a single drop on to her finger and moistened Marco's lips. "Leave us."

"But I can help."

"Giulietta. Your aunt said go."

Lady Giulietta ignored her uncle. "Will Marco live?"

"He will if I have anything to do with it," her aunt said. "Now I want a word with the Regent . . ."

Giulietta left reluctantly.

A few minutes later Alonzo left too.

Although he didn't spot her in the shadow of an arch, glaring at him with such anger she found it impossible to put her hatred into words. He'd had Dr Crow use a *goose quill* on her.

Her uncle had ruined her life, had her inseminated with his own seed, treating her pregnancy as nothing but a move in his political games. Since Janus could not provide an heir, Alonzo would provide one for him.

Only Giulietta and Janus never married.

And now she was someone else's widow, with a child she

adored, by a father she hated and whom magic prevented her naming. Was it any surprise she was unhappy? Wiping a tear from her eyes, Giulietta went to pack.

Not even Marco falling ill was enough to make her stay.

9

By night, rumours of Duke Marco's sickness filled the streets. They were whispered, and then only between friends, because rumours involving the Millioni were always safer whispered and only friends could be trusted.

But everyone in the city was friends with someone and the rumour spread so fast that agents had to be sent by the Council of Ten into the taverns to spread counter-whispers that the original whispers were part of a plot.

This had the desired effect.

As the discussion turned to whose plot this might be.

First the explosion at St Lazar, then false rumours about the duke's health. Everyone agreed the city's enemies were trying to unsettle the city but few agreed on which enemy was responsible. The Castellani, comprising those from the parishes nearest San Pietro di Castello, declared the German emperor was behind the outrages. This was enough for the Nicoletti, their natural enemy, to claim it was the Basilius, and only fools and traitors would say otherwise.

The battle between red caps and black caps was quick and brutal, and as quickly and brutally broken up by the Watch. By the time the young man Duchess Alexa called *that boy* made his way through Dorsoduro around the left bank of the Grand Canal towards San Polo the city was still again.

He walked steadily, his eyes fixed ahead.

Tycho was not thinking about Giulietta. He'd very carefully not been thinking about her since he woke two hours before in his cellar room in Ca' il Mauros and went up through the evening darkness to the piano nobile to bid goodbye to Lady Desdaio and pay his respects to his old master. Could he help it if Atilo thought he was being mocked?

"Sir Tycho . . .?"

"*What?*"

"I thought you said something."

"I was talking to myself."

The two carters carrying his possessions had the sense to stay silent.

At a butcher's shop hung with widows' memories, fat saveloys skinned in an indecent pink, Tycho stopped to watch a merchant's wife choose her supper. He felt envy for a life so normal.

What must it be like to have lived in only one place? To know this was the step where you tripped as a child, that was the wall you climbed for a bet, the bench there was where you had your first kiss, that doorway your second. Would it be wonderful to belong? Or did those who belonged dream of coming from somewhere else?

The narrow canal ahead of him was edged by a mean quayside that crumbled into green and stinking water. The bridge over it was rickety, made from wood that was rotting rather than from stone. The houses lining his route were old, their thin red brick left unplastered. In a *sottoportego* – a covered passage linking one alley to another – two children rutted against a wall. A better choice than the crowded tenement their families undoubtedly shared, where every ecstasy would be accompanied, like as not, by jeers.

"Almost there," one of the carters said.

Saint Apollinaire was patron of those who fled to Venice from Ravenna four centuries before. Here he'd become San Aponal, and his church formed the north-east corner of a slightly better square.

The late Sir Tomas Felezzo's Republican sympathies showed in the statue over the door. Pietro Gradenigo, the last freely elected doge of Venice. In as much as Gradenigo's election had been free. If the man was remembered at all, it was as the doge replaced by Marco Polo.

Pulling a key from his belt, Tycho let himself in.

The hall was dark and dusty, smelling of emptiness and rotten vegetables. The first thing he noticed as his eyes adjusted was another pair staring back at him from beneath an oak bench. The creature looked starved and intent on escaping the house where it had been trapped. A strip of ham stopped it dead.

"What's *that*, my lord?"

"A lizard of some sort."

The carters glanced at the dagger in Tycho's hand, thought about the magical speed with which it moved from his belt to his fingers, and looked at the previously whole ham. Tycho grinned as they decided not trying to rob him had been a wise choice. "You can go."

They took his silver gratefully.

After they vanished, Tycho dragged his supplies inside and stacked them by the door. He'd only brought provisions because Lady Desdaio insisted.

Ca' Bell' Angelo Scuro.

He had a palace named after him.

A small and narrow palace admittedly, with crumbling brick walls and fronting a smelly canal, hemmed in on one side by the church of San Aponal and opposite a wine warehouse, but a palace all the same.

Four floors high to judge from the windows he'd seen outside.

His hall was narrow with oak benches along one wall. A stone fireplace opposite the land door still held ash. To his right, a grander door led to a ramshackle landing stage. The gondola tied there looked expensive.

Since Tycho hated water he was unlikely to be using it.

Back in the hall, he turned a slow circle and frowned. The room looked right but felt wrong; as if he somehow shouted and his echo was bouncing off a different wall. Looking down he noticed the lizard staring with open interest.

"Well you might," Tycho said.

Well I might what? its insolent stare replied.

Tycho considered the things he could see. A freshly painted door to a storeroom. A double-fronted oak cupboard. A marble roundel of the Felezzo arms. A fresco of a naked martyr with breasts like apples that looked glued on. As if Sir Tomas had changed his mind about the martyr's sex at the last minute.

The cupboard contained a single bolt of rotting silk that felt sticky to the touch. The storeroom had a smaller cupboard beyond, filled with cobwebs and dust. A stain inside could have been blood or oil or paint or anything else he chose.

This one, Tycho thought.

The lizard looked more interested still.

Trying to remove the cupboard's back achieved nothing. So Tycho tried several other ideas, ending up with him pushing the back down with the flat of his hand to feel it shift a little and then stop with a click.

Pushing it sideways let in night air.

He thought he'd find a passage of the kind Lord Atilo used to move unseen through Ca' Ducale. Instead, he was in a doorway looking at a weed-strewn little garden with another door directly opposite.

Even the lizard seemed surprised.

The walls looking down lacked windows. At least, windows through which anyone might look. The stuccoed end of San

Aponal had a stained-glass window set so high no one had cleaned it for years. A key jutted from the other door.

Tycho used it to let himself in.

A screw-turn printing press stood in the hall.

The walls around it were hung with layer upon layer of rags, until the hall looked papered with giant leaves. The door itself was thickly padded to reduce the noise of the press. The alley door beyond was bricked up and there was no water door, the little house being too poor.

Piles of printed pages stood on a table, some collected together and a few already sewn. Picking up a sewn booklet, he flicked through and discovered the lizard was standing on the press beside him, also staring.

Return the Republic . . .

The pamphlet called for the overthrow of Marco Polo's dynasty and a free and secret vote to select a new duke for all those owning property worth more than 10,000 ducats. The reasons given included the Millioni's profligacy, their reliance on assassins, the late duke's love of war, the current Regent's love of wine and the Mongol duchess's interest in witchcraft.

The first engraving, cut with surprising skill, showed a peaceful noble stabbed by masked assassins. The second had Prince Alonzo with a merchant's daughter, his wine bottle empty, his hands not. The lizard froze as Tycho flicked to a third engraving to find the new duke depicted spider-like and drooling on his throne. A fourth showed a brave merchant hog-tied and bleeding, being ripped apart by wild horses. A pamphlet jutting from his belt read *Republic*.

Until then, Tycho had believed the famed Republican conspiracy an invention of the Millioni; an excuse to justify how tightly they clung to power. It seemed, however, there was a conspiracy of sorts. At the very least a swelling of dissent among some of the lesser nobles and richer merchants. So, enemies circling outside the city and wolves waiting within. It almost made him sorry for Alexa.

It was the engraving after that which made Tycho stop.

Alonzo again. And Alexa, still veiled but otherwise naked.

Upturned breasts and slim thighs, her head thrown back to look at bats circling her ceiling. She crouched like a jockey above the barrel-chested figure of her hated brother-in-law. In case anyone didn't recognise the bearded man, Alonzo's plumed helm was visible on the floor.

"Burn it," the lizard demanded.

Tycho turned in shock. The lizard glared back at him, eyes wide and a frill of skin erect around its neck, delicate half-wings spread.

"What are you?" Tycho demanded.

The lizard simply hissed.

10

Looking around the piano nobile at Ca' Friedland, Lady Giulietta opened her mouth to disagree with her cousin Eleanor's opinion that the grandest of the palace's upper rooms needed bloody good clean – and decided to save her breath.

While she'd been in Cyprus her lady-in-waiting had grown up. Lady Eleanor had already made it clear she didn't *have* to return to her old position. She would visit Ca' Friedland and decide.

Giulietta was so shocked she agreed without protest.

And her cousin was right. After Lady Giulietta was abducted, Eleanor joined Aunt Alexa's household. She could stay there or attend Giulietta. The choice was hers. "Leopold lived here," Giulietta said, as if that explained why she wanted to return.

Giulietta stared out of a window and across the Grand Canal to the buildings beyond. Anything but look at the young woman watching her. She couldn't bear Eleanor to see the fear in her eyes.

Here I can keep Leo's true nature hidden.

She couldn't say that, not even to Eleanor who was her cousin as well as her lady-in-waiting and the closest she'd had to a friend before she met Leopold. Because then she'd have to admit that Leo was *krieghund*. And even Eleanor would find it hard to keep a secret like that.

Krieghund were beasts, they lacked souls; full-grown *krieghund* turned into monsters under the full moon. Good Christians killed them on sight. That was her baby people were talking about.

"Who will prepare your bed and heat water for washing?" Lady Eleanor asked, changing the subject.

"I can do that myself."

"And I suppose you'll wash the floors too?"

Crossing black and white tiles, Eleanor threw open the shutters of a huge trefoil balcony that let on to the Canalasso. Then she folded back the shutters of a narrower window overlooking a side canal. The gondola that brought them was still tied to its post, the gondolier resting on his pole.

"How many rooms?" she demanded.

Giulietta had no idea. She avoided saying this was because the only rooms she knew were those Leopold had ringed with salt to keep her safe from Dr Crow's magic. There were things Eleanor didn't need to know about her life then. Things that nobody knew. Except *that boy*.

"We'll need servants," Eleanor said.

Giulietta recognised this as surrender. "No we won't," she said. "We can manage on our own." Now was the point at which Eleanor should stick out her bottom lip, complain loudly, or announce in that case she wasn't going to stay. All things Giulietta did at fourteen. Instead, she simply said, "We can't."

And before they could begin one of those *yes we can/no we can't* spats so much a part of their childhood, Eleanor told Giulietta why. If she didn't hire servants her aunt would. Servants provided by Alexa would be loyal to Alexa first and Giulietta second. Did Giulietta want that?

"You've changed."

"I had no choice," Lady Eleanor said tartly.

Giulietta had the grace to look ashamed. In the months she'd been gone she barely thought of her young cousin. "What do you think we'll need?"

Lady Eleanor suggested a wet nurse for Leo, a cook, a gondolier, and an ex-soldier or two to guard the doors. A general maid to prepare the beds and carry water. If they found they needed anyone else, Giulietta could hire them later. "No one will stop you cleaning cobwebs if you want. No one would dare. But . . ."

"I agree," said Giulietta, surprising them both.

Then she asked the question that had been bothering her all week. The one that helped provide the determination to face up to her aunt and leave the Ca' Ducale while everyone was still worrying about poor Marco.

"Marco will recover, won't he?" That wasn't the question. Just what got in the way of the question she wanted to ask.

"Of course he will. Aunt Alexa says so."

Giulietta swallowed hard. "This sounds strange . . . You don't think Aunt Alexa had me abducted, do you? I mean, she's never said anything?"

"*Giulietta* . . ."

"I'm serious. *Has she?*"

"No, of course not. She was really upset. She offered money, titles, patronage for news of you. No one's seen her like it. It's a ridiculous thought."

Giulietta decided Eleanor was right.

Tycho had suggested it. That night on the *San Marco* when he made up his story about arriving in Venice to kill her aunt at her uncle's orders. Just another thing he said to upset her.

11

"You have servants for your house?"

Giulietta made herself pick up a tiny cup of fermented tea and sip it before answering. "Yes, thank you. A cook, a wet nurse, a porter, a guard. I've been hiring staff for days."

"Because if you haven't . . ."

"That's kind. But my household is hired."

She sat with her back to the fretted screen of a marble balcony overlooking the small gardens at the back of Ca' Ducale. The beginning of June was the perfect time for flowers in Venice: bocca di leone, gloriosa and bouvardia filled tubs and fell over the edges of stone urns older than the city itself.

Giulietta could swear her aunt was smiling.

"How's Marco now?" The question wasn't intended to deflect attention from whether she'd accept one of Aunt Alexa's spies. It managed it all the same.

"Better than yesterday, which was better than the day before . . ."

"I'm glad."

"Yes," said the duchess dryly. "So am I." Leaning back, she added, "You know my favourite memory of the boy?"

"No, my lady."

"Sigismund sent him a toy wolf made from real fur." Seeing Giulietta's surprise, she added, "We weren't always enemies. And he is Marco's godfather, for what that's worth. Back then I thought the toy sweet. Now, of course . . ."

Since the emperor turned his *krieghunds'* attention on Venice anyone could recognise the toy for the double-edged offering it was. What lesson was she meant to take from this, Giulietta wondered, before discovering her aunt hadn't finished.

"One day I went to Marco's nursery. You know what he was doing?"

Giulietta shook her head.

"He was playing chess with the wolf. Making moves for both of them. Good moves, real moves . . . A week later the fever took him. It turned a bright boy of six into a stumbling idiot who needs help dressing or washing."

"A fever like this fever?"

Alexa stared through her wretched veil. If Alexa hadn't been her aunt, Giulietta would have been scared of her. Well, more scared.

"You're calling this a slight fever, aren't you? I assume so because that's what the common people are saying on the streets."

"And you know this how?"

"Because I've been there."

It was hard to explain the excitement that sparked. Simply mixing with women in the market, walking through half-deserted *campi*, visiting out-of-the-way and unimportant churches to light candles for Leopold in front of Madonnas who'd gone ungilded and unpainted for years.

Aunt Alexa had never known such freedom.

Would never know it. Her marriage swapped one captivity for another. The death of her husband tying her to different responsibilities. Being Leopold's widow freed Giulietta. Baby Leo might be a prince but no throne awaited him. The death of a man who'd loved her, albeit strangely, had given Giulietta a house and added the power of his name to hers. Reducing her own family's hold.

"You're thinking . . ."

"About how the world works."

"And how does it work?"

"Subtly," said Giulietta, and Alexa laughed so loudly a boy pruning roses in the garden glanced up, then looked away and kept working, hoping his indiscretion had gone unnoticed. It hadn't, of course. Nothing in Ca' Ducale ever did.

"Do you know . . .?"

"Who poisoned him?" Her aunt hesitated on the edge of saying something and decided against it. When Giulietta swallowed her disappointment at being treated like a child, Aunt Alexa nodded her approval and Giulietta then wondered if she was wrong about being treated like a child. Life in the palace was complicated.

Leopold had told her that life in all palaces was complicated.

It should be thought of as being like trying to play chess when you could only see the board in a mirror and half the pieces you did have were invisible.

"I'll have my guards see you home."

Giulietta understood what calling Ca' Friedland *home* must cost her aunt, so she smiled, shook her head gently, and said, "I have two of my own."

"Well, take care of yourself. After Marco . . ."

Giulietta scowled. She wanted her aunt to finish the sentence. *After Marco I love you most. After Marco I couldn't bear if something happened to you.* Or simply, *After Marco we need to take care . . .*

She wished she knew which.

Did her aunt love her? If she did, why didn't she ever say it? Giulietta needed the comfort of knowing someone other than her baby loved her. Her husband had. And Tycho . . .

But being loved by someone you hated was no use to anyone.

"Aunt." Kissing Alexa's cheek, Giulietta bobbed a curtsy as

befitted a niece bidding a duchess goodbye and left, taking with her thoughts of how hard being Aunt Alexa must be. When she'd arrived in the city, Alexa was the daughter of a minor khan and called something else entirely.

She found herself, a Mongol girl, in a strange city that still had nightmares about the Golden Horde. Now Prince Tamburlaine – who was a distant cousin, for all he addressed Alexa as *aunt* in his letters – had conquered China and ruled an empire stretching from the Yellow Sea to the edges of Byzantium.

Silks flooded into Alexa's adopted city from Cathay, spices from northern India and silverwork from Samarkand; while Western goods went east, carried by Venetian caravans, and the profits returned to Venice's coffers.

Venice *needed* Aunt Alexa for her kinship with the khan of khans. It made Giulietta thankful to be herself.

As she walked home accompanied by her guards, Lady Giulietta spotted Dr Crow on some jetty steps near San Giovanni in conversation with two men shabby enough to be beggars. "Fresh, this time," she heard him say. "I'm not paying for . . ."

"No, sir. Of course not. I promise you that the . . . That tonight's catch will be better."

She hurried on, glad the alchemist hadn't seen her and suspecting his blindness was simply because he didn't expect to see her. Well brought up Venetian women used gondolas, one of the reasons Giulietta liked walking. It was only later she wondered what Dr Crow was doing talking to fishermen and why he didn't buy from the market like everyone else.

12

Burning the dead was forbidden by tradition and religion. Of course, religion tended to be given short shrift in Venice unless it agreed with the city's own views. (Even excommunication, and the threat of an eternity in hell, wasn't enough to make the city obey the Pope.) Tradition was another matter.

Venice liked tradition.

And then there was *resurrection*. Which wasn't really religion or tradition. More a matter of common sense. How could you come back from the grave at the last trump if your body had no skeleton to hang its flesh on?

The sexton at San Giacomo, a parish in the slums between Cannaregio and the dockyards of Arzanale, didn't worry about such niceties. He'd have happily burnt bodies if the city paid him. Unfortunately the city wanted its dead buried.

Still, there was money in burying the bodies. And for the sexton's cousin, if not for the sexton himself, even more money in digging them up again.

"This one," the sexton's cousin said.

"You're sure?" His half-brother glanced between moonlit pits.

Both had roots trapped in their recently turned soil. A sprinkling of grass covered the tops.

"That one's smallpox."

The words silenced his helper.

A wave of smallpox had swept the Orseolo hospital. As ever, most of the patients died within ten days and their bodies had needed dousing with quicklime before burial. Smallpox meant the graves couldn't be used again.

"Besides," the sexton's cousin admitted, "I left Giorgio's spade as a marker." An old spade jutted from one of the mounds on the grave island, its cracked blade and splintery handle making it barely worth stealing. "Dig."

"You dig. I dug last time."

The half-brother headed for a small boat pulled up on the mud flats. It was a fishing boat but then he'd trained as a fisherman. It was just that stealing corpses produced more profit. Pulling free a wicker sledge, he dragged it up the slight hill.

The sexton's cousin had found a corpse. The grave pit was old, had been in use for years and was already overfull. There was barely a skin of baked earth over the hand he uncovered.

"Too rotted," his half-brother said.

Their employer didn't accept old or rotten. He demanded young, fresh and recent. What he really wanted was for these two to cream off the best of the bodies before they were buried. So far they'd resisted his threats and bribes.

Tonight's moon was half full, and half hidden by cloud, which made conditions just about perfect. Any fisherman on the lagoon who noticed two shadows moving across Pauper Island would cross himself, mutter a hasty *Ave Maria* and row in the opposite direction.

Sinking his spade into the mound, the sexton's cousin started again. He had to dig for a full minute before hitting something.

"Careful . . ."

"You do it then."

His half-brother shook his head.

Both men were married, both in their thirties and both about to become grandfathers. They'd apprenticed as fishermen under the same uncle and begun to dig graves in their spare time ten years before. Both had been happy to discover there was more money to be made digging up corpses than burying them.

Dropping to his knees, the sexton's cousin put down his spade and reached into the hole, brushing damp earth from a face. "This one looks good."

She came up slowly, the earth releasing her with a soft sucking sound. Everywhere in Venice was near water. Few understood that as well as its gravediggers. As she came free, the hole she'd been pulled from began to fill with foul liquid. Thorn bushes and wild roses blossomed richly around them. It wasn't hard to work out why.

"Check her then."

Turning her head, his half-brother made sure her ears hadn't been cropped for thievery and opened her mouth to check she hadn't lost her tongue to treason, then lifted each eyelid in turn. She'd lived and died without seeing something she shouldn't.

"And the rest . . ."

Arms unbroken, legs the same. Skin surprisingly unmottled for someone buried three days; although neither could remember this one. She had to be from the last batch given how near the surface she was.

"Told you they'd be all right."

His half-brother had only wanted to wait two days. The sexton's cousin had insisted on three. Since he owned the boat he got his way. Pulling up the corpse's mud-soiled shift, his half-brother grunted in annoyance.

"What?

"Stabbed . . ."

A dagger wound to the heart. Worse still, a half-healed gash ran from her left shoulder, between slight breasts to her right hip.

"What do you think?"

"So what . . . She still looks good to me."

Dr Crow complained if the corpses were too thin, too sickly before death to be really useful, too battered by life to fit his standards. He only paid his top price for healthy corpses. No missing limbs, no missing organs, no rot . . .

Venice's great enemy, Emperor Sigismund, had put a price on his head. Venice's other great enemy, the Byzantine emperor, once tried to have Dr Crow killed. The Pope in Rome had excommunicated him for heresy. (Mind you, the Pope once excommunicated all Venice. It didn't seem to do anyone much harm.) Only Millioni patronage kept him safe.

"Nothing less than three silver."

"And if he offers two?"

"We take it. What else are we going to do?"

When the sledge he was dragging towards the mud flats suddenly lightened the sexton's cousin thought the corpse had fallen off. He died without realising his mistake. His half-brother wasn't so lucky.

She bit out his throat.

Her eyes had changed since the girl last saw the world. The colours were deeper and there were more of them than there used to be. The stink of the grave was stronger than she expected, the scent of the mud richer, the water saltier. She knew this instinctively because her knowledge was animal.

Her rebirth had been slow, and she had not been conscious to see it, feel it, or understand it. Inside her body, invisible fingers unravelled threads and changed the knots in the very fabric of what once made her human.

Only then did they repair the flesh they found.

The fingers moved swiftly for their size; but their size was so impossibly small even Dr Crow, looking through his most powerful glass, would have seen nothing. And they worked in the worst of conditions: without light, without air, without what they usually needed to do what they did.

All the same, they'd persevered.

As the horizon brightened, the girl looked at the light and glanced behind her. The hole she'd been dragged from would provide shadow; but the stink of bodies was close to unbearable and she'd had to shovel aside the dead while sensing which way led to freedom. The groundwater had weakened her. In fighting to escape it she'd found drier earth, which became warm earth, ending in a baked crust that stopped her digging free.

Until the sexton's cousin came.

As the girl scrambled into the pit and pulled earth over her, she thought of nothing. She had no sense of what she was. No sense of why she was there. Her fear of daylight was atavistic. The old her would have feared the grave's dampness, realising the groundwater might steal too much of her strength to let her dig free again. This her had no room for such worries. It simply knew darkness was better than light. Wet earth safer than facing the sun.

It was unusually hot that day.

The first of three dawns that warmed the lagoon and made even the wider canals begin to stink. Mud banks hardened and fishing nets grew brittle. Beggars died of the heat as they died of cold, because beggars always died.

They died and needed burying.

Giorgio, the sexton at San Giacomo, was happy with this. His parish was poor and its closeness to Pauper Island its only asset. The money he made as sexton from the burials kept his wife fed and his house standing.

On the third day after his cousins went missing, Giorgio was ordered to bury those who had died in the recent heat wave. It was only when he reached Pauper Island with his cargo of dead beggars that he discovered his cousins.

When he reported their deaths to the Watch and said he believed demons haunted the island, they suggested he keep that opinion to himself. And across the island city, in the dampness of his cellar, Dr Crow accepted his bodies weren't coming, cursed the inefficiency of the locals and wondered, not for the first time, where else in Europe a man of his brilliance might be welcome.

13

Tycho missed the sunshine. He missed the daylight. He missed its warmth and its brightness and its brilliance. His memory of bright days and blue skies fuelled his longing for something that would kill him if he let it.

Glancing at the horizon he found it lacked even a stain of the sun's afterglow. Reds and oranges had paled through yellowy purple into cold blue before he woke. The blues had turned to velvet black.

She will need protecting.

The note was unsigned but the hand was Alexa's own.

And Tycho didn't need telling who *she* was. The sun might be denied him but his other longing remained. So he'd walked the streets for the last three evenings, from this very edge of sunset to just before the arrival of dawn. And Alexa's note gave him the excuse for what he would have done anyway, being unable to stay away from this side of the Grand Canal and streets around Lady Giulietta's house.

In his year spent training with Lord Atilo, he'd learnt the matrix that made up each tiny neighbourhood, discovered which bridges were private and enforced tolls, which of the many squares were controlled by gangs.

In the end, of course, all gangs owed allegiance to the Nicoletti or the Castellani, the red caps or the black. And Tycho suspected both were controlled at arm's length by the Council of Ten. It was easier to control the city when one bank of the Canalasso was always ready to go to war with the other.

Shaking his head, Tycho pushed his way into a tavern in a narrow street behind Giulietta's house. The wine was sour, the goat on a spit so greasy that drop after drop of melting fat ignited with a whoosh. The patrons were hard-eyed Rialto stallholders who watched him with suspicion. They were talking about a demon that inhabited one of the grave islands.

Tycho felt a shiver run down his back.

"This tastes like piss."

"Drink elsewhere then."

"Good idea . . ."

He was pushing his way out, his soul soured by more than the taste of bad wine, when he heard Giulietta scream. Everyone heard it, everyone except him ignored it.

Colours sharpened behind his eyes, hard edges found the world around him. He became the thing he hated, the other Tycho. Anyone looking would have said he vanished. That he fluttered into nothing in the flapping of a cloak. He didn't, he simply moved faster than their world towards the sound.

As the second of Giulietta's guards gurgled and died, Tycho looked down from the roof of the house he'd climbed without realising. The blade held by the assassin below was triangular in section and wickedly pointed.

The man smiled.

"My uncle will kill you," Giulietta said. "You'll be torn into quarters by wild horses on the Molo. Fifty thousand people will watch you die."

He laughed at her.

"Take this." Lady Eleanor pulled a bracelet from her wrist. It looked silver, inlaid with jet. Lady Giulietta wouldn't have put it on, never mind believe it might buy her life. "We'll give you everything we have."

"Everything?"

Lady Eleanor blushed.

As the man moved forward, Eleanor stepped in front of Lady Giulietta to protect her. And Tycho decided he'd seen enough. Spreading his arms, cloak billowing behind him, he stepped off the roof just as Eleanor tried to grab the blade. Twisting away, the man jabbed once and she gasped.

"*Gesù Bambino,*" she whispered.

The assassin's second blow never landed.

Behind him, a falling shadow became a black-dressed figure that crossed the courtyard so swiftly he had no time to turn. In the gap between the assassin's wrist bones breaking and his stiletto hitting the floor, another movement . . . The whipcrack sound of a breaking spine.

"I'm wounded," Eleanor said.

Tycho knew. He could practically taste it.

As Lady Giulietta fumbled for her key, Eleanor began to shake as shock set in. Her olive skin paled and her eyes became unfocused. Tycho could smell fear, urine and blood. Mostly blood.

"I'm going to die."

"No," he said. "You're not."

She froze as he slipped one arm under her to lift her from the ground. Her hip sharp and childlike, the tear in her gown ragged and bloody. Saliva filled Tycho's mouth and his upper jaw began to ache.

"The door . . ."

"*I'm trying.*" Lady Giulietta fought the lock until she realised it was unlocked already and pushed her way in before Tycho could stop her. Inside was dark, the hall lamps smothered burnt out. Giulietta was so busy shouting for servants that she didn't spot the night's underlying stink.

Tycho did, though.

Dropping Eleanor, he stepped over her, pushing Giulietta behind him. The darkness of the hall, which he'd seen as daylight turned scarlet as his gums ripped, dog teeth descended and his throat tightened. It hurt every damn time.

"Tycho, what is it?"

Me, fighting myself.

He was Fallen. He was human.

Someone in here was wounded but still alive.

They must be for their blood to have this effect on him. He could see a dead steward dragged behind a chest, a serving girl rolled beneath a bench, her throat cut and life bled out in a cooling puddle across the marble floor.

Giulietta's staff.

At a sound from halfway up the stairs, Tycho ripped free his dagger and threw. He hoped the man who tripped and stumbled was their leader. He certainly wore a clean jerkin and carried a new crossbow. When this hit the floor Lady Giulietta realised something was badly wrong.

So did those in hiding.

"Down," Tycho ordered.

When Giulietta didn't move, he spun round and kicked her legs from under her, hearing her grunt as she hit the ground.

"Leo," she gasped. "Where's Leo?"

Grabbing Giulietta before she could stand again, Tycho forced her down, tightening his grip until she froze. "Leo's safe."

"How do you know?"

Because I can't smell Millioni blood.

Prince Leopold zum Bas Friedland had left his wife and baby in Tycho's care. The fact Tycho loved Leopold's young widow and feared what the baby would become just made it . . . complicated.

"What do you want?" Tycho shouted.

"Who are you?"

"Someone passing."

"Then leave while you can."

Tycho watched the intruder edge into view, believing himself hidden by darkness and shadows. A dagger jutted below his ribs, proof that one of the servants had died bravely. It was the intruder's blood Tycho could smell.

"Offer him surrender."

"*Giulietta.*"

"*Surrender,*" Giulietta shouted. "You'll get a fair trial."

"No, I won't." The man's accent was too rough to be convincing, and in it Tycho could hear hope that she'd offer her word. Like an idiot, she did.

"I promise."

"I'm making my bow safe."

A dropped bolt, a twang of bowstring, and the sound of a crossbow being put down told them he'd fulfilled his promise. Helping Eleanor to her feet, Eleanor steadied the injured girl, who swayed on her feet.

"Arrest him, then."

Tycho was too busy watching the intruder edge from behind a stair post. One hand at his side, the other behind his back.

Dagger?

Five steps brought them close, and the man froze as he realised someone was near. He screamed when Tycho broke his arm.

Screamed, then backed away, cursing.

"*Tycho . . .*" It would be better if she didn't shout his name all over the place. Out of the corner of his eye, he saw a tiny crossbow appear in the man's good hand. It aimed for Giulietta's voice.

Time froze, and Tycho moved.

He reached her in time to take the finger-sized arrow in his shoulder, and the shock of it snapped him back to almost human. The last thing he remembered was hurling his dagger in return.

"*Wake up, wake up, wake up . . .*"

Waves of agony locked him into darkness. He was so far inside his head his only company was ghosts and a vast expanse of wasteland. A red-painted Skaelingar watched him from a distance. The savage who killed Afrior, his sister.

That happened in his final days at Bjornvin.

Afrior's death was the last thing he remembered before finding himself here. He still wasn't sure this world hadn't been created to punish him.

"*Wake up* . . ."

Tycho forced his eyes open.

Lady Giulietta was crouched over him, tears rolling down her face. Angrily she brushed them away. Her face was pale, her body quivering with horror.

"Take the arrow out," Tycho snarled.

Giulietta rocked back in shock. Suddenly an older woman was behind her, someone Tycho hadn't seen before. Leo's wet nurse, he imagined. She handed Giulietta her child and took a lamp from Eleanor's trembling fingers.

"My ladies, let me . . ."

"You kept the baby safe?" Tycho asked.

"I bolted myself in his nursery."

Tycho tried to smile but pain rubbed away his ability. Waves of darkness were breaking over him; the ghosts in his head were as loud as shingle being dragged down a beach. "You must remove the arrow."

"You might die."

"I'll die if you don't. Its point is . . ."

He was going to say *poisoned* but the truth intruded. "Silver."

Maybe they simply had silver-tipped arrows. Maybe they knew to expect him. Any arrow would kill Giulietta, her lady-in-waiting and the guards. Only a silver-tipped one would put him out of action.

"Please," he added, surprising himself.

"This is going to hurt."

"Not as much as leaving it there."

He screamed all the same. A long howl as barbs ripped free and the oak-panelled walls of the hall lacquered themselves with pain. He should have ordered her to widen the wound first.

"Stay there, my lord. My lady can send for a surgeon."

"No need . . ." His shoulder was healing. A fierce itching said flesh was knitting and muscle remaking itself. The trickle of black blood lessened and stopped as they watched. Always, Tycho imagined spiders. A hundred, a thousand, whatever came after a thousand spiders spinning webs inside him.

"Are you all right?" he asked Giulietta.

It was a stupid question, given her hall was full of dead servants and her two guards lay dead in the courtyard outside.

"You were spying on me," she said.

"I was passing . . . Let me help you clear up. You'll need to call the Watch. And you should probably tell your aunt."

"Did Aunt Alexa send you?"

Tycho shook his head.

"Are you sure?"

"Of course I'm sure." She hadn't exactly sent him, more suggested he keep an eye on things this side of the canal.

"Swear it," Giulietta said. When he didn't she pushed him away. "All my life people have spied on me. Everywhere I went as a child I was watched, everything I did was written down. *I will not be spied on.*"

"Giulietta. I just saved your life."

"You almost got my lady-in-waiting killed." The argument went downhill from there.

14

In the knot of canals behind Ca' Ducale the water had turned to the green of old copper and its smell become so brutal it would cure leather. The Regent appeared to notice neither the smell nor the fact that Dr Crow was breathing through his mouth.

"The robber confessed."

Dr Crow was careful to keep his face neutral. "That's good, my lord. What did he confess to?"

"Being a Republican. We were right. The Republicans were behind the explosion at St Lazar. Just as they were behind Marco's poisoning. And this outrage is simply their latest attempt to destroy my family. The man was a fool. He kept saying my idiot niece had promised him a trial. He kept saying it right up to the point he died."

Dr Crow smiled thinly. The alchemist wanted to say that seemed a big conspiracy for three people but had more sense, contenting himself with, "Were there others?"

"Sympathisers, certainly," Alonzo said. "I have a list of names."

Dr Crow decided he'd heard enough. That the Regent had decided to question the man himself was warning that he should let the matter drop. So he gave Prince Alonzo good news instead. Lady

Giulietta's fury – so fierce it followed Tycho to the door of Ca'
Friedland – showed no sign of abating. A messenger from Tycho
had been turned away.

"Why is this good news?"

"It buys you time to entice him."

"God's man. Why would *I* want to entice him?"

"He would make a useful addition to your party, my lord.
And," Dr Crow played his ace, "better he follows you than Alexa."

Dr Crow's vices were unusual enough to make life complicated.
He liked dressing up in women's gowns, preferably silk. And he
liked cutting open corpses to see what was inside. Had he done
one while indulging in the other even Alonzo couldn't have kept
him safe.

If these were the only things about him of interest, his life
would have long ago stopped being complicated and become
very simple. The Church burnt men who dressed as women, as
it burnt those who dissected bodies. The two vices in one man
would have made for a very impressive bonfire indeed.

Luckily, Dr Crow had other skills.

Most alchemists spent their lives moving from country to
country, usually just ahead of guards sent by whichever prince
they'd drained dry. His genius had been to announce early – on
first meeting Marco the Just – that he couldn't turn lead to gold
and doubted any man could. What he offered were surprisingly
effective forms of magic.

"This quarrel was fierce?"

"She stood in the doorway screaming at him like a Rialto
fishwife."

Alonzo laughed.

"So Sir Tycho told her she was spoilt, brattish and embarrassing.
At which your niece burst into tears, which only made her angrier.
And the boy walked away without looking back." Absent-
mindedly, the alchemist took a honeyed almond from a platter
and seemingly missed the prince's irritated scowl.

"Tycho is unusual." Dr Crow weighed his words.

"What are you saying?"

"Better your man than Alexa's."

The rules governing the Regent's access to Dr Crow mirrored those governing his access to the Assassini. Neither could be used against a co-Regent. Lord Atilo and Dr Crow were required to report any attempt to break this rule.

It was no secret Lord Atilo favoured the duchess, as surely as Dr Crow favoured Prince Alonzo. Sometimes Hightown Crow wondered if his hatred of Alexa's skills with poison simply mirrored Atilo's dislike of the Regent's military training. And the matter of Lady Giulietta *was* tricky.

The Regent had refused to involve Alexa in his plan to have Giulietta impregnated with his seed to guarantee she bore Janus a child. An entirely reasonable plan given the king's previous failures. Had his niece's marriage taken place all would have been well.

Now, obviously, Prince Alonzo needed to be sure Dr Crow's original magic would prevent Giulietta telling Alexa herself.

"With Giulietta, you're sure . . . ?"

Inside himself, Dr Crow sighed. "My lord. We've been through this."

"*I want to know for certain she can't tell anyone.*"

"And I've told you, my lord . . ."

"Then why did he say he knew? *Tell me that.*"

Dr Crow was puzzled. "Who, my lord?" Deciding this wasn't sufficiently clear, he added, "Who said he knew?"

"That white-haired freak you want me to recruit. At the banquet when I questioned him he said, *Some things are best left unspoken.* He knows the child isn't Leopold's. I asked him if Giulietta had ever said . . ."

Dr Crow felt himself tense.

"He replied, *Some things are best left unspoken.* Condescending little bastard. He knows and he's going to use it."

The Regent's next glass of wine was huge. The gulp he took almost large enough to empty it. He was a big man, given to living in his breastplate, and he'd been drunk, more or less, since the night of the banquet. He needed a bath, a change of clothes and a shave. Dr Crow had no intention of being the man who told him that.

"Forget subtlety. I want you to kill him, Hightown. I don't care how you do it. Call up demons from hell for all I care."

"My lord."

"That was a joke. Suggest it wasn't and I'll give you to the Pope myself. You know how badly he wants your company." At the far side of the table, the alchemist stole the last remaining almond.

"Consider, my lord. You don't want to . . ."

"Don't you dare tell me what I want, damn you."

"May I suggest," Hightown Crow said, "that a wise prince thinks carefully before acting. Unless the matter is such that he needs to act immediately?" There was a touch of vinegar in his voice.

"Quote another of my brother's maxims at me and I'll burn you myself."

"I wouldn't dream . . ."

"Of quoting Marco? Then you're the only person who wouldn't. The sainted duke did this. The sainted duke said that."

The Regent really was very drunk indeed and Dr Crow was glad of that. Yes, the man was more dangerous drunk. All men were more dangerous drunk, and all women for all Dr Crow knew; although he didn't, because he tried to avoid having anything much to do with them. But the Regent was also more suggestible.

And for that Dr Crow was grateful.

There were levels of danger in this that made the city's usual levels look positively benign, and much of that danger was for him. The Regent simply bedding his niece would be incest. To have had Giulietta inseminated with a quill by Dr Crow and magic used to guarantee a boy was witchcraft. That would see the Regent excommunicated, which would make it impossible for him to protect Dr Crow from the Church. And then there was Janus of Cyprus. His wife had been poisoned to make way for Lady Giulietta. Janus would be unforgiving if he discovered that. The man had been a Black Crucifer, for God's sake; being unforgiving was part of their job. He might kill Alonzo cleanly but he was unlikely to be that kind to him.

Alonzo couldn't claim the child because he couldn't afford for the news of how the child was conceived to come out. The prince's only hope was to muddy the waters and deny flatly he had anything to do with its conception should he be accused.

"My lord, consider carefully. There is no proof Tycho knows what you did to Lady Giulietta."

"What *we* did."

"At your orders," Dr Crow added. "But, yes, we."

"You have a point to make?"

"Either he doesn't know. Or he knows and hasn't told Alexa. The first is good and the second is better. It suggests he's not her creature, as we thought. And he is . . ." Dr Crow wondered how to put it. "Excellent at what he does and what he does is more than simply kill. I watched his training, remember?"

"He looks like a Moorish merchant's bumboy."

"My lord, his looks are not the question. He kills as if born to it. Although I agree there is a certain angelic quality to his features."

"You're telling me you refuse to kill him?"

"I'm telling you I'm not sure I can."

The Regent would have answered had not heavy footsteps in the corridor outside stopped him. Guards came to attention, halberds hit marble tiles and were crossed as tradition demanded. And then, the intruder having proved her credentials to interrupt the Regent during a private meeting, swept through the opening door, her entourage behind her.

"We have a problem," Alexa said.

Had the Regent's mouth not already been open, the shock of Alexa visiting his office to share this confidence, rather than demanding they meet on neutral ground, would have been sufficient to open it.

"What problem?"

"My spies say Sigismund intends to suggest Giulietta marry Leopold zum Friedland's half-brother."

"Frederick . . . ?"

Alexa nodded. "The emperor will make him a prince imperial. Recognise Giulietta's baby as his own grandson. Our two countries will be bound close by the child." Alexa's clippedness emphasised her worry.

If it annoyed Alonzo that Alexa's spies knew this before his had time to report he swallowed his pride. They both knew Germany and the Byzantine Empire wanted Venice and her colonies.

Milan, Genoa and Florence?

Venice could fight those and win. When philosophers wrote about how rich the Italian republics were they meant Venice. The mainland city-states were mere shadows of Serenissima's glory.

The empires were something else.

These needed to be treated with visible respect. And while the khan of khans might call Alexa aunt, Tamburlaine was on the far side of the world stamping his authority on China, a conquest bigger than the whole of Europe. His mind would be elsewhere. "We keep this to ourselves for now, agreed?"

The Regent nodded. "What do you suggest?"

"The obvious. A personal letter to Sigismund. Our niece is still heartbroken at the loss of her beloved husband. Let us talk about this in a year."

"Sounds right to me. You write it."

"I intend to," Alexa said.

15

The city could be read in the shape of its lights, the up-glow of torches on high walls above, the harder light of oil lamps in windows, the glow of lit gondolas and the lights on barges that vanished and reappeared behind gaps in walls. When the beast woke, Tycho saw life differently.

The world was light in perpetual motion. Flickers of fact that wrote shapes on his retinas in the darkness. Even crowds, maybe especially crowds; they were lights, darker and brighter. Restless bundles of light, constructed from infinitesimally small flames making bigger flames making bigger flames still.

Constantly flickering. Ever flowing.

This was not how he saw himself and Tycho wondered at the difference. And wondered once again if this was really his world. All this flow of multicoloured, unobserved emotion, burning with love and anger.

All this food.

He knew how he looked to the brawlers on the night street. A scowling youth with high cheeks, his hawkish nose in contrast to the soft mouth beneath. They'd swagger towards him, hands on their daggers and falter at the darkness in his eyes.

And the women?

Gentlewomen, whores, Nicoletti . . .

They just saw his strangeness and shivered. Tycho felt them watch him, saw them blush as he brushed past in narrow alleys.

About ten days before, without thinking, he'd blocked the path of a *cittadino*'s red-haired daughter. She froze where she stood. Let his hand touch her at the front through her dress, watched him inhale the musk on his fingers.

The brother meant to be chaperoning her was gaping at a bare-titted whore. When he turned and saw Tycho, he began to move. A purposeful stride that faltered; hesitation turning to relief at Tycho's unexpected bow.

"My house is your house," Tycho said. "Have supper with me."

Next morning he rolled the girl out of his bed, kissed her fingers and slapped her bottom, telling her it was time to leave. In a discreet bloodstain on his sheet was proof of her virginity brought to Ca' Bell' Angelo Scuro and left there.

As the days passed so the rumours grew. He was a Nordic prince's son taken prisoner and enslaved. He was a *Romaioi* noble from Constantinople, where the princes who ruled the Greeks and the Turkic tribes claimed to be Roman still.

That he was *Romaioi* worked its way into ballads.

The ballads became impromptu acts by strolling players, licensed and unlicensed. Until that rumour fell to a better one. Tonight Tycho had watched a young boy in a white wig and ragged finery announce, "I am Sir Tycho of the Angels, Marco the Just's brave bastard." As shuffling crowd of Nicoletti wondered if this was treason, the boy added, "The Mongol bitch fitted me with an iron mask and had me thrown into the Pit. Good Prince Alonzo freed me . . ."

And then they knew it was.

The Watch broke the play up shortly after that.

Smiling sourly at the absurdity, Tycho chose a tavern behind

San Nicolò dei Mendicoli to buy two jugs of cheap red wine, which he took to a rickety table in the corner. The night was late, the room darker than the moonlit square outside and his face enough in shadow to remain unknown.

Having decided he was one of them, because nobody who wasn't would be stupid enough to use the tavern, the Nicoletti returned to their whispered conversations. There was little of interest. A howling heard from an island where paupers were buried.

Ghosts, said one.

A lunatic cast adrift by her family, said another.

Talk touched on the Republican conspiracy that had twice tried to kill Lady Giulietta. To burn to death so many monks and then attack her in her own home proved the Republicans would stop at nothing. A street battle against the Castellani was planned for the following week . . .

The Nicoletti planned to arrive early.

Tycho was willing to bet the Castellani would try to arrive even earlier. It was the small talk of bad men in rough taverns everywhere. If that was the way you wanted to describe them.

And who, he asked himself, *am I to judge?*

Finishing his wine, he nodded to the tavern keeper and squeezed past the man's daughter in the doorway. He took her scent, the brush of full breasts and her giggle with him. It was time to take his hunger home.

"You're drunk," said the woman who answered his door.

"If only it were that simple . . ."

The dark-haired Jewish girl who said Duke Marco sent her struggled as he pulled her close. She sounded so sure she wasn't for the likes of him that he let her go again. "What's your name?"

"Elizavet, sir. Same as yesterday."

"I need you to hide me, Elizavet."

"Who from, sir?"

"Myself – and the moon."

Herding her in front of him into the small storeroom leading off the hall, he told her to wait while he shifted the back of the cupboard and slid it to one side to reveal night air, the ruined garden and the print works beyond.

"What's through there? she asked.

"The truth."

16

Elizavet had unlocked the little house to let him out after three days, as instructed, and neither of them had mentioned it in the weeks since. Although he'd noticed that Elizavet had taken to glancing at the ever-swelling moon. The girl was smart enough to make the connection. Mind you, she was smart all round. Which was more than he could say for the girl currently sharing his bed.

Rolling her over, Tycho said, "Kneel up."

"Sir, first I need to . . ."

"The privy?"

Tonight's girl blushed fetchingly. Given what he'd been doing a few minutes earlier it seemed an odd reaction. But, then, he wasn't a sixteen-year-old Venetian of careful parents with known ambition.

"Through there," he said. "I'll join you."

At that, she looked doubtful and blushed deeper. "My lord . . ."

"What?"

"I'm embarrassed."

"You needn't be. And I'm not *my lord*, the name's Tycho and I've told you to use it." The girl simpered, as if he somehow flattered her. So Tycho pulled a curtain aside to reveal two holes in a plank and pissed through the nearest.

This was easy since he was naked. She had to pull up her shift before joining him, and then sat there looking awkward.

Tycho sighed. "I'll see you in a moment."

An hour to go before dawn, which left him time enough to enjoy her again. He'd be glad when winter came and the nights grew long. Summer nights were too short and the days too long for his comfort.

"I'm sorry," she said, kissing him on the lips.

"For what?"

"For being childish."

"You're not. But I'd like you to lose this."

Perhaps it was a trade-off. He'd let her use the privy alone and this was his reward. Perhaps she was simply more confident. Wrestling the undergown up to her waist she began to pull it over her head and hesitated.

"I'll put out the lamp."

Her body was lush without being overblown. The Venetian ideal was full breasts, soft hips and a gently curving stomach. The girl came close enough to be guaranteed her share of admirers.

"Where's your father?"

She froze.

"I simply wondered."

"With my mother in Pisa. Trading salt for olive oil and buying cloth to trade with the Germans this autumn. They make the trip every year."

Trading had a special place in Venetian life. The great merchant houses were noble, the smaller houses like her father's hoped to be. Trading was the only way a man could become rich. Unless he was a Jew. Christians were banned from lending money by the law of usury.

"And he left you alone?"

"With my cousins. They're downstairs."

Tycho had taken to sex like a fox to slaughter, it being as close as he'd come to finding something to sate his other hunger. He no longer bothered to count his conquests any more than he counted the ducats he won at cards.

Each night Tycho would wait to see which bank of the canal his latest lover favoured. That of ferocity, animal passion and raw excitement? Or of slowness, kindness and quiet restraint? Either was fine with him. The next night he would choose someone likely to head for the other.

So Tycho's reputation as a fierce and kind, dark and gentle lover was confirmed. No one saw the contradiction and every woman thought they'd seen the real him. As if he dared show what that might be.

This time, though, he let his guard down and took her more brutally than he intended, surprising the merchant's daughter into tearful protest. What Tycho really wanted was not what he took, but he took what he could.

When he was done, she hid her face from his kisses and he tasted salt and sadness. So he gentled her, muttering that he was sorry, her beauty had carried him away; and slowly, very carefully, brought her back to the side of the canal she favoured. How could he admit he'd been on the edge of ripping out her throat?

"You're sweet," she said.

Tycho sighed.

She was shocked when he said no husband would know what she'd done unless she chose to tell him. Men did not *know*. That was a lie mothers told daughters to keep them in their place. She was even more shocked when Tycho slid a diamond from his finger. "For your dowry."

She was the last of his conquests.

Although Tycho didn't know that as he closed the shutters half an hour later, drew his curtains against the coming day, remade the bed himself and tossed his soiled sheet outside for Elizavet to wash.

Waking to sadness, and the noise of friends gathering at his front door, he went downstairs to greet them. He was as surprised as they were when he sent them away. He could not afford to have them around in the next few days.

Think, he told himself. *Either you come up with a solution or Elizavet locks you away again.* And the solution when it did come was so obvious that he was surprised he hadn't thought of it earlier.

This was Venice: *everything* was for sale.

There were darker trades beyond the sale of wine barrels offloaded at Riva dei Vin, or iron ore from the German barges that docked on Riva del Ferro, beyond even the slave markets of Riva degli Schiavoni. Since he craved blood, and since he'd taken a decision not to kill to feed, though he doubted he'd keep that unbroken, what he needed to do was buy it.

In a city like Venice how hard could that be?

A single jump carried him from the *altana* of his house – a rooftop terrace – across the narrow *rio* beyond and on to a warehouse roof. A feral tom froze, pigeons woke noisily, a nightwatchman stumbled from his warehouse to stand blinking in the darkness. Tycho was already gone, rooftops beneath his feet as he raced towards the abject poverty of the slums on Venice's western edge.

A hundred squalid streets where each day's battle was simply to stay alive. He wore his drabbest clothes and discarded his sword, taking only a sharp knife. The money in his belt was copper, plus a few silver coins it hurt to handle. A single ducat coin was hidden in his mud-spattered boots.

He wore a stolen Nicoletti cap.

"My patch . . ."

The beggar girl reached for her crutch.

She moved too easily for someone who really needed it. A rancid blanket provided her bed. A filthy dog on a frayed string bared yellowing teeth as she reversed the crutch to use as a weapon. Tycho tossed her a coin.

"What's that?"

"A coin," Tycho said.

The girl looked him and then dropped to a crouch and snaked out her hand to grab the greasy copper grosso. Tycho waited. When she looked up, he tossed her another and then another after that.

"Flat, standing or bent over?"

"My tastes are more complicated than that."

She scowled at the three copper coins as if working out how complicated she was prepared for his tastes to be. Tycho tossed her a fourth and a fifth and watched her decide they must be very complicated indeed.

"What exactly do you want?"

"I want you to fill that." The pewter bowl he handed her once held ink in the print room beyond his house. It was cheap and anonymous, without monograms, crests, patera or family marks. The kind of bowl anybody might own.

"You want to watch me while I . . . ?" She looked almost comically relieved as she decided she knew exactly what he wanted.

"I want blood."

When Tycho slashed open her hand he got to see her piss anyway. Only by then she was shaking too much to notice.

"Too deep," she said. "You cut too deep."

Blood frothed from her palm into the bowl and Tycho could smell it and imagine it sliding down his throat. Turning away to hide the teeth that descended, he bit his own finger, drawing blood.

"Who did that?" he asked

A livid wound crossed half her face.

"Whip slash. Got in the way of a carter."

Yes, he thought he recognised it. The wound was deep in the way of whip cuts, ragged at the ends, too. Leaning forward, he pulled the cut open, her sudden scream stopping footsteps in a street behind. He ran his finger down the side of her face before she could pull free and smeared his blood on her palm.

"Both will heal cleanly."

"They will?"

"Go now," Tycho ordered, his voice hoarse.

The girl scrambled to her feet and her ragged dog hurtled after her.

Crouched in her deserted doorway in a squalid part of town, squatting on her rancid blanket, Tycho drank from the frothing bowl and felt the streets and night sky come into focus around him. Her blood carried fear and sadness, loneliness and hidden hopes but no memories. Maybe for memories he needed a death. Drinking her blood was like tasting his childhood, and he hoped, without expecting it to be true, that she could fight free from her misery, too.

The next night he let it be known his house was permanently closed to friends and guests and would remain so. He suggested everyone make other arrangements for losing their money.

17

Tycho dreamt of late afternoon daylight darkening with the arrival of high-banked cloud over the edge of the lagoon. An early July storm as fierce as a flash flood washing the island city and soaking its inhabitants, falling so hard that stalls closed in the Rialto market and those selling food from trays on the Riva degli Schiavoni took any shelter they could find to protect themselves and their wares.

The rain bounced on herringbone brick in Piazza San Marco, poured in pulsing streams from the stone arsehole of a gargoyle on San Pietro di Castello, splashed from the lead roof of the ducal palace, and ran like a glaze down the copper domes of the basilica. It fell fiercely and for longer than normal.

Until the sun began to set and the skies darkened and what should have been a summer shower still fell. What Tycho could see of Venice altered as the lagoon swivelled beneath him and he found himself above a small island to the north-east of the city. Wild roses bloomed in bloody abundance over grave pits. Without being told, he knew hundreds of bodies were buried in each.

As he watched, a girl half crawled from beneath the newly

sodden earth. She hesitated, then ducked down. A minute or so later, she emerged into the twilight, shielding her eyes against a last blood-red ribbon of sun.

For a moment, he thought it was the beggar girl he'd fed on the previous week. Dreams were such a rarity in the dreamless blackness he called sleep that this one had snapped him into a fugue state halfway between walking and not.

The girl's hair was mud-slicked and filthy.

Her mouth was clogged with earth she scooped and spat free. An instantly sodden grave shroud stuck to her body. Standing unsteadily, she ripped at its cotton to stand thin and trembling in the rain. Her breasts were tiny and her ribs a row of sticks, her hips hollow enough to belong to a starved dog. Tycho recognised her immediately.

Rosalyn had been thirteen when they met and fourteen when Atilo ordered him to hit her and Tycho caused her death by refusing. He felt guilty about that, guilty enough it seemed for her death to haunt him.

She stared up at Tycho.

Her mouth opened in a snarl to reveal dog teeth, and Tycho shivered. The girl's eyes were blood-red, glowing with a fire that faded. Whatever she thought she saw when she glared at the sky was forgotten.

Dropping to all fours, she hurled herself along the beach like an animal. Unsteady at first, then finding her stride and jumping broken boats, catching her heel and falling in a tumble. Her laughter lunatic-wild.

"*My lord . . .*"

The voice was at his door.

A knocking, hesitant. Becoming harder as the boy in the corridor found his courage. "My lord, are you *decent*?" What, Tycho wondered, was Atilo's page doing here? And why would Pietro ask a question like that? First, he dreamt of the boy's dead sister and then the boy himself appeared . . .?

"Pietro?"

"Yes, my lord . . ."

"It's Sir Tycho," Tycho said, rolling out of bed and reaching for a gown. Unlike most, he slept naked. If sleep was what you could call what happened when this world faded away. "What day is it?"

"Saturday, my lord. Late Saturday."

Tycho sighed.

"My lady Desdaio wants to know if you're awake and decent . . ." From the way the boy said it, Tycho knew he had no idea what that meant.

"Ask her to wait downstairs."

"She's in the street."

"God's name. Why?"

"The Hebrew girl who came to your door . . ."

Struggling into his pair of hose, Tycho grabbed a linen shirt and slid his arms into a black velvet doublet that changed to near invisible as shadows caught it. The garment was cut short and stopped at his hips. Like most young Venetians, Tycho wore his codpiece padded in the latest style.

"What about her?"

"She tried to send Lady Desdaio away. Said you'd turned into a monk and stopped bedding pretty little virgins. She should try elsewhere. I don't think Lady Desdaio was . . ."

No, Tycho didn't think she'd be happy about that either.

He'd grown up in a world where his drunken owner rutted slaves where he found them. Desdaio's upbringing was more careful. Buckling his dagger to his hip, Tycho slid on a ruby ring he'd won gaming and opened the door. Pietro followed him down to the land door and they found Desdaio outside.

"I wondered if you were all right? People are saying . . ."

That she was worried enough about the wellbeing of an ex-slave to cross the city at night to ask about it was so absurd it had to be true. What other reason could she have for standing alone in front of his doorway?

"*Desdaio* . . ."

Her chin came up defiantly.

Tycho sighed. "You'd better come in."

18

Lady Desdaio visited again the following week, accompanied by Pietro and unannounced, as before. She brought a wicker basket of fresh figs, saying Tycho looked pale, and a manual of warfare from Atilo's library, which he read in a single day, decided was mostly rubbish and put it by the door for her to take away on her next visit. It seeming likely there would be a next visit.

The daughter of Venice's richest man and Tycho's Jewish maid quickly established a friendship based on the absurdity of their first meeting. Only Desdaio could turn something like that into a fond memory.

She brought Tycho a change of clothes the week after, plus a pair of new kidskin boots she said he'd forgotten he owned, and cold chicken for the winged lizard that refused to leave his house.

"It watches you."

"Lost from a Mongol boat probably. Elizavet feeds it. It stays."

Desdaio shook her head. "Look at its eyes."

Tycho did and found himself looking away. The winged lizard followed him even more closely that night, sleeping on his bolster, so Tycho woke to the next night's darkness with the creature a finger's breadth from his face.

It was a day or two later that he realised Desdaio's visits always coincided with meetings of the Ten. The Council of Ten held Venice in its liver-spotted hands. Old men like Atilo were swift to send young men to their deaths, young women, too. Tycho wondered if Lady Desdaio knew the risks she was taking.

On her fourth visit, when he suggested using the *altana* as the night was hot and the wind over the roof would cool them, she looked surprised. "The moon no longer troubles you?"

"A new moon tonight, my lady."

"But the moon no longer troubles you when full?"

She was remembering another night, when the faintest sliver of a full moon seen over her shoulder had driven him half mad. So he lied. "That's changed, my lady."

"What changed it?"

"Getting older, I suppose."

Desdaio liked that answer. She nodded with the superiority of someone aged twenty-four talking to someone not yet twenty. Age had not cured Tycho's hunger, of course. The beggar girl's blood had.

"What are you thinking?"

"How strange Venice is."

She smiled sadly. "Of course you are."

Five years older than him, Desdaio read fluently, spoke three languages and had a figure to make men turn so fast they walked into walls. She was also – as people never tired of pointing out – the richest heiress in Venice and once suggested as a suitable wife for Marco IV. That was why it had been such a shock when she moved herself into the house of the late duke's Moor . . .

It was Atilo she wanted to talk about.

Tycho knew that the moment she began to talk about him instead. Asking where he gambled, if he still kept mistresses. Telling him his sudden disappearance from society had only made him appear more mysterious.

"I've reformed."

"So I've heard," she said tartly. "You've stopped collecting Venetian virgins. I suppose that makes me safer."

"*Desdaio* . . ."

Seeing the pain in her eyes, Tycho folded his fingers into hers. She turned away on the edge of pulling her hand free.

"What's troubling you?" he asked.

"Giulietta."

"What about her?" Maybe he sounded sharper than he intended, because she removed her hand and her face shut down. "Sorry," Tycho said.

"You've heard about Sigismund's envoy?"

"Elizavet said a German noble arrived this morning with five knights and ten servants, demanding half the Fontego dei Tedeschi be cleared for his personal use. What about him?"

"I should be happy for her. Instead . . ."

Tycho felt shocked. He'd once heard Desdaio described as sugar with added honey. It was hard to imagine what made her scowl so fiercely. "What's he got to do with Giulietta?"

"Sigismund is suggesting a marriage."

Tycho put down his glass.

"I'm jealous . . . All right?" Desdaio said. "I've said it. I'm jealous. She's been married once and now she's going to be married again. Why should she be the next? I've been engaged to Atilo for over a year."

"She's agreed?"

Desdaio's shrug said that was irrelevant.

To Tycho whether or not Giulietta had said yes was the only thing that mattered, but even upset he knew he couldn't say that to Desdaio, so he asked a different question. "You've quarrelled with Atilo?"

Desdaio nodded mutely.

Risking a sideways glance, Tycho noticed her figure was a little fuller, her skin a little less glowing, her chestnut hair, which she famously refused to rinse with urine and potash to turn Venetian-red, less striking than he remembered. She was young, beautiful and rich. Just not as young or as beautiful as she once was.

"Like what you see?" she demanded.

"Desdaio . . ."

She scowled. "They say the number of virgins in Venice halved in a month. That maidenheads fell like petals."

"They lie."

Desdaio glared at him. "You didn't want mine?"

"My lady, you don't mean this."

"Why not?" Desdaio said furiously. "He won't bed me."

"*You asked?*" Tycho tried to imagine Atilo's appalled reaction.

"I asked when we would marry and he said when the time was right. So I said I would go to his bed if that was what he wanted; that we were betrothed and could swear an oath that we would marry and so be free to . . . All my friends are married, and half have children. And now Giulietta is going to be married *again*."

As she leant forward, the neck of her gown fell outwards, revealing the upper swell of her breasts and the valley between. He smelt sweat from her walk through Dorsoduro, what she'd eaten for supper, the sudden scent of longing as her breast shifted beneath her silk gown and her nipple brushed his wrist.

She kissed him hard, her mouth opening and her lips softening. And then she was pushing him away to sit back, too appalled at herself to protest.

That was how Lady Giulietta found them a few seconds later.

Sitting on a bench on Tycho's wooden roof platform, under the starlit bowl of a moonless sky, leant back from each other in shocked silence.

"*My lord,*" Pietro said loudly.

Giulietta lifted the candle she carried and glared into their faces, until Tycho stood to snuff the wick with his fingers.

"We're trying to watch the stars," he said.

"She's here to watch stars?"

"Why do you think I'm here?" Desdaio snapped.

Lady Giulietta glared. That wasn't the way one addressed a Millioni princess. "How would I know? All I know is Tycho's maid didn't want to let me in unannounced. And your boy didn't want to bring me up here."

"Maybe you should have listened."

Stepping between them, Tycho touched Pietro on the shoulder to tell him to stop staring. "Take Lady Desdaio home and use my gondola. Leave it in one of the side canals and I'll have someone collect it tomorrow."

"I can walk."

"You'd be safer by gondola."

"Not to mention," said Giulietta, "it being more fitting than walking the streets at night without a proper escort. Assuming you still care about such things."

"Says the woman who . . ."

"Pietro," Tycho said tightly.

The boy almost herded Desdaio towards the *altana*'s ladder. At the hatch, Desdaio stopped, turned and hesitated.

"We'll talk later," Tycho promised.

Nodding, Desdaio left without curtsying to Lady Giulietta or even acknowledging she was there. A clatter of feet in a corridor below, steps on the piano nobile stairs, Elizavet's voice, the rattle of a hall door opening, silence, then sobs . . .

"Do you have to be such a bitch?"

"What did you say?"

"You heard me . . ." He stared at where the moon should be, and heard a rustle of silk. "Don't," he said, "because I will slap back."

"Real noblemen don't hit women."

"I'm not a real nobleman."

"The king I should have married made you a knight. My

husband stood by you in battle. Marco gave you his friendship. My aunt gave you this house . . ." She stared at him, her eyes bright and her hands on her hips, and then the fight went out of her like wind from the sails of fishing boat. "What have I done to deserve this?" Her bottom lip was trembling.

Tycho realised she meant it.

"I saved your life," he said almost gently. "And you threw me out of your house and told me not to come back. You said I took advantage of you . . . That you never wanted to see me again."

"So you turned to Desdaio instead?"

"She's a friend and lonely. That's the only reason she was here."

"Everyone but Atilo knows about this *friendship*. What do you think people say about her? What do you think they say about you?" The tremble was obvious now. Lady Giulietta was fighting tears and losing.

"Desdaio loves only Atilo."

"You're an idiot. You must realise she loves you too . . ."

"She thinks I'm a demon."

Giulietta shut her mouth, swallowing a question, although her gaze sharpened, and Tycho knew she was waiting for him to explain.

"I told her about my childhood once."

"About which I know nothing."

"I spent seven years chained to a gate as a dog. I slept in ditches. A noble kicked me in the guts for being in his way and saved my life by pissing on me. I was freezing to death and his anger made me hide in a stable."

Tycho stared across the rooftops and wondered how to describe the Skaelingar's nightmare wars of attrition now Bjornvin seemed so far away. The Skaelingar had been winning long before he was born.

"Our enemy fought naked with axes, bows and knives. Their skins bright red and oily in the night. They gutted us, cut breasts from our women, skewered babies on spits. Their leader had horns . . ."

Tycho recognised the look on Lady Giulietta's face.

It had been on Desdaio's face the night he told her about Bjornvin. He expected Giulietta to fire questions at him or warn him to keep this secret. Instead, she crossed herself, and left without looking back.

Tycho let her go.

Only later did he realise he didn't know why she was there.

19

The suggestion Sir Tycho Bell' Angelo Scuro present himself by noon at the Ca' Ducale for a meeting with Prince Alonzo wasn't exactly an order, nor was it a simple request. The guards in the alley below were proof of that

"The black doublet."

Elizavet took the garment from a wooden box, her thumbs brushing the garment's strange surface.

"Oiled silk made by Dr Crow."

At Tycho's mention of the alchemist, the girl scowled.

"And the black hose, the matching gloves and the boots."

He stripped easily, oblivious to Elizavet's blushes, and dressed slowly, almost as if conducting a ritual. The shirt first, followed by black hose, laced codpiece and padded doublet. His expression in the glass was unreadable, his gaze turned inwards as he wrestled with what the summons could mean. A visit from Lady Giulietta followed by a summons from her uncle. Both in their way his self-declared enemies. And Alexa had not been in touch since he admitted to Giulietta that she'd asked him to watch out for her.

That had been well over a month ago.

By the time Tycho had finished belting on his daggers and

was turning for the door his face was stripped of emotion and his eyes cool. He looked what he was. A man trained in the use of weapons. No one would see the beast inside. Or the slave boy he'd been before that.

"Go tell the lieutenant I'm almost ready."

Elizavet did as ordered.

The soft-faced *cittadino*'s son who'd knocked imperiously an hour earlier had refused to believe Sir Tycho was not yet awake or out of bed, his temper worsening when told Tycho must prepare to meet the Regent.

Tycho had not faced the sun for months, and though he knew Dr Crow's spectacles and what remained of the alchemist's unguents would protect him, he still feared daylight for all he missed it.

Rubbing the dregs of the ointment into his face, Tycho slid smoked-glass spectacles on to his nose, and smoothed his wolf-grey braids and hid them under a wide-brimmed hat. As he walked downstairs, past closed shutters and curtained windows, he let his eyes adjust to the gloom.

He wanted to be ready for the shock of the sunlight beyond.

"Oh, so you're finally . . ." Having taken a second look, the lieutenant decided the rumours barely did Sir Tycho's strangeness justice and kept the rest of that sentence to himself. "Sir . . . You need to leave your daggers here."

"Alonzo wants me?"

The correct address was *Prince Alonzo*. The *cittadino*'s son wondered that a new-made knight would ignore such niceties. He wondered so obviously Tycho almost smiled.

"People generally want me for my weapons."

"I have a gondola waiting."

"And I'll be walking," Tycho said. "You can join me or we can meet there."

As they set out for the old wooden bridge at Rialto, where they could cross the Canalasso for the lanes leading south to the ducal palace, Tycho felt his shoulders tighten. His Assassini training turned on remaining unseen; on embracing the shadows like a lover and spreading them around him like a willing cloak. He hated being visible. Hated it so fiercely he almost *felt* the whispers of *look at him* as he turned into Vecchio San Giovanni and saw children playing football.

It helped that the alleys beyond were narrow and the tenements high. Little direct light reached him in Calle de Madonna although the open quayside of Riva dei Vin unnerved him, with its sunshine beating down on the sullen waters of the Grand Canal to make molten patches of silver.

Crossing at Rialto was hardest.

Ponte Maggiore was the city's widest bridge and the only one to span the Grand Canal, and they arrived to find the walkway raised to let a flotilla of small boats row a lumbering Genoese cog upstream. Perhaps Tycho pushed through the waiting crowd too hard, because a broad-shouldered man swung round, saw his strangeness and began apologising for being knocked aside.

"Now you see why I avoid daylight."

"Is it always like this?"

"My looks," Tycho made himself step aside for a nun, who crossed herself and hurried on, "are unusual even for Venice."

"And if you look unusual among them . . ." The lieutenant jerked his chin at the mix of Moors, Mamluks and Mongols who bartered on the Riva del Ferro, their eyes on profit and the next deal. "Then . . ."

"Yes. Exactly."

Venice was where worlds met to sell what others lacked. Information, spices and silks, jade from Cathay, weapons, armour. Merchants bet on the next Seljuk harvest, on rates of brigandage along the Silk Road, on discovering new mines in Africa. Every skin tone, shape of the eye and hair colour could be found more than once. Except for his own.

*   *   *

Lord Roderigo was waiting at the top of marble stairs on which Greek statues posed in various states of nudity and disrepair. Most were chipped and a few were armless. Tycho imagined those must be the really old ones.

"You're late," Roderigo said.

"We walked."

"Why?"

"Because I wanted to."

"Gentlemen, please . . ."

Half turning, Tycho saw the Regent in a doorway.

He held a wine glass, which was not unusual, and appeared to be relatively sober, which was. Stepping back, Alonzo ushered Tycho inside. Swords decorated one wall, captured battle flags hung from another. A suit of richly chased Florentine armour stood in the corner. It would be hard to miss the Regent's history as a *condottiero*.

When the Regent shut the door, Tycho realised he was alone and fully armed, daggers to hand, with someone he'd long wanted to kill. This man had sent him south as a slave. And, despite the claims it was a Republican plot, Tycho imagined he also planned the explosion at St Lazar; unless Lord Roderigo thought of it himself, because Tycho was damn certain Roderigo was involved. The Regent must realise he suspected that? There was something Prince Alonzo didn't suspect, of course. That Tycho knew he was behind Tycho's arrival in Venice all those months ago, stripped of his memories and with a single aim . . .

To kill Alexa.

So why was he here?

"I think we should be friends," the Regent said.

Taking a sweetened almond, the man popped it into his mouth and looked quizzically through a window into the distance. Tycho wasn't sure if Alonzo was considering the sweetmeat's taste or if it was done for effect.

"Really, my lord?"

"Surprising as that must seem."

The prince turned his back and walked to the window to stare at the glittering lagoon and a dozen ships sweltering impotently in the quarantine line. The early August sun was hot enough for the Molo below to be almost deserted.

"You saw my niece last night."

"Her new guards are your spies?"

Alonzo laughed. "One of them. And I had a *cittadino* boy frequent your hazard games until you abandoned those. I have to say you cost me a fortune covering his lost bets and Antonio assures me he is lucky. Do you cheat?"

"I find it hard to lose at anything."

"I'll keep that in mind." There was amusement in the Regent's voice, although Tycho wondered if it reached his eyes.

"How many hidden crossbows cover me?"

"None. What we must talk about can't be reported and even I draw the line at slaughtering half a dozen of my own men afterwards."

Turning from the window, Alonzo half filled a wine glass with compacted snow he said was brought down from the Altus inside bales of straw, and poured white wine into the glass until it brimmed. Then he handed the glass to Tycho and prepared another for himself. The real discussion had begun.

"Why did my niece visit you?"

"My lord . . .?"

"If I'm to trust you then you must answer my questions clearly. So I'll try again . . . Why did my niece visit you last night?

"She came to my house to shout at me. At least, I think that's why she was there. She left before I discovered any other reasons."

"That sounds like Giulietta."

Tycho sipped the iced wine and realised it was good. As if Prince Alonzo would drink anything else. "Lady Desdaio had visited earlier."

"As she does."

The Regent was smiling, leaning forward slightly, and appeared to be giving Tycho his full attention. Yet Tycho couldn't shake the feeling there was a darker purpose to his words.

"We're not lovers."

"You're the only man in Venice who'd admit that. A thousand would happily claim they'd been between her thighs."

"She's a friend."

"Just as well. Atilo would kill you." The Regent thought about that. "He'd probably kill both of you. Could he kill you, do you think?"

"It's possible."

"But by no means certain?"

Tycho shrugged, talking a second sip of wine.

"I'll bear that in mind, too." The Regent sounded as if he meant it.

"Why am I here, my lord?"

"Besides the chance to earn the favour of a prince?"

When Tycho said nothing, the Regent sighed theatrically, chewed at a handful of almonds and washed down the fragments with iced wine.

"You've heard about Sigismund's suggestion?"

"You want me to kill the envoy?" For the first time since being woken Tycho felt the day might be heading in a direction he liked. Killing the messenger wouldn't change the message but it sent a strong reply.

"No. I want you to listen."

Tycho couldn't help but scowl.

"Is it true you and Prince Leopold were friends?"

Since Prince Alonzo had been the man who sent Tycho to kill Leopold this was a loaded question. In sparing the *krieghund*'s life Tycho turned traitor. "We were friends by the end," Tycho said carefully.

"And he died well?"

"Magnificently. He went to his death so Giulietta could live. His men died as bravely. It was glorious . . ."

116

"Good man."

Tycho had known Alonzo would approve.

The Regent was a powder-keg mix of spoilt child, pampered prince and experienced soldier. Had his talents not rotted in his elder brother's shadow, and were he not kept from the throne by that brother's idiot son, his life might have been exemplary. Understanding this didn't make him any less devious, simply easier to read.

"They say you fought beside him. That you fought . . ." Alonzo looked puzzled, too puzzled. "No one really says how you fought. Only that you won the battle." His eyes narrowed when Tycho simply nodded. "You killed many?"

"Enough."

"How many?"

"I didn't count. There was no time and less point. Every time a Mamluk tried to stop me I killed him until there was no one left." He could see the Regent was unsure about that answer.

"You fought in a blind fury?"

"Ice-cold," Tycho said. "As if I wasn't even there."

"Ahh . . ." Reaching for his wine glass, the Regent allowed himself a sip. "It seems Alexa is telling the truth. She saw your fight in one of her dreams. Which, I must say, are becoming more frequent . . ."

"My lord. Why am I here?"

"Because I've wasted a month wondering whether or not to have you killed. And, though I may regret this, I've decided you're more use alive. Emperor Sigismund's suggestion is . . ." Alonzo sighed.

"Unhelpful?"

The Regent crammed almonds into his mouth, chewing noisily. *How much of this is calculated?* Tycho wondered.

"I'm going to be honest," said Alonzo, answering Tycho's question. Everything about this meeting was calculated. "Venice cannot afford to have Giulietta marry Leopold's brother."

Tycho waited to be told why.

"It will upset Byzantium. That's the first. The second is it's a small step from her marrying Frederick to Sigismund suggesting his bastard become duke and Giulietta duchess, thus bringing Venice under German influence. He'll probably suggest Leopold's son become heir."

This time when Alonzo reached for his glass it was to empty it and pour himself another. That done, he put it on the table and turned to Tycho. "But there's a problem with that, isn't there?"

Tycho could think of several.

"Gods," Alonzo snapped. "You play your cards close. Don't blame you, I suppose. You and I *know* the brat isn't Leopold's, don't we? You said as much at the banquet."

"You're suggesting he's mine?"

Prince Alonzo looked at him strangely.

"Is that what you're suggesting? That I'm Leo's father?"

The Regent's heavy face broke into a grin and he pulled the rest of the sweetened almonds towards him. "Dr Crow was right," he said. "You're good at this. Very good indeed. That's even better."

Prince Alonzo's proposal was simple. The newly made Sir Tycho would woo his niece, relying for favour on their shared experiences, her unhappiness and Tycho's friendship with her late husband.

He would bring her to the point of accepting his proposal and the Regent would quietly let it be known that Tycho had fathered her child. A shocking lapse on her part, obviously. But since the whole of Venice had already convinced itself Tycho was the bastard of a prince . . . And there were rumours that he and Lady Giulietta had been lovers aboard the *San Marco*.

"I'll have the Council start proposing she accept Sigismund's suggestion. Give her a week to get desperate and then make your move. I'm relying on you to be subtle."

Around Giulietta?

His tongue always became lead.

If Alonzo's plan worked, Sigismund would lose interest in the baby. In return, Tycho would have the Regent's favour, climb the ladder of Venetian society and see his name in *The Golden Book*, that list of nobles with rights to sit in the inner council. No one would refuse this to the husband of a Millioni princess. Tycho could look forward to a secure future. A favoured future. A future in which he could count the Regent as a friend . . . And in which, Tycho imagined, the Regent believed he could control his niece through his new-found friendship with her future husband.

Walking home through alleys that looked both familiar and strange in the late afternoon sunlight, Tycho had the feeling Prince Alonzo believed he'd already agreed to the plan. The Regent was dishonest, self-interested and devious. Tycho had no doubt of this. But he'd just offered Tycho what he wanted more than anything else in the world – *Giulietta*.

So maybe he had agreed after all.

20

"You've heard about the demon?"

Tycho looked at Atilo's page. The boy was growing, his shoulders were broadening. Training with Atilo had put muscle on his slight frame. Lady Desdaio obviously saw to it he was properly fed.

"Your master knows you're here?"

The boy stopped, shuffled his feet for a second and resumed walking. Tycho took that as a no. Lord Atilo didn't know where he was.

"Lady Desdaio knows."

"She does?"

Pietro nodded fiercely, devotion in his eyes.

"She said not to trouble the master with my every move."

As an apprentice assassin, the boy had every second Saturday of the month off. Tycho should have realised he'd find Pietro waiting at his door as evening fell. "Anyway. My lord is busy in Council."

Pietro sounded proud to be serving a member of the Ten, as well he might. It was a major step up for a street boy. One Tycho had made happen earlier that spring. He had the boy's friendship whether he wanted it or not.

"He's considering Sigismund's proposal?"

"Indeed. My lord is barely home."

So, Atilo was dancing attendance on Duchess Alexa, the woman from whose bed he'd been banished? Desdaio would find that hard. If only because the Moor's approval was the star that carried her through the world's disdain. "Is there any date for Lord Atilo's own marriage?"

Pietro's mouth set to a tight line.

It was right Pietro showed loyalty to his master; and that he was devoted to Desdaio was a given. He was just old enough to be her son had she married at the same age as her friends. It was his conflicting loyalty to Tycho that troubled him.

"It's fine," Tycho promised.

Pietro relaxed. And in the narrowness of an almost deserted alley a few minutes later, Tycho heard a double echo to their feet, which had fallen into step as the footsteps of friends sometimes do. He counted down from fifty.

"Who's following us?"

Tycho had to grab Pietro's head to stop him turning to look. Ahead was a bridge that would take them across Rio di San Felice to Lady Giulietta's house. Around them evening crowds were spilling from a tavern door.

"Walk on."

The boy did as he was told.

A minute later, in front of families leaving late mass, Tycho snapped out Pietro's name. The boy looked up to be cuffed lightly across the face. As Tycho did so, he tripped Pietro with a sweep of his foot. It happened so fast anyone watching would have thought his slap felled the boy.

"Now look," he hissed.

Dragging the tearful boy to his feet, Tycho raised his hand again and apparently changed his mind, releasing him with a shrug. Just another noble angry with his page. Those watching went back to their business.

"Right. Who is it?"

"Iacopo . . ." Pietro said unhappily.

"You're sure Lord Atilo hasn't forbidden you to visit me?"

"He said what I do on my day off is my own business, but use it well."

That sounded like Atilo. "Then who is he following?"

Pietro thought about it. "You?"

Atilo's bodyservant had been above Tycho in Atilo's household and jealous of the speed at which Tycho learnt *assassini* skills. Knowing the man, Tycho imagined it was a grudge he'd hold for life. He'd worry about that later. He had far more important things to worry about now.

"My lord," Pietro whispered.

Tycho glanced down.

"Are you unwell? You're shivering."

"I'm nervous."

The boy looked shocked.

At Lady Giulietta's door, Tycho gave him into the hands of the servant who answered and told her to take him to the kitchens and see he was fed. And to inform Lady Giulietta that Sir Tycho was here.

"If you'll wait in the hall, my lord. I'll send someone."

"I'll wait out here."

"My lord . . ."

"Ask her," he said. "Say it's about Leo."

"You've replaced your guards."

"Hardly surprising."

Since he'd watched the first two die he guessed it wasn't.

Lady Giulietta looked as nervous as he felt. Dressed in her widow's black, she sat stiffly in the middle of the piano nobile, on what had been Prince Leopold's favourite chair, a high-backed walnut seat with carved arms.

In front of her rested a silver plate, a silver fork and a pie of pigeon pasta with its top removed but the meat untouched.

A single glass glittered in the light of a dozen white candles. For all Leopold had been born a bastard, he'd been born an emperor's bastard and kept a rich house. All of its contents hers now.

Tycho tried to remember her age.

Fifteen when they met in the cathedral. So either sixteen or already seventeen. In the candlelight and the glitter of her riches she looked both older and far younger. She didn't ask him to sit or offer him a drink.

"Where's Leo?"

"Asleep," Giulietta said. "Why?"

"I was wondering . . ."

As he looked at her Tycho tried to ignore memories of the first time he'd visited this house. That, of course, simply made him remember them so clearly he might as well have been there.

You're like Leopold, Giulietta had said that night.

She'd turned to face him and lifted her baby to hide her breasts. *A beast inside a man. At war with a man inside a beast.*

"No," Tycho had warned her. "I'm nothing like him." And wrapping one hand into her hair, he'd dragged back her head until her throat was exposed.

You are.

He'd bitten savagely, spilling blood across her child and on to her sheets. And as she'd screamed, and Prince Leopold begun to hammer at the door, Tycho had taken the sweetness her life had to offer.

He walked her to the very edge of death.

Addicted himself in the process and completed what began that night in the basilica when she knelt half naked, a knife to her breast before a softly smiling statue of the Virgin. Had he been wrong?

Tycho dug his nails into his hands until they hurt.

Of course he'd been wrong.

He hadn't known that then, and the dark and bitter beast that hid behind the bars of his ribs and broke free to save Giulietta during the battle against the Mamluks, refused to admit it now.

Without him, she would be dead. Now here she sat, watching coldly as if there were no fierce memories between them. As if he really was the *demon* his tales of Bjornvin and its horned enemies made her think

"Why are you here?"

The inverse of the question he'd asked Alonzo, before he and the Regent reached an agreement that Tycho should propose to Giulietta, a suggestion so strange that Tycho wondered which one of them was really using the other. One look at Lady Giulietta's scowl withered Tycho's prepared speech in his mouth.

"Well . . .?"

"Leo needs a father."

He should have found a better way to say it.

"You've come all this way to tell me to accept Frederick? That's what the Council wants, you know . . . They want me to marry Leopold's half-brother, because one emperor's bastard or another, what's the difference?" Her voice rose, her temper barely in check. "I suppose Aunt Alexa sent you?"

"I haven't seen her in weeks."

"That doesn't answer my question."

"The duchess didn't send me."

"But you think I should accept Frederick? My uncle does. I thought Aunt Alexa less keen. Probably because Uncle Alonzo likes the idea so much. He likes it, she doesn't. She likes it, he doesn't. I'm sick of their games."

"*Giulietta*, listen."

She sat back, scowling.

I love you. I can't survive without you. Our lives were linked from the moment I first saw you. All the things he'd never told her. How hard would they be to say?

"Well?" she said finally.

"Look, I . . ." He hesitated. "We were friends once."

She snorted. With most people, Tycho knew what they were thinking before they thought it. He could read the feelings that burnt off them. He had trouble reading his own thoughts around Giulietta. "Has your aunt trained you?"

"In what? The arts of love?"

"*Giulietta.*"

"Aren't those what she used to keep my late uncle enslaved? You must have heard the gossip. Is that what you're asking?"

He'd meant to shield her thoughts.

"Anyway . . . What business would it be of yours?"

"You don't have to marry Leopold's half-brother."

"*I know that.* I've been saying it all week. So why tell me Leo needs a father?"

"Because he does."

"Well, that's too bad. His father's dead."

"Except Leopold wasn't his father."

"*Who told you that?*"

"You did."

"I lied."

"Leopold told me also. He wanted to know if the child was mine."

"As if he would be," Giulietta said furiously.

Tycho flushed. "Listen," he said. "Marry me and I'll be as good a father to him as Leopold was. No one can make you marry Frederick if you're already married."

"That's what you came to say?"

No, what he came to say was, *I love you. Your smile lights my darkness, your scowl makes me hate myself.*

But he'd left the words too late.

"How do you dare . . .?" Giulietta buried her head in her hands. "Do you really think I'm that stupid?"

"Why would I think that?"

"You think I don't know you could have saved Leopold?"

"*Giulietta . . .*"

125

"You could have saved him."

"He gave his life for you."

"*And you let him.*" Her shout was furious. "You saved everyone else, God knows how because we're not allowed to ask. But you let your *rival* die first. You think I don't know that? *You let Leopold die.*"

"I didn't . . ."

"Yes, you did. I wish you'd let me die too."

"And your baby?" Tycho said. "You wished I'd let him die too?"

"Yes," Giulietta said. "I do. You know *nothing* about Leo. Nothing about how . . . About where I . . ."

"So tell me."

Her mouth shut in a tight line of misery.

"Tell me," he said. "I won't tell anyone. Whatever happened, whoever's child he is, I'll keep your secret."

"Why would I tell *you* anything?"

"That night on the ship when we . . ."

"*Don't you dare use that against me.* You let Leopold's ship burn. You let him die. You let them all die. Leopold, Sir Richard, his crew. Why didn't you save him?"

"I couldn't."

"*Yes, you could,*" she shouted. "*You just didn't.*"

21

The four bronze horses frozen in the act of leaping from the basilica balcony were old, really old. Made by the ancient Greeks and stolen by the Romans, stolen back by Romanised Greeks when Rome was failing, and stolen from them by Venice when it sacked Constantinople two hundred years before now.

Tycho had visited them in his first week in Venice.

They were what carried him up to the balcony that first time. Giulietta's sobs had been what carried him inside to where she knelt before a statue. This time when he rolled himself over the balcony's balustrade he landed lightly on his feet to discover he wasn't alone.

"Well, that was a really stupid idea . . ."

"Climbing the basilica?"

"Upsetting Giulietta."

Green eyes held his gaze. The small girl astride the nearest horse smiled mockingly. Her rags were a sail snapping in the wind. Her red hair a torn pennant in the storm that tried to unseat her.

"Tell me it wasn't stupid."

Tycho recognised her instantly. The high cheekbones, the emerald eyes, the picked-clean bird's skull on a thong round her neck. A'rial was Alexa's *stregoi*, her child witch from Dalmatia.

"What are *you* doing here?"

"Waiting for you, of course. So predictable. *He follows her here, he follows here there, the poor boy follows her everywhere.* How could you be stupid enough to think any girl would accept an offer like that?"

Tycho had been asking himself the same.

"You think she hates you already? How's she going to feel when she discovers you went as Alonzo's errand boy?"

How did A'rial . . .?

"Asked yourself why he wants you to marry her?"

"The Regent told me. Sigismund is . . ."

"His *real* reasons. The ones that reduce a Millioni prince to begging favours from an ex-slave. Maybe you should consider those?"

"He's not begging."

"Gods." A'rial's green eyes hardened. "You think he regards having to deal with you as anything else? He's a Millioni and you're a freak."

"Leopold was no better."

"Gods, still upset he had your girl first?"

"He never had her."

A'rial sighed. "So simple. So simplistic. So unwilling to live up to his talents. You promised Alexa an army of immortals. You promised me a kill of my choosing. Now look at you, weeping like a girl in the rain. Just because Leopold . . ."

"I saw her first."

"*I saw her first . . .*"

Tycho knew the mockery in her words was deserved. He still hated A'rial for it, though. He could leave Venice behind him. Abandon his life here and start again somewhere else. Where?

Beyond Dalmatia . . .?

Where could he go the moon didn't swell each month to birth

his terrifying hunger? His current choices were kill, buy blood, which he now realised carried a risk in leaving the person he bought from alive, or ride out his hunger in self-captivity.

This was not living.

But then some days he doubted he was really alive.

When he looked up A'rial was gone. The horses and the night wind, the rain and the chant of plainsong from inside the cathedral were still there but Alexa's little *stregoi* was not.

What did she want?

Did he mean A'rial or Giulietta?

Tycho wasn't even sure which he meant, as if that even mattered. He'd failed Alonzo and ruined his chances with Giulietta, Alexa's *stregoi* had turned up to give him a warning he was too stupid to understand, and that probably meant Alexa knew he'd failed too.

Unless A'rial was acting on her own?

Yes, that was possible . . .

Wiping rain and tears from his eyes, Tycho glared around him. Bjornvin had been hell. This felt the same, simply with better food and scenery, unless the hell was him and he carried the darkness inside?

The more he thought about it, the more he decided Alexa didn't know.

He would ride out this week's pregnant moon locked away in the printing works with their back-to-front engraving plates of Millioni deceit and Republican virtue that came gifted with his house, and then he would visit her.

Tell Alexa exactly what he'd done.

22

Around suppertime, Alexa decided the third Wednesday of August was turning into the strangest of days. Her niece, already reclusive, now refused to answer letters. A summons sent that morning to attend her aunt had been returned, unbelievably enough, by the messenger sent to deliver it. Asked why, the man stammered some excuse about no one answering the door.

Alexa had him whipped, obviously.

And then there was Alonzo . . . A day's worth of drunken fury last week had spawned forty-eight hours of hangover and sulking, followed by this week's skulking in corners with Lords Roderigo and Bribanzo. This morning Roderigo and the Regent had left the palace together, with all the subtlety of men wearing signs reading *plotting* round their necks.

That Roderigo was on Alonzo's side worried her. The customs office taxed the goods that flowed in and out of the city, remitting the money to the treasury. All it would take was for their captain to tell his men to remit the money straight to the Regent and Alexa's life would become very complicated indeed.

She really did need to know what was going on.

Closing her shutters against the late sun, Alexa poured water from a silver jug into her jade bowl and shut her eyes and concentrated on what she wanted her magic to reveal to her when she opened them again. So she was surprised to discover the reflection showed Atilo's servant, Iacopo.

At the very least she'd been expecting Roderigo.

She let her fingers brush the water and Iacopo's face trembled. The table he sat at was clean and the unfilled glass in front of him expensive. So not a common hostelry, then. Maybe this boy was the key to Alonzo's fury?

Only Iacopo was no longer a boy.

He had a beard and armour, and had dressed himself in his best clothes for whomever he was meeting. But he looked like a boy to Alexa. And, as he sat there, nervously shuffling his feet and talking to himself, she felt almost sorry for him. How terrible to be a pawn in someone else's game.

Only whose pawn and which game?

Those were the questions that had seen her banish her ladies-in-waiting before filling the bowl with rainwater. Any water would do but jade this perfect deserved the best. Alexa smiled as Iacopo stopped staring round the room and composed himself as the man who'd invited him returned from the privies.

Now she was getting somewhere.

It was doubtful Roderigo's choice of meeting place could be called a tavern at all. The floor was clean, the tables steady, the food good. An ambitious young servant like Iacopo must dream of being welcome in clubs like this.

"Sorry," Roderigo said, sliding himself into place. "Thought I might as well get that out of the way before." He reached for his glass, then noticed his guest's was still empty. "You didn't pour for yourself?"

"It seemed rude, my lord."

Roderigo nodded approvingly.

". . . And I must congratulate you."

"On what?"

"Your ennoblement."

Close to an insult, Alexa thought.

Iacopo paled at his mistake. "I meant your title."

"No offence," said Roderigo. His family had been noble for generations and his new title of baron was merely proof of the Regent's favour; as was the gold being spent to reroof his palace on the Canalasso.

"My lord, this is an honour . . ."

"But you're wondering why I asked you?"

The young man flushed, considered lying and decided honesty was his only option. "Much as it's a pleasure to drink with you. And this place is . . ." He glanced round.

"Very different from that brothel in which we first drank?"

"Yes, my lord. Very . . ."

Not a bare-titted whore in sight. Excellent wine, whispered conversation. Even the hazard players had managed to avoid going for their knives and accusing each another of cheating. There was something else . . .

All the serving staff were male. Strange in a city where overflowing bosoms brought in business. "What is this place?"

"A club," Roderigo said. "A Republican club."

"My lord . . ."

"God's man. No one here is a Republican. Or if any of the older members are they have more sense than to admit so. That's how the club began, though. In the brief reign of the Second Republic. The owner had the sense to drop his politics and keep his customers."

"The Censors allow it?"

Roderigo looked at him quizzically. "The Regent is a member. It would be hard for the Censors to accuse a club of treason given Prince Alonzo uses it for his less formal meetings . . . Drink up. This is good wine."

"Very good, my lord."

"Spanish, strangely. But you probably knew that."

"No." Iacopo resisted the urge to lie, and when he glanced up from his now empty glass his host looked thoughtful. Roderigo filled Iacopo's glass himself, waving away a servitor who came hurrying.

"You still work for Lord Atilo?"

Iacopo nodded

"And you're still unhappy . . .?"

"My lord."

"A year ago you told me some days you felt little more than his slave. Remember – the day you won the regatta?"

"I was drunk. I apologise."

"*In vino veritas*. People tell the truth when drunk. For most it's the only time they do. I heard the bitterness in your voice and saw it in your eyes."

This was a test, Alexa decided.

Iacopo realised it, too, because he nodded.

"Yet you've been promoted?"

"I am now Lord Atilo's body servant, his secretary and his bodyguard." The young man smiled to show how ridiculous he found the idea of a hardened warrior like the Moor needing a bodyguard.

"What do you know of Prince Alonzo?"

"What everyone knows, my lord. He is the late duke's brother. The new duke's uncle. A brave man and experienced in war." Iacopo hesitated. "It is said he likes his drink as much as the rest of us. And that he and Alexa . . ."

"Hate each other?"

"That wasn't what I was going to say."

"It would be the truth."

Indeed, thought Alexa. She regretted the promise she'd made to her husband when he was dying. If not for her promise, Alonzo would have died years back of a convenient fever.

In her bowl Alexa watched Iacopo hesitate.

Unsure how to respond, the young man covered his uncertainty by reaching for his glass and sipping thoughtfully. He'd grown up since Alexa last noticed him. His breastplate no longer looked as if it had been polished by a stallholder trying to sell cheap goods to a Schiavoni. (The Schiavoni were like jackdaws and had to have anything shiny.) He'd also learnt to speak less and listen more. Second only to the first lesson a man should learn: watch more and speak less.

"We face great dangers," Roderigo said. "The Byzantines and the Germans want our city. And the city itself is divided. On one side is the Regent, who has fought in battle and is loved by his people. On the other side we have the Mongol duchess who is not."

"My lord . . ."

"It is time for you to choose sides."

Looking up, unable to believe what he was hearing, Iacopo obviously wondered how he'd even come to Alonzo's notice. It was a good question and Alexa was dying to discover the answer.

"He's offering me patronage?"

"He needs to know you're his friend first."

Iacopo took a few seconds to think about that. When he didn't object or look discouraged, Roderigo nodded. "I'll be honest. The Regent doesn't trust your master. Lord Atilo is rumoured to have been the duchess's lover . . ."

All knew it was more than a rumour.

"And he took Lady Desdaio to Cyprus against the Council's orders. She was meant to live at Ca' Ducale while he was gone. Even the duchess had agreed. And then, of course . . ."

Quite, thought Alexa.

Atilo won his victory over the Mamluks.

The Regent would be a fool to try to punish the hero of the hour openly. And thwarting the Moor in Council would look petty. So petty the duchess would be forced to side with her lover publicly. Alonzo needed another way. She wondered if Iacopo was smart enough to realise that involved him.

"You know Sir Tycho well?"

From the instant stiffening of the young man's shoulders, Alexa realised Iacopo hated even hearing the boy's name. "He was Atilo's slave," Iacopo said shortly.

"You dislike each other?"

"He turned Lord Atilo against me."

"Then you will be delighted to know that Sir Tycho has disappointed the Regent badly . . ." Seeing Iacopo scowl, he added, "You're not his replacement if that's what you think. I'm simply saying Prince Alonzo has been disappointed once this month. It would be unwise to disappoint him again."

Tycho disappointed the Regent? Alexa thought.

"What do you need me to do?"

"Nothing, for the moment. Watch your master and note whom he talks to. If possible, remember about what. Watch my Lady Desdaio and learn what you can of her movements, who she sees and what they talk about."

"You know she visits Tycho?"

"I thought that a rumour."

"Once she visited three times in a week. Always when Lord Atilo is in Council. She'd probably be visiting tonight if not for Lady Giulietta."

Roderigo's face stilled. "Explain."

"My lord, three weeks ago Lady Giulietta visited Tycho to complain he risked blackening Lady Desdaio's name. I'm told the argument was fierce."

"You're told?"

Iacopo stared at the table.

"I assume following Desdaio was not on Atilo's orders?"

"No, my lord."

"You didn't take Lord Atilo this information?"

"The last time I told my master the truth, he slit my face and made me sew the wound myself." Iacopo's voice was flat and the hand he put to his face unthinking as he traced the scar.

"What truth was this?"

"That Desdaio visited Tycho's chambers at night."

"This is when he was a slave?"

Alexa leant over her bowl in her anxiety to have the answer. That Tycho and her niece had been lovers was a rumour unwisely whispered by crew from the *San Marco* in their cups. More than one had gone to sleep afterwards and woken not at all, his throat cut and body floating in a canal. That Desdaio Bribanzo, the most famous, not to mention richest, virgin in Venice was also his lover . . .

"Yes, my lord. This is when he was a slave."

Roderigo looked disgusted. "And Atilo doesn't know about Desdaio's visits to his house in San Aponal?"

"Not from me. There's more."

"Well . . . ?"

"Tycho recently visited Lady Giulietta's house."

He did? Alexa thought.

"I know about that," Roderigo said.

That was when Alexa decided she should be worried. She didn't know about Tycho visiting her favourite niece? Yet Alonzo's man did . . . ? Alexa was so busy thinking this through she missed Roderigo's next question; though it was easy to read from Iacopo's answer.

"I followed Atilo's new apprentice."

"Why do that?"

"He's Tycho's spy. Unless the brat's his catamite."

"That might be too much for us to hope for."

"You dislike Sir Tycho as well, my lord?"

Roderigo's mouth set. "It's enough he let the Regent down and misused his trust. A mistake he will regret."

The third part of Iacopo's night was probably the strangest – to him at least. To Alexa it was obvious that Roderigo was working a simple three-point entrapment. Entice, bribe, flatter . . . The first part, the drink in a club on the Canalasso, where Lord Roderigo treated him like an equal simply because Iacopo was there, was strange enough. The second part was not strange at all.

Simply glorious and unexpected by Iacopo.

Roderigo took him to a brothel for nobles behind Giovanni e Paolo, a small palace reached through a *corte*, one of those tiny private squares. The whores were young, well-mannered and undoubtedly shy compared to those Iacopo used.

Having ushered him through the door, Roderigo told a serious-faced major-domo that Iacopo was a trusted man of Prince Alonzo's who should be looked after, then tossed a farewell to Iacopo and vanished up marble stairs, leaving his guest open-mouthed in the richly decorated hall.

The poison flower was unfolding as Alexa expected. Her brother-in-law was thorough in his seductions.

Iacopo was bathed, massaged and invited to watch two girls sport with each other. By the time they finished squirming he was clearly desperate to do the one thing he hadn't yet done. Slide himself between a woman's thighs.

"Which one of us do you want?"

He chose the youngest, prettiest, stupidest. Exactly as Alexa expected. When the blonde girl caught him gazing longingly at her buttocks in a mirror she simply smiled. "This is your first visit?"

Iacopo flushed.

"It's all right. Many are never invited at all."

Iacopo chose the grandest of the bedrooms he was offered.

Huge silvered mirrors, a vast Persian carpet hung on one wall, a semi-circular table topped with horsehair marble and set with a jug of red wine and a dish of grapes. Seeing his wide-eyed glance, she took one, turned away and tucked it discreetly inside her. Then invited him to extract it. With his tongue.

* * *

Many Venetian rooms looked grand by candlelight. Just as candle-light made most faces look younger than their owners really were. The room where Iacopo woke looked grand in daylight as well. And the girl who shared his bed still looked as young and as beautiful as he remembered.

"Will I see you again?"

She smiled at him. Her smile said this wasn't the first time she'd been asked that question. Rolling out of bed, she shrugged herself into a silk wrap and tied it around her. Then she combed out Iacopo's curls with her fingers, wiped his mouth and stepped back before he could lift a hand to her breast.

"It depends if you come here again."

"We could meet anyway . . ."

So little imagination, Alexa thought. And that didn't just apply to his suggestion or the awed sadness with which he took a final look around the over-gilded and gaudily furnished room. It applied to everything he'd done to the girl over the previous six hours.

Or those bits Alexa bothered to watch.

It was while being escorted downstairs that the third part of Iacopo's entrapment occurred. Already washed and dressed, prob-ably wondering how he'd explain his night's absence to Lord Atilo, he almost jostled a barrel-chested man heading in the other direction. Iacopo's shock was complete when the Regent clapped him on the shoulders as if they were companions.

"Lord Roderigo's friend?"

Iacopo bowed low. "Iacopo, my lord."

"Come eat with us. You must be hungry after . . ." The Regent grinned and steered Iacopo back up the stairs into a room full of breakfasting nobles. Only Lord Roderigo bothered to return Iacopo's greeting.

Iacopo took his place at the far end of a bench.

The table offered hot bread, goat's cheese, salted beef and fish so fresh it had to have been pulled from the lagoon that morning.

Small beer, white wine, and fermented milk that was only drunk by a dark-skinned Seljuk.

Finally, Alonzo's companions began to drift away, given their cue by a discreet wave of the Regent's hand. In the end only Roderigo, Alonzo and Iacopo were left.

"Join us," Alonzo barked.

Abandoning his place at the far end, Iacopo sat where Alonzo pointed. The Regent's face was darker now, his eyes less kind. He examined his half-emptied wine glass with anger.

Here it comes, Alexa thought.

"The Red Crucifers have written to me."

Iacopo thought it best to wait until one of them told him who the Red Crucifers were and why they made the Regent cross. It turned out they were a group of Teutonic knights that Venice had hired to fight heathens in Montenegro, who now claimed to have founded a new order.

"They look for a commander."

"My lord . . ." Roderigo sounded appalled.

"Indeed, Roderigo. Traitors inviting me to fight heretics! I've a good mind to set sail immediately to destroy them both . . . I could do with a good battle before I get old. All this politicking wearies me. All these council meetings about monopolies and taxes. All this grubbing after money. Even when Venice does fight, it's off Cyprus, which we practically own. And we have to rely on a turncoat Moor for victory."

Iacopo was shocked.

"You think I'm wrong?"

The question was aimed at him.

"Well?" Alonzo barked. "Do you? Think I'm wrong to want to leave this sewer and get back to battle? To have honest Christian soldiers around me?"

"My lord," said Iacopo, then stopped.

Since there was no right answer he fell back on flattery.

"My lord, you might want to leave Venice. But I'm not sure

Venice can afford to lose you. Even if it is to conquer heretics."

Prince Alonzo snorted.

"I mean it, my lord. You brought the Castellani and Nicoletti together when Lady Giulietta went missing. If you were to go that would leave Venice in the hands of . . ." He hesitated.

"Duchess Alexa?"

"She's a woman. Also she's . . ." Scrying in her water bowl, Alexa wondered how he'd word it. "Not Venetian, my lord."

"You mean she's a Mongol?"

Iacopo nodded.

"Others feel like you?"

"Oh yes, my lord. Among the commons most people do. And there are many rich merchants and nobles who look to you."

It was the right answer.

23

Tycho had woken at twilight to a demand from the Duchess Alexa that he present himself immediately. The guards at the Porta della Carta had admitted him without fuss. One of Alexa's staff had hurried him past petitioners. That was how he found himself in Marco's chamber, being asked by Alexa why he'd sent a petition asking to be allowed to talk to her, what he'd done to upset her brother-in-law, the Regent, and why her niece had locked herself in Ca' Friedland . . .

He was now wondering if saying all three questions had the same answer, and then telling her the answer was a good idea.

"*You did what?*"

Tycho stepped back from the anger of the woman who sat on a low throne in front of him. Anger flared from her like flame. He imagined his skin shrivelling, his flesh burning away. Only his bones remaining.

"Go," Alexa announced.

It turned out she meant everyone but him.

Even Marco, who trailed from his chamber looking somewhere between puzzled and sad. He was the last to leave, having dawdled to check his mother really did mean him too. Having discovered she did, Marco trailed after the ladies-in-waiting, Alexa's maid and two guards. Although first he touched one finger to his chin, raising it slightly. *Chin up*, his gesture said.

Tycho wondered if he imagined it.

"Well . . .?" Alexa demanded.

"I met with Alonzo, here . . ."

"Why?"

"He offered me what I want."

"Riches?" Alexa said contemptuously. "A bigger palace? Gold chains to hang round your neck and embroidery in your cloak? A fake pedigree proving you've been noble all along? It wouldn't be the first time."

"Giulietta."

Alexa looked shocked.

More shocked than if he'd said yes to all her previous questions. Lady Giulietta was a Millioni princess. This whole problem was because she'd married one prince and another now wanted to marry her.

That someone like him might think . . .

He watched her catch her temper. It was impressive and a little unexpected. Alexa put her hands on the marble top of a table and held them there as if letting the fury flow from her body through her fingers. When she sat back, her shoulders were relaxed and her voice almost normal. "You realise Alonzo will kill you if he discovers you've told me this?"

"He said the same about you."

"You're very sure of yourself."

Believe me. That is the last thing I am.

If his face showed courage he didn't feel he was grateful. He'd been offered a chance to woo Lady Giulietta, to win her. To get the one thing he wanted before all others. The thing he still wanted. And his craven cowardice had destroyed his chances. How hard was it to say *I love you*?

Too hard for him, apparently. He could stand here now, and

tell Duchess Alexa to her face he loved her niece and risk arrest. When it came to Giulietta, however, he hadn't dared say the same.

The mockery in her eyes had undone him.

Pushing a pale bowl filled with water away from her, Duchess Alexa draped a cloth over the top. "My niece is sulking."

"She is unhappy, my lady."

Alexa sighed. "Our spies say Sigismund's offer is talked about in Constantinople. Do you know what that means?"

How could he possibly know?

"It has been brought to the attention of the Basilius."

When Tycho looked blank, Alexa scowled. "The *Basilius*," she said. "Emperor John V Palaiologos. In true descent from the Caesars . . . A self-opinionated and superstitious old man. He has been a thorn in my side for years."

"Why have you not sent someone to . . .?"

Alexa smiled. "I do believe you'd try."

"I would prefer to travel by land. If possible."

"That you can cross water at all is impressive. Your kind need bare earth beneath their feet to prosper."

"My kind?"

"Everyone has a kind," she said. "One of my nephew Tamburlaine's scholars was recently good enough to confirm yours. Unfortunately the Basilius is so well protected I doubt even you could get through his defences though I'm tempted to try. Now, I'm going to ask you a question and I want a truthful answer."

Tycho waited.

"What have you done to upset Giulietta?"

"I asked her to marry me."

"You're not listening. I don't mean what was your last idiocy. Nor am I asking what you called her when she found you with Lady Desdaio." Catching Tycho's shock, Alexa said, "Yes, I know about that, too."

"Nothing happened with Desdaio."

"I doubt my niece believes that . . . I mean before all this, before you even landed at St Lazar, something happened. You will tell me what."

"I told her a secret."

"You told her what you are?"

"My lady," Tycho swallowed. "I don't know what I am."

"I've heard you call your self *Fallen*."

"That's what my mother called herself. So I was told by a woman before . . . before I found myself here. No, this is different. On the night of battle off Cyprus I gave a Mamluk prince his life. In return he told me of my origins."

"How would he know anything about that?"

"He said his father bought me from Timurid mercenaries and had mages fill my head with only one thought, *that I must kill you*. He did so at Prince Alonzo's request. Venetian gold sweetened the request."

"You did not say that. I did not hear it."

"No, my lady."

"I'm not surprised my niece is upset if you go around telling her things like that." Raising her gauze-like veil, Alexa stared at Tycho with dark eyes set in an unlined, almost ageless face. She had the flawless tallow skin most Mongol women in the city seemed to have.

The more he stared the younger she became.

Until he was looking at a Mongol girl with huge eyes. She smiled as if amused to be recognised and his heart flooded with sadness when she lowered the veil again. "You love my niece." She sounded surprised. "I thought you simply ambitious."

"My lady . . ."

"Yes, yes, I know. Your heart bleeds to be without her. The fact marriage would make you a prince means nothing." Alexa sighed. "You should understand that marriage is impossible. However, you could be lovers."

144

Holding up her hand she stilled Tycho's protest.

"If that becomes true, so be it. I'll summon Giulietta again, tell her I won't brook refusal. In the meantime, we tell Sigismund's envoy it's a fact."

"Will saying we're lovers be enough?"

"It will be for the envoy," Alexa assured Tycho. "He'll need to report back. Sigismund will want to discuss this *fact* with his advisers."

"And Giulietta's baby?"

"What exactly do you know of that?"

"May I ask what you know?"

For a moment it looked as if the duchess would order him to answer anyway, and Tycho had little doubt she had the magic to compel him. Instead she said, "I know nothing. You have no idea how worrying that is."

"Surely, my lady. You must . . ."

"Oh, I've held the brat, looked deep into its eyes. It's hers all right. My husband's blood runs thick in its veins. But Leopold's part. Sigismund's bloodline . . .?" Alexa shrugged. "I have no sense of Leopold's part."

"The child is not his."

"You know this?" Alexa said sharply.

"The prince asked if Leo was mine."

"How could it be yours? When did he ask this?"

"On the day he died. We were talking before the battle and Leopold . . . He was troubled," Tycho finished lamely.

"A strange and brilliant man. Who liked other men, bedded women he hated, and therefore mistreated, because the bedding was expected and he resented what he felt the world required him to do."

"I did not know."

"Why should you? Giulietta falls silent if we talk about this. I assume Alonzo knows that Leopold asked?" Alexa took Tycho's silence as answer. "Then his offer makes more sense. You were to claim the child?"

"Yes, my lady."

"And you would do this?"

"Willingly."

Duchess Alexa sighed. "I repeat, marriage is out of the question. But I will consider the alternatives. In the meantime what have you heard about a demon on the island off San Giacomo?"

"Very little, my lady."

"That's about to change."

24

The sexton for San Giacomo lived with his wife and daughter in a squalid house at Three-Sided Square, slightly to the west of Arzanale, and as far north as it was possible to go without hitting water. The square's name came from its northernmost edge having collapsed into the lagoon.

The night air stank of rotting canals and sulphur from the iron foundries to the west, and of human shit from a night-soil dock a hundred paces away. It smelt no better ten feet above the ground than it did at ground level, but at least Tycho had a slight wind to soften the night's heat. Sliding his knife between shutters, he lifted a wooden latch free.

When no one stirred, he opened one side.

A man slept on a narrow bed, with a woman on a low cot beside him and a baby in a crate at her feet. All three were covered by cloth cut from a single sheet. The sexton and his woman were younger than Tycho expected.

Tycho stilled as the sill settled slightly under his weight, but the room remained silent and the three remained sleeping, so he sheathed his own knife and took the dagger from the floor beside the sexton's bed to place it out of reach.

Then he knelt beside the woman, tapped her face and watched her stir. The childish smile filling her face in the brief gap between sleeping and waking revealed the girl she'd once been. A split second later, she opened her mouth to scream and Tycho put his finger to her lips.

"Bid me welcome . . ."

She stared at him.

He had to order her a second time before she did and the ache gripping him began to fade. "Wake your man."

"We're married."

"Then wake your husband."

He could have knocked at their door, demanding entry. What he wanted, however, was the sexton off guard. One glance at the woman as she tossed her sheet aside to kneel by her husband told Tycho he had all the leverage he needed.

The woman was heavily pregnant, her stomach stretched to splitting, her breasts overfull. When the baby in the crate began wailing, she shut her eyes.

"If it's hungry, feed it."

She looked at him.

"Duchess Alexa sent me."

Mentioning the duchess's name drove all emotion from the woman's face. He'd simply scared her more deeply. Blindly, as if asleep, she lifted the wailing baby, opened her shift and exposed a breast.

A second later the baby was feeding.

"Now wake your man."

"Giorgio . . ." When he didn't wake, she shook him. "He drinks." Touching her belly, she added, "These are difficult times for him. And there's something else . . ."

"I know," said Tycho. "That's why I'm here."

The drunk scrabbled for his dagger, fingers digging at the filthy floor like a man trapped inside a coffin. Tycho pointed to a table and watched Giorgio's eyes focus. There was enough moonlight for him to see his dagger.

Giorgio judged the distance, looked at his wife to give himself courage and hesitated when she said, "The duchess sent him."

"Cover yourself, woman."

"I'll be downstairs." She levered herself from her knees.

"Maria . . ."

"It's not me he wants to talk to."

Both men listened to her heavy steps on the stairs, the sound of a door banging and the splash of someone pissing outside. The door banged as she came back and then there was silence.

"She's almost due," Giorgio said.

Maybe he thought to excuse her. Maybe he thought to excuse the bruises on her face. The night was hot and sticky, the air foul from the moored shit barges. It was a bad time of year to be pregnant, and the separate beds, snapped words and tight silences said tempers were frayed between them.

"You're the sexton for San Giacomo?"

The man nodded, his eyes watchful. A tic at one corner said he knew there was more to Tycho's question than the words implied.

"Then you know why I'm here."

For a moment Giorgio almost denied it. He opened his mouth to say he had no idea, only to hiccup instead. "Three barges," he said. "Five of my men."

"No one's come back?"

He shook his head.

"And that's why paupers' corpses are piling up in the crypt?"

"I have no men," he said simply. "No men, no barges. You think I can find men when something like this is known?"

"It's known?"

"How not?" said Giorgio, losing his fear. "You can hear her howling from here."

"On moonlit nights?"

"Any night. Every night. Listen . . ."

Tycho did. All he could hear was the slap of distant sails, the strum of wind-plucked hawsers, the snuffle of rubbish pigs cleaning up in Three-Sided Square below. That was all Giorgio could hear too.

"Idiots," he said.

Tycho looked puzzled.

"Some of the men said they were going to hunt her down. If she's silent that's because she's eaten. She's always silent after she kills."

"You know she kills?"

"They don't come back, do they?"

"Have you told the Watch?"

"My cousins were killed on the island and I found their bodies. The Watch didn't want to know."

"You said *her*. You've seen this creature?"

The sexton looked nervous. "I went out after the second barge didn't return. I used my brother-in-law's fishing boat and stopped offshore. She came down to the water's edge to glare at me."

"Describe her."

"Naked, my lord." That was the first time Giorgio had been polite. He'd probably just worked out that if his secret was known to those in authority it wasn't his secret any more. "Moves on all fours like a dog."

"You've seen her clearly?"

Giorgio nodded. "Stick-thin, my lord. With huge eyes and black hair. A scar runs from shoulder to her hip. Another scar . . ." He hesitated "It looks like she was stabbed in the heart."

"She was."

The sexton paled. "Say you're joking, please."

"I was there when she died. I will need your help."

"To do what, my lord?"

"Kill her a second time."

The sexton crossed himself.

25

"We're off," Giorgio shouted into the darkness of a tiny room behind him. An irritated grunt and the wail of a newborn child answered him.

"We meet your brother-in-law at the jetty?"

"Yes, sir. And he's bringing his cousin." Before Tycho could protest, the sexton added, "The man who owns the barge you wanted filled with earth. You do have his warrant for this trip?" Giorgio paled at his own bluntness.

"In my pocket," Tycho lied.

Boats were forbidden to move on the lagoon after dark without a warrant from the office of the Dogana and proof of taxes paid. Boats did move, of course, smugglers and lovers, those disposing of bodies and those on their way to other dark deeds.

"The boat is over there, sir."

A shit barge had been emptied and slopped down.

It still stank like a public latrine and had stains to make Tycho fear for his doublet. However, its usual cargo had been replaced with earth, freshly dug and still moist, with worms wriggling blindly on its surface.

"That's my brother-in-law, Mario."

A squat young man in a Castellano smock, his cap greasy with age, bowed clumsily in Tycho's direction and busied himself with a rope.

"And that's his cousin."

The owner of the barge stank even at a distance. He stank with the vigour of a man who spent six days each week up to his waist in excrement. Venice had strict rules regarding both water and shit. Fresh water was drawn from one set of cisterns in the city, and shit deposited into another set. When the cisterns were full the shit was dug out and shipped to the mainland as night soil for the crops.

Freeing his sword, Tycho jabbed the earth at his feet.

His blade sank through dirt and touched the wooden hull two feet down, which was better than he'd demanded. Maybe even deep enough to stop his sickness over water. "It'll do," he said.

To the men's surprise Tycho sat himself directly on the earth rather than the crate they'd provided. "Tell him," Mario whispered.

"Later," hissed another.

"Now's better."

"Tell me what?" Tycho demanded. "My hearing would embarrass an owl," he added, when the three men turned in shock. "Talk more quietly or move away." Truth was, he'd hear them even if they stood on the far side of the square. "Better still, say what you want to say."

"Sometimes, my lord. We . . ."

Silence followed Mario's words. Either side of Mario, his companions shuffled their feet. It turned out they robbed the dead of anything not taken by those who found them.

"The bodies arrive naked?"

Giorgio looked shocked. "No, my lord. They arrive in the rags they were wearing when found. Some bodies are fresh and others rotten, depending on the season and how long before someone reported them. We search all but the worst."

"Their rags?"

"And their bodies."

One of the others muttered something.

Actually, thought Tycho, *I wouldn't be surprised where you found things hidden*. The poor undoubtedly hid things in the same places slaves did; different for men and women, but not that different.

"That's what you wanted to tell me?"

"There's more. There are people who . . ."

Tycho knew he wouldn't like what was coming. Although it turned out to be not what he thought. Mario didn't want to talk about dark practices. Well, he did, but not the necrophiliac kind. Greed was behind their sins.

It took the three men halfway to the island to get to the heart of it.

They took trinkets from bodies. Occasionally they took the bodies themselves. Mario said he didn't dare say who bought the bodies. Which was fine, Tycho didn't need telling. Only one man in Venice was likely to want a steady supply of cadavers. Hightown Crow.

26

Her uncle Alonzo was still out whoring, gambling or whatever he did with Sundays these days. Tycho was . . . Lady Giulietta didn't care where he was. And Aunt Alexa was pouring tea, and radiating smugness at finally having Giulietta to herself.

"Come late afternoon," her note said.

It arrived along with the duchess's own red-lacquered palanquin. She'd even sent her best men to carry her through the streets. Lady Giulietta made them wait while she changed, and drew the curtains on the chair so no one could see inside. It was, she had to admit, a comfortable way to travel.

She'd come dressed as a grown-up.

Because I am a grown-up.

She'd had her maid tie back her hair with barely a strand escaping, had put on a black gown of raw Chinese silk, shaved into complicated patterns. She'd half hidden her face behind cobweb lace, and hung a silver chain of overlapping scales across her bosom. It made no difference. Even dressed as a grown-up she'd walked straight into her aunt's trap. This meeting was serious.

It had to be. Her aunt was so slow getting to the point.

For someone who prided herself on her ability to navigate the hidden rocks of court life, Giulietta had run aground on rather too many in recent years. Tycho appearing when she'd been about to kill herself was the start of it. She'd been begging the Virgin for help for days . . . And the Virgin sent him?

Then Leopold, elegant and slightly mocking on the Riva degli Schiavoni that first time they met. *Eggs have no business dancing with stones.* He'd known who she was. While pretending not to. *I know quality.*

She'd fallen for his line and his smile.

And he'd left her, left the world and left her mistress of everything he once owned. Lands, tithes, titles.

"Are you listening?"

"No," Giulietta snapped. "I'm thinking."

Nudging aside a copy of *Liber Igneum*, whose full title roughly translated as *A Book of Ways to Burn Enemies to Death*, Alexa reached for an ivory-handled jug. Her book contained a recipe for gunpowder that Giulietta had once learnt by heart. She'd been eleven and Uncle Marco had been dying, and Giulietta was going to blow a hole in the garden wall and escape.

For a month, she saved her piss to distil saltpetre, adding charcoal from the drawing box and crushed sulphur from the pills her nurse took for the flux. But the hidden urine stank so badly she finally tipped it into the privy and explained away the stink by complaining Lady Eleanor wet the bed. Eleanor was whipped, of course. She'd refused to talk to Giulietta for days.

"Why did you whip us as children?"

"Everyone's whipped as a child."

"As often as we were?"

"Let me tell you a story." Taking a slow sip, Aunt Alexa appeared to vanish inside herself for a few seconds. "A girl of Eleanor's age was discovered talking to a boy in a corridor after dark. Talking, nothing else. She was not whipped, she was strangled with a silken rope. The boy was not whipped, he was impaled on a steel spike that had been heated to cauterise the wound. It took him two days to die. Her lady-in-waiting was not whipped. She was hung, being too common for a silken rope. The girl was my sister and I was whipped."

"For not stopping her?"

"I wasn't even in the same city. You think your uncle wouldn't have had you strangled if he could? My son impaled if he could get away with it?"

Giulietta had never heard her speak like this.

"I kept you *alive*," the duchess said. "I kept you both alive. If you leave Venice – and I'm told you want to – how will I protect you? Although maybe Tycho could help with that."

"Tycho?"

"There are murmurs . . ."

"He means nothing to me."

"So he won't be going with you?"

Won't be . . . ? Lady Giulietta shook her head fiercely. *How could her aunt even ask such a question?* "Of course not."

"Then I doubt the Council will give you permission to retire to your mother's mainland estates. Nor can you count on my support."

"*My lady . . .*"

"You will remain in this city."

They sat on opposite sides of a small table on scissor chairs with embroidered cushions that looked more comfortable than they felt. Alexa's room was as Giulietta remembered. The one unchanging room in a palace that was forever being rebuilt, improved and redecorated. Although the table stank of turpentine, having been recently revarnished with amber dissolved in spirit. The only unusual thing in the room, which Giulietta glared round trying to regain her temper, was an iridescent lizard in one corner.

"What's that called again?"

"Don't change the subject."

Lady Giulietta's chin went up. "I think it's time for me to go."

"We should finish our conversation first."

Why should we? Giulietta thought. But obedience had been beaten into her, for all that obstinacy had never been beaten out. Her aunt's assurance she would be obeyed undid Giulietta's resolve.

"All right then . . . *Who* said something about me?"

"There are murmurs."

"About Lady Desdaio," Giulietta said viciously. "Not about me. Why would there be rumours about me? It's Desdaio who practically lives there. Every time Atilo leaves for a council meeting she sneaks out to see his ex-slave."

"You're jealous."

"*I'm not jealous.*" Giulietta dug her nails into her hand hard. All the same, she felt her eyes brim. She would *not* cry in front of Aunt Alexa.

The lizard thing looked up as Giulietta came closer. It eyed her warily as she knelt beside it, her back turned to her aunt. Lady Giulietta's voice was steady by the time she trusted herself to speak. "What is it?"

"A dragonet."

"Never heard of them."

"They're common in China. My nephew sent it with his last letter. He thought it would remind me of home."

"Does it?" Giulietta asked, hoping to be cruel in her turn.

Alexa nodded. "My dear," she said. "We must talk about Tycho. Reports say the two of you were close on the ship."

It was half question, half statement.

Lady Giulietta didn't bother to deny it. "After the battle I was tired and distressed. Leopold had died and . . ."

"A man can laugh a woman into bed but sadness will take her there quicker. Be careful. With creatures like that you become responsible for what you tame."

Giulietta was pretty sure they weren't talking about the dragonet. "We didn't . . ."

"But it was close?"

Blushing, she tried to shrug aside the question.

"I need you to tell me . . . Believe it or not, this has become a matter of state." Perhaps it was coincidence Aunt Alexa moved to stand between the door and where her niece crouched by the dragonet, although Giulietta doubted it. Her aunt retained her ability to make Giulietta feel twelve.

She could lie or tell the truth. She'd always despised people who lied. "Leopold was dead. And I," Giulietta shrugged, "was desperate, alone, scared. There's something about Tycho . . ."

"And there's something about being sixteen. I have two questions, both important."

Giulietta waited.

"Is that child Leopold's? Were you lovers? Because his tastes usually ran in a different direction. And, did you really love him? Or is this dressing up in widow's clothes play-acting?"

"That's three."

Alexa scowled.

"No, no, yes." Giulietta got her answers over quickly. So quickly she barely gave herself time to think. "And it's not acting. Leopold was a friend and kind to me when I needed . . ." She hesitated. "Help."

"So who is Leo's real father?"

Giulietta was up and running for the door.

She couldn't even remember deciding to leave. Only Aunt Alexa's shockingly strong grip on her wrist prevented her turning the handle. She was younger and should be stronger. When she couldn't free herself tears came.

"Was it Tycho?"

"*No, it wasn't.*"

Putting her other hand to the fingers that gripped her, Giulietta contemptuously peeled them off her wrist. Alexa let it happen.

"This is the last time I visit you," Lady Giulietta said tightly. "If you wish to contact me you may write. I don't guarantee to reply."

Alexa stepped back and Giulietta opened the door.

"Keep in mind," Alexa said. "We've told the envoy you and Tycho are lovers. That you cling to him in your grief. I suggest you act in public as if that is true."

"I'd rather die."

"Gods," said Alexa. "He really has got to you, hasn't he?"

Giulietta gripped her silver chain tightly. She also slammed the door on her way out.

27

The first trip to the island produced little. The sexton, his brother-in-law and cousin being too terrified to put ashore. Since all Tycho could see were wild roses, thorn bushes and grave mounds, and all he could hear was the wind through wild grass, and all he could feel was an eerie emptiness, he allowed them their cowardice.

They put ashore the next night and found three dead Castellani bravoes in straw-stuffed leather jerkins with rusting pot helms and boar spears. There was no sign of the demon.

As darkness fell the night after that, Tycho rolled off his slab in the crypt of the church Giorgio served, about the only place in the near-derelict building out of direct sunlight, and unlocked the door from inside, not bothering to light a candle. The three men were already waiting for him at the jetty.

"Tonight we find her."

"How do you know, my lord?"

"I just do . . ." How could he explain this ache in his gut, his sense that tonight was different? Low wisps of summer fog waited above the glistening mud flats as they approached. The entire lagoon was banks and shallows, and since the dukes refused to allow maps to be made showing the channels that knowledge had to be learnt by heart and no one but a trained pilot knew them all.

The grave island had been made by driving staves around a mud bank, weaving willow branches along the staves and back-filling with dirt planted to grasses to help the ground set. Five hundred years of burials had raised its height.

"Is this fog usual?"

"What fog, my lord?"

That was an answer in itself. "You're certain it was here you first saw her?"

"My lord, I'm not likely to forget."

He'd give the man that. They led ordinary lives for all it involved shovelling shit or burying bodies. A creature from hell howling at the moon was likely to leave its mark on the memory. "Tie up there." Tycho pointed at a jetty.

His order had them scrabbling for their oars.

Tossing a rope around a spar, one dragged the barge close and tied off in that lazy way all Venetians did as easily as breathing. Then Giorgio looked around at the dark lagoon and the thorn-covered slopes of the island and shivered. "Perhaps we should wait offshore, my lord."

"You'll wait here."

"This is our island." The protest echoed inside Tycho's head.

In the fog were faces who all said the same.

Hollow-eyed faces with open and miserable mouths. He could see through them to wild roses beyond. A flicker of lights beyond that had to be stars on the horizon or a town on the mainland.

"You can keep it," Tycho said flatly.

"This is our . . ."

"I've come for the girl."

"Ahh . . ." The voices stilled, though the faces kept forming and fading, looming and retreating as they considered Tycho's statement. He was in a dream, unless the dream was the three men in the barge behind him too blind to see that the ghosts they feared were already here.

"She is dead," the voices said.

"Then I am dead."

The faces stopped, solidified.

White masks with dark hollows where eyes should be. They smiled and scowled at him, looked impassive, angry, intrigued and finally puzzled.

"*You are not us.*" With those words the mist faded, the low litany of misery fell into echo and then silence, and the ghosts vanished as if in agreement that their job here was done.

Kicking over one of the three Castellani he'd found the night before, Tycho examined the corpse. Even putrid and split by gases it was obvious the man had been eviscerated, his guts dragged from his body. His throat was ripped out and his head flopped from side to side so easily his neck had to be broken.

The kill was crude, probably swift. Blood had dried to splatter on the grass around him. It was unlikely she'd left herself enough to feed.

It wasn't hard to track her movements.

A footprint in the mud showed where she stood by the water before looking along the shore in both directions. Her prints ran right round the island. Tycho could read frustration in their pattern.

She'd walked the shore more than once. Walked down to the water's edge, headed in one direction and returned to this point before heading in the other. Always her prints returned here.

So, why this spot?

He could see one answer.

A line of light glimmered from Cannaregio's foundries, and linkmen's torches could be seen as they lit journeys along a distant *fondamenta*. This part of the island looked south towards Venice's northern shore. If he listened carefully he could hear the clock in Piazza San Marco strike ten.

The girl would have his hearing.

The other answer lay behind him. A grave pit, the earth of its surface trampled, the half-shell of a small boat covering one corner. Heaving away its rotten wood revealed the entrance to her own private hell.

All he had to do was entice her out.

Not a single mouse ran from Tycho's approach as he headed back to the jetty. The salt grass was quiet, the wild roses and thorn bushes undisturbed except for a shiver of wind. All the birds, rats, mice and voles were missing.

Tycho could remember what it felt like to be that hungry.

At the jetty, he pointed at Giorgio and told him to come here. The sexton looked unhappy but did what he was told, helped by hissed instructions from the other two.

"Hold out your hand."

He looked even more unhappy at that.

Tycho drew his dagger, slashed once and returned it to its sheath before the sexton even had time to yell. Blood welling between the man's clenched fingers dripped on to the dirt around his feet.

"Now run," Tycho told him.

She came out of the grave pit hard and fast, earth fountaining around her as she sprang free and dropped to a crouch, mouth wide and dog teeth descended. Nothing human stared from her eyes.

"Run," Tycho shouted.

The wild girl hit him full-on, bowling Tycho backwards into thorns, scrawny limbs wrestling his as she struggled to fight free and go after the man hurtling towards the boat. Tycho refused to let go.

"Run, damn it . . ."

Poised above him, the wild girl howled in fury as the sexton jumped into the boat, and his friends cast off, frantically rowing from the jetty.

In life she'd been fourteen.

In death she looked no older. Hunger made the poor age more slowly as children and faster as adults. It had been the same in Bjornvin; a starveling childhood looked the same everywhere.

He needed to work out how to kill her.

But the beast behind her eyes wanted feeding and she was furious.

Everything on this island she could eat was gone, and now her prey was escaping and it was his fault. It was like looking at himself, the otherness in her face, her skin under the pale moonlight sickly alabaster.

She dipped for his throat.

So he rammed his forearm under her chin and worked one foot under her, kicking her off so viciously she arced through the air in a wheel of limbs to land a dozen paces away. Only to pick herself up and charge again.

She closed on him so fast that Tycho slid back as he was rising to his feet, his toes digging into the dirt. He punched for the throat and she blocked without thinking. A second punch was blocked as fast. Dark eyes glared at him.

He could read their hatred.

Hurling her away, Tycho watched her stumble and turn to attack as swiftly as before. There was frustration in her eyes as he sidestepped and she hurtled into thorns, flesh ripping as she dragged herself free. She'd never faced someone as fast as him before. *She'd never faced someone as . . .*

He was missing the point.

Her frustration *proved* she was not mindless. Fear, madness, voices, despair . . . He could recognise those emotions. His stupidity at not recognising them earlier hit Tycho as hard as her next attack.

She felt what he'd felt.

164

In killing her he would be killing a version of himself, perhaps the only version of himself there would ever be.

She kicked, and he moved out of the way. She slashed, and he blocked and kept blocking until the wild roses became a blur and the stars a scribble of lines across the sky. They fought in the stretching length of seconds, then in the seconds themselves, and finally in the gaps between. The world was theirs, and no other existed. Eventually Rosalyn's breath became ragged, her eyes went wide and she knew she was losing.

Drawing his dagger, Tycho hesitated . . .

His orders from Alexa were to kill her, and to disobey and be discovered would cost him his patron. Why would he be stupid enough to risk that? This *thing* was filthy, once dead, barely human.

Once dead, barely human.

All the things he'd been. And besides . . .

Who'd pulled him from the Grand Canal the night he arrived in Venice? She had. In return he got her killed. He refused to be responsible for her second death. Despite knowing he might regret it, despite suspecting strongly he *would* regret it, Tycho sheathed his dagger. The next time she attacked he grabbed her. Picking her up, he carried her to the jetty and tossed her into the sea.

She screamed.

He let the girl crawl up the mud flats before he grabbed her again. She was scrabbling, fighting and hissing as he returned to the jetty to throw her back in. It was brutal, Tycho knew it was brutal. But he kept doing it.

Every time she reached the mud flats, he dragged her upright as if helping her, carried her back to the jetty and hurled her in, until the lagoon finally stole what little remained of her strength and left her unable to crawl ashore. Somewhere in the process, like the alchemical change that transmutes lead to gold, her animal howls became sobs. She still howled, but now she knew who she howled at.

He held her tight as she fought him.

You let them kill me.

Up to his knees in mud, aware he was being watched in horrified fascination, Tycho carried her ashore one final time. For all she'd fought like a demon – snarling and baring her teeth – she weighed almost nothing. Exhaustion caught her within seconds and she fell asleep in his arms.

"You will tell *no one* what happened here tonight."

The three men stared at Tycho, glanced at the naked girl and looked at each other. In their eyes was the flat anger of those who'd become embroiled in matters beyond them and knew they'd be lucky to escape.

"You understand me?"

They nodded.

28

The trip back to Tycho's house was as uneventful as any trip through midnight Venice could be. He'd given the sexton and his friends gold, which they weren't expecting, and a reminder their lives would be forfeit if they spoke of the night's work, which they were. No one stopped Tycho on his way through the city.

No one tried to catch his eye.

The Night Watch turned into a squalid square as he was crossing, hailed him and raised their torches. One look at Tycho's rich black velvets, the sword across his back and the near-naked girl in his arms had them retreating the way they'd come, muttering apologies.

On the Ponte Maggiore, where a guard snored on his three-legged stool, two mastiffs raised their heads to watch Tycho, sniffed the scent from Rosalyn's borrowed shift, considered their next actions and slumped back on all fours.

As he and Rosalyn passed emptying taverns and filling brothels, a young priest locking the doors of an old church crossed himself, and a sharp-eyed Mongol outside his Khan's *fontego* grinned. The stink of canals filled the air, mixed with acrid smoke from tavern grills and the sulphuric devilry of local foundries.

And for Tycho, at least, was added the scent of the gown Giorgio's wife surrendered so reluctantly. Salt fish, poverty and breast milk. The smell of Castellani women everywhere.

"*Tycho . . .*"

He turned, caught unaware.

The elegantly dressed young woman hurrying towards him had been hiding in a doorway. She faltered at the sight of the girl in his arms, and froze when she realised the unconscious girl was near naked.

"My lady?"

Desdaio just stood there.

"Where are your guards?" Tycho asked, already guessing the answer. She'd come out on to the night streets without protection, and, much as he hated Iacopo, he would have preferred Atilo's body servant to be here rather than have Lady Desdaio walk the streets unprotected.

"Is she dead?"

"No . . ." *But she was.*

And she would be again if Alexa got her way.

Tycho's orders had been clear. Hunt down and kill the demon. That was what he'd have the duchess believe had happened.

"She's just a child." Desdaio chewed her lip, looking increasingly unhappy. "And she stinks. That shift has holes in it. She's not decent. Tycho, what are you doing carrying an almost naked . . .?"

"*Desdaio.*"

She stopped talking.

"Go home," Tycho told her.

Tears brimmed in Desdaio's eyes and her bitten lip started trembling. Instinctively she hunched as if expecting a blow. And Tycho wondered about her childhood. About Lord Bribanzo, the richest man in Venice and one of the most ambitious. "You hate me," she said.

"I don't. But it's late and you shouldn't be here."

"Nor should you," said Desdaio crossly. "At least, not carrying that. What are planning to do with her anyway?"

"Wash her," Tycho said. "Feed her."

"And then bed her?"

"*Desdaio.*"

"That's not an answer."

"She saved my life the first night I was in Venice."

"Where's she been since?"

"Prison," Tycho said without thinking.

To be trapped between life and death in the darkness, and smothered by earth, barely able to move, to fight to the surface, having left all humanity behind, how could it be anything else? When he looked up, Desdaio's expression had softened. He knew what he was about to say before she said it.

"I'll bathe her. It's not proper for you to do it."

29

After Elizavet got over her surprise that Lady Desdaio had not, in fact, gone home after being told Tycho was not there, she hurried away to heat water, prepare cloths for washing and fetch soap. And though Tycho accepted Desdaio's order that he sit outside the bedroom door, his price was that she leave the door slightly open. So long as Rosalyn was unconscious Tycho was prepared to leave Desdaio to her cheerful chatting. Should Rosalyn wake he wanted to be nearby.

I should have killed her.

Tycho pressed his back against the wall and unpicked his worries. *If Desdaio hadn't turned up I could have killed her.* Except why bring her here when he could have obeyed Alexa's orders and killed her on the island? Sparing Rosalyn had been stupid. One monster was enough; the city didn't need two.

She wasn't him, anyway.

He was born and she was made.

Closing his eyes, Tycho fought the sudden sickness that thought brought. He'd made her. First of all, he'd been responsible for her death then he'd been responsible for bringing her back to life. If she was monstrous it was because he was monstrous. Of course she was dangerous. He was dangerous. But his stubbornness refused to let her die again.

If she lived the night he would look after her.

Having discovered Tycho really didn't want to bed the ragged girl, Desdaio now found his concern for Rosalyn touching, further proof he could be redeemed from the creature he'd declared himself the first time they talked.

She took credit for his change. Not understanding there had been none.

"You can come in," Desdaio said.

Rosalyn lay on the truckle bed, dressed in a silk shift that was too big around the bust. Seeing Tycho look, Desdaio covered her with a sheet and frowned when he pulled it down again.

"You gave her your own undergown?"

"She needed something decent."

Tycho could smell the old shift from where he stood. Mind you, he could smell everything in that room from the wood ash, lavender and mutton fat in the soap Elizavet provided to Desdaio's sweat from working to get the girl's dark hair clean. Even the fresh sheet smelt of the cedar wood chest in which it had been stored. Going to the door, he called for Elizavet.

"Take that shift and burn it."

"I could have done that."

Tycho wondered how lonely you had to be to want to undertake menial tasks for someone who'd been your slave. That was how lonely Desdaio was. He realised Desdaio was staring at the bed.

Rosalyn stared back.

Without even stopping to consider, Tycho untied the belt from around Lady Desdaio's waist and lashed Rosalyn's wrists together, tying her to the head of the bed. "In case she hurts herself."

Desdaio looked puzzled.

"We don't want her having a fit."

Never full, the street child's face was thinner than ever. Her cheeks bruised shadows tied to the skull beneath. Her shoulders sharp enough to jut through the silk of her borrowed gown. It was her eyes Tycho noticed.

He hoped Desdaio hadn't.

Only to glance back and realise she had. Her gaze flicking between Tycho's eyes and those of the girl on the bed. Lifting a candle, Desdaio checked she was right. Amber flecks really did dot Rosalyn's eyes.

"That's impossible."

"She has the same illness." Maybe his words would be enough to explain away the strangeness?

"She will be unable to stand daylight?"

"And the sun will burn her as surely as it burns me."

Tycho knew Desdaio believed him from hell, either an escaped demon or a fallen angel. The paleness of his skin, the strangeness of his eyes and the extremeness of his beauty had helped persuade her she was right. And looking at Rosalyn, her translucent skin as glorious as rain-slicked marble, Tycho realised the street girl had become unnervingly beautiful.

"Is she mute?"

"She wasn't before she . . ."

Before she died and was buried, before she was thrown into the sea by me. Every northern parish in Castello and Cannaregio must have heard Rosalyn's howls of fear and anger. Little human had stared from Rosalyn's eyes before he dunked her. Little of anything at all remained afterwards. "Before she became ill."

"So she needs medicine?"

"She needs feeding."

Desdaio looked exasperated. "Then fetch her food, and quickly. If you don't have anything suitable I can make something."

"Where's Atilo?

From her look you'd think he'd slapped her.

"In Council, so he says." Although her chin came up, the

defiance didn't reach her eyes, which flooded with hurt. "Seeing his duchess, I imagine. They seem to be friends again."

"Who told you about Alexa?"

"Since you didn't?" Desdaio said sharply. "Since you pretended Council meetings were where Lord Atilo was going all those nights he took you with him?"

"Most of those had nothing to do with the duchess."

"So what had they to do with?"

Tycho shook his head. "Not my secret to break, my lady."

He could hardly say that on those nights Atilo watched him hunt and kill released prisoners who'd been promised freedom if they could escape the city, critiquing his every move until he'd learnt to catch them fast and kill them quickly. That he began with pigs so he could kill humans, and with men so that he could progress to women and children. That he did this under Atilo's instruction, at Duchess Alexa's orders and watched by Dr Crow.

For Desdaio, her beloved was an occasionally stern but mostly kindly and retired soldier. For the rest of the city he was a turncoat Moor who'd successfully bewitched a girl less than half his age. This begged the question why he didn't take her to his bed when he happily went to the beds of others.

"Alexa wasn't involved?"

"No," Tycho promised. "She wasn"t."

"Atilo told me his *friendship* with Alexa was necessary, a matter of alliances and politics. I could live with that. But this . . . The more time he spends with her the less he has to spend with me."

Desdaio was how old? Tycho wondered.

Twenty-three? A virgin, rich and unmarried in a city where those were strange and unlikely bedfellows. She'd simply replaced her father's ambition for her with Atilo's devotion, which was just as constricting; no wonder she was lonely enough to find comfort in the fact Atilo had betrayed her less than she thought.

"Food," she reminded Tycho.

"I have nothing suitable."

"I'll make something." Desdaio stood, happy to have something to do. "Broth . . . You can make broth from anything."

"She needs blood," Tycho said. Seeing Desdaio's shock, he added, "It's a symptom of the illness. I'll send Elizavet to an abattoir in the morning." And if Rosalyn refused pig's blood – which he suspected she would – he'd have to find her human. Although, heaven knows, keeping himself fed was hard enough.

"Send Elizavet now."

"It can wait."

"No, it can't. What if she dies in the night? How will you feel then?" Desdaio glared at him and Tycho looked away. If felt as if she saw more than she should. Her next words confirmed it. "You're lying about sending Elizavet."

"It's not really pig's blood Rosalyn needs."

This Desdaio was frightening. Having asked for a small bowl and a sharp knife, she told Tycho he could go or stay, it was all the same to her. And having pulled up her sleeve, she scrubbed the skin of her upper arm, tightened a ribbon around her elbow, and cut carefully into bulging flesh.

She'd cut herself before. Tycho could see that from the neat run of scars like struts to a garden gate. Most looked recent, a few had healed and one was fresh that morning. "Dr Crow," she told him.

"He did those?"

"The first. The rest I did. It was that, or . . ." She blushed, unwilling to describe the alchemist's alternative suggestion. "My humours have been worsening. So I thought . . . Well, Dr Crow seemed the obvious person."

As she spoke, blood trickled from her elbow into the pewter bowl Tycho had brought her.

"Are you all right?" she asked suddenly.

No, he wasn't. Obviously not.

His jaw ached and sourness filled his mouth, he wanted the pleasure and taste of Desdaio's blood almost as badly as the girl who thrashed on the bed.

"You think this will be enough?"

Tycho looked at the half-full bowl. So thick and rich and warm he could smell its sweetness, almost taste its savour. "Bind your arm now."

Rosalyn watched him drop to a crouch beside her. Although he spoke in the barest whisper he knew the girl could hear.

"You will not harm this woman. Try to fight free and I *will* kill you." To Desdaio, he said, "Drip it between her lips."

"Where are you going?"

"Downstairs."

In the event Tycho clattered down half a dozen and crept up again silently; on guard outside the room where Rosalyn lay. Through the door came Desdaio's low chatter. Sweet and funny and full of hopes the girl would get better soon. "There you are," she said finally. "That's the last of it."

Rosalyn's moan said she understood that bit.

"Maybe I could give you more."

"No," Tycho said.

"I didn't hear you come upstairs." Lady Desdaio looked paler than usual. A handkerchief was now tied around her upper arm and the ribbon she'd used to constrict her elbow rested on the table.

"You were concentrating."

Tycho wrapped his arm about Desdaio's shoulders to steer her from the bed, and for a second she bridled at his familiarity, and then rested her head against him, her body softening under his touch.

"I don't think Rosalyn's going to have a fit."

"Not now," Tycho agreed.

"You should untie her."

"Elizavet can do it in a moment."

Tycho and Desdaio descended the stairs together with Desdaio still leaning on his arm. At the front door she hesitated. "You said once you hated me."

"I hated everyone."

"So," she said, ignoring that, "do you hate me still?"

He kissed her hair. The effort it cost not to react to the smell of her blood made his gesture clumsy and Desdaio looked at him strangely. Standing on tiptoe, she kissed his forehead in turn.

"I lied," Tycho said. "I never hated you."

"I didn't think so."

She rested her head on his shoulders one more time. And, looking round, signalled to a linkman in a doorway in the alley that ran down one side of San Aponal and led to Tycho's little palazzo. She might not have brought her servants but it seemed she'd brought someone after all.

"Where did you find him?"

"San Marco . . ."

"You hired a man off the streets to light you through the city?"

"Pietro's ill. I could hardly ask Iacopo."

That wasn't what Tycho meant. "What will you say if Lord Atilo discovers this and asks where you went?"

"I was with the duchess." Desdaio's chin came up. "We were taking tea in her private chambers. He's hardly going to tell me I'm lying, is he?"

30

Alexa was impressed. Who knew the girl possessed that kind of cunning?

The Moor had just gone when she filled her bowl from habit, planning to while away an hour before bed. What it showed was more interesting than that night's council meeting or her unsatisfactory chat with Atilo afterwards.

He's hardly going to tell me I'm lying . . .

Maybe the little chit's engagement to Lord Atilo was some kind of deep power play that would let her combine her father's fortune with the Moor's reputation and connections . . .? That would make life much more *interesting*.

Of course, if it were true Atilo's doe-eyed little beloved would need killing. Since it was just amusing fantasy Alexa let the thought go.

Follow Desdaio or see what Tycho was doing?

Or concentrate on tonight's hidden player? Because it was Iacopo, her brother-in-law's lurking little protégé, who focused Alexa's vision on Tycho's house just before the end of that touching little scene.

All the world might be a stage, and all the men and women

mere players with their exits and entrances, but the jade bowl let her follow one player only. Their exits and entrances were branching points.

Iacopo . . .

She would follow Atilo's servant, who had gone muttering after Desdaio. While Lady Desdaio, of course, strolled through the back alleys without a worry in the world. *Taking tea with the duchess, indeed.*

Alexa smiled as she drew her bowl closer.

"Got you," she heard Iacopo whisper. "Hooked deep to the gullet, and that other place. How long have I waited to nail you? And now I have . . ."

A real charmer, Alexa decided.

She'd watched Iacopo climb the outside of Tycho's house. Seen him mutter and rub at his groin as he tried to peer past locked shutters.

She'd heard what Iacopo heard . . . Desdaio's gasp. Loud enough to rise above the murmur of conversation. Heard the gasp, followed by a whimper and Tycho's sympathetic murmur.

"As if," Iacopo muttered, "you aren't the one making her whimper."

His fury had shocked Alexa.

How far did she want to go into his mind?

Did she want to watch him and only that? Did she want to watch and hear what he heard? Or did she want to delve deeper, see what he saw, feel what he felt, think what he thought? Looking at him in the shadows, falling back and darting forward, hearing his venom as he followed his master's beloved, Alexa debated cutting him free altogether and sleeping instead.

But her mind was too restless and the air at court thick with plotting and unspoken words. Alonzo was secretive, half drunk and hiding so obviously in corners to discuss matters with Lord Roderigo that she suspected his real attention was somewhere else entirely. With this young man perhaps?

There was only one way to find out.

Opening her mind to the city, Alexa flinched at its cacophony of noise and then found Iacopo among myriad thoughts by watching him in her bowl, and filtering the voices until she found one that matched the contempt he mouthed.

The Moor should have listened to me.

That night I told him I saw Lady Desdaio go to Tycho's room when he was still a slave . . . Oh, I was mistaken about one thing. I thought Tycho took her then and the bitch's famed virginity was a lie. I was wrong in that. They talked probably, discussed, kissed, petted. All the little luxuries unrequited love allows. But her virginity held. When the bitch declared herself chaste, virtuous and true on the deck of the bucintoro, *before assembled nobles, she told the truth.*

Well, not any longer.

Unless she planned to go down to breakfast and say, Remember Tycho, your ex-slave and favourite apprentice? Well, he had me last night.

Let Atilo try to ignore this.

Not pretty, Alexa thought, jerking her mind free from the rancid mess of Iacopo's jealousy. She wanted to know what the young man thought, wanted to follow him and discover if Alonzo had stoked this anger; she just wanted to do it without having to wade through such stench.

Following Lady Desdaio through the lanes beyond San Aponal, some of the narrowest in the city, unescorted but for her skulking Schiavoni linkman who barely knew this part of the city, Alexa heard Iacopo gloat over what he knew.

"And why shouldn't I?" he muttered. "Why shouldn't a man have revenge for wrongs done him?"

Iacopo's thoughts were simple.

If he couldn't bring down the master he'd served for scant reward, the freak who'd stolen his place, and the whore who looked away every time he smiled at her then Iacopo was less a true-born Venetian than he thought. He would have both his revenge and the Regent's favour.

At the thought of Alonzo, the duchess decided to stay with the sliver of world she was watching.

"Now what?" Iacopo demanded.

It was a good question. Lady Desdaio had ordered her Schiavoni linkman to walk ahead to the end of the narrow alley. Glancing at the *sottoportego* behind her, he recognised the carved sign that indicated it as a *corte*, with no other way out, and decided his hirer wasn't trying to escape without paying.

Iacopo trailed Lady Desdaio into the darkness.

Atilo's servant probably expected a hike of her gown, a flash of buttocks and the splash of a woman's piss hitting herringbone brick. That was certainly what Alexa expected. Instead, with her back to where he hid, she undid the neck of her gown, reached for her upper arm and fumbled, producing a handkerchief a second later.

Tossing it into a corner as if it was a rag rather than Maltese lace, she turned to go and hesitated, and Iacopo was rewarded with the sight he'd hoped for when she dropped to a squat and urinated heartily.

She wore no undergown.

Retrieving her handkerchief, Desdaio regarded it critically and turned it in her hands until she found a patch that satisfied her needs. Having discarded it one final time, she turned to go so fast Iacopo only just found shadows.

And he was trained in that art.

Iacopo should follow immediately so he could swear in court he had unbroken sight of her after he let her pass but he was unable to resist the lure of the handkerchief in the corner of that small courtyard.

Alexa re-entered his mind as he lifted it to his nose.

It stank of woman and urine, and from being close to a body on a warm summer night. And something else . . . That was when Iacopo realised the cloth in his fingers was tacky. Although it was not what he first thought in a single revolted and excited moment, this was blood. This was better.

Tycho's seed would simply be evidence of wrongdoing.

Lady Desdaio's blood, however, after hours alone with Tycho in a bedroom during which she'd lost her undergown . . . And the gasp to which Iacopo could swear. Revenge was sweet but the thought of Prince Alonzo's patronage was sweeter.

Indeed, thought Alexa.

Everyone knew how sweet her brother-in-law could be.

Lady Desdaio was nearly home, her beloved must be nearly home too. It would be interesting to see which arrived first, and what developed.

Ringing a small bell, Alexa called a maid who knocked diffidently at the door. Having told the girl to enter, Alexa ordered more water and a fresh brazier to make tea. She also gave orders she was not to be disturbed.

31

"My lord . . ."

The Moor put his hand to his dagger, looking older through Iacopo's eyes than Alexa remembered him. She obviously saw Atilo through a filter of fondness and familiarity. She'd need to watch that.

Behind Atilo was Alexa's own craft in which he'd been delivered home. Her man helped him on to his jetty, saluted and pushed away into the night currents to row for the distant lights of Ca' Ducale.

That the Moor had not seen Iacopo first said his intake of wine at the council meeting was greater than it should be. He was old enough to have collected enemies. Letting his guard down like that was a mistake.

"My boy, it's nearly dawn."

The young man glanced to the east where the sun would cut streaks in the retreating night. A sultry midnight had given way to a humid pre-dawn and the day would be hot again.

"Some hours yet, my lord."

Atilo looked as if he wondered at the insolence.

"Why are you here?"

"Waiting for you."

Atilo's mouth tightened. His beard and hair might be grey but Alexa knew his temper was as youthful as it had ever been. She watched him fight to be its master. As usual, he won.

"I can see that. I want to know why."

"Ahh . . . Of course."

It was almost as if Iacopo intended to provoke him.

"*Out with it.*"

And as Iacopo stepped back and found himself at the water's edge, with the dark swirl of a side canal behind him, he looked for a second the grubby orphan he'd been on first entering Atilo's service.

"My lord. I hardly know . . ."

"Tell me."

"It's about Lady Desdaio. Only the last time . . ."

Atilo went still. The last time Iacopo spoke out of turn about the future mistress of Ca' il Mauros Atilo had slit his face and come near to murdering one of his own servants. Others might kill their servants in rage but he was not one of those. If not for the Moor's pride Iacopo would have been dead.

Alexa wondered if either of them realised that.

That she might find the story of Atilo protecting Desdaio's honour less than touching had obviously not occurred to the Moor; any more than Atilo really understood her depth of anger when he took Desdaio to Cyprus against the Council's orders. The only reason she'd even consider taking him back to her bed would be if she needed allies.

"Iacopo," Atilo said. "Be careful."

"My lord, I hardly dare . . ." Reaching into his pocket, Iacopo pulled out a scrap of cloth and offered it mutely. His lips were trembling and he looked to be about to cry.

"What it is?"

"Take it to the light, my lord."

Atilo ignored him and turned the rag over in his fingers; linen with a Maltese lace trim. His fingers found embroidery, tracing two initials twined together like strands of ivy on one corner. Instinctively he brought the rag to his nose.

"Take it inside, my lord."

The lamp Iacopo lit threw back shadows as wisps of wick smoke drifted across Lord Atilo's dark-panelled hall. Ca' il Mauros had been recently remade to look as if Atilo's family had lived there for ever. Alexa understood it was that vanity which first took him to her bed. His desire to be one of the only two men to have her body. Marco the Just, duke of Venice . . . And Atilo il Mauros, his High Admiral.

The light confirmed what Atilo already knew.

The initials in the corner of the handkerchief had a D and a B intertwined, and you didn't kill as many people as Atilo without recognising blood. Where it was dry it flaked beneath his fingers, in the crumpled centre it clung like dough.

"What does this mean?"

"It is my lady Desdaio's."

"I know that. I gave it to her. Is she all right?"

"Safe in her room, my lord. Resting."

"Not sleeping?"

"I've heard her footsteps on the stairs. She went down to the kitchens to get food and then returned to her room . . . Perhaps she was hungry."

"Where did you find this?"

The young man hesitated.

"I won't hurt you for telling the truth."

"You did last time," Iacopo replied, unable to keep the bitterness out of his voice. Instinct made him touch the scar disfiguring his cheek. He probably claimed it as a battle wound and his new beard hid most of it. In years to come it would make him look distinguished. For now its memory was too raw.

"Are you saying . . .?"

"Smell it again, my lord."

The elderly Moor did as Iacopo suggested. He closed his eyes, put the handkerchief to his nose, inhaled deeply, using his skill to identify the scents he found there. Though he numbered them so softly his lips barely moved.

"Sweat, womanhood, blood, urine, rose water."

The bleakness in Atilo's eyes said he knew he held Desdaio's handkerchief. That she had been the one using it.

"You swear you told me the truth last time?"

"On my soul."

"Then speak freely."

"I returned tonight to find the house empty. Almost empty. Pietro in bed with fever, the cook in her kitchen. I'm not sure where Amelia was . . ."

"She has work."

"Of course, my lord. Lady Desdaio was gone. I imagine she left shortly after you did. She was at Sir Tycho's house."

"How did you know she was there?" Atilo missed the irritated glance that said Iacopo considered him a fool.

"This is not her first visit, my lord."

"How often?"

"Every time you're . . ." Iacopo appeared to consider his words. "Almost every time you're called to the palace unexpectedly. She makes a visit of her own."

Does she now? Alexa thought.

"You're saying Lady Desdaio is unchaste?"

"I wasn't certain until tonight. But now . . ." Iacopo shrugged. "I'd better tell you what I saw and heard."

He told the tale simply. He had arrived at Sir Tycho's house and heard muffled voices behind shutters. Employing Assassini skills he had used the alley's gap between Tycho's building and that opposite to climb level with the bedrooms, positioning himself right outside the window. He had heard Lady Desdaio gasp in pain and heard Tycho comfort her.

In the street as Tycho and Lady Desdaio said farewells she had clung to him as he kissed her hair. And later, Iacopo had watched her discard the handkerchief in a deserted *corte*. How, though Iacopo was ashamed to admit it, he'd watched briefly as she squatted to piss and noticed, in the split-second before he turned away, that she lacked an undergown.

"That bastard took her . . ."

"My lord, I cannot say for sure."

"You don't need to. He stole her virginity. She wiped maiden blood on the handkerchief I gave her and discarded it in the dirt. Sneaking back here to pretend nothing happened."

Perhaps Atilo saw Iacopo shiver.

Perhaps he simply remembered cutting Iacopo's face for himself.

Either way, Atilo turned his gaze from inner blackness to the young man in front of him, eyes downcast, looking as if he'd rather be anywhere than the hallway of Ca' il Mauros with its enraged owner.

"I should have believed you."

"It was the truth, my lord. I saw Lady Desdaio leave the slave's quarters and make her way upstairs. I retracted my statement because you would have killed me otherwise and I wanted . . ." His chin rose. "I lied to save my life."

Atilo nodded slowly. Reaching out, he clasped Iaco by the shoulders. "I wronged you then. As she has wronged me now."

The Moor didn't see Iacopo's smile as he said this. Two other people did. One of them watched in a water-filled jade bowl and knew the other existed. The other was a small, fever-struck boy who thought he was on his own.

Ducking, Pietro rolled himself under a bench as Atilo swept past on his way to the floors above. The boy looked small and frightened. Although less small and less frightened than the first time Alexa saw him.

The stamp of Atilo's boots would have woken the dead.

At the kitchen door, Pietro glanced inside to see a grinning

Iacopo breaking open one of Atilo's better jugs of wine. He sprawled back on the cook's chair, his dusty heels on the table.

Alexa could see Pietro wonder what to do.

Iacopo was bigger, better armed and better trained. The boy was not grown-up enough to make Iacopo take back the lie so someone else would have to do that for him. Alexa could already guess who that would be.

At the side canal's edge Pietro crossed himself. In case that wasn't enough he kissed a cheap spelter medallion he wore on a string round his neck, Saint Gennaro, patron saint of orphans, then crossed himself one more time, took a deep breath and dived into the black waters.

32

Look into the seeds of time and say which will grow and which not . . .

Something Alexa's mother used to say. A bad mother but a great witch from a race which produced those who walked with the dead almost as often as they produced those good with a bow. Did the rest of humanity really think stout horses and good bows were enough to conquer the world?

Should Alexa stay with the boy or return to Ca' il Mauros?

She wondered briefly how Tamburlaine would react to a request for a second jade bowl and smiled at her own greed. The khan of khan's present was beyond price. That he offered it at all said how much he valued his empire's links with her adopted city. At least she hoped that was his reason.

She would stay with events at Ca' il Mauros for now.

Dropping dried leaves into her tiny iron pot, Alexa shook it slightly to distribute the leaves evenly before adding boiling water. A brief wait, a longer one to prove she could, and she poured with the slowness and grace Abbot Eisai demanded in his treatise on tea drinking.

Observing ritual cost Alexa the sight of Lord Atilo reaching

Desdaio's bedroom door and knowledge of what he first said. Outside or inside that locked door? The bowl was making Alexa aware of how many times in a single story she had to ask herself that question. *Inside.*

"Open this door . . ."

"My lord. It's long past midnight."

"We need to speak now."

"Tomorrow, my lord. When the wine has worn off."

"I'm not . . ."

"I can hear it in your voice." Desdaio obviously expected to hear Atilo turn away, perhaps mutter a half-drunken apology before making his way to his own quarters to sleep off supper at the palace.

"Open. This. Door."

She flinched as his fist beat out the order. He hit her door so hard that flakes fell from the whitewashed wall and furniture rattled.

"What troubles you, my lord?"

"You do, my lady. Your behaviour does."

"What have I done?" Desdaio scowled at herself for asking, for the tremble that asking put in her voice. From what Alexa heard, if she'd wanted to be afraid or beaten she could have stayed at home. Desdaio dug knuckles into her eyes, dashing away tears. "What do you accuse me of?"

"You ask me that?"

A kick at the door made her step back.

"Wait . . ." Iaco's voice came from beyond, sounding sly. "My lord, this is not seemly. Talk to my lady when your fury has cooled."

"You *know* she betrayed me."

"There may be a simple explanation," Iacopo said. "I might be wrong in what I saw. I might have misunderstood. It was dark, my lord."

"It's no use . . ." Atilo snarled. "I know the truth when I hear it."

"What am I meant to have done?"

"Where were you tonight?"

"Here . . ." Desdaio shouldn't have faltered. People like her were bad liars; and hers was a life of little lies. Her lips had twisted and her expression become shame-faced. It was as well she had the door to hide her.

"You swear it?"

"My lord . . ."

"You swear it on your soul? May it destroy your hope of salvation for ever if you lie. Do you?"

"Atilo, my lord . . ."

"Swear it."

"Why?" Desdaio wailed.

"Because I want to hear you damn yourself."

This was obviously an Atilo unknown to her. Not the warrior who'd faced down Prince Alonzo and asked for Tycho's life on her behalf. Nor the serious, poetry-quoting suitor who'd wooed her. This man had sacked cities and hung mutineers. This was Duke Marco's Admiral of the Middle Sea.

"I have done nothing wrong."

"Why would I believe you this time?" His voice was bitter. "I trusted you once when you'd betrayed me."

"Nothing happened."

"You lied about going to his room."

"I told you the truth."

"Having lied first. Show me the shift you put on this morning and the handkerchief I gave you. The linen one with Maltese lace and your initials."

Lady Desdaio put her hand to her mouth. She clearly wanted to say something but the words weren't so much not coming as stuck in her throat. She looked locked into panic. "Why?" she managed.

"Because I'm asking you."

"*How* . . .?" It was a whisper.

Alexa knew what Desdaio wanted to ask. How did Atilo know

she'd lost it . . .? Except the little fool hadn't lost it, had she? The only way her beloved could know was if someone had followed Desdaio and told him. And if someone had been following then that person knew where she'd been.

And so did he, clearly.

"Let's talk about this in the morning."

It was the wrong thing for her to say. A heavy thud shook her door on its hinges, dropping plaster like snow to the boards at her feet. And in the fall of snow Desdaio's happiness withered and died.

Alexa was worried enough to sweep her fingers across the water in her bowl and pull a small boy's face from the broken reflection. She wanted to stay at Ca' il Mauros but she wanted to track Pietro more.

Where was Tycho when she could use him?

Ringing the little bell on her table Alexa told her maid to wake one of her spies. The spy should discover Dr Crow's whereabouts and report straight back. A palace messenger was also to be woken and told to wait to discover if she would need him.

It was a difficult balance between observing and changing, between discovering what she needed to discover about Alonzo and stopping a man she'd taken to her bed making a dangerous fool of himself. Alexa understood the temptation of simply letting what wanted to happen happen. Just as she understood that every change came at a price and a short-term gain could cause a long-term loss. The Venetians were so used to thinking in terms of gold that they often forgot other people dealt in more complex currencies.

33

"Where do you think you're going?"

Swinging round, Pietro put his hand to his belt, ripped free the blade he carried and dropped to a fighter's crouch. Only to have the dagger swept from his fingers with a roundhouse kick that left him clutching his wrist.

Duchess Alexa recognised his opponent instantly.

Silver thimbles danced at the end of her hair and she could swear the Nubian girl had blood on her hands. Licking her fingers, Amelia rubbed them on her ragged dress. Boy and girl stared at each other.

"You should be in bed."

"So should you."

Glancing at the new moon, the Nubian said, "No. Tonight is mine, and tomorrow I leave for Paris. Lord Atilo's orders."

"To kill the king?"

Amelia snorted. "To kill the only doctor who might cure him of madness. A mad king of France is a safe king. Although with the Valois how can you tell? Go home, let me about my business."

"*Lady Desdaio . . .*"

"What about her?"

"My lord Atilo is drunk and shouting for her. He means her harm and Iacopo is behind this. I must find Sir Tycho."

The Nubian girl's gaze sharpened. "What's Tycho got to do with this?" Her fingers became hooks in Pietro's shoulder. "Tell me."

"Lord Atilo thinks Tycho bedded her. He's drunk and beside himself with anger. He has . . ."

Amelia waited.

"Blood on a handkerchief."

"Sweet mother." The Nubian checked to make sure Pietro was serious, and then the boy found himself being dragged through Dorsoduro towards San Polo at speeds that intrigued Alexa. The girl used back alleys the duchess didn't know existed, took *sottoportegos* so dark they looked like mouths to hell and cut through squares full of Nicoletti bravoes, who glanced over and looked away.

A few crossed themselves.

Before Alexa realised it, the Nubian girl was hammering at a black-painted door. Not bothering with the knocker, she pounded her fist to a rhythm Alexa suspected was an Assassini signal. When Tycho answered the door he was wide awake and fully dressed. In his hand was a dagger. Behind him hovered a dark-haired servant who returned upstairs the moment Tycho ordered.

"Invite me in," Amelia demanded.

Startled by the sound of a knock at her own door, Alexa covered her jade bowl with a cloth despite knowing only she could see its other reflection. A spy had returned to say Dr Crow slept in his own bed.

"Fetch me a pen, ink and paper," Alexa ordered. "Tell the messenger he's to take a note to the alchemist."

Pushing Pietro ahead of her, Amelia entered Tycho's house as if she owned it; turned in a swift circle and sniffed the hall air like an animal, her nose wrinkling and her mouth twisting. There was a strangeness to her eyes Tycho barely recognised.

"Did you fuck Desdaio?"

"Did I what?"

"Didn't think so," she said. "Not your type. You'd need to be a poor little rich boy who wanted to fuck his mummy. So what did you do to her?"

Tycho stared at her.

A slow gaze that saw her for the first time. Tycho had the sense of being trapped in a bubble where time moved differently and colours changed to new hues. A rattle overhead made Amelia and Pietro glance up. The noise grew louder.

"What's that?"

"First tell me what this is about."

Amelia did. Relaying what Pietro had apparently told her; but using shorter words and briefer sentences. Amelia was angry, viciously angry. And it was obvious to Tycho that she loved her mistress. Desdaio had that effect on people.

"What did you do to her?"

"*Nothing*," Tycho said fiercely.

He led Amelia upstairs to where a girl lay hunched on a bed, Pietro trailing after them until he stepped through the door.

"*How did you . . . ?*"

Before Tycho could stop him, Pietro threw himself across the room and wrapped his arms tight around the girl, burying his face in her neck. At which she twisted her head, opened her mouth to bite and hesitated . . .

Intelligence flickered in her eyes.

"Thank you," the boy said. "Thank you. Thank you . . ." There was such devotion in his voice that Tycho looked away.

"This is my sister," Pietro told Amelia.

"Your sister is dead."

The boy shrugged.

"You let *this* feed on Desdaio?"

194

Pietro obviously didn't understand the turn the conversation had taken and Tycho wanted to keep it that way. Tycho also needed to consider how freely Amelia talked about feeding. She was not whatever he was. He would have recognised that. All the same, it would require thought. Just not now.

"Desdaio offered."

"She would." Amelia rolled her eyes.

Just don't, Alexa thought. *Really, don't be that stupid.*

Desdaio's fingers trembled as she found the key and turned it until the lock clicked with a finality Alexa knew was in her own imagination.

On Desdaio's face were written questions to which she would never now get answers. Why had she believed she could find happiness here? How could she have imagined she'd escape the bars life erected around her?

"It is unlocked, my lord."

Atilo tried the handle as if not believing her. Light from a lamp he carried cut like a knife round the edges of her door as it began to open. Stepping to one side, she indicated that Atilo should enter.

"Iacopo remains there," she said.

"He is my witness."

"To what?"

"Show me the handkerchief I gave you."

Desdaio might have been one of his servants who'd failed in her duties, his tone was so brutal. Her chin came up and fire entered her eyes. Only to fade as she accepted what she'd always half known.

Happiness was not hers.

"It's lost."

"That's it," Atilo growled. "*It's lost?*"

"What do you want me to do, my lord? Pretend to search for it? Turn my wooden chest upside down? Claim that Amelia,

195

wherever she is, must have stolen it? Along with the undergown that is also missing?"

Digging into his pocket, Atilo found the rag. "Do you deny I gave you this?"

"I've never denied the truth in my life."

"How can you say . . .?"

"Not when it mattered," Desdaio said, refusing to let him finish. "Not when it was a matter of honour."

"You talk to me of honour?"

"And you talk to me?" she spat back. "Who goes running back to the duchess's bed when called, fucks his servants and uses brothels?" Desdaio glared at him. "You think I don't know about Amelia? About your whores?"

Desdaio's voice broke as the duchess was still digesting that. Her voice broke, her courage failed and tears put out the fire in her eyes. Atilo began pushing his way into her room. Iacopo followed.

34

The land gate to Ca' il Mauros was unlocked. That was warning in itself that something was badly wrong. A light burnt in the entrance hall and in the kitchen that Atilo had moved down from the attics.

The house itself was in utter silence.

"Upstairs," Amelia said.

The stairs flowed beneath Tycho's feet and he was at Desdaio's door, his fingers twisting the handle before he registered Pietro behind him.

"No," Amelia insisted. It was too late.

Twisting past, Pietro halted at the tableau in front of him. Desdaio was slumped in a chair, with urine spreading in a circle on the boards around her feet. Her throat was purple with finger bruises and her lip was split. It was Atilo's dagger in her chest that froze the boy in his tracks.

"Don't," said Tycho.

Desdaio's gaze met his.

Wrapping her fingers round the dagger's handle she dragged it free. The man who'd stabbed her barely noticed the blood begin to flow between his beloved's fingers. All his attention was on Tycho in the doorway.

"*You dare come here?*"

In Atilo's bloody hand was the companion to the dagger he'd used on Desdaio. In true Venetian tradition the man had strangled her, then stabbed her to stop her ghost passing into him through the touch of flesh on flesh.

"She's still alive," Amelia said.

"Not for much longer." Pietro's voice trembled. He was holding Lady Desdaio's hand, stroking her fingers, his eyes locked on hers; the tears rolling down his face.

"How could you?" Atilo asked.

"Do what?"

"Dishonour me."

His beloved was dying, the Assassini were disgraced and maybe destroyed and this man still thought he had honour? When Tycho took a dagger from his belt he knew he intended to use it.

"Don't I deserve an answer?"

"You deserve nothing and *her* honour is untouched. I don't know what Iacopo told you but nothing happened tonight that besmirched her."

"Her maiden blood . . ."

"*What?*"

Atilo dragged a rag from his sleeve and Tycho recognised the handkerchief Lady Desdaio had used to stop the bleeding.

"Where did you get that?"

"Iaco found it. He followed her to your house. Saw her discard this in the dirt on her way home. I gave her this handkerchief. And she used it to . . ."

"She bled herself."

"You lie." Atilo's voice trembled.

"No," said Tycho, stepping forward. "I don't. You have killed the thing you loved. What else can you expect from a man who betrayed his family for a place at Duke Marco's side?"

Atilo's face tightened. "It was not like that."

"It was always like that. Not only have you killed the person you loved, you have killed the one person in Venice who truly loved you."

"Iacopo said . . ."

"He lied."

Atilo did nothing to block Tycho's blow.

As Tycho's hilt thumped to a halt, his blade deep in the Moor's chest, Atilo muttered, "Finish it. *Always finish it.*"

And Tycho cut his heart in two. Although they both knew it was already broken.

Iacopo's pleas for mercy could barely be heard over Pietro's sobs.

"Keep the bastard quiet."

Amelia's knife edge against Iacopo's throat did the job. "Just say the word," she told Tycho. "I'll be happy to oblige."

Pietro had found his sister and was losing the closest thing he'd had to a mother in the same day. He knelt at Desdaio's feet, his look so anguished even the dying woman had been forced to turn her face away.

"Please," Pietro begged. "Help her."

When Tycho dropped to his knees Desdaio tried to look around him to where Atilo lay. A single tear on her perfect cheek matched a drop of blood on her lip. Touching the drop, Tycho felt his throat sour.

"I can save you."

"Demon magic?" Desdaio barely had strength to speak and her voice was too ruined for clear words. Tycho understood her question all the same.

He nodded.

"Too high a price."

"*Desdaio* . . ."

"How else can I see Atilo again?"

Reaching out, Tycho touched his hands to the sides of her head and felt pain flow into him like water into an empty jug. The anguish left her eyes, her mouth stopped trembling. The blood from the wound in her chest lessened to a trickle and he let her go; his throat tight with hunger, his face aching where dog teeth fought to descend, his body demanding to change.

What hurt most were his tears.

"You die next," Tycho said. He wasn't fool enough to think that killing Iacopo would lessen his anger or take away the pain.

He would do it all the same.

At his nod, Amelia stepped back and sheathed her dagger. The fear in Iacopo's eyes said he knew what was going to happen. "You won't kill an unarmed man . . .?"

"Give him back his dagger."

Amelia returned the blade grudgingly. She'd been the one to disarm him and the scowl on her face said she wanted to be the one to kill him.

"You owe me a death," she said.

Tycho read the room.

The north of the circle he trod as he and Iacopo faced each other – blades drawn and eyes locked – was Atilo's body. Desdaio's corpse marked the south of the circle. Pietro and Amelia were east and west respectively.

Amelia had put herself between Iacopo and the door and was chanting softly under her breath, prayers for Desdaio probably. Pietro's attention was on Tycho's blade. Which was why neither of those watching heard what Tycho heard, boots on the stairs beyond and the sound of a handle turning . . .

"*Hold,*" a voice barked.

The Regent stood in the doorway. A nervous Dr Crow hovered behind him, and behind him Lord Roderigo, his half-Mongol sergeant and five Dogana guard. In Prince Alonzo's hand was a letter. Alonzo's gaze swept the room and he swore at the sight of Desdaio, his scowl lessening when he saw Atilo was also dead.

"Apparently my sister-in-law has had another dream." He held up the paper. "Her letter to Dr Crow is strangely precise and conveniently vague. Someone want to tell me what's really going on here?"

"Murder, my lord." Iacopo's voice was beseeching. "Tycho killed his old master and mistress. He should stand trial."

"That's a lie," Pietro said.

"The brat's his catamite and that's his whore." Iacopo jerked his chin at Amelia. "They'll say what he tells them. Look, my lord. You can see it was him. There's blood on his blade."

"You will die," Tycho said. "I swear it."

"Not here he won't." Alonzo nodded to Roderigo and the Dogana guard filed into the room, raising their crossbows to cover Tycho, Amelia and Pietro. "I'm arresting you for the murder of Lord Atilo and his beloved. I doubt the courts will be kind to such monstrous behaviour."

The Regent's gaze settled again on Atilo's corpse and he smiled.

35

Rumours swept the city faster than runaway fire, licking into tavern corners, inflaming the narrowest of streets. The authorities let the rumours spread until there were a dozen versions of the truth and a hundred people to swear that each was true. When the conflagration faltered, tapsters in taverns and costermongers in the market refanned the flames with chance comments, dropped hints and outright lies.

Desdaio Bribanzo had poisoned Lord Atilo and stabbed herself.

The Moor had strangled her and cut his wrists like a Roman, leaving a note explaining he'd only ever loved his first wife. Mamluk assassins had landed at night to slaughter Atilo's entire Venetian household . . .

Atilo's proper family, the one he abandoned in Tunis to serve Venice, had finally taken their revenge. No, it was Emperor Sigismund removing the Ten's wisest voice. It was John V Palaiologos, the Byzantine emperor, unnerved by Lord Atilo's great victory over the Mamluks.

Within two days, the truth was as muddied as if Tamburlaine himself had ridden his conquering army through the middle. Tycho knew none of this, being held in the dungeons behind Ca'

Ducale. Pietro had been returned to Tycho's house on Alexa's orders.

Amelia rode north for Paris.

That she should go and go now was the only thing on which Alonzo and Alexa agreed. Alexa's fury with Dr Crow had come close to fracturing her truce with Alonzo. The duchess having stated coldly in Council that Dr Crow had betrayed her in involving the Regent. Alonzo insisting in turn that Dr Crow simply did his duty, the situation at Ca' il Mauros was such the responsibility for containing it lay with both rulers.

"John V Palaiologos is behind it, you say? The Byzantine emperor?" Tycho sounded interested.

"For certain, Excellency."

The turnkey pocketed the coin that opened his mouth, and Tycho used the moment to consider the *facts*; which were anything but. Not one of the rumours the turnkey so contemptuously dismissed nudged the truth any more than the rumour he'd decided was fact.

That the man had not simply stolen Tycho's valuables was how he'd known he'd be given a chance to speak and the game was not yet lost. He'd be sent for and Iacopo would be sent for too. It seemed that moment had come.

"Excellency, my apologies . . ."

"For what?"

The turnkey gestured at the cell's stone walls and stale straw, the brimming bucket and plate of rancid pickles. "You must be used to much better."

"Compared to the Pit this is paradise."

The man gaped at him, obviously wondering what kind of noble survived the dreaded Pit and joked about it afterwards. The kind with wolf-grey hair who dressed in black and slept the day flat on his back on cold stone, untroubled by where he found himself, apparently.

Tycho smiled. "You'd better lead the way."

That night the Council met in an upper chamber where ten gilded chairs had been arranged in a horseshoe, broken at the top where a throne stood flanked by two simpler seats that were halfway between thrones and chairs.

Duke Marco was missing.

Sleeping, Alexa said.

Since everyone in the room could hear howls coming from his room they knew the truth was less simple. Marco's fondness for Desdaio was known; and he liked the familiar and Lord Atilo was a familiar part of his life.

So two seats stood empty that evening. Duke Marco's throne, and the place where Atilo should sit. Tycho doubted he was the only one to notice how often Alexa glanced at his chair. The Council had agreed that only Tycho and Iacopo should swear their versions of the story. Alonzo, having backed Iacopo's, claimed that Amelia was Tycho's whore and would simply perjure herself to order.

Iacopo was the first to be called forward.

"Are you willing to swear the truth of what you say?"

Prince Alonzo's hand was on the Millioni bible. Hand-scripted and lovingly illuminated in gold leaf and precious pigments, the book was heavy and old and supported on a wooden frame itself black with age.

"I am," Iacopo said.

"Then put your hand on the book and swear your account is the truth, the whole truth and nothing but the truth."

Iacopo did.

Alexa was watching keenly. So keenly she leant slightly forward. Maybe seeing Tycho notice made her lean back and maybe it was Alonzo's quizzical glance. A second later no one could have known from her posture that she wasn't bored.

"Now Tycho," Alexa said.

Alonzo held up his hand. "We don't know he believes."

"Do you?" Alexa sounded genuinely interested.

"No, my lady."

Around him the Council scowled.

"My lady Desdaio tried to teach me but I'm not sure I always understood what she was saying. I read the books Desdaio gave me, though. And she swore that she would talk to me more of it . . ."

A couple of the Council looked less disapproving after that.

"Why bother anyway?" Alonzo said. "Iacopo has sworn to the truth already. That should be enough."

"My lord . . ." A soft-faced man stood.

Desdaio's father was a merchant prince of infinite ambition and near infinite wealth; and now, it seemed, infinite sadness for the daughter he'd disowned. "It would be best if they both swore. We need the truth of this."

It was a poorly kept secret that Alonzo owed Lord Bribanzo several thousand ducats from a loan.

"Desdaio's father is right," Alexa said. "Anyway, I insist."

"What will your man swear by?"

"My man?" The duchess glanced at Tycho, who realised he was meant to answer that for himself.

"By the thing I hold dearest."

"And what is that?" Alonzo demanded.

"I cannot say."

The gauze of Alexa's veil stopped Tycho from seeing her face but he could swear she watched closely. "How much," Alexa said, "does this *thing* mean to you?"

"It is sweeter than life."

Tycho swore the truth of his account and stepped back knowing the Council now faced two conflicting versions of what happened that night; both sworn with soul-damning and inviolate oaths. Even Alonzo looked slightly shocked.

"One of you is damned."

No, thought Tycho, *two of us*. He'd been damned already. Iacopo had just joined him.

"My lords . . ."

As usual, Dr Crow was dressed in dusty robes that made him look as if he should be working as an apothecary.

"Perhaps neither one is damned."

"How is that possible?"

"Childish spite makes them blame each other. That both your protégés have sworn their innocence simply proves what the city already knows. This outrage was committed by outsiders. Both should be allowed to go free."

36

The first day of September was a Sunday and the day chosen for Lord Atilo's funeral. It was also as hot as Lady Giulietta could remember September being, certainly too hot for the mourners around her.

The Basilica of San Marco formed the shape of a Greek cross, with a large dome over the centre of the cross, and slightly smaller domes over each arm. Each one featured biblical scenes made with intricate mosaic.

A thousand people filled the cross below, with more spilling out through the great doors and down the steps outside. Those not important enough to merit a place in the basilica filled the great square beyond. Though guards stood ready to hold the crowds back, the solemnity of the occasion turned out to be enough to do that on its own.

Prayers were said and psalms sung.

The new patriarch spoke at great length about the Moor's life and his love for his adopted city. In Giulietta's opinion he passed rather too swiftly over Atilo's early years as one of the greatest pirates in the Mediterranean. Naturally enough, he also glossed over Atilo's job as Duke's Blade.

Had those foreigners around her known the Blade was dead and a new Blade yet to be appointed, which was not a fact Giulietta should herself know, they would have stood there plotting instead of mouthing pieties.

Only she, Aunt Alexa, Uncle Alonzo and Marco sat.

Everyone else – and that included nobles, foreign ambassadors and Lady Eleanor – had to stand. The incense and the stink of the mourners made the air so thick that Giulietta was scared she'd faint when the time came to stand.

It was sheer luck her widow's black rendered her discomfort invisible. Her Uncle Alonzo, in his purple doublet, blossomed sweat like a Castellano loading a barge. As did most of those around her. Her aunt, of course, looked as cool as always. Although what she found to watch so intently was harder to guess.

Giulietta risked one glance at a censer on its chain high overhead before ruthlessly suppressing the memory of the night Tycho leapt from a balcony to land on top of the censer, dropping to the floor like a cat.

"B-behind you," Marco whispered. "Five rows back."

She wished her cousin would stop doing that. For an idiot he knew entirely too much of what she was thinking. The thought of Tycho's finger tracing a trickle of blood from her hip to the underside of her breast made Giulietta melt in a way the cruder memory of him kneeling at her feet, her gown raised to her hips, a hot Cypriot night wind swirling around them, never would.

She knew Marco was watching and blushed.

Enough, Giulietta told herself. A great-aunt had ruled a kingdom at sixteen, another died in childbirth having defended her city from besiegers. Why should Giulietta let the memory of a boy dropping from the sky turn her life upside down?

Until that night her life had been bearable.

No. That was untrue, and now Aunt Alexa was staring at her strangely as well. It hadn't been bearable, it had simply been unbearable in an ordinary way. Since meeting Tycho . . . A tear began to trickle down her face.

Not now, not here.

She was so unhappy she hadn't even dared say hello to the Madonna on her way in and she always said hello. She'd said hello every day she came here since she was a child.

The stone mother, Tycho called her.

Feeling arms grip her, Giulietta tried to shake them off and realised the service had stopped because Marco was standing. She watched horrified as he came round to the front of her chair and dropped to a crouch in front of her. His hand came up to wipe a tear from her face and he pressed his forehead against hers.

"Better to love unwisely than n-not at all." Letting her go, he turned to his mother, and said, "J-julie's upset. She's c-crying."

Duchess Alexa nodded.

It was obvious to everyone Giulietta was upset.

"Atilo carved her a b-bear when she was small." Marco made it sound as if the two intertwined and Giulietta nodded gratefully.

"You must sit now," Alexa said.

Marco did as he was told.

It was a long service on a hot day in a cathedral ripe with mourners gathered below its central dome. And though the basilica was really the Millioni's private chapel and open to others on high days and holidays only . . . And though Lord Atilo's funeral was neither, Atilo had been Venice's Admiral of the Middle Sea.

Since he had no heirs the city now owned his house, its contents and the treasure chests found there. Prince Alonzo had gracefully agreed to return any chests Lord Bribanzo could prove belonged to his daughter.

Also being buried was Lord Atilo's beloved. They would lie together beneath the mosaics as they never had in life. Side by side, on one bed of earth, their hands clasping each other's. Marco had demanded they be married first.

Nothing the archbishop could say dissuaded him.

Faced with the duke's disapproval or that of the Pope, the archbishop sided with the ruler of the city in which he lived. Since the Pope was negotiating a truce to reunite the competing papacies it was unlikely two corpses married at the request of a lunatic would worry him overmuch.

As for Tycho . . . Preparing himself for the service had used almost the last of his ointment. He had one more day's worth, maybe two if he was willing to take the risk. Tycho knew how out of place he looked in his oiled silk and black leather, with smoked glass spectacles to hide his eyes from the daylight.

Had it simply been Atilo he would have stayed at home.

Desdaio, however . . . That was different. She had befriended him when few thought his friendship worth anything; when most doubted he could be tamed at all. She'd taught him to read and given her jewellery for his freedom.

Tycho owed Desdaio his respect.

Beside Tycho stood his new page, dressed in a livery of black doublet, black hose and black boots, of which the boy was ridiculously proud. Pietro had little right to be there and his presence attracted scowls of disapproval. So Tycho had announced he needed the boy's guidance through daylight and dared his neighbours to disagree.

"What now?"

Tycho put his finger to his lips.

Now the double coffin would be lowered into a trench.

The fact the coffin was lead-lined had two advantages: it helped seal in the smell of corruption, and its weight would stop the coffin from trying to float to the surface and ruining the mosaics the next time Venice had an *aqua alta*.

Prayers having been said, the trench would be filled, the earth compacted and the underfloor replaced. After which a master mosaicist would reset the tiny glass tiles removed to allow this burial. That a mosaic in the floor of San Marco had been disturbed showed how seriously Venice took this crime.

"Soon," Tycho whispered.

Pietro looked at him.

"It's ending. You'll be free to go."

The boy nodded gratefully. It had cost Tycho gold to buy out his apprenticeship, and have evidence of the boy's earlier crimes removed from the records. Alexa's patronage had helped.

"Go straight home."

Pietro nodded and kept his silence. He was learning.

Having given his name, Tycho was allowed into the upper chamber where he had sworn his oath two days earlier. Again, chairs were set in a horseshoe for the Council, with two lesser thrones and one greater throne showing where Alonzo, Alexa and Duke Marco would sit.

A marble table laden with sweetmeats was set against one wood-panelled wall. Wine stood in tall silver jugs and small beer in an oak half-barrel. Alexa had a brazier for making tea. All the gathering lacked was servants to pour for them. These had been banished. Only one person was now missing.

Duke Marco shuffled into the room without looking at anyone, slumped on the throne without being told and sprawled back, kicking his heels on marble tiles to a beat only he could hear. His brief exchange with Giulietta in the basilica had obviously exhausted him; or exhausted his supply of common sense.

Before everyone's eyes, he forced his fingers into the waistband of his hose and scratched his crotch, then examined his nails.

"Alexa . . ."

"Yes," she said. "He does."

Alonzo shut his mouth again. The protest was for form only. They were there to choose the next Duke's Blade. Marco *had* to be there because his presence gave the choice legitimacy. How could it be made if the duke was missing?

"If I may?" Alonzo said.

Marco said nothing.

"We're assembled to choose the next Blade and discussion is allowed." He smiled at the Council. "Indeed, you know with me that discussion is encouraged. Tradition makes the choice Marco's, however. Since my nephew is unable to choose, the choice will be made by his Regent and by . . ."

"By his *Regents*," Alexa said.

Alonzo sneered.

It was known he barely tolerated her co-rule, although Tycho imagined the fact Alonzo was usually referred to as *the Regent*, and Alexa styled herself *duchess* went some way to sweetening it.

"The Regents," he said heavily. "Once the Blade is chosen all those in this room will swear to keep his name secret unto death." Alonzo glanced round the panelled chamber, his gaze skimming over Marco, stopping on Iacopo, fixing for a few seconds on Alexa and dismissing Tycho altogether.

It seemed studied.

"To me," Alonzo said, "the choice is obvious."

Duchess Alexa's shoulders stiffened and then she relaxed, sitting back in her carved chair to stroke Marco's hand, settling him.

"Do go on . . ."

"Venice cannot be without a Blade."

The Regent's slight pause suggested he was waiting to see if Duchess Alexa would object. When she remained silent, he nodded. Tycho imagined the duchess knew he was leading her like a horse to the jumps and that any minute now the small jumps were going to turn into bigger ones.

"That means we should choose now."

Alexa kept her silence and waved her hand as if to say that Prince Alonzo should go on. He flushed.

"There is only one member of the Assassini in Venice."

The duchess looked at Tycho.

"No," said Alonzo, shaking his head. "Tycho is *not* Assassini. He failed his apprenticeship and was dismissed. It is true we have Blades in Constantinople, Vienna and Cordoba but only one here. Another, a Nubian ex-slave, already tasked with a job, has ridden north. I would suggest slaves have not been a good choice recently." Alonzo smiled. "So our choice seems simple."

"*My lord!*" Iacopo said.

"Alonzo . . . This needs discussion."

"What's to discuss? We need a Blade and we need one now. The only suitable candidate in Venice stands before us. This is the son of a man who died fighting for this city as a free oarsman on one of our war galleys. The fact more experienced members are abroad is a poor excuse for not acting."

"Sir Tycho . . ."

"Is not qualified to be an Assassini."

"He defeated the Mamluks."

"So everyone says. How exactly did he defeat the Mamluks? How could *that* possibly defeat an entire navy? It was Atilo, your husband's admiral."

On the throne Marco stopped kicking his heels.

"S-so," he said. "We're d-done?"

As if answering his own question, he stood up, helped himself to a handful of his uncle's sweetened almonds, finished his mother's tiny cup of tea in a single gulp and staggered towards the door.

"Marco . . ."

"D-done," he protested. Only returning when Alexa took his hand and led him back to the throne.

"You insist on Iacopo?"

"I thought you'd approve. After all, he was body servant to your . . . old friend. They worked closely and Iacopo had many opportunities to study Lord Atilo's methods. And, let's face it, *we need a Blade . . .*"

The Blade was as much a part of government as the Great Council, inner council and the Ten themselves. As totemic for the city as the *bucintoro*, the duke's ceremonial barge, the battle flag of San Marco and the chalice and ring the duke used to marry the sea.

"He's not noble."

"At least he's Venetian. Besides, that's easily solved."

Walking to a fireplace where an ancient sword hung as decoration, Alonzo reached for its handle. The sword's edge had been blunted to make it safe but he didn't need sharpness.

Returning to Iacopo, he commanded, "Kneel."

And in that moment, seeing the smugness and false modesty on Iacopo's face as he knelt, Tycho hated him more than ever. Iaco had brought Atilo to the point of killing Desdaio. How could he not hate him?

"Rise, Sir Iacopo."

Iacopo bowed low to the thrones.

In the sly smile that flickered across Iacopo's face was everything Tycho loathed about the man. Looking up, he found Marco staring at him.

"T-t-tycho . . ."

He thought he was being called. Then realised he was being talked about. Although what Marco was trying to say was near impossible to tell. The duke was so tongue-tied he began pounding his throne in anger. To Tycho it seemed studied. If not studied then exaggerated. Everyone said the duke's senses came and went. Tycho was beginning to wonder if they went quite as often as people said.

"H-h-he has s-s-something to s-say."

"You have?"

Maybe there was warning in Alexa's question. There was certainly warning in Alonzo's scowl. Iacopo simply smirked. He was the Blade, the weapon Venice wielded against its enemies. How could Tycho touch him now?

"They're e-equals?"

"Yes," Alonzo said heavily. "Equals."

The duke smiled happily.

Beyond the window, gulls squabbled and the waters darkened as the sun sank into the horizon. It would be night within an hour and Tycho could feel at ease again. Fishing boats would be lowering their night nets. Somewhere in the back canals smugglers would be stacking contraband knowing the Watch had been bribed or threatened into looking the other way.

Venice was Venice.

As it was and maybe always would be.

If he couldn't truly mourn Atilo's death Tycho was surprised to discover he could regret it. Desdaio, however . . . He mourned that and hated her refusal to let him save her, while understanding her reasons.

"T-t-tycho?"

Iacopo's jealousy and Tycho's own carelessness had killed her. He wasn't sure which he despised more. Stalking across the room, he backhanded Iacopo to the floor. "You murdered Desdaio."

The new Blade stood up.

"They were your hands around her neck, your blade between her ribs. You drove Atilo to murder her," Tycho said.

"They were killed by foreign assassins." Alonzo shot a warning glance at Alexa, who nodded. Desdaio and Marco were childhood friends. She'd once hoped they would marry. The last thing she wanted was Marco upset again.

"You can fight me," Tycho said. "Or I can kill you here."

"A d-duel?"

Tycho bowed in Marco's direction.

"Among equals." The duke smiled. "S-s-so clever of my uncle to make that p-possible." And Tycho realised this was what Marco had intended all along.

37

His note from Lady Giulietta was brief. *You loved her?* Tycho tried to imagine the Millioni princess saying it, and found it impossible to read her meaning from between the words. For an hour he considered ignoring it.

Having decided he needed to answer, he spent another hour wrestling with what to say. Challenging Iacopo was easy; answering a three-word note from a girl who hated him made demands Tycho barely understood. In the end he settled for the truth. Compressing it into three carefully chosen words of his own, in letters he could only write because Desdaio taught him.

"She loved me."

It was true. A complicated and unfulfilled love. The love of a rich young woman betrothed to an older man for a slave a little younger than her. She gave her jewellery for him. Braved shame to buy him in Limassol slave market when he was bound and weakened and before he could be sold to a brothel.

She was the closest he had to a true friend.

Iacopo had to die.

Opening another jug of his best wine, Tycho sipped it slowly as the hours slipped away. As he expected, the messenger he sent to Ca' Friedland returned with no note in reply. So he sharpened his sword, then sharpened both his daggers and considered and then rejected the idea of adjusting the straps on a breastplate he'd bought but never worn.

He would fight without armour.

That was how he felt about Giulietta, Tycho suddenly realised. He went into every fight with her armed but without armour; and came away not knowing until later how badly she'd wounded him.

Prince Alonzo and Sir Iacopo arrived at the duelling site together. The site being a ruined square beyond Arzanale, almost over the bridge into San Pietro, the island at the eastern edge of Venice ruled by the patriarch.

The pair arrived flanked by Lord Roderigo, his half-Mongol sergeant and a half-dozen Dogana guard carrying lit torches. All the guard carried ready-cocked crossbows, except for Sergeant Temujin who wore a curved sword. Iacopo's breastplate glittered in the torchlight and he proudly carried an open helm in the Florentine style. The fact Lord Roderigo and his Dogana guard accompanied the Regent and Iacopo said sides had been taken, as if anyone needed telling.

Alonzo said something and Iacopo laughed.

A church with a broken tower, a cracked wellhead, herringbone brick rooted up by rubbish pigs, the fate of ruined squares everywhere . . . Tycho let Alonzo and Iacopo determine the square was empty before dropping from a broken balcony. Pietro crawled from a filthy tunnel leading to an old cistern.

"What's he doing here?"

"He's my page."

Alexa was the last to arrive in her red-lacquered palanquin, the velvet curtains carefully drawn. Her two Mongol carriers put down the chair and retreated to the edge of the square without being told. Pulling back the curtains, Alexa opened the light wood half-door herself and stepped on to broken brick.

She said nothing, simply glanced at where the sun would stain the horizon and looked at Tycho, who nodded. He wore ointment. When the last of the pot was gone so would be his ability to face even weak sunlight.

"You're here," Alonzo said.

He made it sound as if they'd been waiting hours.

At his nod, Roderigo had his men form a circle and raise their torches, lighting the makeshift arena.

"This is an affair of honour."

Lord Roderigo nodded at Alonzo's words while looking puzzled. Not being a member of the Ten, he lacked the vital information that Iacopo was now Duke's Blade. Tycho imagined Roderigo was wondering why the Regent and Duchess Alexa would so openly involve themselves in something so slight.

"The usual rules apply," Alonzo said. "You fight until one person begs for mercy. If neither does this ends in death . . ." He glanced at Iacopo, who nodded.

"Are we done?" Tycho asked.

"Yes," Alonzo said. "I think we are."

"Good . . ."

Tycho hurled his sword.

Dropping his new helm, Iacopo stumbled on broken brick as Tycho's sword ricocheted off his breastplate. It spun away towards a Dogana guard, who had to jump out of the way. By then Tycho had already closed the gap to side-kick his boot into Iacopo's sword hand. He moved so fast Iacopo had barely let out a yell before Tycho caught the falling weapon, flipped it round and prepared to strike.

"*Hold*," Alonzo shouted. "That was cheating."

"You said the talking was done."

"*You will lower your sword.*"

"How long do you think he'll last as your Blade?"

Anger and shame filled Iacopo's face at the question, and Tycho realised Iacopo also doubted his own abilities. Doubt, vanity and pride. It was a dangerous mix. Iacopo was fingering the dent Tycho's sword had put in his breastplate. His scowl said he would not be caught like that again.

"Step back from each other."

Tycho tossed Iacopo's sword contemptuously at his feet and collected his own, raising it high above his head as Atilo had taught him. The circle around them stilled and even Alexa held her breath.

"You may begin."

This time Iacopo attacked first. A heavy-handed slash at Tycho's hip.

Their blades met and shock radiated up Tycho's arms. A brutal rally followed, with swords blocking vicious blows, the noise of steel echoing off the walls of the square around them. The blades were sweeps of light reflected in the flickering torches. Iacopo should have kept up his attack but retreated, gasping.

So Tycho pulled back his blade, slid his arm under it and lanced for Iacopo's groin, the point of his sword grating against the edge of Iacopo's breastplate. As Tycho half hoped he would, the fool glanced down.

When he looked back up, Tycho's elbow found his throat. Alonzo's howl of protest said he knew his man was beaten.

Iacopo stepped back with a hand to his neck, his breath coming in ragged gasps. His sword hung loose from his other hand. He was trying to say something.

"I can't hear you."

"He's surrendering."

Tycho ignored Roderigo. "You lied about Desdaio. You tricked Atilo into murder. You said Amelia was my whore and that boy my catamite. You stole the office you hold from a better man."

Iacopo let his sword fall at his feet, and spread his hands in obvious surrender. Silent words formed on his lips.

"I can't hear you."

"Tycho . . ." Alexa said.

But Tycho was already moving. He spun once, adding speed to the weight of his blade and dragged its tip across Iacopo's throat, looking away before blood even began to fountain.

I will not turn.

"Arrest that man," Alonzo shouted.

Lord Roderigo stepped forward, stopping when Tycho raised his sword. Tycho's gaze locked on the man. Only Tycho knew he glared fiercely at Roderigo because the smell of Iacopo's blood filled the air so richly he could barely control his desire to feed before Iacopo finished dying.

Hunger and indecision rooted him to the ground.

"Arrest his catamite, too."

"*Alonzo.*"

"What?"

"That is not necessary."

"The courts can decide."

"Not on this." Alexa's voice was firm. "I'm taking the boy with me . . . He is protected," she added, in case Alonzo needed help with what she was saying.

"Gods, woman . . ." Alonzo gripped his sword. Decided in that second to take his anger out on Roderigo instead. "Too afraid to arrest him?"

Roderigo stepped forward and hesitated.

And then Roderigo's Mongol sergeant solved his captain's problem by nodding to his men, who slotted steel-headed bolts into their ready-cocked crossbows and aimed them at Tycho.

"Your choice," Temujin said.

When Tycho put down his sword, Roderigo looked relieved and Alonzo disappointed. "You will stand trial," he said.

"For what?"

"Killing a man who was surrendering. It was clear this was a fight to the death or until either combatant demanded quarter."

220

"I heard nothing."

Alonzo flushed. "You murdered him."

"A matter for the courts." The duchess's voice was calm.

"He is stripped of his knighthood and the house in San Aponal returns to the city." Alonzo glared at his sister-in-law, daring her to object.

She nodded reluctantly.

"And you and I should ask ourselves," Alonzo added, "if we really want this matter to reach the courts?" Tycho wondered if he was the only person to hear in those words an invitation to his murder. "In the meantime, Roderigo can arrange Sir Iacopo's burial and that Mongol can take the slave back to prison."

38

Tycho looked Sergeant Temujin in the eye and saw the desert wastes and snow-capped mountains the sergeant barely knew he hungered for. He saw Temujin's fear, far back and hidden, at finding himself face to face with a monster.

"You know what I am?"

Temujin nodded reluctantly.

"You were right," said Tycho. "That night on the boat . . . Roderigo should have killed me. Remember what you said? The Khan owned something like me and it killed him. You were right and Roderigo was wrong."

The ruined square was empty.

Alonzo, Alexa and the others were gone.

Knowing his hatred of water and fearing he'd escape if taken through the back alleys, the Regent had ordered Tycho be shipped along the northern shore and delivered to the Pit via the canals. It was slightly longer than walking but carried him over water almost the entire way.

Ropes bound Tycho's hands behind his back.

Sergeant Temujin had found a sack once used for dry fish to go over his head. The sergeant was taking no chances. The lugger he'd commandeered floated squat on the edge of a *fondamenta* lining the city's eastern edge.

"Fill the sack with earth instead," Tycho suggested. "If you want to stop me turning into a demon seat me on dry dirt."

"Why would you help me?"

"It hurts," said Tycho, meaning it. "Changing to a demon hurts. My bones crack, my flesh rips, muscles tear . . ."

Around him Dogana guards crossed themselves.

"Fill that with earth," Temujin ordered. "And find me another sack for his head."

"There isn't another one."

"Find one."

"Took long enough to find that."

The man disappeared muttering into a couple of ruined houses around the square where Tycho's duel had been fought and returned empty-handed, protesting the area was too poor to waste anything that valuable by discarding it.

"He escapes, I'm holding you responsible."

Only once did the black waves along the city's northern edge threaten to swamp the lugger and Tycho turned his back to the spray, feeling it splash across his shoulders as Temujin's men cursed and steered their boat into the wind.

When they turned it was for a wide canal that separated the district of Castello from Cannaregio. At a sharp-prowed house that stood where the canal divided, they took the wider of the two canals on offer and came ashore a few minutes later.

"Follow me," Temujin said. Had the last guard been watching properly he would have seen Tycho test the rope round his wrists and nod thoughtfully.

Could be worse . . .

Luckily the hemp was wet, his wrists thin and the guard who tied the knot was in a hurry. All three helped. It helped too that the pre-dawn crowd on the landing stage swelled as pie sellers and women with grilled fish on skewers decided Temujin's men needed breakfast.

"Boss, let's . . ."

"No," Temujin said. "We'll eat later."

The alley he chose was narrow enough for Tycho to have touched both sides if his hands hadn't been bound behind his back. So Tycho counted paces to steady himself and take his mind from the pain of twisting one wrist against another.

After a hundred paces, the alley turned right abruptly, ran for another fifty and then opened into a narrow courtyard, where bricked-in windows stared blindly down at them from high walls. Even at noon the courtyard must look gloomy. Right now it was ink-black.

Fear crawled up Tycho's spine as he opened his senses.

Bitter misery coated the flagstones under his feet like slime, and pain like mould varnished the thick brick walls that climbed blindly around them. In a city of ghosts, where he'd grown used to being watched by what could not be seen, he knew even the ghosts were afraid to haunt this place.

How could he not be afraid? He'd been here before. Although that time they brought him blindfold. This time Tycho *knew* where he was. Silently, he fought the ropes as fiercely as he fought his fear.

Once a day Venice's high tide flowed down culverts into the Pit, raising its level until those on a small central island crowded tight, and those in the fetid shallows crept closer, and those already up to their necks at the edges of the circular prison knew that the oldest, tiredest and weakest would drown.

It was hell with added water.

Luck and ruthlessness carried him through last time. This time? *I'm not sure I'm even the same person.*

"Let me talk to Alexa."

Sergeant Temujin growled at him to remain silent. Stepping up to the heavy black-painted door, he prepared to knock.

Don't let him knock, Tycho told himself.

He twisted his wrists so hard rope scraped flesh from bone, and he buckled at the pain, toppling sideways to black out as the world exploded against the side of his head. He woke a second later to a kick in his gut.

"Stand him up."

Hands gripped him. Tycho felt himself being lifted as a guard struggled to obey Temujin's order.

Do it now.

Time slowed as Tycho's wrists slicked free from bloody rope.

Lifting a dagger from the man's belt, he flipped it and slammed the pommel into the other man's temple, dropping him. Shock crossed the second guard's face as Tycho spun, driving rigid fingers into his liver. The man shat himself before he hit the ground. The next two went down just as quickly.

"*Shoot him.*"

Catching the bolt, Tycho threw it back hard enough to pierce the wrist of the one who fired. And then, grabbing his crossbow, Tycho used it like a club on a guard beyond, and the one with the wounded wrist ran. This was good since he took the temptation of fresh blood with him.

The fight was finished in seconds.

"I knew you'd be my death," Temujin said.

Tycho saw dark eyes and leathery skin, a sour grin of bravado in the face of expected defeat. Behind it Temujin's skull glistened yellow in a grin of its own. The young man and skull stared at each other.

"I'll tell your boss you died to let him live."

The sergeant's mouth twitched.

The sword Temujin drew was old and its blade pitted with the evidence of more battles than sharpening could remove. Mongol script ran down its length like rusting swirls.

"Your father's?"

"He left it with Ma as proof he'd return. He lied." Raising the weapon, Temujin grinned. "I'll be calling him on that when we meet."

His opening blow would have beheaded an ox.

Only luck, fear and hunger gave Tycho the speed to drop under it. He dipped his fingers in blood spilt by the crossbowman who ran, scooped cooling liquid into his mouth. Temujin's second blow seemed slower.

His third moved so slowly that Tycho had time to choose a target for the dagger he punched so hard through Temujin's armour that the point split buffalo horn and pierced boiled leather as if it were paper. Pain twisted the Mongol sergeant's face and his eyes widened as his mind caught up with what had happened.

A clatter said Temujin's sword had dropped to the ground. Very slowly, Tycho touched the trickle of blood that ran from the sergeant's lip.

"What are you really?" Temujin asked.

"I'm Fallen."

"What are Fallen?"

"Let me see if you know." Tycho lifted his thumb to his mouth hoping to find an answer in the fragments of a life coming to its end. But there was little in the sergeant's memories Tycho didn't know already. Even the story about the Tycho-like demon that killed the Khan was gossip overheard as a child.

"So, you *were* at San Lazar to . . ."

"Of course I was," Temujin said. "To blow up the girl and her brat. Alonzo's orders. There's something about that child." He smiled sourly. "I'm sure a demon like you can recognise that. Now, I have a fight to pick with my father. End this."

Tycho did.

Taking the first unlocked door he found led to a private yard and an open door to a room filled with half-naked Schiavoni children sleeping in a huddle on a rotting mattress. Tycho exited

226

the room under the gaze of a Schiavoni woman wise enough to stay silent. The blood on his clothes probably helped.

The tenement hall was as squalid as he expected, the lock to its front door broken. Leaving the hall he took an alley so narrow he had to turn sideways. Someone had widened a warehouse into the alley.

He found himself among the early morning crowd in a meat market, where his bloody doublet attracted fewer glances than it might. A church tower stood between the market and the rising sun. The stalls were covered with canvas awnings. For everyone except Tycho it was dark.

His eyes were struggling with the brightness.

He stole a leather apron from a cart and kept walking, the blood-smeared apron flapping around his knees. In his hand was a knife. But then half the people around him held knives or cleavers.

The church door was unlocked and the inside blissfully dark and almost empty. Two old women knelt before a rail that kept them from approaching the altar, where a young man in grey cassock muttered prayers to himself with his eyes fixed on something Tycho couldn't see.

He left the three of them to their prayers and took the stairs to the tower.

There would be a room without windows that would be full of junk too decrepit to use and too venerable to throw away. The door would be locked, in which case he'd break the lock. Or unlocked, in which case he'd simply let himself in. Either way, he would jam the door from inside. This wasn't the first church he'd used to hide from daylight. Only now he was hiding from more than daylight. He was an outlaw. By the time he woke there would be a price on his head.

Darkness and plainsong, the muted clatter of stallholders packing their stalls and handcarts trundling home . . . Tycho found comfort in the sounds that filtered into his hiding place, even if it was only the comfort of knowing he would soon be able to leave. The room he'd found was high in the tower, directly below the bell platform and only reachable through a low door off the spiral stairs.

He went up the stairs rather than down to where the service was being held. From the top of the tower he could see Venice laid out around him. In one direction the north-west corner of Arzanale, with oil lamps burning on the rope walks. Five minutes' walk in the other delivered the squat building of the Tedeschi *fondaco*, where the German merchants kept to their own traditions and laws.

Straight ahead was open lagoon and beyond that mainland. Behind him was the Riva degli Schiavoni, the city's southern edge, where ships re-victualled and crews were hired and brothels and taverns catered for those with a day ashore.

Sergeant Temujin had asked a question that needed answering.

What are you really?

And looking towards the Tedeschi *fondaco* and the warren of lanes leading towards it, Tycho knew where he might find an answer. In the Street of Scribes, where Jews wrote letters for those unable to write and read letters for those unable to read, and studied knowledge it was said no other people had.

Tycho had a name, one Atilo had muttered when drawing up a list of those the Council should have watched . . .

"Rabbi Abram?"

The old man smiled. "Enter," he said.

"My master – my *late* master – spoke highly of you."

The rabbi nodded. Not asking who his master was or why Tycho had just appeared at an upper window.

"He said you know more pateras than anyone alive."

These were the carved signs used by guilds and families and gangs. The roundels could be found all over the city. More than fifty thousand examples were said to adorn the walls of the city. That might even have been true.

"What else did he say?"

"That you can read the stars and see the colour of human souls with your naked eye. That you know the thousand names of God."

"Which must not be spoken in vain and must never be collected. If collected, they must be burnt in the way prescribed." Steel had entered Rabbi Abram's voice. "Pateras, stars, souls, names of God – which one of these very different things brings you through my window at night? Accepting, of course, that in the end all things are the same. Gang pateras?"

"It's said you're the wisest man in Venice."

"So much saying." The rabbi sighed. "So little studying and common sense. What do you want from me?" His tone was softer than the thrust of his words.

"I want to know what I am."

Rabbi Abram picked up a candle from his desk and walked round Tycho, holding the candle close. "A bloodstained boy," he said finally. "Who thinks a dagger in his belt makes him a man. One of a thousand within a spit of this street. That seems the most likely answer. What do you think you are?"

"A demon."

The rabbi took a harder look.

He tapped Tycho's face and examined his fingers, lifted his eyelids and made him open his mouth. Finally, he bent his head to listen to Tycho's chest and froze.

Half an hour later Rabbi Abram put down a star chart, walked to a table and poured two large glasses of blood-red wine. He drank from one and offered Tycho the other. When Tycho refused the rabbi scowled. "Drink."

"What did you discover?"

"Not what I was expecting."

Tycho waited.

"I should be able to read your past, where you now stand and your future from the stars and my calculations. And yet, if they are to be believed you did not exist until a year ago, two years at the most."

"You didn't see deserts and madness?"

"Should I have done?"

"So I was told."

The rabbi finished his glass of red wine. A glance said he wanted another. Instead he sunk on to a stool. A second later, he ordered Tycho to drag his seat closer. "Before you did not exist you existed somewhere else."

"Bjornvin."

"You know about this?"

"I have memories," Tycho said.

"Old memories? Memories from many lifetimes ago?"

"To me they feel like yesterday." That was the truth. Bjornvin was no further away than just beyond his first memory of this city. So close that he felt he should be able to taste the smoke of the great hall burning.

"What is the worst you've done?"

"Taken life."

"Half of Venice does that daily."

Tycho looked doubtful.

"Some with a knife, other with words. Most by stepping over a beggar or turning away when they hear a scream. If killing makes you a demon this is a city of demons in a world of the same. Tell me of yourself."

"I can see in the dark. Sunlight hurts me."

The rabbi's mouth tightened to a line.

"So, you come to me?" he said finally. "Who should probably have come to you? My niece Elizavet has mentioned you, she says . . ."

He saw Tycho's surprise.

"You didn't know I was her uncle?"

"No," Tycho said. "I thought she was Alexa's spy."

The rabbi looked pained. "So maybe you're more than a boy and maybe not. Only God can judge. What is the best thing you've done?"

"I saved Pietro. He'd have drowned in the Pit otherwise. Either drowned, been murdered or wished he had been."

"Where is he now?"

"I found him a home."

"Would a demon do that?"

It was a real question, Tycho realised. His answer was a shrug.

"Do you believe in God?"

"No . . ." The first thing he'd said not needing thought.

"You should. If you're part of this world then you're part of him. He means for you to exist. So two questions: what is the ugliest thing you've seen and what the most beautiful?"

"I didn't see it but I was it."

"The monster . . . And the most beautiful?"

"A young woman half naked kneeling in the darkness."

"Not my niece?"

Tycho shook his head and the rabbi relaxed slightly. "So," he said. "This girl kneeling half naked in the darkness . . . You love her?"

Beyond life. How could this longing be anything else?

"Answer me," the rabbi's voice was sharp.

"Yes . . . I love her."

"You want to marry her?"

Tycho stared at his hands. "Yes," he said, when he allowed himself to think. "More than I have ever wanted anything."

"That is as it should be . . . Go to her and make your peace, if making peace is possible. Beg forgiveness for whatever monstrous thing you think you've done." The old man smiled. "But next time you want to talk to me use the door."

39

The sound of a harpsichord drifted through a balcony window high above. No light showed from the room and though the dying light of the sun stained distant roofs the colour of drying blood it would be dark inside.

The notes were fierce, impassioned.

Until a missed note made Giulietta crash her hands down in anger. Tycho heard a sob, a slam of a door, footsteps vanishing upstairs.

Old memories slowed his climb. A hundred tiny hooks pierced his flesh, attached to unseen wires that dragged the barbs so hard he wanted to turn back and abandon this idea for the stupidity it was. In places ivy had been ripped away and the walls beneath mended. Patches of brick had been remortared and some bricks replaced altogether. The fact the building work was unfinished suggested Giulietta had grown bored with it or quarrelled with her masons. Money could not be the problem. With the death of Desdaio Bribanzo she'd become the richest heiress in the city.

He climbed towards a balcony he already knew was hers. A narrow, high, pointed window, a simple marble balustrade half lost under twisting fingers of ivy that still had to be removed. Its wooden shutter was bleached with age, frayed along the bottom with rot and in need of repair.

It rattled when the rubble he threw landed. A second later a bolt was withdrawn and the shutters pushed open.

"Who's there?"

Her voice touched Tycho more than her music, and that had left him clinging to a rotting wall and close to tears. Simply hearing her made his stomach lurch, his heart tighten. He had blood on his clothes, his own description of himself as a demon in his ears and he was worried she'd opened the shutters so readily. How did she know it was safe?

Foreshortened against the night sky, Giulietta leant from her balcony as if intending to make herself a target. Tycho wanted to order her to step back into shadow; or abandon his climb, drop down to where her guards stood either side of the front door and shake some professionalism into them.

"I know you're there." She held up a stiletto to show she was armed.

"I hope it's sharp . . ."

"*Tycho?*" The figure above him froze.

"I'm coming up," he said. Grabbing a fat stem of ivy, he hauled while finding purchase with his feet. He moved at normal speed so as not to frighten her.

"This blade's silver."

Tycho halted.

"Silver doesn't take an edge. That's what the armourer said. But I'm a Millioni princess and who was he to disagree? My money spoke loud enough."

"Giulietta . . ."

"Go," she ordered. "While you can."

The shutters slammed loud enough for a drunk on the *fondamenta* to look up, shake his head and go back to pissing. The dragonet on a parapet above their heads took longer to look away. Tycho listened for a door slamming, for footsteps up to a bedchamber or down to the halls to call her guards . . .

All he heard was silence.

Ca' Friedland had been old when Leopold's grandfather bought it. Most palaces on this stretch of the Grand Canal were equally shabby. That Giulietta had started redecorating and then stopped told Tycho enough about her state of mind. Rumour said she was holed up in cold, patrician splendour. Tycho suspected it was misery. Rolling himself over her balustrade he landed lightly.

"I know you're in there."

"Leave now."

"Giulietta . . ."

"I will send to the palace. They'll arrest you. *Execute you.* They'll strangle you between the lion and the dragon, cut open your stomach, rip away your manhood with iron claws . . ."

Tycho felt his balls shrivel. She'd given some thought to this.

"You want me dead?"

A single sob edged between locked shutters.

"Uncle Alonzo says you killed Lord Atilo. You murdered Atilo's servant who was surrendering. You killed the Dogana sergeant. The whole city is talking about your treachery."

"It wasn't like that."

"What was it like?"

"Iacopo killed Desdaio."

"You *did* love her."

Sliding his dagger between shutters to lift the latch, Tycho pushed them open to stand in the window staring at the darkened room. There were candles everywhere, unlit ones. An untouched jug of wine sat on a marble table. An abandoned plate of bread and cheese looked hard and stale. The red-headed girl who glared at him had eyes that burnt him like fire.

"What do you want?" she demanded.

His fingers were steady as he undid jet on his soiled velvet doublet and unlaced the neck of the silk shirt beneath. Dropping the doublet, he pulled the shirt over his head, holding it loosely in one hand.

Giulietta sucked in her breath.

"Here's my heart," Tycho said, touching his breast. *It should be there beneath his fingers.* Tycho wasn't sure if he could feel it or not.

She glared at him.

"So kill me," he said.

"Don't you dare mock me."

"You don't mock the people you love."

Her bottom lip trembled. Her eyes softened and then she scowled. "I don't believe you." Her glare dared him to ask about what. Instead he stayed silent and watchful as she stepped towards him.

She was beautiful.

Sorrow and loneliness had thinned her face. Her flame-red hair was shorter than he remembered, and the slight moonlight heightened its colour. Her clothes were as severe as he recalled. Her black silks and sombre jewellery a disturbing mockery of his own costume. The blade she drew shone silver. Its workmanship was the best Venice could supply.

"You killed Lord Atilo."

Tycho stared at her. In her eyes were anger, confusion, a wish to believe something she didn't believe. The confusion left her statement on the lower slopes of a question. She was waiting for him to deny it.

He stayed silent.

"And you killed Leopold. You could have saved him but you let him die because . . ." she gripped the dagger harder, "because of me. And on the *San Marco* I let you . . ." Her words drained away.

"Giulietta."

"You took advantage of me."

Tycho shook his head. Her words belonged to someone else. He didn't recognise the girl speaking or the traitor she spoke about. *He couldn't have saved Leopold.*

"I couldn't . . ."

"Yes, you could. You saved everyone else. While we were locked below you called up waves and a storm. Leapt from one ship to another and killed every Mamluk who tried to stop you. That's what people believe."

She looked uncertain as she said it.

When Tycho nodded she'd raised her dagger a little higher as if to remind herself how dangerous he was. A slow step brought them together, and she put the point to his chest, her eyes widening as his flesh sizzled.

"I'm not human."

Stepping back, she lowered her blade. "What are you then?"
If I knew I would tell you.

The second time Lady Giulietta lifted the blade she pushed deeper and held it there, her eyes never leaving his. Whatever she was searching for he doubted she found it. "He was a better man than you."

I know.

"Swear you couldn't save him."

Opening his mouth to swear, Tycho shut it again.

Lady Giulietta stepped back and let her dagger sag, holding it loosely in shaking fingers. *Gods*, Tycho was shuddering with pain as his flesh took longer this time to begin to heal. Giulietta waited for him to speak. It took him a full minute to find his voice.

"May I put my shirt on?"

Probably not what she expected him to say.

Her gaze never left him as he pulled the shirt over his head, tying its ribbons with shaking fingers. All he had left inside were emptiness and truth, so he offered her those. "When Leopold asked me to take you to Atilo's ship I thought we'd all die. That he was simply banishing you so he could die with dignity, and wouldn't have to kill you himself."

"Leopold would never . . ."

"He asked me to do it."

"*What?*"

"Leopold couldn't do it himself. So he begged me to. Lord

Atilo also asked. He wanted me to kill Desdaio and I told him that was his job." Tycho couldn't keep the bitterness from his voice. "We thought we were going to die."

"And Desdaio and I would prefer being killed to captured?"

"Believe me," Tycho said. "You would."

"How do you know?"

"Because I've been captured." Tycho had come to Venice with no memories, and the ones he'd regained made him grateful most were still missing. He thought about putting on his doublet and didn't bother. Instead he asked if he might come in.

"Yes," said Giulietta, standing to one side.

"Thank you."

"That night, I would have liked a choice." She took a look at Tycho's face, and added, "So would Desdaio." Tycho lifted a wine jug and looked to Giulietta for permission; she seemed surprised he gave the first glass to her.

"I didn't know," he said carefully. "Until I began fighting that I could alter the course of battle. I didn't know I could save you until I did."

"*You could save me?*"

"Why do you think I did it?"

He was careful not to catch her gaze. Not to think too deeply about what he was saying and what happened that night, what he became. For a second it seemed what he'd said was enough, but doubt re-entered her eyes.

"Tell me how you won the battle."

"Does it matter?"

He let her slap him. He could have caught her wrist, brushed it contemptuously aside or held it with iron fingers. He let her blow land and in the following silence saw a different kind of doubt behind her eyes. It ebbed as he watched, taking care to make no movement to scare her.

"All right," he said. "Why does it matter?"

He hoped for an answer he could live with. The longer he

stood there the more trouble Giulietta had framing any answer at all.

"We're alive," she said finally.

Tycho waited.

"And Leopold's not . . ."

"You feel guilty to be alive?"

She wanted to say that wasn't it, only he could see in her eyes it was. "You should have saved him," she said sadly. "You saved everyone else."

"Thousands died."

Lady Giulietta almost said those thousands didn't matter but caught herself. Tycho had long since realised only one life lost in that battle mattered to her, the one for which she held him responsible.

There was the rub.

"You're right," Tycho said.

Lady Giulietta's eyes widened. Fury rose inside her so fast its edges flared purple in a halo. Tycho knew only he could see it.

"I could have saved him. But I didn't know that."

"You thought you were going to die?"

He nodded.

"So what changed?"

"I did," said Tycho, forcing out the words.

The Venetians had a word for the hell he inhabited: limbo.

It was as if nothing existed beyond Ca' Friedland's walls; its foundations were built above a void, the sky over it was empty. The city was something he created. It had cracks because he did, if he could only find one he could slip through to hide on the other side. There was probably a word for that feeling too. "I made a deal."

"Who with?"

"The deal was simple."

"Victory . . .?"

"You lived."

"In exchange for what?"

"My soul," he said, watching Giulietta cross herself. He was about to say he wasn't even sure he had one. Only she had tears in her eyes and a rare softness smoothed the harshness in her thin face.

"You offered your soul for me?"

"It was always yours."

Tears magnified her pale blue eyes until he thought he would vanish into them. "*Tycho . . .*"

"From the night you knelt before the stone mother."

She smiled at his name for the Virgin, and blushed to recall their meeting. Tycho saw her embarrassment and realised this was the first time in months he'd seen her unveiled. When she held out her hand he thought she was taking him to bed.

He was wrong.

"This is older than the Wolf Brothers."

As Lady Giulietta raised the long lid, her fingers brushed a gold lock plate decorated with a naked man holding a pelt of fur. Inside was a simpler box and no gold decorated this one. The hinges were brass, however. The walnut sides lovingly polished.

"Lift it out."

Tycho was surprised by its weight.

He could swear he felt the box shiver. A shutter banged in the hall above, and wind whistled around a rusting trap door overhead. Trying to remember if the wind had been there before, Tycho realised he couldn't. Maybe it had.

Inside the box was a sword.

"The *WolfeSelle*," Giulietta said. "I shouldn't even know its name."

"May I . . .?"

She nodded.

He took the handle and this time the shiver was unmistakable. The sword roiled under his fingers as if alive. A high note broke the air, way beyond Giulietta's hearing. Inside his body something answered. Dark and primal. Something that gloated in being the monster Rabbi Abram had looked for. Tycho could feel a hungry joy and longing he didn't recognise as any part of himself.

"What's wrong?"

"Where did Leopold get this?"

"It belongs to the Wolf Brothers as the highest of their objects. Every chief has owned it since . . ." She named a Hunnish prince he'd never heard of. Tycho only knowing what *Hunnish* was because she told him.

By then thread-like fingers were reaching for his thoughts. Instinctively he brushed them away and pushed back when they kept reaching. He put the *WolfeSelle* down with a bang.

"This belongs to your son."

"No." Lady Giulietta was firm.

"You heard Leopold at the christening. He named Leo his heir in all things. This was Leopold's. Therefore it belongs to Leo."

"It belongs to the Wolf Brothers."

"Then give it back to them."

"How? I can't go to them. I can never let them come to me."

"Because they'd discover Leopold made your son *krieghund*?"

She stared at him in shock. "You know that?" Lady Giulietta shook her head, irritated at her own stupidity. "Obviously you do, given your question. You know what my Uncle Alonzo would do if he discovered . . .?

Tycho knew exactly what the Regent would do. Tycho didn't doubt Alexa would have the child killed, too. How could either of them let Leo live? The *krieghund* were Sigismund's shock troops, Venice's deadliest enemy.

"No one must know."

"I promise."

"Leo is *mine*," Giulietta said. "Whatever God thinks of what he is. Whatever he thinks of how Leo was conceived. He is *my* child and I won't have him harmed or taken from me." Beneath her determination she sounded young and frightened. Young, frightened and very, very stubborn.

This was the girl he loved.

240

PART 2

"Now could I drink hot blood, and do such bitter business, as the day would quake to look on . . ."

Hamlet, William Shakespeare

40

Alta Mofacon

"My lady." The mayor of Gorizia bustled forward, looking both flustered and puffed up at his chance of impressing his long-absent mistress. "The local girls . . ." His hopes collapsed as Lady Giulietta stepped from her litter and he saw her black gown and gloves, the widow's veil covering her face.

Spurring his horse, her escort hurried forward and slid from its saddle, offering Giulietta his arm. After a moment's hesitation she took it.

"My lady will not be . . ."

"Roderigo."

Her escort hesitated.

"Let's be kind," Giulietta muttered.

A statement so unlikely from the lips of a Millioni princess she knew he instantly believed she'd loved her German princeling – which she had – and was as grief-stricken as rumour said. Watching him decide this she hid a sour smile.

Her grief was real enough to have brought her to Gorizia, a town on the mainland between Port Monfalcone, where she'd recently landed, and Alta Mofacon, the hill village where she was heading.

Lady Giulietta's very public display of grief was not so much play-acting as the simple result of letting down her guard. Once she'd decided to mourn Leopold properly the tears came. It had taken less than a week of public weeping, at a meeting with the duke, on her way through the streets, navigating the Canalasso in her gondola for a note from Aunt Alexa to arrive.

On that occasion Lady Giulietta dispensed with her retinue and guards and accepted the palanquin her aunt sent for her. She arrived at the palace at dusk, almost alone, simply dressed and in tears.

The meeting was brief. Mercifully, her uncle had been absent. These days he found her presence as hard to stand as she his.

"You loved Leopold that much?" Aunt Alexa asked.

Lady Giulietta had blinked. "It's complicated," she said finally. And her eyes had overflowed and spilt the tears she tried to hold back, her throat tightening as she turned away. It was a long time since Aunt Alexa petted her but strong arms wrapped Giulietta and held her.

Only when the sobbing stopped did Alexa let her go; although first she stroked Giulietta's hair and kissed her forehead as she used to do when Giulietta was a little girl. "So young," the duchess said.

"I'm seventeen."

"That's what I mean. You think your life is over. It's barely begun. What do you need?" Absent-mindedly Alexa wiped a tear from Giulietta's face and carried it on a fingertip beneath her veil to taste.

"There are potions for sadness and ointments for grief. However, I cannot make sadness disappear without deadening some of who you are. And you are too much yourself to like that. So tell me what would make it bearable?"

"I want to go home."

"You want to return to Ca' Ducale?" Duchess Alexa sounded surprised. "I'd understood you were happy to get away."

"No," Giulietta said. "I want to go *home*."

Aunt Alexa said nothing. She was good at that.

"Alta Mofacon."

"You stayed there for three summers as a child."

"It felt like home," Giulietta said fiercely. "And don't tell me I have bigger estates because I know that. I've looked at the list. Two cities, three market towns, five ordinary towns, a dozen manors, thirty-six villages, two oak forests . . ."

The duchess nodded approvingly. The forests were worth as much as all the villages together. Shipyards needed oak, the Mamluks needed wood of any sort, having cut down their own supplies, foundries everywhere needed charcoal, which was expensive to buy and rewarding to sell. Duchess Alexa approved of forests. She approved of forests as much as she approved of silver mines.

"All that," said Giulietta, "before I include Leopold's lands or my father's estates in Carpathia."

"You're rich."

"I've always been rich."

"Well, now you're richer . . ." Hesitating on the edge of saying more, Alexa chose not to and Giulietta pretended not to notice. She had Tycho's words fresh in her head. He'd insisted – again – her aunt was behind her abduction.

Having made Giulietta tea, which was Alexa's answer to most things, she called a scribe and demanded he write a passport allowing Giulietta to leave. Then she took the paper and Giulietta went in search of Marco, who was on the roof feeding pigeons with scraps of pie. He signed without bothering to read it first.

"Sweet c-cousin . . ."

Giulietta looked back to see him smiling at her. "Have f-fun," he said. "Say h-hello to the p-pine trees for m-me." Having blown her a kiss, he went back to shredding sweetmeats into little piles. Feeding raisins to one pigeon, candied peel to another and barely edible pastry to a third.

"How does he . . ."

"Know what he does?" Alexa shrugged. "Fools are different. Sometime's very different. Marco is more different than most."

Lady Giulietta knew that wasn't the full answer.

All the same, that was how she found herself in Gorizia, a fortified town at the foot of the Julian Alps on the mainland north-east of Venice. It was half a day's hard ride above Port Monfalcone, which the Germans called Falconberg and the local people something unpronounceable. Her mother had owned Falconberg, Gorizia and Alta Mofacon and all the land in between. Lady Giulietta owned them now.

"Let the girls dance," she ordered.

Half were fair, most were big breasted and red-cheeked. What their dance lacked in skill it supplied in enthusiasm. Hating herself for her own stuck-upness, Giulietta made herself clap when the dancing was done.

This meant they wanted to do it again.

"Very gracious, my lady." Lord Roderigo took it for granted she wouldn't want to see a third performance. In this he was right. She also didn't want him accompanying her to Alta Mofacon.

"This is where we part."

"My lady, my orders . . ."

"Are irrelevant. We're on my land now."

She was correct and he knew it. Lady Giulietta held the county in her own right. The laws were her laws not those of the watery city they'd left behind.

"Roderigo," she said, sweetening the pill. "Look at them. I grew up here. These are my people. It's half a day's ride through my own fields. What can happen?"

Scowling, the Dogana captain let his gaze rake over her litter, the three huge-wheeled ox carts loaded with her goods, and the two dozen local guards who accompanied her. Uncle Alonzo would have a spy among them. Aunt Alexa, too. If Cousin Marco hadn't been an idiot he'd also have had one.

"Will you send a man, my lady, when you've arrived?"

"And you'll wait here?"

"If that's acceptable."

Lady Giulietta hid her smile. It was better than she expected. "Thank you," she said. "I'm sure the mayor will make you comfortable while you wait."

At her side the mayor nodded.

Lord Roderigo was having trouble adjusting to this new version of her. Giulietta liked that. She liked being here in her hill town, on the way to her favourite place in the world; but she wasn't stupid, she knew half her happiness came from having cried herself out.

What began as a ruse took over until she thought her tears would never stop. Tears for Leopold, tears for her son and what his future held, tears for her own childhood's unhappiness. Even, though it filled her with guilt to remember it, tears at how badly she'd treated her lady-in-waiting, and tears for Tycho . . .

She'd cried so much her eyes were empty and her milk salty with tears.

It was whispered she'd said goodbye to her dead husband in a frenzy of grief more suited to the death of a barbarian chief.

"Leo . . ."

"Is sleeping, my lady."

Lady Eleanor had appeared at her side at the exact moment Giulietta wanted to ask her a question.

"The wet nurse is with her?"

"Yes, my lady."

"And he's . . ."

"More interested in stewed fruit." Lady Eleanor grinned and stared around her, taking in a fortified tower, built by one of the Hunnish kings, and the hills rising to mountains beyond. "Strong as an ox, that child."

Lady Giulietta smiled.

* * *

"You," she said.

The man she picked looked surprised. He was small, untidy and barely noticeable to someone like her. Giulietta imagined that helped in his line of work.

"You're to take this to Lord Roderigo."

He took her letter reluctantly.

She'd spent half the afternoon's journey to Alta Mofacon deciding which two of the three most anonymous guards was Alonzo's spy and which her aunt's.

"I ride poorly, my lady."

"You won't be riding. It's mostly downhill, which will help with walking. You can walk back or wait for a carter to come this way."

She'd left her letter poorly sealed to make it easier to read, although if he were any kind of spy at all he'd be able to melt and refix the wax without it showing.

The man bowed low.

That just left Aunt Alexa's spy.

"Take those two soldiers," Giulietta told her sergeant. "And set up a watch post there." She pointed at a broke-backed mountain that rose to a peak on its right, with a gap like a missing tooth near the top. Below falls of grit and gravel was a goat path that climbed through summer scrub. It would take half an hour to navigate, maybe more; in half an hour it would be nightfall.

"Tell the men to find wood, build a beacon and light it if they see movement on the plains below. You return but they remain."

She was her own captain.

This had been explained to her guards. They answered to their sergeant, who answered to her. She expected them to obey without hesitation.

Giulietta smiled. That took care of Alexa's spy, and if the two her sergeant was taking were innocent, then no problem; her other choice was the sergeant himself. "Perhaps I should stay," he said.

"No," Giulietta said.

She watched the three begin their trek towards the scree, and turned to check how Alonzo's spy was doing on his return to the coast. Any minute now he'd be hidden in an orange grove. The trees that hid him from her would hide her from him.

"Get my carts into the courtyard."

The man she addressed grabbed an ox collar and began tugging the reluctant beast into action. With a heavy sigh it pulled the first of the carts under an arch and into an empty square. Although the manor yard would be a nightmare come winter, recent sun had baked spring mud to the hardness of stale bread. As the lead oxen raised its tail to splash shit into the dirt, Giulietta smiled; not even minding how close the beast came to soiling her dress.

This was home.

For all Aunt Alexa's protest that she'd only spent three summers here, this was home because this was where her mother had been happiest, alone on her own little estate. "I'll take the upper room in that corner."

"My lady . . ." One look at her stubborn face and the steward was ordering servants to move furniture from the room they'd prepared to the one she wanted.

"You'll sleep next door," she told Eleanor. "In my room."

Her lady-in-waiting looked puzzled.

"When I was small."

"And Leo, my lady?"

"Put his wet nurse on the other side."

The concerns of her immediate family dealt with, Lady Giulietta turned her attention to wider matters. Within ten minutes her possessions were unloaded, she'd refused a formal supper and demanded fresh bread, cheese and fruit be brought to her room. "But first," she said, "gather everyone in the hall. I want to address them."

* * *

The canvas covering the third cart was so rotten that Tycho's blade cut through it like wind through smoke. The courtyard was dark – which he expected – and as deserted as Lady Giulietta had promised it would be.

Her manor had heavy walls of a yellowy stone that was new to him, red pantiles on the roof and window frames carved from sandstone. Tycho swallowed the details of this place she loved so much in a single glance. The manor house was less grand than he expected, but solid. The walls looking as if they'd been standing for five hundred years.

Around him light bled from half a dozen windows, but the stars still showed higher and clearer in the sky than in Venice. So this was where the girl he loved felt so at home? In a squat manor little better than a farmhouse, with oxen lowing in the distance, swifts skimming the roofs and the sound of a fiddle coming from a nearby tavern. Wood smoke, wild herbs and manure scented the air.

My house is your house. You may enter anywhere.

The words she'd whispered as she passed the cart on her way inside to talk to those who had looked after her lands in the eleven years she'd been away. The people he'd heard greet her with respect, and a nervous fondness that came from remembering her as a child.

Tycho held out his hand to Rosalyn.

She climbed from the ox cart in clothes so ragged they must have come from charity or a corpse. If the first, the Brothers of the Poor were well rid, because Tycho could see lice crawling through frayed seams. If the second, it had been a rich corpse. The original dress was silk dyed to a flat black.

"Where did you get that?"

"Stole it."

He considered asking where but didn't.

Kicking her feet in the dirt, Rosalyn looked sullenly around her. "This is where she wants to live?" Rosalyn's nose wrinkled as if ox dung was worse than the sulphur of Venice's foundries or the urine of its tanners' pits. She sniffed again, this time in disgust.

"You will behave."

Rosalyn gave a little curtsy.

"Lady Giulietta has just saved us."

The girl was obviously about to say she didn't need saving but shut her mouth instead. Reaching up, she combed fingers through her filthy hair and straightened the rancid dress. "Where do we sleep?"

"In the cellars."

She stepped closer and stared up at him, the amber flecks in her eyes glittering in the starlight until staring at them was like looking at the night sky itself. Tycho stepped back slightly and her face hardened.

"Do we sleep together?"

He was too slow to understand her question.

She stepped back, tugging the dress tight against her, so he could see what she was offering. And he saw a scrawny child, with thin hips and slight breasts and filthy hair. There was a fineness to her thin face he didn't remember, and a wildness behind her eyes from a life that had been brutal long before she died the way she did.

"Well?" Rosalyn said fiercely.

He knew she'd had pimps and protectors, what passed for a lover and her time on the night streets had been as grim as anything Bjornvin could offer, just in a different way. He understood she offered more than her body.

"Rosalyn . . ."

The fierceness went out of her eyes as she looked away, staring into the distance at something he imagined she didn't see. Her face when she looked back was stripped of emotion and her voice flat. "You love your princess." It was part statement, part question; but mostly she was daring him to deny it.

"From the moment I saw her."

"Of course you did." Rosalyn stared at him for a second, then shrugged to dismiss the conversation. "I'm hungry. Where can I feed?"

Tycho sighed with relief. "Nowhere within twenty minutes. Twenty minutes your speed. Be back before dawn."

"And you're sure Pietro . . . ?"

"As I said. He's safe at Ca' Friedland."

That she could smile at this touched Tycho.

He imagined there were times she forgot her small brother altogether. There had certainly been times he forgot everyone outside his own darkness. Her foul temper had mostly faded, her humour improved. In the week they'd hidden at Ca' Friedland she'd found many bits of herself that were human.

"Go," he told her. "Feed."

"Yes, master."

Tycho knew he was being mocked.

41

This is what I wanted . . .

The bed was as she remembered it. A huge oak frame with a straw-stuffed mattress at the bottom, a wool-stuffed mattress above, and over the top of those her feather bed stuffed with the finest goose down.

A bolster was there to support her head.

Carved posts rose from the corners of her mother's bed, not quite as huge as Giulietta recalled, but still big enough to have needed a fat oak branch for each. Thick red curtains hung on all four sides, drawn back and tied with velvet rope. In winter they would keep her warm but it was high summer and she wanted to be able to see the sky. Her sky, since it was over her land.

In her head, Giulietta could see her mother on the bed, nursing a headache but still trying to smile at the small girl in her doorway. Zoë di Millioni had been rich enough to afford a three-mattress bed in each of her houses. Most nobles travelled with their beds; her mother had owned half a dozen.

Tonight I will sleep.

For the first time in weeks she would close her eyes to

the darkness and wake to the day without dreams or waking ridiculously early. No falling out of tall trees and jerking herself awake. No being chased by faceless assassins. No Leo to feed. The bed was hers and her body was hers.

She meant it. Tonight she would sleep.

"I'll wash myself," she told Lady Eleanor.

"Are you sure?"

"Yes." Giulietta waved her towards the door. "See you in the morning." She kissed her lady-in-waiting on the cheek, much to Eleanor's surprise, and smiled at the click of the door closing.

Tycho was out there somewhere.

He would be roaming Mofacon's hills. Watching the crescent moon in that unsettling way of his, letting the wind blow through his hair; she liked the idea of that. And the wild girl she'd hidden for him?

Doing the same.

Giulietta folded her clothes neatly, washed her hands and face, and then under her arms using the cloth laid out. Then she knelt, as she'd knelt every night she could remember, and prayed to the *stone mother*.

Leopold had laughed at her for praying.

Asked who she thought was out there in the darkness to hear. It was as close as they'd come to an outright argument. In the end, Leopold stepped back from the breach, saying women often found comfort in religion. And though the argument that statement produced was furious it was not fatal.

All done, and Leopold's memory called up for once without tears, Giulietta bolted her own door, slid under her white sheet and slept like a child.

Wiping her mouth, Rosalyn looked at the old priest's body. His life had been long, hard and happy. She wondered how that was possible. Blue skies, long summers, cold winters, occasional hunger and occasional plenty.

In his memories she tasted life as she'd not known it could be lived. For the moment, minute by minute, contentedly. She was shocked to discover she was crying. Even more shocked to realise she resented being made to feel more human now than she had ever felt when properly alive . . .

Was this what Tycho felt?

Was this why he fought so hard to deny himself food?

Because the vulnerability other people's memories brought wore his anger away? Rosalyn wondered if she should feel sorry for the life taken and decided there was little point. The man had been old, close to dying and wouldn't have lived another winter anyway. Besides, how could she survive if she wasn't allowed to feed?

Time to go home . . .

She reached the edges of the village she'd found in seconds, the harbour at Port Monfalcone a few minutes later and skirted Gorizia, passing the man Lady Giulietta had sent with a message as he was gasping up the final mile to Alta Mofacon.

The man didn't see her but the person watching him did.

Tycho stood between trees in an apple grove, his hair silver-grey in the moonlight and a strange smile on his lips. Rosalyn had a sudden feeling he knew exactly where she'd been and what she'd been thinking.

"That dress is rancid."

More an observation than a complaint. At least, that's how it sounded to her. So she waited to see what else Tycho would say.

"Wash yourself."

"Master.

"Use sand if you can't stand water. And stop calling me that."

"Yes, master."

She felt his gaze follow her as she stepped off the edge of the road to skid down a slope, gravel and scree dragging at her heels. A second later he followed after her; his descent was neater and

less playful. At the bottom a dry riverbed was lined with grit
carried down from the mountains.

"Take off your dress."

She did as he ordered, wondering if he intended to take her
after all.

He would not be her first, obviously enough. But it would be
her first with him, and the first time since she . . . Rosalyn drew
a deep breath and knew she needed to learn how to name what
had happened.

Instead he took her dress, shaking it so hard and fast it cracked
like a whip. Then he slammed it against a rock a couple of times,
and climbed the slope to find a culvert that carried water to the
terraces below. He rinsed the rag quickly, wringing it dry with
a brutality that made stitches pop.

"Didn't the lice offend you?"

What lice? she wondered, hearing him sigh. She took the dress
he threw her, scrabbling into it without really knowing why.

"You fed?"

She nodded.

"Good." Taking her wrist, he bit deep, his dog teeth descending
to cut into her flesh like arrow points. Stepping back he considered the taste.

"Rich," Tycho said finally.

She guessed he meant rich with the life she'd taken from her
kill. Biting into his own wrist, he said, "Now you."

Grabbing his hand in case he snatched it away, Rosalyn rocked
backwards as half a dozen new colours lit the hillside, more
colours than she knew existed. *Oh shit*, she thought. *What Tycho
gets from feeding is way beyond me.*

Vision that could see for miles, hearing that caught the flutter
of a tiny bat overhead, a vixen barking three valleys beyond. As
for the scents on the wind, they twisted together like brightly lit
threads. For a second she saw the world as Tycho saw it. When
she looked up, her eyes were wide.

He obviously wondered if her clumsy curtsy was mockery.

Tycho must know she wouldn't dare. Turning, Rosalyn ran for the slope leading up to the white walls circling Alta Mofacon.

Her needs were simple: his approval and food. Tycho allowed her the second without telling her how to earn the first. She guessed she'd simply replaced Josh with a man who was kinder, if somewhat more dangerous.

Josh had been her first.

She'd been young, very young. He hadn't much cared about that. He found her food, found her shelter and, after a while, when she'd learnt to crave his approval, withdrew it. Well, now Josh was dead and she was . . .?

Not dead, Rosalyn guessed.

Though she remembered dying. Remembered an abject terror so fierce it froze her, and a blow to her chest and cold steel sliding under her rib, as the night sky faded and Tycho's face twisted in misery, because he was unable to stop it happening.

Rats scuttled in the grain pits built into Alta Mofacon's walls. In the little guardhouse, the keeper was locked in an argument with his wife and losing. His beaten tone as he admitted he might have been wrong reminded Rosalyn of someone.

After a second she realised it was her.

A couple in a house beyond also argued despite the night's lateness. Theirs lacked the other argument's bitterness and spite. As Rosalyn listened they stopped fighting and started rutting instead.

A change as swift as a shift in the wind.

A wild dog turned towards Rosalyn looking puzzled. A feral cat arched its back. Rosalyn heard a baby whimper, and a girl stifle a cry, though the two were unconnected. The night breeze rustled the smaller branches and feathered grass growing between slabs in a deserted garden, flicked and teased leaves on a tree. The air smelt different, tasted different.

She liked it here.

Scrambling up a wall, Rosalyn stepped over a gap between house and manor wall, felt a tile shift under her toes and slide towards an alley below.

"What was that?"

"What was what?"

She left two nightwatchmen in a discussion going nowhere.

Fixing her fingers and toes into mortarless gaps, she scaled the side of Giulietta's manor, landed lightly on a ledge and edged towards an open shutter before rolling herself over a waist-high windowsill and landing lightly on her feet in an open passage above the great hall.

The sound of a baby snuffling and a woman snoring came from behind the same door. Sweat soured the air from all those who slept on straw in the hall below.

"You," someone said.

Rosalyn turned.

A shocked girl watched her, face half hidden by a hand to her mouth.

Shocked by the speed of Rosalyn's turn, most probably. The girl's nightgown fell to her knees. Her feet and ankles were surprisingly clean. "What are you doing up here?"

Pretty, thought Rosalyn, wondering if she meant the dark-skinned girl or the embroidered white nightgown she was wearing.

"Answer my question."

"Why?"

The girl flushed.

Instantly, Rosalyn could sense blood beneath her skin and feel a tracery of rivers and rivulets bringing life to her body. So young and sweet, so clean. So very unlike everything Rosalyn was.

"Come with me . . ." The girl held out her hand.

What? Rosalyn was puzzled.

"They'll whip you if you're found up here." Nodding to a door left ajar, the girl added, "I'm Eleanor. That's my room."

Rosalyn was shocked to realise she didn't want to feed on this one. It was a revelation, an unexpected crack in her shell. "I'm Rosalyn."

"Are you hungry?"

Rosalyn shook her head. "I've fed already."

The girl frowned and tiny lines formed along the sides of her dark eyes. Pushing past Rosalyn she looked beyond the shutters, checking the drop to the courtyard below and the sheer wall to an overhanging roof above.

"You came in the window."

"I climb well."

"Perhaps I should call the guards?" If she was asking herself the girl didn't find the suggestion convincing. "But then you'd get whipped and that's never fun. Maybe I'll mention you to Giulietta in the morning."

The girl's room was huge and her bed had two mattresses, one on top of the other. Five white candles burnt in silver holders. *Five*, and *white*. Not yellow and stinking like normal people used when they could afford candles.

"You're filthy."

Not an insult, simply a statement of fact; although Rosalyn was as clean as she'd ever been. Cleaner probably, having scrubbed herself with grit.

"And that . . . dress." Eleanor hesitated between words, unsure how to describe the rags Rosalyn was wearing. Something about the way she spoke . . .

"Do you know the duchess?" Rosalyn asked.

"How did you know?"

"You sound like her."

"You've met?"

Rosalyn nodded. "Once. She was kind to me."

"Really?"

And then she gave me up to be killed.

Now seemed the wrong time to say that because Rosalyn had a feeling Eleanor thought she belonged at Alta Mofacon.

259

"First we must wash you," Eleanor said. "Then find new clothes. After that we can talk properly." Lifting a jug, she poured tepid water into a bowl and picked up a cloth, wetting it and rinsing it out. "Let's start with your face."

42

The wagon jolted up the track towards Alta Mofacon and the two girls giggled, giggles turning to shrieks as the younger slid from her precarious seat and landed on her back in freshly picked hops. The girls were drunk on the smell of the hops, the blueness of the sky and the whiteness of the lamb-like clouds dotting the sky field.

The bailiff had protested, smilingly, that it wasn't really fitting for Lady Giulietta to travel by cart. Then added, a little wide-eyed, that of course my lady could help in the fields if that was what she wanted.

My lady had grinned happily and gone to change into a simple dress of homespun cloth a little better made than everyone else's, and wrap her red hair against the sun in a plain scarf. The silver jewellery was gone. She no longer wore the widow's weeds in which she'd arrived, or the scowls and tempers that began her journey. And if Eleanor had noticed Leopold's ring no longer adorned Giulietta's finger she appeared happy for her, without putting into words what she thought the change meant. Besides, Giulietta knew Eleanor had her own secrets.

Half Eleanor's dresses seemed to have disappeared, her twine and lapis bracelet had gone missing, probably *lost*. In its place oranges, ripe dates, pretty layered pebbles that looked as if they came from a beach. Eleanor smiled more, was happy to leave Giulietta to her own company.

"I've been making friends."

It sounded like one of the local girls to Giulietta.

She'd never had the fierce friendships other girls had because she'd never been allowed. Still, why would she stop her cousin?

Giulietta spent much of her own nights talking to Tycho.

He seemed willing to listen, eager to learn. He asked questions and she answered: about Sigismund's empire, how the trade routes made Venice rich, what might happen to the Byzantine Empire after John V Palaiologos died. Like her, he found Venice easier to like at a distance. In fact, she was sure they could grow to love it provided they didn't have to return there.

Why would they want to? When they had Alta Mofacon.

Her wheat was cut, threshed and stored, her hay was made and straw gathered. Fences were mended, hedges replanted and ditches dug for the coming winter. The stone walls of half her field terracing had been rebuilt. Work had been found for everyone. When the bailiff protested, gently as always, that the estate could not afford such generosity, Lady Giulietta gave him her silver jewellery and told him she wanted apple trees planted and more wheat sown. Her birthday had come and gone in the time they were here. Lady Giulietta had let it pass quietly, not wanting a fuss to be made. Tycho gave her a kiss. Eleanor gave her a pebble. "We're here," Eleanor said.

Giulietta grinned, slid from her seat, which was only a full hopsack in a sea of loose hops, and landed carelessly, laughing as she grabbed the cart's side to save herself.

"My lady . . . !"

"Is fine," she said. Turning a circle, she looked round her court-yard. The manor's walls had been repainted a dark red that would fade to pink and then to ochre, which was the colour they'd been when she arrived.

"What news?"

Her steward looked troubled.

Although she suspected that had more to do with not ruining her sunny mood. Her aunt's spy had already absconded, probably to take news back to the city of how her grief had been cleared by the warm winds, burnt off by the bright summer sun, worn away by hard work. Aunt Alexa would not approve of the work. Lady Giulietta wasn't sure she cared.

"Tell me," she said gently.

"Another dead priest beyond Port Monfalcone. Three now."

"On my lands?"

The steward shook his head, smiled slightly. "No, my lady. Always just beyond your borders."

"Tell me if one of my priests dies. What else?"

"There are wolves . . ."

Giulietta froze.

"There are always wolves," he added hastily. "They come down from the mountains after the flocks. The boys have slings to keep them at bay."

"Then why tell me?"

Some of the happiness had gone from her voice. But she still sounded so reasonable and unexpectedly polite that she knew few people who'd known her in the last few years would have recognised her.

The steward looked embarrassed.

So Giulietta waited.

"You know peasants," he said finally, as if his own family didn't come from such stock. "So superstitious."

"Master Theo . . ."

The man sighed. "A swordsman kills them, my lady. That's what they say. He cuts off their heads with a gleaming blade and tosses the bodies into ravines."

"Has anyone found a beheaded wolf?"

"No, my lady. Exactly, my lady. That's what I tell them. If

263

there was a swordsman beheading wolves we'd find beheaded wolf carcasses."

"Tycho . . . How long has this been going on?"

Pulling up his knees, Tycho wrapped his arms around them and rested his chin on his intertwined fingers. He was sat on the end of Lady Giulietta's great bed, her window open to allow in starlight, the night wind and him.

He was being careful.

He'd spent weeks being careful to do nothing to scare her. So they talked, or she talked and he listened and that was all they did. Or mostly all they did. Sometimes they kissed. Slowly made her happy. Fiercely made her worried. He stayed always just the right side of not upsetting her.

Recently she'd taken to falling asleep in his arms.

Tycho knew she knew it was a waiting game, but he was learning from the things she told him about Venice, and about history and politics. And he fed from Rosalyn when he must, and Rosalyn fed from her priests, because she liked their memories. And occasionally he'd abandon Giulietta to her sleep and go and kill *krieghund* before they could threaten her.

It was as close to perfect as his life had ever got.

The wind through her window smelt of lavender and dung, of hops from a wagon in the yard and wood smoke from a fire still burning in the kitchen range. He knew he would associate that mix of smells for ever with Alta Mofacon.

"For a week or so," he admitted.

"A week or so?"

"All right, longer. The first two appeared the night after we arrived."

"And what do they want?"

"I haven't asked. They come in ones and twos."

"And you kill them in ones and twos?"

264

"I kill the first and the second doesn't usually dare venture further into your lands. They're *krieghund*, obviously enough."

"So was my husband."

Tycho looked hurt, he couldn't help himself.

"Jealous?" Giulietta asked.

"Always."

Her face softened. But she still sighed.

43

"Found him yet?"

Prince Alonzo flushed. And Duchess Alexa watched in amusement as her brother-in-law fought to keep his temper. His vow to capture Tycho within a day was no closer to being fulfilled than when he made it weeks earlier.

They met at Alexa's request in the map room, because she hoped the murals would help remind Alonzo of the dangers they faced. It was a century since the map of Europe had been repainted. She hoped it would be another century before it needed repainting again. She'd given up having the Asia maps redrawn to include Tamburlaine's latest conquests and simply had Marco's cartographer put a translucent green wash over what had been there before.

The Regent was drinking again, which was good in one way and bad in another. Drunk, her brother-in-law was impulsive. Sober, he was scheming and occasionally intuitive.

"More wine?" Alexa suggested.

A servant dashed forward to lift a jug before Prince Alonzo could do more than reach for it. She was young and pretty. Wide-hipped, dark-skinned and wavy-haired. Entirely to her brother-in-law's taste. Alexa saw the girl's face tighten as his fingers found the back of her knee and began climbing.

"You can go," Alexa said.

The girl bobbed her head gratefully. Alexa pretending not to see her shift her hips to dislodge Alonzo's hand.

"What did you do that for?"

"I have news."

"She wouldn't have said anything."

All the servants at Ca' Ducale were well trained and, if training wasn't enough, their families would suffer if they spoke out of turn. The girl would never have risked that.

"She's a spy."

"The Byzantine emperor?" Alonzo was so shocked he put down his glass of wine. After a moment he decided to pick it up again.

"Sigismund," Alexa said. "So I'd be grateful if you could leave her alone." It wasn't true, of course. She was simply a girl from the Veneto whose father, a Levantine merchant, had bought her a place in the palace. Alexa allowed it to happen. Her father was the spy and it paid Alexa to keep his daughter close.

"What's your news?" Alonzo demanded.

"It concerns Sigismund." Alexa was glad about that. The German emperor's involvement would confirm for Alonzo her words about the servant. It was, however, time to stop baiting him and see if he could be brought temporarily to her cause. Which she would present as their cause.

Like most of her husband's race, Alonzo had little understanding of the subtlety needed to keep Venice safe from itself as much as its enemies. Alexa had long since decided Europe's problem was having one god. (And so what if he was split into three, if those parts always agreed with each other?)

How could you learn how to appear to ask for one thing while really asking for another when there was so little need? The Khan's empire had a dozen gods each of which needed to be cajoled and placated, teased into delivering promises and made to feel more important than the others.

"Sigismund's forcing the issue."

"How?"

"Frederick is already on his way."

She watched Alonzo play catch-up through his wine-induced haze. Laying bets with herself on how long it would take for his eyes to widen in shock. She was a second out, in his favour. "Another glass?" she suggested.

He held it out and she poured as if they were old friends, not enemies who'd happily see each other dead if they could find a way that wouldn't leave them dead or disgraced themselves.

"How soon does he arrive?"

"I'm trying to find out. The boy's bringing an army."

Emperor Sigismund was also King of Hungary, Croatia and Germany. Lombardy and Venice were on the list of countries he'd like to add. His ambition was to force the warring popes to accept a single papacy. Thus earning Rome's gratitude, and forgiveness for a multitude of sins.

He'd probably succeed in uniting the papacies. Only his God would know if he succeeded buying off his sins. Either way, Alexa had dedicated the last few years to keeping Venice out of his hands.

It looked as if her plans were failing.

Sigismund had no legitimate children and only two bastards. Leopold, now dead, and Frederick. It was said he adored both and had made them princes not because he wanted to offend his nobles but because he really wished Leopold could be his heir. Frederick was the younger. Sigismund was about fifty now so Frederick had to be eighteen or so. Alexa reminded herself to check. She'd need to discover something else, if Frederick was *krieghund* like his brother.

Neither could have taken the imperial throne. But he had acknowledged them both as his sons, created dukedoms for them and granted them the title and rights of imperial princes. No father could do more.

"What would it take to buy Sigismund off?"

"What do you think . . .?" Alexa caught herself, shrugged apologetically. "Giulietta, of course. And through her, Venice."

Alonzo's mouth tightened behind his beard. This was not a conversation he relished, but perhaps he saw the truth in Alexa's face, or maybe for once the wine dulled his obstinacy instead of stoking his anger.

Either way, he suggested she continue.

"Marco will not produce an heir."

There, she'd said it. Alexa could see from Alonzo's shock that this was something he'd never expected her to admit. She might pride herself on facing facts, but that fact was harder to face than most. She wondered if he could be that brave.

"And no child of mine will be legitimate?"

"To the best of my knowledge none of your mistresses has even fallen pregnant?" At her question, a grimace twisted Alonzo's lips so fast a lesser woman might have missed it. The duchess felt her guts lurch. "Unless I'm wrong about that? Your new one . . . The Dolphini girl?"

"Not her."

"Alonzo."

"None of them."

Alexa was surprised by the vehemence in his voice.

She didn't doubt they were still enemies. In the face of Sigismund's ambition, however, if seemed even such enemies might become allies of covenience, albeit briefly in her experience. She risked a truth.

"I've thought of marrying Marco off, having some noble bed his wife. Or even announcing a pregnancy and substituting a child."

"What stopped you?"

"The brat must be a Millioni."

"Marco shows no signs . . . ?"

"I've even put a boy in his bed," Alexa said tightly. "To see if that was the problem. That small boy Atilo brought me. Theodore's bastard. They played with toy boats in Marco's washbowl. "We have to face it. If Marco dies Giulietta will be duchess."

"And her son become duke?"

Something in Alonzo's voice made Alexa look up.

What was she missing? The duchess had her veil, and Alonzo was three-quarters drunk, which made it hard for him to hide his feelings. As if he'd ever really been able to hide those from her. For once she found it impossible to know what he was thinking. Both waited for the other to speak.

"Her son is Leopold's heir," Alexa said finally.

"Which brings his lands."

"And his lands border Giulietta's own."

"So we extend our power?"

"Possibly. But do we then give Venice to Sigismund? That's the question. She can rule as a widow but Leo is Sigismund's grandson, giving the Holy Roman Empire a claim to Venice in the future. John V Palaiologos is going to hate that."

"Suppose we marry her to a Byzantine prince instead?"

"Then we're back where we started. Only this time the Byzantine emperor has influence. Scylla and Charybdis, Alonzo. A rock and a hard place."

"So we welcome Frederick?"

"Unless you have a better idea?"

"Not me," Alonzo said. "You're the thinker around here."

44

"Are you awake?"

A candle burnt on her bedside table. A candle Lady Giulietta had blown out some hours earlier. Tycho sat at the end of her bed, watching intently.

He smiled when Giulietta reached for her sheet and she blushed. Her scowl said it was still late summer, how could she be expected to sleep in more than the shift she presently wore?

Tycho liked that shift best. It was the white one with embroidery down the front and ribbons at the neck. He particularly liked how thin the silk was.

"No wolves tonight?"

"Not for three nights now."

"What do you think it means?"

"They've given up." Tycho hoped that was the truth.

Outside the night was dark, halfway between midnight and dawn. Rosalyn would be out there somewhere. She'd tell him if anything changed. The stars that lit Alta Mofacon's lands were slight, the moon a day past half full and hidden by mountains. Although Tycho knew where it was. He always knew.

"How long have you been here?"

"A few minutes."

It wasn't much longer than that. Just long enough to fix every line of her sleep-softened face in his mind. Alta Mofacon had been kind to her. She looked more grown up than when they first met, less strained, however.

Sun had flamed her red hair and bronzed her skin enough to produce the freckles she hated and he loved. Scratches from hop picking showed on the backs of her hands and she had dirt beneath her nails scrubbing hadn't removed. He wondered what Duchess Alexa would say if she could see her now.

"What are you thinking?" Giulietta asked.

"Your hands are scratched."

She examined them proudly. "Tomorrow sees the last of it. Then the maltster starts his work. I have a meeting with the brewer at the end of the week . . ." She stopped, seeing his smile. "What?"

"Nothing."

He came further up the bed, took her face in his hands and kissed her gently, feeling his stomach somersault. After the third kiss, soft and small and entirely gentle, he felt her lips soften and her mouth open. His fingers reached for the ribbon at the front of her gown and though she tensed slightly she didn't push his hand away. So he kissed her again and pulled at the first bow.

"No more . . ." Sitting up, Giulietta adjusted the neck of her nightgown and tied the three ribbons she'd let Tycho undo. She touched her hand to her lips. They were bruised enough to make her wince. She was grinning ruefully.

"You're dangerous."

Her words surprised him. "No, I'm not. Well, not to you."

"Yes, you are," she insisted. "I should know if anyone does. I've lived around dangerous people my entire life, you're different dangerous."

Tycho said nothing.

Wait and people will fill the silence. What they say might be what you need to know. What you need to know might save your life. Retaining your life will let you fulfil your mission.

Atilo's lessons remained with Tycho for all the old man was dead. Tycho had other reasons for waiting, however.

She'd kissed him as fiercely as he'd ever wanted to kiss her, and had hooked one quivering leg behind his and pushed against him to lose herself somewhere he couldn't reach as she buried her face in his neck and swallowed rolling gasps he definitely wasn't meant to hear.

Something had changed between them.

His admission that he would have saved Leopold if he'd only known how . . . His coming to her for help when he had no one else to turn to . . . What had just passed between them. Tycho knew something had changed.

"My aunt poisons her enemies. My uncle . . ." Giulietta shrugged. "Killing people is the least of his sins. The Council hang, behead and torture daily. These are the people who brought me up, who have owned me. Yet I don't fear any of them the way I sometimes fear you. You look as if you want to hurt me and then kiss me instead. What happens when it's the other way round?"

"I'll never hurt you."

"You already did." Her words were sharp.

"That was then."

"And this is now? That's meant to make it better? And already I've decided that somehow it does, that I should forgive you. See? What you are is hard to hide and, I should guess, difficult to fake."

"And what am I?"

"As I said. Different dangerous."

She slapped at his hand as he reached for her slip again, then let him undo the first ribbon when he insisted that was all he wanted to do. Sliding one finger under a chain, he lifted it until

273

the gold ring he'd found earlier between her breasts lay in his hand. It was warm from her body.

His silence was his question.

"Marco's ring."

"He wears it."

"He wears the replacement."

"That's the original?"

Lady Giulietta sighed. "We're talking about Venice. The ring he wears is now the original, this is simply an ancient copy. I took it with me the night I was abducted. It was meant to make my aunt and uncle come after me. I thought . . ."

"If they wouldn't save you they'd save the ring?"

"Instead they ordered a replica."

"And had the jeweller killed to keep their secret?"

"I imagine so."

The heart-shaped sadness of the girl in the bed was enough to lock him in place and Tycho knew he loved her. Every man boasted he'd die for love. *I can offer more. I can live for it.* With her help he could keep the other him at bay.

"Tell me of your childhood."

Tycho shook his head. "Tell me about yours."

"I was very young when my mother died . . . When she was killed . . . When my father had her killed." Giulietta forced her words to hold the full truth. "Although no one could prove that, no one doubted it either."

"What happened to him?"

"Atilo had him killed."

"And no one could prove that either?"

She smiled sadly. "Atilo brought me to Venice wrapped in a blanket and carried in his arms. Small, afraid and mostly snivelling. We travelled at night, through mountains. He made it seem an adventure. I realise now we were being hunted. He carved me a wooden bear . . ."

Tycho listened carefully, noticing the gaps and hesitations, the

274

quickening of her voice that carried her over those bits best left unspoken. No boy at court had ever caught her eye. Lady Eleanor was the closest she'd ever had to a friend until . . . *She met Leopold.* Tycho filled that gap himself

He didn't say, *I can be your friend,* because he didn't know if that was true. At least not in the sense Leopold and Eleanor were her friends. He would always want more. "There's no chance Leopold's the father?"

"I told you on the *San Marco.* I never . . . We never even came close. Didn't you believe me when I told you?"

He shrugged, embarrassed.

"I don't lie to you," Giulietta said.

Outside a fingernail of moon crawled the rim of the upturned bowl of the sky, and the stars paled and grew afraid along the horizon where day threatened to chase them away. Only once after that did Lady Giulietta falter, her words running like water into sand. She'd been talking about the abduction. Finding herself unable to talk at all about the hours immediately before.

"That's when . . . ?"

She nodded, unable to say more.

Tycho's first guess had been wrong. Leo's conception had nothing to do with the abduction itself or the days following it. She was pregnant before being taken from the basilica.

Some days Rosalyn really hated the Millioni princess and her brat.

Eleanor's arrival in Venice had been unhappy, the years following it miserable. She served Lady Giulietta as lady-in-waiting as best she could and Giulietta barely noticed. Oh, Eleanor loved her cousin, worshipped the older girl. It was just that sometimes Eleanor didn't like her very much. Eleanor never said that. She didn't need to. Rosalyn could read the silences between her words.

"It's almost daylight," Rosalyn said. "I should go . . ."

"Stay a little longer."

"I can't."

"Yes, you can. Tell me about home."

Lady Eleanor liked Rosalyn's stories about her family. The father who cut wood on the lower slopes of the mountains. The mother who cooked badly but endlessly. Her brother who wanted to learn to be a carpenter. The little wooden house they lived in outside Alta Mofacon. Rosalyn worried what would happen if her new friend discovered they weren't true. She kept telling them all the same.

Rosalyn liked them, too.

"Tomorrow night."

"No, now."

"Hush," Rosalyn said.

"*Why?*"

"Because someone's coming."

The girl lying on the bed next to her froze. "They'd have to be coming from Lady Giulietta's room."

Rosalyn nodded.

A grin lit Eleanor's lips, and she began rolling off the bed until Rosalyn grabbed her. "We'll be caught," she said.

Eleanor stopped struggling. "I can't hear anything."

"You wouldn't." Rosalyn smiled to soften her words. "And I know whose footsteps they are. I recognise them."

"You can recognise footsteps?"

"Those ones."

Having rolled off the bed, she darted back to give Eleanor a goodbye-for-now hug, grinned at Eleanor's answering grin, and followed Tycho down a flight of stairs through a pre-dawn others would have considered darkness.

Her steps matched his exactly and Rosalyn was proud of that. Everything he'd been taught by Lord Atilo he was teaching her. She was surprised, all the same, he didn't notice. Although not as surprised as the fact he used the stairs at all. Something must have changed that he would come from Giulietta's bedroom so openly.

And something had changed for her. As Rosalyn made her way down a twist of stairs towards the cellars she realised she felt almost shockingly happy. She should have known it couldn't last.

45

Tycho woke at dusk from dreamlessness into the dusty darkness of a brick vault that fed from an empty wine cellar into a stocked wine cellar, a vast meat locker and two rooms containing brick-lined pits used for grain. In the middle of the empty wine cellar was a low well, capped with an old millstone.

The footprint of the cellars under the manor of Alta Mofacon matched the floor plan above. With the manor's heavy walls, arrow slit external windows and huge underground storage capacity it would be possible to withstand a siege.

None of this mattered to Tycho.

He knew instantly that Mofacon was empty. It *sounded* empty. Scrabbling upright, he cursed the bladder that left him hard and pissed awkwardly, not worried that Rosalyn was waking. "Quiet," he hissed.

Behind him Rosalyn froze.

He could hear no sounds beyond the door.

Somewhere overhead footsteps crossed oak boards. A single pair of stolid feet. *Not empty then, just emptier . . .* The front door opened and he heard low conversation, too far away to pick out words but the person talking sounded upset rather than panicked. That was something.

Turning, he found Rosalyn behind him.

She'd moved quietly and grinned as he smiled his approval. Their relationship was changing. She'd hated him for getting her killed. Now she seemed grateful he'd been the instrument to bring her back.

"We're locked in?"

Tycho tried the door to confirm it. The lock was turned and the key missing from its slot. Enough of a gap showed between door and frame to reveal that both outside bolts had been slammed into place. The lock plate was thick, the door strong and the hinges almost new. They needed another way out.

"There's an air shaft."

"Go," Tycho said. "Find me the key."

She became smoke; a twist of dark velvets flowing through the gloom to sweep upwards, leaving a falling trickle of dust behind her. Alone in the cellar Tycho considered what could have happened and found no answers.

Had he scared Giulietta away? She would have told him if she was planning to leave, surely? Either way she'd have left the cellar unlocked, since she alone in her household knew that was where two people slept. Every second of every minute of the previous evening replayed in his brain.

He swallowed the images, froze the memories.

Turned them around inside his head and looked at them from different angles. Seeing himself as someone else, someone treading so carefully not to make happen what had seemed to have happened. Giulietta fleeing.

Unless it was worse. Unless the *krieghund* . . .

His throat tightened at the thought and he inhaled deeply, tasting dust and damp and stale air. The scent he was afraid of finding was missing. No rank if distant smell of death to say her servants had been slaughtered.

A scrape beyond the cellar door told him Rosalyn had found the key. A click of the lock was followed by the crash of two bolts being shot back. "No one saw me," she said before he could ask.

The huge hall was deserted.

A broken cart stood in the darkened courtyard. Blood had dried on the front door's lintel. Dropping to a crouch, Tycho winced at its staleness. Not Giulietta's, which was all that worried him.

"Bring me someone."

Rosalyn nodded.

"Quietly."

She came back with a small child.

Snot-nosed and willing to stop sobbing once it realised nothing bad would happen. Marco worked in the kitchens. His mother was a scullery maid, his father long dead. Everyone except his mother and the cook, the steward and a groom had returned home, not being needed.

"Where's Lady Giulietta?"

Marco said her family had taken her.

Unpacked, that meant soldiers had arrived with orders for her immediate return to Venice. The great lord who brought the order sounded like Roderigo. When Giulietta refused he said he had orders to bring her anyway. That was when Giulietta's sergeant stepped forward. His was the blood on the sill.

"Who gave orders to lock the cellar doors?"

"The steward, after my lady left."

Lord Roderigo had arrived at dawn with a small crowd of cavalry behind him. He brought a letter from the Council and spare horses for Ladies Giulietta and Eleanor. The others in Giulietta's retinue would have to make their own way back. The galley in the harbour couldn't be expected to wait for them.

"Who's in the house now?"

The steward was out, apparently. The groom had gone to the

tavern. The cook was getting drunk in the kitchens. And his mother . . . The boy stopped to glare at Tycho.

"No one's going to hurt her."

She was tending the sergeant who'd been hurt trying to protect my lady. She'd asked the groom to help carry the injured man to her quarters. It sounded to Tycho as if she and the sergeant might have met before.

The door to Lady Giulietta's bedroom was unlocked. Her three-mattress bed was still there. Although the feather upper mattress lay rolled for safekeeping. Nothing was rolled in its middle. So Tycho tried a chest and found old blankets and a mildewed bear pelt. Her money chests were gone, obviously returned with her. The *WolfeSelle* he already carried on his back.

So why did he think she . . . ?

Tycho found what called him in an alcove behind a tapestry. The original of the ring Marco used to wed the sea. Threaded through it and tied in a bow was a neck ribbon from Giulietta's nightgown. The boy went wide-eyed when Tycho slid the ring on to his finger and tied the ribbon round his wrist.

"We weren't here. Understand me?"

"It's a secret?"

"Lady Giulietta's secret."

Her name was enough to make the boy nod fiercely.

"Now go and do whatever you're meant to be doing and promise me not to tell anyone about this . . ."

"Atilo would have killed him," Rosalyn said.

"I'm not Atilo."

From the twist of Rosalyn's lips when she looked back to where the boy stood at the top of the unlit corridor he knew she saw her own brother in the small boy. A happier, safer, less damaged version. The boy Pietro could have been.

"He probably lives in a wooden house outside Alta Mofacon," Rosalyn said. "He's going to grow up to be a carpenter."

Tycho looked at her.

Adjusting the *WolfeSelle* on his shoulder, he checked the leather straps that held the soul of the Wolf Brothers in place and made sure the courtyard was empty. Then he slid into the darkness and heard a rustle as Rosalyn joined him.

A streak of blood still lit the far horizon.

It would fade within minutes, paling through blues to the black of a cloud-filled sky. He missed the sun. How perverse was that? He missed the thing that could kill him and hoarded memories of kinder days.

"Are you all right?" Rosalyn asked.

"Remembering."

She had the sense not to ask *what?*

"Can you run in that?" Her long, dark gown looked shadow-black in the darkness under the arch of the deserted gatehouse.

"Run?"

"A ship will be too slow and booking passage too complicated. We take the shore." Besides, they both hated water.

"Tycho . . ."

He knew she was serious. Rosalyn hardly ever used his name.

"You're an outlaw. If you're captured they'll kill you."

"If I don't kill them first."

"It's not a joke."

"I'm not joking."

She looked at him and her face was thoughtful.

She seemed older so Tycho took another look. No, just cleaner, better dressed, her hair somehow different.

"Could you?" she asked "Kill a city?"

For Giulietta? He could certainly try.

Biting into his wrist, Tycho offered it to the girl and watched sudden hunger banish the softness he'd just noticed. She drank fast, his fingers tightening in her hair in warning she'd taken enough.

"Now me," he said.

Grabbing her wrist Tycho fed in turn, tasting his blood in hers. The night brightened around him, the courtyard fell into sharp focus around him. High overhead the stars flared and glittered.

"What now?"

"We run . . ."

Forested slopes fell away to ploughed fields as they passed the tree line. Below this lay towns, orchards, hop fields and finally shore. They ran south-west through a fishing village and past drying racks, with the sea to their right and a plain on their left. Scrub broke the fields, rice paddies had been dug here and there. Then marsh grass whipped them, and splashed under their feet as fertile farmland gave way to a salt wilderness of runt bushes and crippled trees.

The run was placeless and timeless. For the first time he could remember Tycho belonged to this space and state of being on the edge of everything, being between this everything and everything else.

Then an expanse of inland water glittered in front of him and lights showed through the shutters of a fisherman's hut on stilts. The air smelt of smoke, brine and salted mackerel and mullet.

"That was fast."

"Laguna di Grado," said Tycho, remembering the map he'd seen in his first weeks in Venice. "Not halfway yet."

Rosalyn grinned.

They faltered only once when a path beyond twisted back on itself to deliver them to where they'd already been. A woman sat in the shadow of a fish-drying rack, one breast protruding from a white pearl-buttoned gown. At her nipple was a crow wrapped in seaweed. Its beady eyes regarded Tycho coldly.

"Who are you?" Rosalyn demanded.

"I should ask that of you."

Switching her attention to Tycho, she added. "Be careful the weights you choose to carry. You will not be allowed to put them down."

He stared at her.

"You wear my ring. You run my shore. You will fight a man who claims to be my mage . . . My sister talks of you."

"Your sister?"

"A'rial. She says you are Marco's . . ."

The last words Tycho heard were *grievous angel*, said in a tone so sly it was hard to know if it held amusement or contempt.

This time the same path led onwards.

So they jumped marsh pools and tidal rivulets, landing on swaying tussocks, before leaping for firmer ground beyond. Filled with the power that feeding on each other gave them. When marsh turned to track they increased their speed.

Eighty miles separated Alta Mofacon from Venice and he and Rosalyn covered half of that with barely a stop. A wild fowlers' camp approached and disappeared behind, an arrow failing to catch them as they raced away. Water appeared on both sides as they reached the spit circling Venice's lagoon.

If he couldn't escape his fate he'd run towards it instead.

"Lights," Rosalyn said.

And people. A small group around a battered boat drawn up on a mud bank. They swirled as Tycho approached, daggers in their hands. Their courage vanishing as he yanked the *WolfeSelle* from his shoulder.

"My lord," said a man who held a light. "We're simple fishermen."

"And those bolts of silk in your boat are fish?"

The man's face slackened. Behind him Tycho heard one of his company swear and another begin to take slow steps as he tried to blind-side the newcomers.

"I wouldn't," Rosalyn said.

From the way the companion went still she had her dagger

to his back and was prodding firmly enough to guarantee his attention.

"What's the news from Venice?"

"News, my lord?"

Tycho growled in irritation. "What is happening in the city?"

"A feast," the man said. "At the palace."

"Huge," one of the other men agreed.

Tycho wanted to say there was always a feast. Half the time it seemed all the nobles in Venice did was eat, drink and bed each other's wives.

"That's where we're going," Rosalyn said.

Tycho glanced at her.

She smiled. "My master needs to reach Venice as swiftly as possible. You can take him and he'll pay. Or we can kill you now."

They chose their lives and saved Tycho the trouble of trying to sail a boat himself, the very thought of which made him sick. He had them scatter earth in the boat's bottom, rip a single length of cloth from the silk, fill that with dirt and put the makeshift cushion on the boat's cross-slat.

It was better than nothing.

Three of the gang were to remain behind to lighten the boat, their chief unloading the rest of his silk with hissed warnings about what would happen if it got muddy or he returned to find his men not there.

Tycho was a lord, a rich one.

He was holding a sword. A purse of gold had been promised. The smuggler chief decided it would be polite to help Rosalyn into the craft, stepping back when she bared her teeth. "Push us off," Tycho demanded.

Strong arms forced the boat into a willing current.

Tycho only discovering how low it rode in the water when its lateen sail caught the wind and the craft began to skim towards the distant light, its gunwales bare inches above the waves. The two and a bit miles to San Pietro felt like an eternity, each watery second dragged out to the point of pain. From the sick look on Rosalyn's face she was having as bad a time of it.

"Almost there," Tycho said.

"Indeed, my lord. We're approaching San Pietro."

"Drop us at the nearest jetty."

"My lord. The monks . . ."

"Will not mind." The island of San Pietro belonged to the patriarch, who guarded his rights jealously. Tonight he'd be a fool to enforce them. "Put in over there."

"Where, my lord?"

"There's a jetty ahead."

Tycho rolled himself out of the boat before the man even tied up. Crawling to the shore, he crouched on all fours in the dirt, feeling his dizziness fade and focus return. Had anything been left in his guts he'd have vomited it.

"My lord . . ."

"Wait." Tycho dragged Rosalyn from the boat and carried her to dry land, leaving her sack-like in the dirt. "I travel badly. So does my servant."

The man had enough sense to stay silent.

Digging in his pocket for a purse, Tycho considered counting out coins and tossed the smuggler the purse instead. The man had kept his word. Tycho would keep his. "You didn't see me."

"No, my lord. Indeed not."

The gang leader pushed out from the jetty, and then hung in the current. Squinting at the coins in the darkness to see if they were real.

"They're real," Tycho said.

The man began rowing.

The stone bridge from San Pietro to Arzanale's eastern edge lacked rails at the sides, as did most bridges in the city. Unlike most, this one was wide enough and strong enough for an ox cart to cross from the Riva degli Schiavoni into the patriarch's territory.

Tycho and Rosalyn went in the other direction, keeping to the middle and grateful for the heavy stone under their feet.

"Got your strength back?"

Tycho pointed to the roofline of a warehouse edging Arzanale and Rosalyn nodded. Seconds later an outer boatyard lay below them. Beyond it was an inner yard, with a dense cluster of streets and canals beyond that. And then the domes of San Marco's basilica, the roofs of the palace and a sliver of the campanile.

As a distant bell began to number the hour, Rosalyn counted the second bell as the first to muddle the devil, added one to her total and told Tycho what he already knew. It was three hours until midnight.

"*Look*," she added.

And Tycho's guts lurched.

A barge in the lagoon flew Prince Leopold's flag.

As Tycho examined the flapping yards of cloth he began to see differences; the same black eagle squatted in the flag's centre; the same jagged border indicated bastardy; but over the eagle's head hung a simpler coronet, and its claws clutched an orb rather than a sceptre.

He forced his eyes to focus beyond the city on the low line of mainland in the far distance. Campfires where there should be darkness. Smudges of white that could be pavilions. Leopold's brother had brought an army.

"Oh, shit."

Tycho knew why Giulietta had been called back.

A Millioni princess by birth, she belonged to Sigismund's family by marriage. Leopold had named Leo as his heir. Who, other than Tycho, Alonzo and Alexa, knew Leo was not Sigismund's grandchild? To free herself she would have to say whose child he was. And she could not or would not. He found it hard to know which was worse.

Dust and ashes, dead and done with . . .

"What?" Rosalyn asked.

His glare made her flinch. Outstripping the wind to leave marsh grass swaying behind him seemed mere childishness now. Giulietta *would* marry again. She could not do otherwise, for all her brave words.

Not bothering to check Rosalyn was following, Tycho ran the shipyard wall and leapt a wide canal, landing on the roof of an outbuilding. Scrambling up a church porch – there was always a damn church – he cut along a low warehouse, negotiated wood stacks in a rotting brick and tar paper timber yard, jumped another canal, ran more houses . . .

"Should I let you go on alone?"

"I say if you stay or not."

Rosalyn bobbed her street girl's curtsy. "Yes, master."

"I'm not your master."

"No, master."

"Come here," Tycho ordered.

She approached slowly, placing her feet carefully on the tiles. She would survive a drop to the small square below easily. It was Tycho's anger she feared and not the fall. Gripping her face, Tycho stared into her eyes as he looked for the street child who'd been the first person to see him in this city. She had saved his life and he had turned back death for her, by accident admittedly.

There the debts should end.

"That night," he said. "When you found me floating by the stone steps . . ."

"Stone steps?"

"You found me in the Grand Canal and pulled me to the steps, cut silver manacles from my wrist . . ." Her nod simply meant she was listening. The watchfulness in her face remained. "You remember?"

Rosalyn tried to shake her head but he gripped her face too tightly.

"I know nothing about that at all."

Tycho let her go.

46

"My lady . . ."

Having knocked again at the door, Lady Eleanor turned to look beseechingly at Duchess Alexa, who stood rigid with such fury there was a clear space in the crowded passageway around her.

"What do you mean she won't come out?" Alonzo's question only just preceded him, so fast did he push his way through the people.

"She's locked herself in."

Alonzo turned the handle, pushed and then pushed again. Having demanded loudly that his niece leave her room immediately, he took it on himself to hammer on the door in front of half a dozen courtiers when she didn't obey.

"Come out."

"No," Giulietta said.

Alonzo's next demand contained so many swear words he could have been a Schiavoni sailor.

"W-w-what's happening?"

Duke Marco had edged his way through nervous courtiers so quietly his mother only realised he was there when he stood beside her. He was carrying a kitten that seemed to be wearing a bonnet.

"Giulietta doesn't want to come out."

"B-b-but it's her party." Pushing past Eleanor, he put his ear to the door. "She's crying," he said. "I think you should a-all g-go. Everyone should g-go. Except m-me. I'll talk to her."

The balcony of the basilica had been Tycho's first choice to set up camp.

Only that proved too exposed to the view of the crowd in Piazza San Marco, so he abandoned the balcony and climbed to the south-west of the basilica roof, which let him look out at the square, or south across the *piazzetta* to the lagoon where Frederick's imperial barge was anchored.

He was trying not to look in that direction, but found that was the only direction in which he wanted to look. Sailors were moving on deck, others preparing to lower a smaller but no less ornate boat over the side.

Stay here or enter the palace?

Arsenalotti filled Piazza San Marco, drunk on free wine and cutting slivers from half-roasted oxen that would give them bubble shits for a week. Between the fire pits and the colonnades of Ca' Ducale stood the Watch, glaring at any of the ragged crowd who dared push too close.

The Dogana guard occupied the Molo, the little terrace between Ca' Ducale and the choppy waters of the Bacino di San Marco. They were better armed than the Watch, and more experienced than the palace guard who mustered at the water's edge below the lion and the dragon.

Sigismund's son would be greeted in style.

The rich and the noble had obviously been arriving for hours, most probably in reverse order of importance. The gilded palanquin now entering the square faltered as those carrying it found themselves facing the Arsenalotti. A drunken shipwright left his friends to yank back velvet curtains.

His nod let the chair begin its slow journey through the crowd, during which other self-appointed protectors of the city inspected the latest guests for themselves. Only a fool would upset the Arsenalotti by protesting.

On the Molo, the Dogana guard came to attention with Lord Roderigo commanding. Even if the clouds hadn't cleared to reveal a moon half full, the lamps on the boat leaving Prince Frederick's barge would have let them see it coming.

More nobles entered the piazza.

Each palanquin more ornate than the one before.

The servants carrying the litters wore doublets grander than most *cittadini*. The livery of great houses being excused the sumptuary laws that ruled the lives of servants and *cittadini* and even lesser nobles.

"*Tycho* . . ."

Yes, he'd caught it.

A rat-like scratch from a dome above.

Rats he might ignore because they got everywhere, but the dull scratch of steel against lead? That he would never miss.

When Rosalyn stood, Tycho grabbed her wrist and held it until she understood he needed her to become stone and blend into the darkness of the parapet they hid behind. She understood immediately, wrapping the shadows around her until even Tycho found it hard to see she was there.

Atilo would have been proud of her.

From a little way above came the noise of armed men trying to stand silently. One of them swore softly at the knots in his muscles and the aches in his bones and was hissed into silence. Four sets of footsteps departed.

"Follow me," Tycho said.

Their hide had been beneath a black sheet between a dome and a slope of lead-lined roof. That it had taken Tycho five minutes to realise they were there worried him because it meant they were good and he'd almost blown it by sulking; but their skills didn't worry him as much as the circle of salt around their encampment.

"Magic?" Rosalyn asked.

"Protects them from scrying."

Leopold used it to keep Giulietta safe.

Below them the gilded boat drew parallel with the Molo and Lord Roderigo bowed to a young man with a slight beard and a smile. Dark, curling hair fell to his shoulders, and Leopold's brother stared at Roderigo with dark, if slightly nervous eyes as he stepped ashore. He looked like Leopold without the brashness.

Roderigo's men closed ranks, the palace guard fell into place beside the Dogana guard and the whole group swept across the salt-sprayed brick of the Molo into the nearest palace gateway.

Heavy doors shut and Prince Frederick was safe inside.

It would have been too risky for the men to try to kill the prince from that distance. They had simply wanted to see their target, discover if he'd brought his own guards and confirm for themselves he'd arrived. That they intended to kill Giulietta's suitor seemed obvious. Tycho's question was, should he let them?

A grappling hook over the parapet above the back of Ca' Ducale dropped a rope to a balcony below. Tycho followed it over the edge, landing silently. A dark-haired girl lay with her neck broken just inside the window.

"Bastards," Rosalyn said.

The passage Tycho found was narrow and its plaster crumbling. Rotted tapestries and peeling frescos indicated that only servants used it. There had to be any number of these to let household staff move through the palace unseen. When laughter came from ahead, Tycho grabbed Rosalyn and spun them both into a storeroom, leaving the door slightly ajar.

Three grinning servitors passed carrying a wine jug, a plate of pears and a pie, spoils from the kitchens. A fourth trailed behind, holding nothing and looking uncertain. An uncertainty that turned to fear.

"Where's Prince Frederick now?"

Not knowing how he suddenly found himself in Tycho's store-room and terrified by the dagger at his throat, the man had trouble speaking. When he did it was to show more courage than Tycho expected.

"I won't tell you."

"Then you will die," Rosalyn said.

Tycho sighed. "We're *assassini*," he said, slipping into the lie. "Here at the duke's orders. What's your name?"

"Tonio."

"Well, Tonio. I need your doublet, your cap and your help. What is the quickest way from here to the banqueting hall?"

"Down those stairs. Through the kitchens."

"Did you see strangers earlier?"

Tonio shook his head.

"Keep an eye out for them. Find me and tell me if you do."

"There were three palace guards with longbows," Tonio admitted. "And their sergeant. They were going downstairs as I came up." It had obviously only just occurred to him to wonder why.

Tycho sighed.

Between them, Rosalyn's scowl and Tycho's borrowed livery carried them past a dozen chefs, cooks, potboys and kitchen maids, between open griddles, past glowing ovens and grimy half-barrels used for rinsing pans. All looked as it should, except for Dr Crow, stood by a peacock pie. He was watching an apprentice paint yolk on its pastry tail.

"You go ahead," Tycho told Rosalyn.

She kept walking and, despite her dusty velvet gown, the certainty in her face and the steeliness in her eyes made kitchen boys look away without her having to glare at them.

Tycho watched her go and turned back in time to see the apprentice scurry away. A second later Dr Crow pulled a box from his doublet and extracted two glittering beads that he almost dropped when Tycho's dagger nudged his spine.

"No fuss now," Tycho said.

"This is unwise." Hightown Crow's voice trembled. "Alonzo's orders are that you're to be killed on sight. And I had no choice, you know. The Regent can be very . . ." His words drained away.

"Alonzo ordered this?"

Relief flooded Dr Crow's face. The alchemist nodding as he hurriedly agreed Alonzo made him do this . . .

What did I miss?

Dr Crow's ability to manipulate relied on his ability to control himself as well as others. A dangerous truth had nearly been spoken and Tycho could read its ripples in the air the way an eel reads the wake of fish recently gone. It was Dr Crow withdrawing whatever thought first occurred to him.

"That sword . . ."

"Is not at issue. That is."

Dr Crow looked at the gilded eye he'd removed from the pastry peacock, and then at two replacements in his hand.

"What are those?"

A jab of Tycho's dagger told him to answer. When he didn't, Tycho asked a little harder and the alchemist's face whitened. He understood what would happen if he shouted or tried to move.

"Well?"

"Lady Giulietta is upset. So upset she's locked herself in her room. Prince Alonzo thought . . ."

What are they?

"Love pills. The gold is for him and the silver for her. They're truffles," Hightown Crow added, as if this excused it. "Soaked in brandy and wrapped in gold or silver leaf. Real gold and silver leaf."

"They fall in love if they eat those?"

"My life depends on it." The rawness to Dr Crow's voice made Tycho look again. The fat little alchemist was scared. As Hightown Crow opened his mouth to protest Tycho took both pills and dropped them into his pocket.

*   *   *

Candles lit each table and torches flared in their wall sconces.

A thousand people sat in the banqueting hall at places laid for that night's feast. Almost half that number of servants hovered. Fifty guards stood by doors and flanked windows, lined the walls and crouched atop scaffolding left by the builders who'd vacated the nearly finished hall to let this event to take place.

The carnival usually found in San Marco had been brought inside.

Wise-cracking dwarves lewdly caressed their codpieces. Fire-eaters blew great plumes of flame above the guests' heads. Tumblers rolled themselves under tables and acrobats somersaulted over them. Contortionists clambered on to the tables themselves, tying their limbs in such knots they bent backwards to stare from between their own thighs.

A dozen half-naked children balanced on plinths set against the panelled walls. They were gilded or silvered, wearing feather necklaces or strings of seashells. A few were swaying with tiredness.

Tycho imagined they'd been there for hours.

Many of the guests looked bored, a few of the more choleric ones looked openly exasperated by the banquet's late start.

As the bell in the duchess's clock began to chime the hour Tycho read the room, found where Rosalyn crouched atop scaffolding and joined her there before the last ring echoed into silence.

"Ten by the clock." She said it without looking round.

Her choice was good. The scaffolding covered half an end wall, almost directly above the kitchen door and in near darkness because the kitchen end of the great room was unused except by servants. Even better, silk drapes meant to conceal the scaffolding helped keep them both hidden.

A carpenter's chisel lay next to her. From this height, dropping it would kill the boy below who carried wine to the *cittadini*'s tables. More smartly dressed servants attended the grander tables. The real feasting had yet to begin.

"Where are they?"

Rosalyn bit her lip and looked worried.

Tycho read the room for friends and enemies; except he had no friends in that room, so he read it for Frederick's enemies first, and those most likely to kill him as an outlaw second. Fifty guards, four of which were probably imposters . . .

Two either side of the great doors staring straight ahead. Tycho dismissed them as there to look impressive. The ten Dogana guard along the far wall were out of sight of the high table but able to see the whole room. Four guards occupied a high window-sill on the *piazzetta* side. That would be a good place if you wanted to kill someone at the top table. But they were guards, not a sergeant among them.

Three more occupied a *piazzetta* window closer to Tycho's end of the room. Others stood in pairs along the opposite walls. The Millioni were taking no chances.

But the four he wanted?

Having dismissed the oak beams that would support the final ceiling, Tycho tried to listen for a noise that shouldn't be there, see a shape pretending to be something different. His problem was that noise, emotion and expectation blasted off the assembled guests as they readied themselves for the largest feast Venice had thrown since the last one.

A blare of trumpets met the slam of halberds.

The great doors crashed open and Alonzo and Frederick entered with Duchess Alexa walking a step behind. As the guests stood, Alonzo showed the German princeling to his seat, a hand resting on his elbow. The boy looked nervous and Alexa troubled. Well, she walked stiffly and sat reluctantly. What she really thought was hidden by her veil.

Everyone at the tables looked towards the door and waited and then waited some more. Eventually the great doors shut and Alonzo glared at Alexa. He would have said something if not for Frederick. Lady Giulietta was obviously proving harder to extract than they'd imagined.

In the sudden stillness of disappointment, Tycho found what he was looking for, a single note of purpose. It came from the three guards cross-legged in a *piazzetta* window. At first glance they seemed to be watching the guests. But a shadow line behind one showed where his longbow was hidden. Unless they'd brought uniforms with them, three women in this city were already widows without knowing it.

"We need to identify their sergeant."

Tycho could almost feel Rosalyn begin scouring the room.

The sound of guards coming to attention beyond the main door distracted her. As halberds banged, one of the three guards put down his crossbow and shifted deeper into the shadows. He picked up a yard-long arrow and untied a leather cap at its point.

Poisoned, unquestionably.

Reaching behind him for the longbow he nodded to his companions, who scanned the room for anyone watching. They shook their heads.

And as the noise in the corridor became louder, the man slotted the arrow around the twisted sinew of his bow.

47

In the corridor outside the banqueting hall Lady Giulietta stopped, turned to her smiling cousin and said, "The sad thing is . . . It's not like you really understand a word I'm saying anyway, do you?"

Nodding enthusiastically, Duke Marco turned back to a Roman lion stolen during the sacking of Constantinople two hundred years before. The majority of the most interesting treasures in Ca' Ducale had been. He stroked its face tenderly, and kissed it lightly on the forehead.

"I don't know why I'm even talking to you."

"Because you have n-no one else?" Her cousin's voice was firmer, clear and sympathetic. "We're a lot alike, you k-know."

She stared at him in shock.

For a second Marco looked entirely normal, no twitch to his eye or slackness to his mouth, no drooling or rubbing at his groin. He stood straighter and looked her firmly in the eye. Neither the guards five paces behind him nor those at the doors ahead could see the transformation.

"I have m-moments of clarity."

"I'm sorry," Giulietta flushed. "I didn't mean . . ."

Even now, she thought. *I can't help messing up. I don't want to be here. I don't want to go in there. I don't even want to be at Ca' Friedland any more.*

"Everyone needs an Alta M-mofacon," Marco agreed, although she'd said nothing about her mother's estate or, indeed, spoken at all. "The fact you h-have somewhere to h-hide makes you luckier than me."

Her mouth fell open.

"I have to hide inside my h-head."

"Inside your head?"

"Where else . . . ? I c-can't leave. For that I need permission from both R-regents and the full C-council. What are my chances of that? So I t-twitch and drool and disgust my d-drunken uncle and exasperate my m-mother. And he s-suspects nothing and she can't tell suspicion from hope and allows herself neither. So far it's been enough to k-keep me alive."

"You pretend?"

Marco shrugged. "Not entirely. I embellish a l-little. You have your anger and t-tears and I have my t-twitches."

"But why?"

"Alonzo nearly killed me as a child."

"The fever that took your senses?"

"It was Alonzo. I saw him p-poison my cup."

"They say you should have died." And that only having a witch for a mother saved you. Lady Giulietta didn't add the last bit.

"I k-know what they say," Marco said. "She guarded me day and night. Alonzo w-watched and waited to see what I would r-remember. And I said n-nothing. I never remembered. I b-became Marco the Simple."

"Marco the Harmless?"

Reaching out, Marco touched his fingers to her cheek, then twisted his hand gently into her hair, leant forward and kissed her lightly on the lips. The guards at the door carefully looked away. "Such a p-pity we're cousins," he said. "And that I'm not someone else. You understand I love you? That if I d-didn't I would never have shown you the real m-me? I wouldn't be saying this?"

Tears spilt down Giulietta's face.

"But you don't love m-me. And you c-certainly don't love Frederick, how c-could you before you've even met him? You loved Leopold, of course. Only even that wasn't s-simple, was it? I mean, he didn't even b-bed you."

"*You know?*"

Marco shrugged. "It's obvious."

The waves were dark beyond the Molo, the sea air through the window rich with salt and spray and the salt stink of the sea. She could smell smoke from fire pits in the piazza. She stared at the familiar view and blinked back tears.

"My love . . ."

He'd never called her that; it was not appropriate.

"You do understand why Sigismund wants F-frederick to marry you? Because I won't have children and your child will r-rule one day. That makes you Regent when my m-mother dies. Frederick would be Regent with you."

"Why won't you . . . ?"

"I'm not s-sure I love even you like that. Leopold, or your p-pretty angel, perhaps. If he d-didn't love you." Marco smiled wistfully. "I always k-knew you loved him."

"That's why you made Aunt Alexa sit us together?"

"At the victory b-banquet? You were m-meant to make f-friends." Marco's mouth twisted. "Didn't work, though. D-did it?"

"Leopold . . ."

"Was d-dead. And would have p-preferred T-tycho anyway."

"That's . . ." Lady Giulietta wasn't sure what Marco saw in her eyes but he reached out and dried a tear with his finger, then pulled her close in a tight hug.

"Be h-happy. Be brave."

"Marco . . ."

"Most days I w-wish I wasn't m-me. Most days I wish my father hadn't been m-murdered. He could have had other s-sons. Then the Council could confirm a d-different heir . . ."

"*Murdered?*"

"You m-must know that?"

"Who would dare . . . ?"

"My uncle o-obviously." Marco seemed shocked by her surprise. As if this was the commonest gossip. "He was having an affair with my m-mother."

"That's impossible." Lady Giulietta expected him to deny it, but the face he suddenly turned to her was lopsided, a twitch pulling at his eye. Looking up, she saw Roderigo approaching. As he reached them, Marco pushed free from Giulietta and grabbed a marble faun, throwing his arms happily around its neck.

"You're here now, my lady."

"It would appear so."

Roderigo flushed. "Is there a problem?"

"I'm waiting on the duke."

"Ahh . . ." The question of what to do next was answered when Marco suddenly let go of his marble faun, grabbed Giulietta's hand and began to drag her towards the banqueting hall.

"We're l-late. Mustn't be. Ma doesn't l-like it when you're . . ."

As guards began to drag the great doors back, a young girl in mud-splattered velvet somersaulted through the opening gap, spun once to kick the doors shut and slammed Giulietta and Duke Marco to the tiles.

With a snarl, she dragged them from the doorway, tossing them behind the base of Marco's marble faun. When Roderigo hurtled forward, the girl ripped a knife from her belt, bared her teeth and stood over her captives hissing.

"Hold," Marco barked.

It took Roderigo a second to realise she was protecting them.

48

A handful of seconds before Rosalyn bundled the two to safety, the guard on the windowsill inside the banqueting hall began to lift his hidden bow, his gaze never leaving the great door.

"Marco and Giulietta," Tycho said.

Dropping from the scaffolding, Rosalyn landed cleanly and sprinted the length of the room, hoiking her dress to her thighs as she somersaulted over a table and then slid between the legs of a stilt-walker.

The four genuine guards in the furthest window were too busy watching Marco's guests get drunk to worry about those on a window behind them. Anyway, they believed the three pretenders to be legitimate.

Rosalyn's drop from the scaffolding and her spin between fire-eaters, her tumble through the rapidly shut door, was noticed by few. All of whom undoubtedly thought she was another enter-tainer. The man with the bow might have had his doubts. Tycho would have done in his place.

Tycho was so busy watching the bowman he barely noticed the tug at his sleeve. But he still flicked out his hand and swept the air with a dagger that only just missed a red-haired child who dropped beneath it. Thin shoulder blades showed through her rags, one buttock showed thinner, her feet were filthy.

She grinned contemptuously.

"You're not here."

"Indeed," said A'rial. "I'm abroad on orders from the duchess." She nodded at Tycho's knife, adding, "Can we talk sensibly now?" Eyes old as the moon glared at him and then she nodded, somehow satisfied. "You'd have shivered once. Now you hold my gaze."

"What does your being here have to do with me?"

"Everything and nothing."

"I don't have time for this."

"Look around you," A'rial said crossly.

Smoke from a torch on an opposite wall had frozen to twists of black marble. The bowman crouched unmoving in his high window, his actions still hidden from those below. A *cittadino* hesitated in the act of lifting wine to his lips. As Tycho watched him the goblet lifted enough to let the first drop touch.

"See? We have all the time in the world."

The glass masters of Murano said glass was a liquid and windows flowed downwards over the decades, so they became thicker along the bottom. If glass was a liquid so was this smoke. It shifted on its old trail at a fraction of the speed.

Cold, green eyes watched him.

Ancient and knowing, carrion-cruel.

"It seems you met my oldest sister. She liked you."

The bare-breasted woman with the crow was A'rial's sister? Everyone said A'rial was Alexa's *stregoi*. Tycho wasn't quite sure what a *stregoi* was but he strongly suspected this wasn't really one of them.

"Just as well. Since without her help I'd never have sunk the Mamluk fleet. I owe her that debt, as you owe me . . ."

Tycho's guts tightened as he recalled his conversation with A'rial on the deck of the *San Marco* in the darkest moment of the Mamluk battle.

"*One kill. At my choosing.*"

"*Alexa's choosing?*"

"*Mine.*" Her voice had been hard. "*One time, I will ask for a kill. You will grant it without question.*"

"*Not Giulietta, not Desdaio, not Pietro.*"

Her smile had been sour. "*You're not in a position to bargain. All the same, I agree. None of those three.*" Now Desdaio was dead, Giulietta hid in the corridor outside, and Pietro . . . was safe, Tycho hoped.

"Yes," said A'rial. "I'm here to collect."

"Who, then?"

The German princeling he could live with. Hell, Tycho would welcome it. Alonzo. He hoped it wasn't Alexa, wondering if A'rial had it in her to order her mistress's murder.

"Hightown Crow."

Tycho gaped at her.

"Everyone hates their rivals."

He doubted it was that simple. Little in Venice was.

Tycho spotted his missing sergeant against one of the walls. He'd positioned himself almost directly between the two *piazzetta* windows opposite and occupied a squat marble plinth meant for some statue. He was signalling to his men in the window, his fingers flicking in a code Atilo never thought to teach Tycho or hadn't known.

The three pretenders on the sill looked at the row of gilded thrones where Alexa, Eleanor, Frederick and Alonzo already sat. Nodding slightly as the sergeant began to raise a crossbow.

Tycho moved.

Colours changed and lights brightened, the hall falling into hard and brutal focus around him as he almost flowed along a beam to which the painted ceiling would eventually be bolted. A small girl looked up, puzzled; and he dropped, grabbing the sergeant from his plinth on the way down.

Blood spurted on to a table behind him in a fine spray and a woman screamed. Tycho could swear his thumbnails grew as he took out the man's eyes. Screaming exploded as Tycho put a dagger into the throat of the archer in the window. Watched him begin to tip backwards and put another into the man next to him.

On Tycho's back the *WolfeSelle* shivered.

Everyone else in the room was a bit player, even those who thought the play was about them and believed history turned on the decisions they made. As he began to move again the very city came alive.

It waited to discover what Tycho would do.

He was flame.

Cold as ice, hot as fire.

Tycho saw a *cittadino* child look up, face slack with shock as the entire chamber dipped briefly into darkness. A giant beast passing in front of the sun. A moth casting a vast shadow on a wall beyond imagining. If fear of the sun was his weakness then darkness was theirs.

Their light poisoned his world. His darkness could fill theirs. There would be more darkness in the world than light; the city held its breath as Tycho considered this for the infinity of a split second. And then the longbowman finished tipping backwards and fell out of the window.

Alonzo was scrabbling for his dagger. The Dogana guard behind him raised their crossbows. Shouts of outrage filled the *piazzetta* outside.

"Kill him," Alonzo screamed.

And Tycho stopped beside Dr Crow, dragged him upright and put the man between himself and the bows. Ripping the alchemist's dinner knife from his grasp, Tycho held it to his throat.

"Fire," Alonzo ordered.

Lord Roderigo's guards hesitated, scared they might hit the duke's alchemist. Alonzo looked panicked, that much Tycho noticed in the moment that passed before he gave Dr Crow his own order. "Make it dark."

"It takes . . . I can't."

"I've seen you create fire."

"Quenching it is harder."

"*I don't care if it kills you.*" Tycho tightened the blade under Dr Crow's chin and drew it sideways, blood beading along its edge.

"Do it," Tycho ordered.

All around him torches guttered, candles flickered and lamps shrivelled. The veins stood out like highways on Dr Crow's forehead, his face scarlet as a cardinal's gown. When the light began to return Tycho twitched the blade.

With the guards hesitating and Alonzo shouting, the alchemist uttered a strangled cry and every torch, candle and lamp in the hall went out.

"This is for Giulietta."

Tycho cut Dr Crow's throat. He'd find someone else to tell him what was done to Giulietta. Alonzo, if necessary.

High above he heard a longbow creak.

And Tycho flowed through the darkness, avoiding tables and the Dogana guard to catch Prince Frederick full-on, knocking the boy backwards as a woman screamed close by. The arrow had hit blind.

Prince Frederick fought; not well and not effectively but with fierce determination. His sobs of frustration rather then fear. Grabbing his wrists, Tycho growled, "I'm protecting you." And the princeling went still.

Stupid but understandable.

A huge bat swept through an open window, brushing the hair of a *cittadino* woman who howled loudly enough to make Tycho flinch. It swept a circle around Tycho and Frederick and froze midair, crashing to a clumsy heap.

"*Eleanor,*" Alexa shouted.

The arrow aimed at Frederick jutted below Eleanor's breast, blood trickling in a slow run down her white silk gown. She tried to stand and slumped, one hand on the arrow's shaft, uncertain whether to remove it or not.

"Light the lamps," Alexa ordered.

"My lady, we're trying."

The dining hall was in chaos. Nobles standing in the darkness with drawn daggers. Alonzo shouting endlessly for guards. A *cittadino* worked flints as he tried desperately to light a single candle, his strikes as flashy as cheap magic.

It would be so easy to kill Frederick . . . *Giulietta would have no prince to marry*. No one would know. Well, perhaps Alexa, if her damned bat was still watching.

"Thank you," Frederick said.

"Go, while you can."

"Who are you?"

"Tycho Bell' Angelo Scuro."

"Giulietta's . . .?" He heard the boy swallow.

"Return to your barge and guard yourself well. There are people here who would happily kill you."

He led the princeling down the darkened halls towards the door to the kitchens, telling him which tables to avoid and when to step over the body of a bowman. The corridor between hall and kitchen had one lamp at the far end. The last Tycho saw was a cook giving Frederick directions. A thin, fair-haired boy trembling like a reed and doing his best not to be afraid.

Because he left by the Molo door, Prince Frederick avoided meeting Duke Marco, Lady Giulietta or Rosalyn, who still stood guard on the first two, knife in hand and teeth bared . . . She nodded abruptly at Tycho but he looked past her.

"I knew you'd come," Giulietta said.

49

Alexa looked from her son to a girl in a muddy dress who knelt on the bed in front of Lady Eleanor. In one hand she held a knife, in the other what remained of Eleanor's clothes. As Alexa watched, the girl tossed rags to the floor, put her fingers to the blood flowing from Lady Eleanor's ribs and hesitated.

"Who is she?"

"M-my friend."

The girl's feet were mud-encrusted, her dress slashed to the knees. Alexa wasn't even sure how she got into Eleanor and Giulietta's old bedchamber on this floor. She imagined Marco had something to do with that.

Alexa's night eyes were exhausted, hanging upside down in a wardrobe in the duchess's office. The shock of seeing her niece injured having snapped Alexa free from her tame bat's mind. "There's something about her that's . . ."

Familiar, Alexa wanted to say.

But the girl turned to glare as if Alexa's voice irritated her and she didn't care if Alexa was the duchess. Grabbing the arrow, she snapped the shaft without asking permission. "Well d-done," Marco said.

He sat in the open doorway, his knees to his chin.

No staff could enter and only Alexa had dared step over him. His mother's sharply voiced suggestion that he might want to move simply earned her a defiant shake of his head. "I'm w-waiting."

"For what?"

"Angels."

Prince Frederick was safe on his barge and Alexa was grateful for that. The only thing worse than an attempt on the life of the emperor's son would have been an attack that succeeded. She was already trying to judge Sigismund's anger when he heard. It would be fierce.

Leopold, his first son, had been lost fighting beside Venetian troops. Sigismund had almost lost his second to assassins in Venice itself. He would hold Alexa and Alonzo responsible.

"Where's h-horrible Dr C-c-crow?"

"Dead." The ragged girl didn't bother to turn round.

Marco clapped. "How do you know?"

"I just do." She said nothing else, simply turned to the bed and washed Eleanor's ribs in cold water from a jug on the side. The blood trickling from the injured girl's mouth was black, sticky like treacle.

"The arrow is poisoned," the girl said.

How do you know that? Alexa wondered.

Rising from her chair, she walked to the bed, felt Eleanor's forehead and sniffed heavily at a sourness that was beyond sweat. Touching her fingers to the trickle, Alexa tasted it and turned to find the strange girl glaring at her. Almost as if daring the duchess to remember who she was.

"My dear . . ."

What made Alexa say that?

The girl smiled, then glanced at Eleanor and her happiness fled. In her eyes Alexa could see such anger she shivered.

"I know poisons," Alexa said gently.

"I know blood."

All the same, the girl surrendered her position.

Lady Eleanor's body had been poisoned with a mixture of belladonna, wolfsbane and foxglove. When the arrow was finally removed they would find its head drilled through and the tiny holes filled with paste. Alexa would give good money on it.

A second later there was a commotion outside.

Guards beyond the door scrabbled for their swords but the newcomer brushed them aside as if they were not there. His eyes were black, flecked with amber. His hair wolf-grey and set in braids capped with steel end pieces.

He carried fury like its own thundercloud.

A shimmering darkness Alexa she was glad only she could see. He wore black, except for a doublet in Millioni livery thrown over his shoulder. At his side walked her niece. Lady Giulietta's hand twisted into his, her knuckles white from the fierceness of his grip.

Duchess Alexa understood why her guards hesitated.

Standing to embrace his cousin, Marco whispered something that made her blush. He gave Sir Tycho a slow stare. Then clasped him on the shoulders, looking more like his own father than Alexa could ever remember.

"Without this m-man I'd be d-dead."

"Marco . . ."

"Believe it," Marco said.

He let go of Tycho's shoulders and stepped into the room he'd been refusing to let anyone else enter. Reaching the ragged girl, he turned her face to a lamp and smiled when he saw her eyes. "I'm M-marco . . ."

He left a pause.

"Rosalyn," the girl said.

Alexa was glad of her veil.

When her shock was gone Marco was still smiling, and two people now stared at her. Tycho, who appeared to be waiting for something. And Rosalyn.

"Mother," Marco said. "M-meet . . ."

"We've met."

"Really?"

"A year or so ago. There was an . . ."

Words were power and defined the world, sometimes Alexa suspected they wrote it. Either way, they mattered. "An accident is not quite right. Something happened that shouldn't have done. Rosalyn was . . . hurt. I was furious. Mostly with myself for letting it happen."

"But she's b-better now?"

"So it would seem."

There was a feral look to the girl's eyes. Mind you, there was a feral look to half the street children in the city; as if dropped by squatting dams in gutters and left to find the animal in themselves if they wanted to survive.

"You *are* better?" Alexa asked.

"I'm alive."

The duchess nodded slowly.

She'd asked Tycho for this. In the days she believed he'd become Duke's Blade. *Make me an army of people like you*; warriors in Venice's hidden war against the *krieghund*. The city couldn't take another blow like the one Prince Leopold inflicted the day Giulietta . . .

Ran away, Alexa reminded herself.

Her niece ran away to avoid marrying King Janus of Cyprus and almost all the Blade were destroyed in the single night it took to fetch her back. Their near destruction was a secret Alexa worked hard to keep hidden.

She'd also asked him to kill the monster on the island.

If she was right, this *was* the monster and he'd disobeyed her. Or maybe simply decided her early order cancelled out her later one. Unless he made the decision for reasons of his own.

"Tea," she said. "I need tea."

Marco laughed.

"But first . . ." Alexa did as her son had, turned Rosalyn's face to the light and stared into her eyes. As the girl leant into her touch, Alexa realised there was a child inside the animal. Something living inside what had been dead.

"Help Ellie," Rosalyn begged.

"You're friends?"

The girl's nod was simple.

Her muddy dress was Eleanor's cast-off, which was why it looked familiar. Her thread and lapis bangle was one Giulietta gave Eleanor when she grew bored with it. Looking at the anguish in Rosalyn's face as she turned away, Alexa knew boredom was not the reason the bracelet changed hands a second time.

"You knew about this friendship?"

Obviously, Lady Giulietta didn't.

"Rosalyn may stay."

The others took that as their signal to leave.

50

"My Aunt Alexa knows the ragged girl?"

"It's a long story," Tycho said.

"How could they have met? Come to that, how could your ragged girl have met Eleanor, never mind become such friends?"

"Her name's Rosalyn," Tycho said gently.

They were sitting in a window seat, half hidden by a curtain flapping in the pre-dawn breeze. Ignoring Giulietta's scowl, Tycho ran a sharpening stone along the edge of the *WolfeSelle*. The stone was inset in a small cedar block.

"I mean, how could they?"

He shrugged, swiped the stone along the blade and hoped she wouldn't ask again because he had no answer. Luckily, his care for the *WolfeSelle* took her attention instead.

"Does it really need sharpening?"

Plucking a red hair from her head without asking, he ran the strand against the edge and it parted immediately. "The sword likes it."

She snorted.

Tycho envied her faith that Aunt Alexa had antidotes to the poisons used on that arrow, that surgeons could be found to remove the arrow cleanly, that Eleanor would be same person when she recovered.

That life could not be that unkind.

"You realise it could have been . . ." Giulietta put a hand to her mouth, looking sick at herself. "What a thing to say. I almost said . . ."

"It could have been you?"

"I was going to say Aunt Alexa." Lady Giulietta looked ashamed, a rare expression for her and one Tycho wasn't sure he'd seen before. "Eleanor's my *cousin*. When her parents . . ." She shrugged. "It's a messy story and coming here should have made her life better. She was happy to be away from home and I . . ."

Tycho waited.

"I didn't want to share Aunt Alexa so I took my own unhappiness out on her. I don't even know why you're in love with me . . ."

"*Giulietta.*"

"I mean it. She's nice, prettier, kinder."

Tycho smiled. "She's not you."

Lady Giulietta told him she'd be too heavy as he lifted her on to his lap. She weighed almost nothing. In the minutes that followed she told him to keep his hands to himself and he almost managed it.

He couldn't have done so a year earlier.

The control that stopped him feeding on the dying, or turning in the presence of spilt blood in the banqueting hall, kept him staring at the lagoon and nodding at her words, though his hand rested on her hip and he could feel her shift on his lap. Her scent was rich with contradictions.

All the things he could say and all the things he couldn't. Most love affairs must be like that, if that's what this was. His love for Giulietta felt as fraught as the situation in the world outside. The emperor's anger would need to be turned aside. Frederick was on his barge. And Tycho was still officially outlawed.

When he said that, Giulietta laughed.

Whatever the new guards outside Lady Eleanor's sickroom had been told it obviously didn't include Tycho's part in saving Prince Frederick, or the fact he was free to roam the palace. On the other hand, there were the clothes he now wore.

He made an impressive officer of the palace guard.

"Sir, you can't . . ."

"Yes," said Marco. "He c-can."

As the duke prised himself from the floor Tycho wondered if anyone else had noticed Marco's stammer and twitches were mostly gone. Wondering also if they'd still be gone in the morning. Giulietta had told him of Marco's change. The fierce intelligence that suddenly confronted her.

"New c-clothes?"

"Temporary. Giulietta found them for me."

"They s-suit you."

"Your highness, I'm told there's a prisoner."

"I b-believe a man was caught trying to escape."

"May I question him?"

"Of course." Marco hesitated. "I'm glad you like Giulietta. She needs someone to l-like her. You will be k-kind to her though, won't you?" They could have been a brother and friend worrying about the first one's young sister. For Duke Marco his guards simply didn't exist. "You need to see my m-mother first?"

Tycho nodded.

The duke knocked on the door himself.

Smoke filled the sickroom from burning herbs on a brazier and the heaviness of the herbs made the air thicker than ever. As Tycho entered, the duchess flicked down her veil and turned crossly. Whatever she'd been about to say went unsaid when she saw his uniform; instead she nodded.

"There are worse disguises."

Rosalyn knelt by Eleanor's bed with a silver bowl and a sponge she used to wipe the body of the girl in front of her. She made a move to cover Eleanor's nakedness and the duchess shook her head.

The injured girl was little more than a child.

The girl at her side not much older, yet the determination with which one cooled the other was so adult it made them look more childish still. When Tycho turned back the duchess was staring at him. "We should talk."

"Later, my lady. I must go to the dungeons."

"To sleep? While your apprentice risks . . ." Duchess Alexa indicated the curtains. Rosalyn would be at the mercy of anyone who decided to open a curtain or throw wide a door to let in sunlight. Although Tycho doubted Alexa would let that happen.

"I'm going to question the prisoner with Marco's permission."

"*Marco's . . . ?*"

Tycho nodded.

"I expect you to bring me answers."

And I expect to deliver my answers to Marco . . . If he is the same man tomorrow. If not, they will be yours.

As Tycho left, he heard the click of a lock and knew Alexa would keep Rosalyn safe from the daylight, as surely as both of them would stay at Lady Eleanor's side. The same guards stood in the corridor. Only now Duke Marco stood at a window staring at seagulls. "Venice," the duke said, pointing at the gulls fighting each other for food. He hesitated, steeled himself to say something. "Would you like me to c-come with you?"

"No, highness. It might be best if I do this alone."

Builders had lined the dungeon with Istrian stone centuries before to stop groundwater from flooding the cells, although moisture still seeped between the blocks, finding its way through mortar that was supposed to be waterproof.

In Rome, the jetties on the River Tiber still stood a thousand years after they'd been built but the formula for *opus signinum* was lost. All the same the Venetian version was close and the gaoler expected Tycho to be impressed by the watertightness of his prison.

Tycho nodded at a locked door. "Total darkness?"

"Absolute. The walls are thick enough to support storerooms above."

"And light from the corridor?"

The gaoler knew who his visitor was. Even if he couldn't read the posters offering a thousand ducats for Tycho's capture, he'd have had them read to him from the pulpit. Now the outlaw was here, dressed in the uniform of a duke's guard and free, confident and obviously expecting to be given the answers he asked for.

"Does light show around the door?"

"A little. At the very bottom."

"You have sandbags?"

Of course he had. Every official building in Venice had sandbags against the effects of the *acqua alta*, the high tides that periodically flooded the city.

"Fetch me some before you go."

"But, my lord, I thought you would need my . . ." He looked at Tycho's uniform. "It will be messy."

"It will be very messy."

The flatness of Tycho's voice and the darkness in his eyes made the gaoler even more nervous. Tycho could read his fear. A further shrivelling of a spirit withered from years working here.

"I sent for a Black Crucifer," the man said.

"Well, unsend for him."

This was too close to blasphemy for the gaoler, so he bowed low and returned a minute later under the weight of three sandbags. After that he left, shutting the passage gate behind him. Tycho didn't need the man to secure the bolt on the prisoner's door; no one would be going anywhere.

The air inside the cell stank of shit curled out on a damp floor, the thick stone walls were layered with centuries of pain, and the darkness was absolute. Well, it was unless you were him. Tycho felt something stir in his gut. Felt the beast he'd been starving for days rattle at the bars of his ribs and grinned.

Tycho ignored it.

"I won't tell you anything."

Mamluk, he thought. Perhaps Greek? The man spoke bad Italian with the roughness of someone from further south.

"Believe me. You won't have a choice."

The only survivor of the assassins stared into the darkness. His training told him to identify where his enemy stood, only Tycho now stood somewhere else, and even if the man could free himself from the heavy block of wood to which his feet had been nailed nothing in his training would be enough to take him past Tycho, or prepare him for what was going to happen next.

"I don't know anything anyway."

That was closer to the truth, but he would know more than he thought and Tycho wanted everything, even things he thought he didn't know.

"I'll take what you have."

The ceiling was arched and the blocks of stone huge.

Slaves, Tycho decided. Slaves lost their lives building this place. It had ghosts before the first prisoner died in one of these cells. As Tycho made himself wait to prove he could, he examined his surroundings and gave his captive time to become truly afraid. Fresh pain the prisoner was expecting; this silence he was not. Both men opened their mouths at the same time.

The prisoner to beg, Tycho to feed.

Every wall around him lit as if flaming coals heaped the cold stone floor. Flesh began to smoulder where Tycho's dog teeth ripped it. Dancing flames reflected from glistening walls and encased Tycho's body without burning him.

Screams filled the tiny cell.

Those of pain and terror, and those of wild joy.

Inside Tycho's chest, his ribs tightened and his legs and arms flooded with pain so vicious every long bone in his body felt as if smashed with hammers as a whip master forced him to climb stone steps on broken elbows and knees.

The beast inside threw itself at the bars and he threw it back. It growled and snarled, tore at his mind to fight free, but Tycho didn't turn. The tearing flesh and twisting bones that remade him into something other on the night of the Mamluk battle never came. The greatest victory of his life to date.

A fight with himself no one else could see.

The prisoner had been a Byzantine spy, highly trained and travelling with amulets that let him avoid triggering all but the strongest watching spell. Even without talismans he'd been good enough to stay alive longer than most of his friends.

A thousand gold coins for every dead Millioni woman, five thousand for Marco, five thousand for Frederick, Marco was to die first . . . He should have known the job was poison, he would miss his family. Let no one say Tycho couldn't purge sins as easily as a Crucifer.

This was what Giulietta must never see.

A blood-splattered cell and the drained husk of something that had once been human. And ready to sleep out the day on flagstones beside it, another husk that feared it had not been human for a while.

51

Frederick's barge remained at anchor in the lagoon for a week following the disastrous feast at the new banqueting hall. His crew remained on board. Messages delivered by the Dogana guard went unanswered. When it seemed likely the barge intended to remain where it was, Alexa sent fresh bread, beef, apples, wine, small beer and three of her most trusted food tasters.

A single line from the prince thanked her for the courtesy and hoped her health was well. Alexa suspected he wrote that himself.

Even those who'd only heard about the attack at third or fourth hand decided he must be waiting for a reply from his father to a report sent shortly after the feast. So, the city waited with him, and Lady Eleanor hung between life and death, feverish and tearful, tended by the best doctors Alexa could find, and guarded by the ragged girl Alexa had ordered be allowed to come and go at will.

The house in San Aponal was once again Tycho's.

That this was Marco's decision gave Alexa hope: he stammered less, seemed more sure of himself and appeared to understand much of what was going on. Alexa half expected Giulietta to return to Ca' Friedland and had wondered if Tycho would go with her and whether she should object. In fact Giulietta slept at Ca' Ducale and so did Tycho, and Alexa was surprised to discover she didn't mind.

All the same, she hadn't slept for three nights and the strain was beginning to tell. Her dragonet was exhausted from over-flying Frederick's barge, looking for something Alexa hadn't spotted last time.

Nero, her huge black fruit bat, had passed from rumour to myth as he plagued the city, swirling over night markets, jagging his way the length of the Riva degli Schiavoni looking for some-thing she might have missed. Alexa *knew* something was wrong; until she knew what she would be unable to sleep.

"My lady . . . ?"

"Boiling water," she ordered, "in my study. And bring me cold water from the rain bucket, white wine and fresh fruit. You may return to bed afterwards."

Her maid curtsied and walked backwards from the room.

The boiled water was to make tea and the cold water to fill the jade bowl her nephew had given her; the wine she would tip away after the first glass. Alexa wanted a clear head for scrying. Fresh fruit was about the only thing in this city she found edible. In the early days of her marriage Marco had suggested she learn to eat his people's food, and seemed surprised she agreed so readily, little knowing this had already been explained to her.

Tea made and bowl filled, Alexa leant forward and willed what had stopped her sleeping to make itself known. Around her feet curled the dragonet, sleeping off its exhaustion. Nero was sulking in a cupboard. She'd named the dragonet *dracul*, meaning little dragon in her mother's tongue.

"Show me . . ." Alexa said.

She expected to see conspirators in a tavern, Republicans wondering how to turn the recent chaos to their advantage, a boat approaching Frederick's barge, carrying a message that would complicate life enormously. All the bowl showed was fog obscuring the mouth of the lagoon. The fog itself was not a puzzle since early morning fog was common in Venice at this time of year, but what was Alexa supposed to take from being shown a spit of land few even visited?

She was still asking herself that question when the fog began to clear. It was the way it burnt off that shocked her.

It parted like the Red Sea to reveal a triple-decked galley, banks of oars above each other sweeping in time to a muffled kettle-drum. The ship was vast, with a brass-bound ram that skewered the waves in front of it.

Alexa recognised it instantly.

The Will of God flew the double-headed eagle under a single crown on a background of scarlet. The family emblem on the eagle's breast was the Byzantine emperor's own. Her triangular sail held more wind than actually blew. Her silver oars sped the war galley through the water more swiftly than their number should allow.

A blond-haired and handsome young man leant against a blue rail wearing a robe hemmed with imperial purple. At his shoulder stood a thin and clean-shaven man in a simple white robe. Alexa doubted Andronikos had ever been handsome, but she imagined he'd always been striking.

The rail was set with slabs of lapis. The sail was oiled silk and the oars skinned with thin sheets of electrum. Once started, the fog burnt back to reveal a war fleet in the mouth of the Venetian lagoon. No trade ships could leave harbour in the face of such a blockade and none enter without agreement.

Alexa had not sensed their arrival at all.

As an old woman on the sandbank turned to run to raise an alarm, the thin man spoke a single word. In the world behind this one something stirred.

Black wings spread and an infinity of cold space was crossed in the time it took to part the veil between them, which was no time at all. On the sandbank the old woman clutched her chest, feeling her heart falter behind frail ribs. Death came for her only a little early and Lord Andronikos's boat glided on.

The Council of Ten had assembled hastily, as well it might. No Byzantine prince had visited Venice since the city broke with Constantinople six hundred years earlier. The odd princess had been traded in one direction or the other. And, notoriously, the Venetians had sacked Constantinople two centuries before, but a visit from one of the emperor's sons in the emperor's own ship . . . ?

In an upstairs room of the Ca' Ducale, the Council were considering Lord Roderigo's report. The guards first sent to *The Will of God* were dead, their boat found floating and not a mark of violence on any of them.

Lord Roderigo had gone himself the second time.

He went alone, wearing the chain of the Dogana captain and dressed in a style befitting a Venetian noble. For the first time since he'd joined the Customs, he boarded a foreign ship with their permission rather than at his demand.

Roderigo's meeting had been polite but chilly. Most of the talking was done by a thin man who introduced himself as Prince Nikolaos's tutor, although Alexa at least knew Andronikos was also the Byzantine emperor's adviser.

The boy whom Alexa assumed was Prince Nikolaos, although he was not introduced to Roderigo, stood in silence. When he thought no one was looking his gaze had apparently slid beyond *The Will*'s side to Venice beyond. He'd seemed unimpressed and disappointed, as if expecting more.

"And they definitely berthed without a pilot?"

"Yes, my lord." Lord Roderigo bowed to Alonzo. This fact worried the Regent, as it worried Roderigo, and Alexa imagined everyone in the Council.

The lagoon was Venice's safety. It was the world's biggest moat and the only reason Ca' Ducale could afford to be unfortified.

One of Sigismund's ancestors ran his fleet aground on its mud banks and had his army slaughtered. Wave after wave of barbarians had failed in centuries gone by to reach the city.

The Will of God had found her way through unaided.

If the fragile beauty of Ca' Ducale – with its pink and cream walls above beautifully carved marble colonnades, and its elegant central balcony looking over the wide stretch of the lagoon, reputedly the most beautiful view in Europe – was a message of defiance, this was the Byzantine emperor's answer.

"Maybe they abducted a pilot," Alonzo suggested.

Pilots were forbidden to leave Venice and the penalty for trying was death; the same sentence passed on fleeing glassblowers. Abductions happened, however. Then it was up to the *assassini* to kill the abductee before maps could be drawn using his knowledge. But pilots were licensed, controlled by a guild and all accounted for.

Besides, Alexa knew they hadn't used a pilot.

She'd seen Andronikos alone on deck apart from the boy, felt the echo of his magic grow stronger as Andronikos neared the city. Tendrils of insight feeling their way through the water to judge which direction was safe and which not.

If Venice was a hundred islands, the Byzantine emperor had a thousand, two thousand, such. Southern Greece was a jigsaw of sea-skirted rock. He took his power from the Middle Sea itself; just as Sigismund's *krieghund* took theirs from the mountains and forests. Why did people think Venice married the sea each year? The city needed all the help she could get.

"They must quarantine. They're . . ."

That would be Lord Corte whose fear of catching diseases from foreigners was infamous. Given his father survived God's Wrath, when the plague cleared Venice of more than half its citizens and swept across Western Europe killing as effectively as any Mongol army, his nervousness was perhaps acceptable. The virulence with which he expressed it less so.

"They will quarantine," Alonzo promised.

"My lord," said Roderigo. "Andronikos refuses."

Indignation filled the panelled chamber.

"Their mission is urgent. And . . ." Lord Roderigo swallowed, his next point being unpalatable. "He guarantees *The Will of God* is free from disease."

"*He guarantees?*"

Alonzo's tone made Roderigo flinch. "There's more, my lord. Once Prince Nikolaos is housed here in the Ca' Ducale, his future home, Lord Andronikos offers his assistance curing Lady Eleanor, whom he gathers is sick."

"His future home, Roderigo? No *guests* are housed here. That is one of our basic laws; only Millioni sleep at Ca' Ducale."

And servants, thought Alexa. *And, God help us, Tycho.* Unless Alonzo already considered him part of the family and she doubted that.

"My lord . . ." Roderigo said.

"*What?*"

"He seems certain his demands will be met."

"Then you'll have to persuade him otherwise."

Lord Roderigo swallowed.

The little dragonet did what Alexa's fruit bat did, only he did it during the day and with greater facility and some unexpected advantages. Those around the palace were now so used to Alexa's Chinese lizard they often fed it titbits, little knowing their kindness was known.

Both Nero and the little dragonet could give her the night and the day skies, though she had to be behind their eyes to see what they saw, which meant she needed privacy and somewhere to concentrate. Being duchess, this was easy enough to arrange. But the dragonet could give her more than this.

What it saw it *remembered* perfectly, whether she was behind its eyes or not. So perfectly she might as well have been there.

The advantage was obvious, an extra pair of eyes where her gaze was not. The disadvantage was that the memories could only be taken later, when the dragonet and she were together.

That the khan of khans had sent her two presents so valuable was flattering and worrying. Far more worrying now she understood the dragonet's full powers. For the first week or so, until their heads bumped and Alexa flinched under the slew of memories, she'd thought it no more exotic than her bat.

Her worry was how to get the dragonet aboard *The Will of God* for Roderigo's next meeting.

In the end, she simply had the dragonet drop into Andronikos's rigging from high overhead at the exact moment Roderigo's boat pulled alongside. As an added precaution, she hung its neck with amulets and, from the way the little dragonet preened, imagined she'd have a hard time getting them back.

And so it proved.

Although trading already drained trinkets was a small price for the flash flow of events, the dragonet gave up when she finally rested her forehead against its own. The difference being she *understood* what the dragonet only saw.

The deck of *The Will of God* was still as stone, even though waves rocked all the other boats in the lagoon. Its sails, earlier filled by winds that didn't exist, now hung furled and untroubled in an afternoon wind that flapped the canvas of Roderigo's own craft. Roderigo had come aboard alone and unarmed, and no weapons seemed to be trained on him.

Maybe Andronikos considered Venice too cowed for Roderigo to be a danger. Maybe he simply couldn't imagine anyone being rash enough to attack the emperor's son. For a moment Alexa wished she'd gone along with Alonzo's plan to have Roderigo kill Nikolaos. If only because failure would have cost the Regent one of his most powerful allies at court.

Lord Andronikos was amused by Roderigo's nervousness.

As Alexa suspected, this did not last beyond his delivering the message; and his argument that if the Millioni housed Prince Nikolaos at Ca' Ducale they would have to house Frederick too produced outright anger.

"*You do not compare them.*"

To Alexa that sounded like an order. One given with such confidence even Roderigo realised Andronikos was more than Nikolaos's tutor.

"My lord . . ."

"Did the German Electors pick Sigismund? No, they were simply too scared to disagree. And a ruler chosen by three arch-bishops and five princes, what kind of mandate is that? *God* has been choosing the Basilius for a thousand years."

It had taken centuries for the Byzantines to recognise the right of the Holy Roman Empire to call itself an empire at all. Andronikos's fury might have lasted longer had Roderigo not mentioned where the city intended to house Nikolaos instead.

"In Lady Giulietta's own house?"

"Yes, my lord."

"Really?" said a new voice. "The house that once belonged to Leopold zum Bas Friedland?"

So Nikolaos had been listening . . .

Alexa had thought the blond youth too busy adjusting his armour.

Pretty, conceited and unlikely to underestimate his attractive-ness to the girls he mistreated, she'd met young men like him before. Most hid a fear of liking other men behind a bullying contempt for women. Her own people's ways were simpler. *Anda*, the practice of blood partners, allowed young men their fierce friendships. Even the great Khan Genghis had bound to his childhood friend Jamuka.

"Yes, highness. Leopold's old house."

"We will take it."

327

The thin man at the prince's side scowled but nodded in the prince's direction to show he accepted the decision.

"I want Leopold's bed," Prince Nikolaos said.

"Highness. I imagine that is where Lady Giulietta usually sleeps."

"She's welcome to join me."

Glancing at his tutor, the prince muttered something and Alexa caught the word, *sweeter*. Andronikos smoothed his disgust when he realised Roderigo was watching.

"And the German?"

"Frederick will be offered a house Alexa owns."

"You may go," said Andronikos, as if he'd been the one to summon the Captain of the Dogana guard. He glanced towards the rigging, scowled. "Next time tell your duchess to keep her eyes to herself."

52

"You offered him what?"

Duchess Alexa continued lighting her candle.

Late afternoon had become early evening as she waited for Giulietta to answer the summons. Hours during which south-easterly winds tossed spray on to the Riva degli Schiavoni and wet those gathered in near silence to stare at *The Will of God*, the largest galley any of them had ever seen.

Now her niece was here and as cross as ever. Apparently unconcerned that between them the Byzantines and Germans had Venice surrounded.

The fanciful whispered they could see the Byzantine fleet at anchor in the mouth of the lagoon. Alexa doubted it. She could barely number them herself from Ca' Ducale's famous fretted balcony using her late husband's leather and brass looking device. Fifty ships, three rows of oars each.

The ships undoubtedly carried mage fire, hardened soldiers and skilled archers, those huge crossbows used to harpoon enemy ships. At speed, any one of them could ride right over a Venetian galley provided the slaves lifted their oars correctly. Alexa hoped their keel depth made them hard to manoeuvre.

Beyond this was a greater worry.

Byzantine artificers were bolting together a floating platform from parts carried on cargo ships behind the war fleet. If she was right they were constructing a gun platform to bombard Venice into submission should it refuse to choose Nikolaos over his German rival.

It would help if so much of Venice's fleet hadn't recently been sunk in the battle off Cyprus. Alexa should have known the Byzantine and Holy Roman emperors would move at the city's first sign of weakness.

We're in trouble, Giulietta, she wanted say. *I need your cooperation.*

Alexa wondered what her niece was thinking as she stood there in tight fury. Instead of asking, she said, "Have a look at their fleet."

Have a look at . . . ? This was ridiculous.

"I don't want a look at their bloody fleet."

Aunt Alexa sighed. "My dear," she said. "We have to house Prince Nikolaos somewhere. And it's not as if you're using the place."

"Ca' Friedland is *not* yours to offer. It belonged to Leopold. It belongs to me now. You have no rights over it." Giulietta felt her stomach knot in anger.

"My dear . . ."

"Don't you *my dear* me."

Giulietta glared at the offending ships in the lagoon.

Frederick's high-prowed barge in the northern style, flying a black eagle on a blood-red background. And Nikolaos's gilded Byzantine trireme, so glittering it made Marco's *bucintoro* look like a night-soil barge. She hated them both.

Hated everything they represented.

On her aunt's desk were letters from the emperors. Both demanded she marry their son. Both claimed first rights over Venice's heiress and stressed their ancient ties to the city, mentioned the many advantages marriage would bring, and left implicit the threat of what would happen if their demand was refused.

Giulietta knew she was trapped.

She wasn't stupid. She'd always known she was an asset, something to be traded. Leopold's death was supposed to free her from that.

The Council of Ten had bought her time by announcing they needed two days to consider the merits of both suits. Their answer would be given the morning after next. Since to choose one made an enemy of the other and a Byzantine fleet waited off the mouth of the lagoon, just as Frederick's army camped along the mainland shore, there was little between them.

They would have to hope the power of one provided counterweight to the enmity of the other. All that remained was for Giulietta to choose which she wanted, and Venice would *live with the consequences of her choice.*

How could Aunt Alexa even say that?

The Regent had left this bit of the conversation to them, arguing that the two women would find discussing delicate matters easier without him. Their contempt for his cowardice was the only thing on which they agreed.

"You have to choose."

"No, I don't."

"Giulietta, listen to me . . ."

"Why would I listen to you?" Swinging round, Giulietta glared at her aunt, summoning the loathing she'd felt a second earlier for the ships. "*You* had me abducted." She said the words coldly, deliberately. Each one a slap.

Alexa froze.

When she unfroze it was to lift her veil and stare Giulietta full in the face, as if daring her to lie. "Who told you that?"

"Tycho."

"A dangerous young man." Alexa's lips twisted. "But you refused to believe him at first, obviously. Because why would I have you abducted . . .?"

She sounded older than Giulietta remembered.

"I mean, why would I have my favourite niece abducted the night before she were due to leave Venice, in tears, for a marriage she would hate, in which she'd be required to kill her husband after he'd bedded her."

Lady Giulietta felt her eyes prickle.

"You knew I was unhappy?"

"The whole palace knew. I simply decided to do something about it. I couldn't tell you because I needed you unhappy. If you'd suddenly stopped being miserable it would have made Alonzo suspicious. I couldn't risk that."

"Why didn't you . . ."

"I've just told you why. It was a good plan, too. Mercenaries disguised as Mamluks. A pavilion in the Mongol garden my husband gave me when we married to hide you. My old lady's maid to look after you."

"I'm sorry," said Giulietta, remembering how the woman died trying to protect her. Her husband also. "Leopold killed them."

"I know."

"He was going to kill me, too."

She wanted to say more but couldn't decide how to frame it. Although Aunt Alexa was obviously prepared to wait until she found her courage and her tongue. "I guess he decided I was worth more to him alive."

"And maybe it was more complicated than that."

Lady Giulietta ignored her. "He kept me caged in an upstairs room, until I escaped the night . . . The night you captured Tycho."

Looking into Aunt Alexa's unveiled face Giulietta realised how much went unsaid, how much she knew but didn't dare share. She'd grown up. Not as much as she thought, perhaps not as much as she should have done, but she'd grown up all the same. Having a child did that.

The one single light in any darkness.

"You're thinking of Leo?"

Lady Giulietta nodded.

"Now you understand how I feel about Marco. Every time I look at him, I see all his father's weaknesses and none of his strengths. It breaks my heart . . . Can you tell me yet who Leo's father is?"

Lady Giulietta shook her head.

"Sometime between the original abduction and Leopold's attack you met Leo's father?"

"I met him before."

"Tycho?"

"Why do you say that?"

"This tension between you. He has a claim on your soul. The kind a young girl's first lover . . ."

"Tycho is not Leo's father."

"Then who is?" The words were sharp.

"I cannot say."

"Giulietta . . ."

"*I cannot say.* Don't you understand?"

Giulietta fought as Alexa grabbed her face and turned it to the candlelight. Whatever she found there shocked her so deeply her grip slackened and she barely scowled when Giulietta slapped her hand aside. By then Giulietta had reached the door. Not even bothering to greet Nero who hung from a picture frame.

"Wait," Alexa said.

"I'm going back to Eleanor's room."

"I can have my guard prevent you leaving."

"And I can call for help." Beyond the window dark spread across the lagoon. "And your guards will die because Tycho will come. Wherever I am. Wherever he is. He will come."

"Ask Tycho about the prisoner he questioned."

"What prisoner?"

"Before you become too infatuated, ask him what he did to

the last of the assassins after the banquet for Frederick. And remember, that's the man you're in love with. You'd be better off with Frederick. Nikolaos, less so. Though we could always have him killed later."

"I'm not going to . . ."

"*Listen to me.*" Alexa said. "The Byzantine fleet blockades the lagoon. The army Sigismund sent with Frederick controls the rim. The poor in the city are already going hungry. How long do you think we can hold out?"

Giulietta shrugged.

"I've fought for years to keep this city independent but that's no longer possible and, much as I hate to say it, your Uncle Alonzo agrees. He favours the Byzantines slightly. I hate them both equally. Frederick will make a better husband, and Nikolaos's father a less demanding ally."

"Aunt Alexa . . ."

"The choice is yours. Venice's fate is in your hands."

"And what," Giulietta asked, "did Venice do when my fate was in its hands?" She was pleased with herself for not slamming the door.

"My lady . . ."

"*What?*"

"Sir Tycho is in there."

"Then let me in immediately."

The young guard twisted under her gaze, wondering if he dared object again. All he said was, "Yes, my lady."

There were now as many rumours about Tycho as there had been about Dr Crow and most were equally inaccurate. When the guard looked away as he opened the door Giulietta thought it was because Tycho scared him. It turned out he was probably just scared of seeing what was going on in the room.

"*Tycho . . .*"

A half-naked couple were on the bed.

Rosalyn stood at its foot, tight-faced, with her fingers clenched into fists. Eleanor was naked except for her bandage, which showed blood again. Tycho wore his hose and nothing else; he was cradling the injured girl.

His muscles were alabaster, his naked chest wet marble. Need lanced through Giulietta and she stepped forward.

"Stay back," Rosalyn growled.

His flesh against hers, his left arm under her. He was stroking Eleanor's cheek, kissing her forehead, crooning strange words. Giulietta didn't know how Rosalyn could stand to watch.

"He's singing her back from the edge. He learnt how from a slave who'd once been his enemy. The Skaelingar can do that."

Giulietta came closer and this time Rosalyn let her. She discovered Rosalyn was telling the truth. Tycho was singing words that were high and strange, and there was an eldritch concentration in his face she found mesmerising.

"I don't think he has enough power."

"To do what?" Giulietta asked.

"Make Ellie want to live."

"How did you meet?"

Giulietta meant how did you meet my lady-in-waiting, and why didn't I know about it? Rosalyn thought she meant Tycho.

"I pulled his body from the Grand Canal."

"His body?"

"In return he brought me back from the grave."

Lady Giulietta crossed herself. It was habit. She'd spent her life crossing herself to ward off bad luck, at the mention of disasters, when someone said something that shocked her. She wasn't even sure why. Mind you, she'd spent a life not knowing why she did most things.

"I'm sorry," Tycho said.

Having rested Eleanor on the bed, he half covered her with a thin sheet and turned to Rosalyn. *I've seen it work* was all he said. Sweat slicked his marble skin, making him look unnervingly like a graveyard statue. When he turned back to stand over Eleanor, Giulietta felt tearful to admit she looked the same.

"She's dying," Rosalyn said.

"My aunt has a new alchemist."

"Unfortunately," said Tycho. "He has few suggestions."

"Then he won't last long. Aunt Alexa likes answers not problems. If he fails in this she'll get rid of him."

"Even your aunt can't stop this."

"*But you can*," Rosalyn almost shouted.

"He just tried," Giulietta said gently. Surprisingly so for her. "And he couldn't do it either. You saw him try."

"I don't mean songs to make her stay."

There was a rawness in Rosalyn's words, and Giulietta guessed some dam was breaking that had probably never broken before in her life.

"I mean, let her go and then bring her back."

She couldn't be suggesting?

"He did it for me. He can do it for her. He owes me that . . . I pulled him from the Canalasso. Without me he'd be dead."

Rosalyn was shaking. Her shoulders hunched inside Eleanor's old dress. When Tycho looked at her, Rosalyn raised her chin and glared defiantly; but even Giulietta could see the panic behind her eyes.

"*Rosalyn . . .*" Tycho said.

"I've never loved anyone before in my life. Never had anyone to love me. Oh, people used me." She glared at him. "But no one *loved* me until . . ."

In a shockingly un-Millioni-like display Giulietta surprised herself by wrapping the sobbing girl so tight Rosalyn collapsed against her.

Tycho left them there.

53

"Wait for me . . ."

Turning, Tycho was aware of guards carefully not watching the princess hurrying towards him down marble stairs leading to the ground floor and out into darkness and fresh air beyond. "I have a question."

"So ask me."

"Not here . . ."

In that second he remembered she wasn't that much older than Eleanor, and Eleanor was almost a child. Then he remembered he wasn't much older than either, and wondered how he could forget that.

"I'm going for a walk."

Giulietta hesitated, and Tycho discovered he wasn't going for a walk after all. She didn't want to go for a walk and she didn't want to be where they were. Since that was on the stairs, not being watched by guards and servants passing in the courtyard below, he could understand that.

"Where's Leo?"

"Do you want to see him?"

Tycho nodded and she smiled through her tears.

He followed her back up the stairs, under an arch and along a narrow corridor. Smaller stairs led to the floor above. Old tapestries covered the stairwell walls. A Mongol guard escorting a golden chair with red curtains. The prince at the front carried a horsehair banner.

"Alexa?"

Giulietta nodded. "She was a child."

"No choice?"

"There seldom is. You know that."

"I was born a slave," Tycho reminded her. "There was never a choice. No marriage either. Women lay with whom they were told. Boys, too. To kill a slave was not murder, to force one was not rape."

"Tycho . . ."

"We were not people even to ourselves. Hunting dogs were more valuable." He shrugged, still not finding it strange. After all, hunting dogs took longer to train.

Leo's room was next to Lady Giulietta's new one and the woman sitting in a chair beside the cot scrambled to her feet as they entered.

"My lady . . ."

"It's all right. I just wanted . . ."

Removing a chamber pot, which the woman covered with a cloth before carrying it past them, she dipped a slight curtsy and hurried out.

"Which one of us frightens her?"

"Both. But where I might have her whipped, you . . ." Giulietta took a breath. "I need to ask. What did you do to the prisoner?"

And how, Tycho wondered, *do you know about that?*

"Well?" she demanded.

"Freed him."

"From what?" asked Giulietta, picking up her child and reaching for the buttons on the neck of her gown, before hesitating.

"From life. Do you need me to leave so you can feed Leo?"

"He's almost weaned . . . And I'm not sure who comforts whom when we feed. Maybe we comfort each other." She let her hand drop. "So tell me about the prisoner, because my aunt thinks I should know."

Alexa was changing allegiances?

Tycho felt invisible sands shift under him.

He knew he'd only ever played a small part in Alexa's plans. All the same, he thought they watched the world with the same dark gaze.

He could lie to Giulietta about the prisoner or tell the truth. Lying offended him. A *finesse* his slave self would regard as ridiculous, had that person known what *finesse* and *ridiculous* meant.

"I took a soul, I think. Or maybe freed one."

"I'm not sure that helps much. What did you *do*?"

Tycho told her. When he finished she was white-faced and gripped Leo so tight Tycho was afraid she'd hurt him. The tears were gone from her eyes and she looked older. As if his words had stolen a final part of her childhood.

"You fed from him?"

"It gave me answers."

"I'm glad to hear it," she said flatly. "Was there no other way?"

"Men lie under torture. Tell you what they think you want to hear and create conspiracies where none exist. Confess to other people's crimes. I wanted the *truth*."

"Why?"

"Because Sigismund's army is camped on the mainland. And there's a Byzantine fleet in the mouth of the lagoon."

"You sound like my aunt."

"Your city is blockaded on both sides." His voice was as flat as hers. And his next words dripped bitterness. "Two princes want to marry you and one will be disappointed. Unless you think they'd be willing to share?"

The sound of her slap set Leo crying.

When Leo was settled, Tycho returned from the window. "This hurts," he said. "You know that. Two men who don't love you can have you with everyone's blessing. The one who loves you can't."

Lady Giulietta didn't protest as he took Leo from her arms. She obviously expected him to return the child to his cot. Instead Tycho unwrapped the swaddling that kept his limbs straight. "You understand what the scar means?"

"He is *krieghund*."

"Exactly. Leopold's heir in all things . . ."

She nodded as Tycho repeated the words Prince Leopold spoke in the chapel on the day she married. And her nod and the memory of Leopold asking him if Giulietta's child was his tumbled a part of the puzzle into place. Leopold must have asked about Leo, and she hadn't told him either.

"Magic stops you saying Leo's father's name?"

She nodded.

"Hightown Crow?"

"Was there when my son was conceived. To ensure Leo was a boy. They said I had to bear Janus a boy."

"They . . .?"

"Yes," she said. "They."

Noble brides were still publicly bedded on the Italian mainland but the custom, designed to prove the marriage valid, had been out of fashion in Venice for years. A memory filled Tycho's head. The Prior saying, *I can sense Millioni blood*. Words he wouldn't have found strange but for Lady Giulietta close to despair in front of him now. "They bedded you with Marco?"

"Marco I could have stood. And no one *bedded* me."

Sweeping jugs from a table in a clatter loud enough to still conversation in the corridor outside, Tycho drew his dagger. Then he stabbed it into the table. "If you can't say it, write it here."

He watched her fingers shake as she gripped the handle, her

340

knuckles turning white as she pulled the dagger free. She cut *Alonzo* into the wood without letting herself hesitate. And before Tycho could react, she said, "I'm not going to marry either one. I've told Aunt Alexa that."

"Of course you have."

"I mean it."

"I know you do."

"Good," said Giulietta. "Because I'm going to marry you instead."

54

Well, thought Giulietta, lying back and catching her breath. *That was . . .* She wasn't sure of the word. *Unexpected?* Tycho hovered above her in half-darkness. His face candlelight and shadow. The act had been clumsy on her part; surprisingly gentle on his. Neither the ecstasy minstrels sang about, nor the hellish horror her nurse hinted at the day she began her bleeding.

She knew it had happened, right enough.

There was a dull ache in her abdomen where her body had yet to adjust to this new her. And for all her trying she hadn't arrived where she wanted to go. She would, though. It was like knowing where you needed to be was round the next corner.

The second time was rougher than the first.

The third softer than either before. A gentle rocking that carried her where she wanted to be and brought release. She wouldn't call it ecstasy, but it was warm and made her happy and she liked the way Tycho sprawled, his head on her breasts, his voice sleepy.

"Thank you," he said.

"For that?" asked Giulietta, unsure whether to be offended.

"For the night in the basilica . . . For not killing yourself . . . For letting us make friends again."

"*Tycho.*"

"Let me say this . . ."

She waited for him to finish his words and realised he had. So she took her turn. And though the clock in the piazza struck four as she began telling him about her childhood, the trip across the mountains with Atilo, her early life at Ca' Ducale, it was five before she came to what really troubled her.

She told Tycho the story of Leo's conception, beginning with her uncle's secretary finding her in a corridor and ending with being made to wait, on her back with her knees up. Long after Dr Crow had gone.

"They used a *goose quill*?"

"Seljuks breed mares that way. They transport the quills on crushed ice when the mares can't be brought and the stallions are too valuable to be moved." Giulietta's voice was matter-of-fact.

She'd already described how Hightown Crow froze her jaw so she couldn't scream and how his magic prevented her talking about it. Although now she wondered if that was really shame.

Tycho obviously expected her to rage.

Instead, she'd kept her voice calm and controlled her temper. She hadn't even cried. It was hard to explain but, for someone who'd spent over a year desperate to tell the truth, simply speaking was enough. She might come to regret telling him this. He might, in time, regret having listened, but not tonight in this room. On this night and in this room her words freed her from misery as surely as if she cut one poisoned rope after another.

There was one thing she still needed to say.

"Just say it."

"You must stop doing that."

"Doing what?" Tycho asked, puzzled.

"Knowing what I'm thinking."

She felt him smile in the darkness. "I don't," he said. "Most times I have no idea. When I think I do, with you I'm mostly wrong. So tell me."

Should she?

"Listen . . . This has *nothing* to do with us going to bed and you can say no and I'll understand. But I *know* you did magic in the battle; everyone knows. Lord Atilo was the last on deck and afterwards he was afraid of you."

"Giulietta. What are you asking?"

"Aunt Alexa says I have to marry Frederick or Nikolaos. And one's got a fleet and the other an army and I thought, *Tycho beat the Mamluks . . .*"

She sensed his shoulders stiffen, felt her heart sink as he rolled away from her. Sitting up, he turned his back to her. So Giulietta sat behind him and wrapped her legs around his hips, resting her chin on his shoulder. His skin was cold, his muscles locked and he felt so closed down she worried what she'd said.

"Tycho. I'm sorry . . ."

"Wait," he said sharply.

But she wouldn't. Instead she rubbed his shoulders and kissed his hair and held him until her warmth became his. Though she knew he wanted her to let go she kept hold of him until he relaxed and she felt him sigh.

"*Whatever I did that night do it again?*"

Giulietta nodded.

"For you," he said.

"For me?"

"Even that."

Since there was neither writing paper, ink nor a pen in her room, Lady Giulietta sent for all three when Tycho asked. She stood at his shoulder when he sat at a table to write a note to her aunt Alexa. He wrote slowly and carefully, struggling to make his letters clear as Desdaio must have taught him.

"All right?" he asked, when she gripped his shoulder.

"Yes," she said.

He didn't tell her what he was about to say. Nor did he ask her not to look. His note was short and to the point. *How much do you value Venice's independence? Enough to risk all?*

55

The shutters, the curtains and the roll of cloth along the bottom of Lady Eleanor's sickroom door were enough to keep out the light and keep Rosalyn safe. The surgeons had stopped coming. Duchess Alexa's new alchemist had admitted defeat. Rosalyn had her friend to herself.

She'd seen enough deaths to recognise what was coming.

Eleanor would be dead before dark. Maybe two hours of life remained at the most. A little of Rosalyn wanted to risk the daylight, discover where Tycho was sleeping and beg him to save her friend. The rest of her remembered the terror of waking in a grave. The horror at realising what sunlight could do. The pain of knowing you were different, really different.

Had her friend been conscious Rosalyn would have asked what she wanted. But, desperate as she was, Rosalyn didn't feel brave enough to make the decision alone. Were she able to die in Eleanor's place she would do that. Had she been able to die too she would. Instead, she held Eleanor's head and stroked her hair and wiped sweat from her eyes while tears rolled down her own face. Eleanor's pulse was butterfly-light and getting lighter. Her heart nervous as a hare.

Soon . . . Rosalyn would be alone again.

The howl that echoed down a marble-floored corridor and spread from the open-sided upper colonnade was so loud that those walking two streets away froze in terror, crossed themselves and kept walking.

Those in the palace knew Giulietta's lady-in-waiting was dead.

No member of Alexa or Alonzo's staff rushed to check, they had more sense than this. The young crucifer who'd arrived the previous day to pray over Eleanor was nursing broken ribs and a dislocated jaw.

Lady Giulietta was the first to the door.

She arrived at twilight. Her hair was down and she looked nervous as she knocked, said her name and waited until bolts rattled and the heavy door swung back. The two young women stared at each other until Rosalyn gestured Giulietta into the room. "I'll wait outside," she said.

"You heard about Lady Eleanor?" Alexa asked.

"Yes," Tycho said flatly. "I heard."

"But that's not why you're here, is it? You're here to say you won't let my niece marry either prince."

"Unless she wants to."

"Since you've both spent last night and most of today behind locked doors I think that's unlikely." Rising from her couch, Alexa muttered, "I hope you were kind about it. That girl needed comfort."

What was he supposed to say to that?

Tycho had intended to ask why she'd told Giulietta about the prisoner. Except he'd already worked that out for himself. Alexa had been checking if the bond between them could be broken. That he came from her niece's darkened bedchamber and crumpled bed with a proposal to kill both princes was her answer.

"You want to slaughter Nikolaos and Frederick don't you . . .?

Yes," she added, seeing his face, "I rather thought you did. Your ideas lack finesse. You'll need to do better if we're going to work together long-term."

Work together long-term?

"How much do you love my niece?"

"Beyond life."

"That will help with what comes next."

She told him where to sit. A leather seat like a saddle with squat wooden legs, its surface worn and legs dark with age. Mongol, he imagined. Small mirrors hung either side of him on opposite walls.

"Look deeply into both."

Tycho did and saw himself. An infinite number of Tychos, wolf-grey hair, high cheekbones, dark, amber-flecked eyes. He stared at them and they stared back so intently he wanted to shiver.

"What do you see in that one?"

"Myself."

And in that one?"

"The same . . ."

Alexa smiled sourly. "How typical. I had Dr Crow make those for me. One shows your greatest weakness and the other your greatest strength. Making them was my price for convincing Marco to employ him. You did kill Dr Crow, didn't you?"

"Yes," Tycho said.

"Want to tell me why?"

"You'd have to ask your niece, my lady."

"Believe me," Alexa said. "I will."

Tycho believed her.

"Your asking for audience saves me sending for you. A blessing, since it might embarrass even me to send guards to my niece's bed."

"She's with Rosalyn."

"You know what I mean . . . You've heard rumours of the

Byzantine weapon everyone talks about? Alexa unrolled a scroll. "It's a gun platform in the Chinese style."

"How far can . . ."

"From the lagoon mouth to Arzanale undoubtedly. Closer to the centre is possible. Maybe even this palace. We'll find out soon enough." She sounded calm for someone describing the possible destruction of her city.

Then Tycho discovered why.

"We're going to attack before they do."

"Prince Alonzo leads?"

"Don't think I'm not tempted. Of course, if the Regent succeeded he'd be unbearable but right now if an Alonzo-led attack would work I'd give it my blessing. It would be a glorious defeat, however. So I'm letting Roderigo and him come up with their own plan while forming one of my own."

"And then you choose?"

"Hardly. Mine will be in action by the time he brings me his." She shrugged. "I know his already. Tell both sides they're our choice. Use the time that buys to hire assassins from Florence or recall some of our own."

Tycho thought about that.

"I've heard worse," Alexa agreed.

"And what's your plan, my lady?"

"We entice Andronikos, Nikolaos and Frederick into one place, and you and that ragged girl of yours slaughter them. You take no prisoners and leave no witnesses. You were never there. The deaths are the result of a clash between units of Frederick's and Nikolaos's forces trying to outwit each other."

"My lady . . ."

"Alonzo never knows about this."

"They say Andronikos has magic."

"And you will have this . . ." Removing the cloth from a side table, Alexa revealed what looked like a matchlock gun, but far smaller. Italian matchlocks were little more than iron poles. And though Mamluk matchlocks were the world's finest even they looked oversized next to this.

This was little longer than his forearm.

Its wooden stock lacked a metal S to hold a length of match.

Where the S lock should be was a drilled-out hole in the wood, with a long wedge shape chiselled into the stock's side. A simple downturn in the oak formed its handle. Lighter wood showed where decoration had been stripped away.

"He'd used silver," Alexa said. A knock at the door made her smile. "Here's the artificer now."

A small Mongol in a leather apron pushed past a palace guard, passed between the mirrors without glancing to either side and fell on his face at Alexa's feet. For Tycho she was the duchess. For him a Mongol princess.

He rose at her command.

Pulling ironwork decoration from his apron, he slotted the end of the stock into it and grunted. Two quick blows from a small hammer fixed it in place. It fitted perfectly. An iron spike now jutted from below the handle.

The man showed Alexa a wheel-like mechanism. At her nod, he used pliers to compress a steel spring that fitted below the wheel. Releasing the pliers let the spring lock into place. The whole mechanism then slid into the pistol's stock, hidden behind a steel side plate that he screwed into place. The handgun's final piece was modelled on a cobra's head. A flint was held between its jaws.

"Marco's idea. The cobra's hood keeps out the rain."

"Your husband?"

"My son." She passed Tycho the weapon and a key.

Cogs clicked as he wound the wheel and felt its hidden spring take up the tension. He could already see how this worked. The flint dragged on the spinning wheel, lighting powder in the pan.

"Now lower the flint."

Alexa looked impressed when he pulled a little lever below the stock. She'd obviously expected him to need the mechanism explaining. A dry grating from the wheel produced sparks that fell around his feet.

"You can go," she told the artificer.

The Mongol bowed deeply, collected his pliers, small hammer and remaining screws and nails and walked backwards to the door, only turning when it was already closing behind him. As he did, Tycho saw a grin.

"Although my people have used cannon for three hundred years this gun is the first of its kind. The second will be sent to my nephew, the khan of khans, as poor repayment for recent kindnesses . . ." How she referred to Tamburlaine changed at will. *My cousin, my nephew, my brave brother.*

Upending her purse, Alexa let two bullets roll on to the table and grabbed Tycho's wrist when he reached for one. That bullet was silver inlaid with red writing. The other black and so scribbled with gold script it looked made from words.

"The gold one you can touch."

Tycho could read Italian. He could speak the language of his childhood and recognise runes. The script on the black bullet meant nothing to him.

"Enochian," Alexa said.

The fleet and the army were two monsters.

Large, powerful, dangerous and hungry monsters. According to Alexa, her adopted city didn't have the power to defeat the monsters in battle or even meet them face to face. Tycho would simply have to ambush them.

He loved that *simply*.

"Andronikos is the power. Nikolaos merely the figurehead. So these kill Andronikos and Frederick." She smiled. "Since Nikolaos has no powers he should die easily enough. Kill those three and the rest is easy."

"It is, my lady?"

"We tell the Byzantine Empire and the Germans we'll side

with the others against whoever attacks first and suggest both withdraw."

"Why would they?"

"Pushing Venice into the arms of the other side would be a worse sin than not taking us at all. Sigismund and the Basilius are not forgiving men. If I were their second in command, I'd want advice before condemning myself to death. You must kill all three by dawn tomorrow."

"My lady . . .?"

"Giulietta will help you."

"Rosalyn and I work alone, my lady."

Raising her veil, Alexa stared at him. Her eyes cold and distant, her face suddenly hard. What he noticed most was her heart-stopping beauty. He hadn't remembered you could be old and beautiful.

"You're meant to be afraid."

"I'll tremble next time, my lady."

Alexa snorted. "You can't do this without Giulietta." Lowering her veil, she settled into a cushion. "My niece is your bait and that ragged girl of yours can cover your back. I doubt you'd be able to keep her out of this anyway. I've already sowed the seeds. All you need do is let them flower."

He waited for her to unravel that.

"The Germans will intercept a spy of mine at midnight. He will reveal you are about to spirit my niece out of Venice on a boat leaving Giudecca before dawn. You plan to take her across the southern marshes."

"How do you know he'll be captured at midnight?"

"He leaves in two hours, his map is inaccurate and it will take him that long to reach their picket line. Since *krieghund* are cruel he'll confess quickly. Having spies of his own in their camp Andronikos will know shortly afterwards. Andronikos and Frederick will race each other to Giudecca to intercept you.

"My attention will be . . ." Alexa glanced at a water-filled stone bowl. "You will be on your own. I cannot afford to draw Andronikos's notice."

"Rosalyn could dress as Giulietta."

"You might fool the *krieghund* but Andronikos will *know*. He can sense where my niece is. He can sense where all the Millioni are."

"It would be worth the risk."

"*Tycho*. The moment Andronikos believes we're spiriting Lady Giulietta out of Venice the bombardment will begin. Take her with you if you want to keep her safe. Oh . . . And take that damn sword I'm not meant to know about."

"My lady. She'll see what I become."

Alexa sighed. "My niece might be spoilt but she's nobody's fool. Lord Atilo feared you. You defeated Leopold zum Friedland on the roof of his own house. You destroyed a Mamluk fleet. You slaughtered the new Blade in cold blood despite knowing you'd face death for it. She knows you're a monster already."

56

A hundred hastily commandeered barges floated in the middle of the lagoon beyond the palace window. Tethered above each were half a dozen glowing globes.

"Magic?" Tycho asked.

"Of a kind."

The globes were tissue wrapped round a coil of split bamboo. Coals in a small bucket kept them aloft and had enough lift to support an oil lamp underneath. The women of the Arzanale ropewalk had been making them for days.

Seemingly Alexa's grandfather, a Mongol general, had seen the Chinese use them on campaign. A captured Chinese artificer told him how they worked and her people had used them ever since. Usually they provided light for attacks. Tonight's lights would pretend to be Venice.

An hour earlier, the Council of Ten had issued orders that all fires in the city be extinguished. Even the foundry furnaces that burnt day and night.

With luck, these would look from a distance like city lights and the Byzantine fleet's cannon men would fire at the lagoon. When the lamps faded the soldiers on the gun platform would think orders had been issued to put the lights out and keep firing through the fog towards where they remembered the lights being.

"And there will be fog. Make use of it."

Tycho took Alexa's advice into the boat she provided.

Her words, two bullets, the handgun her artificer made and her warning that the fate of Venice and the life of her niece rested in his hands. Between worrying about that warning, listening to waves slap against her boat and trying not to think about the depth of the water beneath them, Tycho watched Giulietta.

He wondered if she really knew he was a monster.

"I'm scared," she snapped when he asked if something was wrong. "And you keep staring at me. That would make anyone nervous."

Leo chose that moment to wake up.

Ten minutes passed while Lady Giulietta tried to get him back to sleep. The whole plan had nearly foundered on her refusal to be parted from Leo. If she was safer with Tycho because Venice was going to be bombarded then so was he. In the end Alexa agreed.

Giulietta hadn't left her much choice.

Their boat chose the shortest route between Ca' Ducale and a cluster of fishing huts at Giudecca's eastern end, hugging the edge of Giorgio Maggiore island on its way. The trip was made bearable by the boat Alexa provided; the one Dr Crow built to deliver Tycho to Ca' il Mauros. As before, it moved without oars or sail.

"After you go ashore," Alexa had said, "the boat will find its own way to Giudecca's southern edge, near the Jewish graveyard. Andronikos will sense its unnaturalness and assume it's how you intend to escape. Let the boat draw him there. Cross the island and surprise him."

"And the *krieghund*?"

"Kill Andronikos first. He's far more dangerous."

The memory of her words shocked Tycho into wondering if he was thinking enough about what was to happen. It was hard to concentrate when the girl he loved sat there scowling, and the girl he'd brought back from the grave hunched unreadable on the floor where the cabin came to a point.

"Why am I really here?" Giulietta demanded suddenly.

To keep you safe . . . That was what Tycho should have said. At worst, he should have answered, *Those are my orders.* What he said was, "You're the bait. We need you to draw out Andronikos and Prince Nikolaos."

"Aunt Alexa would never agree."

"It was her suggestion."

Giulietta paled. "Not Alonzo?"

"Your uncle knows nothing of this."

Thunder rolled overhead and everyone instinctively ducked. A second later a splash sounded to one side like a huge ballista shot hitting water. More thunder followed and a second splash. The bombardment of Venice had obviously begun.

"I'm going up on deck."

Giulietta nodded, not offering to join him; while Rosalyn barely bothered to look up, staring inwards instead with dark and vicious eyes. Her anger felt far more dangerous for being entirely cold. On her wrist was the bangle Giulietta once gave Eleanor and she still wore Eleanor's velvet dress.

And on Tycho's wrist?

The ribbon from the neck of Giulietta's nightgown.

The ducal wedding ring was back between her breasts, hidden from him and the world by the gown she wore. Because Tycho was the only one who went on deck, he was the only one to see A'rial on a sandbank calling down fog with imperious gestures. A second later she was gone.

"I think you should go below."

Turning, he found Rosalyn behind him.

"Your woman's crying. She's scared for Leo."

"You're not scared?" asked Tycho, already knowing the answer. Rosalyn confirmed what he knew. She was angry.

"You are here to be kept safe . . ." Tycho shrugged. "That's the truth and what I should have said. I asked Alexa to let Rosalyn dress as you. She said you'd be safer with me than her."

"And Leo? Is he safer here?"

"I will protect you both."

"That's not an answer."

"What else can I say to someone I love?"

He held her while she sobbed, heard Giulietta say crossly she didn't even know why she was crying and let her clean her face against his doublet. A minute later she pulled back and he knew from her expression that Giulietta had something she wanted to say.

"Aunt Alexa loves me, I think. Though she'd never bring herself to say it. Even Leopold only ever said he was fond of me. The last person to say she loved me was . . ."

"Your mother?"

"You have to stop doing that."

Her face was wet beneath his lips as he kissed away her tears. He was him and so was the monster. And this was her, complicated and spoilt, simple and giving. They were together in the eye of a storm neither had chosen. He could not abandon her now, would not abandon her now, any more than she abandoned him the night he came to her after he killed Iacopo.

He still hated her city. Hated the water that was supposed to keep it safe. Hated its overcrowded alleys, its stinking canals, the Castellani's and Nicoletti's simmering anger, the greed of the *cittadini* and the nobles' contempt for everyone else. The sheer need of the poor, which mirrored his never-satisfied hungers.

Only, in the middle of all this hate, was her.

The girl he held and felt settle as her eyes dried and sobs stopped shaking her body as fiercely as if her distress was a furious adult and she its child. Tycho had no real idea of her childhood, its slights and cruelties; just as she had no idea of the sheer brutality of his, the horrors done to him and his horrors to others.

"What are you thinking?" Giulietta asked.

So he told her.

"We can change this."

Tycho tried to decipher which *this* she meant.

"The Nicoletti have brothers and sisters . . ." Her voice broke. "They have children and lovers. So do the Castellani, the Moors and the Hebrews. *If you cut us do we not bleed?* My uncle's treasurer said that before he was executed. He grew up poor and died poor because my uncle took his wealth."

"Marco the Just?"

"If you were noble or *cittadini* or of use to him."

Tycho had never heard Giulietta say such things.

"If I live through this I'm going to be different. And when I'm duchess and Venice is mine I'll abolish the Millioni and make Venice a proper republic again. You can help me."

Tycho wasn't sure what to say to that.

57

Once all of Venice had been huts on stilts, but that was a thousand years before and few such remained on the main islands. The five that loomed through the fog surrounding Giudecca's eastern point looked derelict and deserted.

The cluster of huts stood three feet above the water and ten feet from the shoreline. A narrow walkway stretched from solid ground to the first of them. Shorter walkways stretched between huts.

If Tycho wanted to ambush a boat coming ashore, the huts were where he'd hide. He had everyone disembark on the far side of the boat, keeping its cabin between the huts and his little party.

"We walk together."

He went first, Rosalyn behind him, with Giulietta and Leo beyond them so any archers would have to shoot Tycho and Rosalyn first. The mud shelf was sticky underfoot, and Tycho breathed easier when he reached the shore knowing how badly the mud would have slowed him down.

As Dr Crow's boat backed away to head south to the Jewish graveyard they reached the narrow walkway leading to the huts. Stepping on to it, he felt it sway and heard it creak ominously.

"Tycho . . ."

He looked back.

Giulietta was staring in horror at the walkway.

No sides and half the boards missing, one of the uprights holding it up snapped in half, another cracked . . . He tried to see the walkway through her eyes and imagine himself without his sense of balance and holding a baby.

"Rosalyn, stay with Giulietta."

"Yes, master." Rosalyn's voice said what she thought of that.

Drawing his dagger, Tycho ran the walkway and spun into the first of the huts, the knife in front of him. It was empty, floorboards rotten and single room cleared of anything valuable. Lapping waves showed where planks had been taken to repair huts elsewhere. The next three huts were the same. Tycho was examining the last when he heard a scream, sudden and high.

Choked off instantly.

He went out through the corner of a hut, wood splintering behind him, in the corner of another, through the original hut and on to the walkway. He moved without thought for the water beneath him, walkway forgotten as he closed the gap to where Rosalyn swayed, his eyes already searching beyond her for Giulietta or Leo.

Tycho caught Rosalyn as she crumpled.

"Where is she?" His voice was brutal, his question pitiless. He saw her flinch at its cruelty before he noticed the cuts in her face, the blood dripping from tears in her dress. A thousand tiny slashes disfigured her legs and arms.

"What happened?"

"He shouted at me."

Tycho made her repeat that. His gaze sharp as he turned a slow circle in the drifting fog, hunting for traces of Giulietta's scent on the wind. All he could feel was an absence of where she should be. "Were she or Leo hurt?"

"No," said Rosalyn. "He didn't shout at them."

Her face was already healing. The slashes on her arms stopped
bleeding as he watched, sealing themselves and beginning to scab
over. Rosalyn had his ability to mend. Whatever his blood passed
to her this quality passed with it. Her mouth untwisted as a cut
stopped pulling it out of shape.

"Describe him," Tycho ordered.

"Tall," Rosalyn said. "Thin, dark-red robes. He had eyes like yours."

"Like mine?"

"Hard," she said. "Angry."

That wasn't how Tycho thought of himself.

He recognised her attacker all the same, Rosalyn's description
matching that of Duchess Alexa . . . Andronikos, the Byzantine
emperor's mage. The man their boat was meant to be drawing
to the southern edge of this set of islands. He must have sensed
them coming. Waited until Tycho was out of the way.

Stupid . . .

Actually, Rosalyn was right.

Tycho did feel angry. Bitterly, furiously, unnaturally angry. He
wondered if Andronikos had poisoned the fog around him. If
this flaring anger was a weakness rather the strength he first
thought.

"Tell me *exactly* what happened . . ."

As Rosalyn did he walked her towards a gate in a distant wall
and the looming shadow of a squat monastery. An orchard stood
beyond it, rows of heavily pruned trees clustered with apples.
Some clusters had rotted enough to fill the fog with cider sweetness. The smell masked the scent he needed to discover.

Rosalyn's story was brief.

She, Giulietta and Leo had been alone.

And then they weren't. She didn't see or hear the thin man
appear, didn't even know he was there until he called Giulietta's
name from behind them.

"What happened then?"

"She went to him."

"Just like that? *She went to him.*"

"When he said *turn*, she turned. When he said *walk*, she walked." Rosalyn shrugged. "She took Leo with her."

"And you?"

"I attacked." Rosalyn's eyes were bleak. "Much good it did me."

They found a ribbon from Giulietta's dress on the lowest branch of an apple tree, saw her footprints in mud that edged an irrigation ditch. She seemed to have walked in the muddiest bits she could find and Tycho hoped that was intentional. He tracked her muddy trail into the orchard and halfway through before returning his thoughts to what Rosalyn had said.

"He shouted at you?"

"It was like being hit by a hundred knives. Well, what I imagine that would be like. Only he threw a single word."

"What word?"

She turned away from him.

Tycho's demand she tell the truth only produced silence; followed by the lie that she thought it might have been foreign. He knew that was a lie.

She knew he knew.

That the man threw words made him think of the gold script on the black bullet Alexa gave him. Tycho was about to demand a proper answer when Rosalyn froze and he saw what she'd seen.

"Between those trees."

"Seen it." Not Andronikos, which would have been too simple. The mage was probably halfway to the boat by now.

Instead, a shadow loomed ahead of them.

Another appeared beside it, then another and another. Within seconds a dozen shifting shapes stood in their way. Gangly bodies, twisted claws and vicious fangs. The fog added a sheen to the hunting pack's silver-grey fur. As Tycho watched the figures stood taller, their transformations complete.

"My God," Rosalyn said.

She'd seen *krieghund* the night they slaughtered the Blade as they tried to capture Lady Giulietta. Tycho had heard of that night from Rosalyn, from Lord Atilo, from Giulietta herself . . . Their versions differed in all but the utter viciousness of the *krieghund*. The only Wolf Brother he'd fought was Leopold, and he'd won that fight with difficulty. Now he faced an entire pack.

58

There were days Giulietta felt too old for her seventeen years and others she felt far too young to deal with what was happening to her.

Tonight, typically, she felt both.

Young, and afraid of the man dragging her towards the gates to a graveyard. And so tired of the cruelty of the last few years she'd willingly let life go if she didn't have Leo. But she did, wrapped tight in her arms.

And Tycho was out there somewhere.

Obviously, it was *inappropriate* to love an ex-slave.

A word that had been whipped into her. Hating him obviously made far more sense anyway. He'd betrayed Leopold and he would betray her. If he couldn't even save Leopold how did she expect him to save her?

Of course, he swore he couldn't save Leopold, but he lied. *Except*, Giulietta told herself, *he hadn't. He'd admitted he could have done if only he'd known how.* She'd recognised enough self-disgust in his voice to know it was true. As well she might, because if anyone recognised self-disgust it was her. Lady Giulietta the Useless. Her life was a mess and she deserved what was happening to her. That was it: she deserved this and always had. Looking up, Giulietta realised the sneering contempt on her captor's face matched her own thoughts exactly. Their presence in her head was his doing.

"I *don't deserve* it," she said.

Andronikos shrugged, and she hated him more than ever.

"Nearly there."

"Where?" Giulietta asked, immediately regretting it.

She shouldn't be talking to him. She should keep her silence and plot to escape. But she couldn't find the willpower, so she put one foot in front of another, until the fog-swirled entrance to the cemetery was behind her and grave markers stood like a squat, half-born army around her.

They used a small wooden bridge over a muddy creek that someone would wall on both sides one day, creating new *fondamente*, sinking larch poles into the silt to built houses on top. Giulietta suspected she would not be around to see it.

"As promised," said Andronikos. "I've brought you a present."

The thin man flung her forward. Stumbling, Giulietta took two steps to try to regain her balance and tumbled to her knees. Only just keeping hold of Leo.

"Try not to break this one."

In front of her she saw a pair of legs; muscled and shapely, calves wrapped in sandal straps of purple leather. Reaching down, strong fingers gripped her hair and tipped her head backwards, forcing her to look up at their owner.

Prince Nikolaos looked like a god from one of the Greek stories. Flowing blond curls and broad shoulders. A black breastplate with a Medusa head picked out in gold. A strangely squat sword hung at his side. His cloak was short and purple. The bracelets pressing into her face were ornate and heavy.

"You told me she was ugly." The man spoke Latin, inflected with the Byzantine Empire's accent. "You shouldn't lie."

Perhaps he thought she wouldn't understand.

Andronikos replied in the same language. "And you should listen more carefully, your highness. I said, most reports said she was ugly. Thin, small-breasted, narrow-hipped, bad-tempered . . ."

"But that's how I like my women."

"Then I'm sure you'll do famously. Now if you'll excuse me I should make sure Alexa's pet and our furry friends are busy killing each other to order."

He slipped between the graves, vanishing more quickly than the fog should allow, leaving Giulietta knelt at the young prince's feet.

"Since you're down there . . ."

She looked up, not understanding.

"Oh, you little innocent. And with a baby, too." Nikolaos helped her to her feet, his hands cupping a breast before he let her go. As Giulietta stepped back, mouth opening in outrage, he grinned.

"I'm going to enjoy this. Prince Nikolaos, duke of Venice; and his beautiful, fiery wife."

Giulietta felt sick.

"Still," he said, "time for fun and games later. We'd better behave as Andronikos said. He can get cross and that's not pretty. Of course, I am a prince and he's only an adviser. Still, best be good." Something about Nikolaos reminded her of a darker and dangerous version of cousin Marco. As if reflections could somehow escape from the dark side of a mirror.

"How old are you?"

Prince Nikolaos raised his eyebrows. It looked like something he'd been practising.

"I'm seventeen," Giulietta added.

"You're trying to make friends with me?"

"I'm trying to find out how old you are." She wanted to discover all she could about this man. His flaws, his weaknesses, anything of use against him. Prince Nikolaos was looking disappointed.

"I don't want you to be friends with me. It's no fun if you're friends with me."

"Oh, don't worry," Giulietta snapped. "That's not likely to happen."

He grinned happily.

"Nineteen," he admitted after a while.

Giulietta ignored him. That made him grin even more.

After a while, the prince produced an ivory-handled dagger and began cleaning his nails, humming happily to himself. Nails clean, he produced a tortoiseshell comb from somewhere and carefully combed out his blond hair until it fell evenly around his shoulders. Giulietta imagined he was trying to anger her.

He was certainly succeeding.

The Millioni had been in power for five generations, marrying only other princely families, and they'd produced Marco. Byzantines nobles had been marrying, slaughtering and torturing one other's families for a thousand years. It was a wonder Nikolaos wasn't worse.

"What are you muttering?"

"That I'm probably a Republican."

He laughed like a delighted child. "This is going to be fun. So what shall we do while we wait for Andronikos . . . Any thoughts? If not, I have some ideas."

Hiding her shiver, Giulietta began thinking, hard.

Moonlight and fog made the *krieghund* look enormous, giving them ghostly silhouettes that loomed huge in the final run of apple trees that blocked the orchard's exit. Raising his head, one of them howled eerily.

His fur was the grey of Tycho's hair, his arms tortuously long and his fingers ended in vicious claws. He stank like a polecat, sour and urinous. His glare was on Tycho when he jerked his head, and a smaller *krieghund* at the end of the line dropped to a crouch, used his knuckles to start his run.

As he did, Rosalyn moved.

They hit obliquely, spinning past each other.

The *krieghund* halted, furious to find blood dripping from nail wounds in its chest. She whistled and snapped her fingers as if calling a pet. Their second clash was full-on. Body hit body in a thud that echoed through the trees.

For a split second the two gripped like lovers then spun away.

Blood dribbling down Rosalyn's chin matched a gash in the *krieghund*'s neck, which bled black on to its neck fur. Rosalyn was also injured. Her turn to face her attacker a fraction slower than before. Although both fighters were still moving at inhuman speeds.

Polecat stink behind you.

Tycho dropped to his knees and caught an attacking *krieghund* in the gut with his shoulder, somersaulting it to the dirt. His heel found its neck, cartilage ruptured and the change began. Within seconds a young man lay choking to death in front of him. Whipping the *WolfeSelle* from his back Tycho struck.

The blade sang.

When Tycho turned it was to see Rosalyn with a dead boy at her feet. In the trees the rest of the pack raced forward, all ideas of single combat forgotten. So Tycho ripped free his dagger and threw. A single step closed a gap between him and his target and he slapped the dagger's handle, slicing it through the *krieghund*'s heart. Spinning, he opened the throat of another.

"That was mine," Rosalyn shouted furiously.

Tycho hefted the *WolfeSelle*. "Plenty more."

"So why take mine?"

Ducking a *krieghund* blow, she jumped for the beast, opening her legs to straddle its neck and locking them tight before momentum spun her round. The noise of vertebrae breaking was shockingly loud.

Tycho expected her to attack another.

Instead she dropped to her feet and sunk her teeth into its neck, holding it upright as it began to change. The shuddering figure which hit the dirt was little more than a boy. From the trees came a howl so hideous Tycho looked back. A vast *krieghund* was racing forward, mouth open in an endless snarl.

Tycho's blow cut it in two.

For a second Tycho howled in exhilaration as the sword sang.

The edges of the world hardened and brightened. *This*, he thought, *is what I was born for.* The brutality of his Bjornvin childhood, the hunger and cold and the fight to stay alive made him good at this.

He could kill the way others breathed, instinctively, without thinking. Running his thumb along the blade, he carried *krieghund* blood to his mouth and felt his throat tighten. In his hand, the *WolfeSelle* shivered.

It rang with a note high beyond human hearing and Tycho felt strength flow into him. The strength of the red-bearded giant lying dead at his feet.

Swinging round, he went for the nearest enemy.

The *krieghund* backed away snarling, jaws wide and foul tongue flopping from its mouth. Its teeth were yellow, its breath stank in the night air. Tycho raised his sword as Atilo had taught him. So he could cut in either direction. Or strike down and cleave his enemy in two. Rosalyn guarded his back, facing away.

Tycho's breath rasped in his throat.

She was wounded and he was not. The longer he kept the Wolf Brothers from attacking the longer she had for her recent wounds to heal. But the battle had been as swift as it had been brutal. If he had time he could pick them off one after another. He didn't have time, however. Andronikos had Giulietta.

He needed to kill their leader.

Tycho studied the pack behaviour, watching as they circled. All of those remaining glanced, now and then, at a broad-shouldered beast which glared and circled without making its move, seemingly unnerved by Tycho's sword.

That would be Frederick. Killing him would scare the rest. If not enough to break their spirit then he'd settle for leaving them leaderless and kill the next most senior after that. "Take the blade for me."

"Tycho . . ."

"I know what I'm doing."

Rosalyn lifted her hands above her head, fumbled for the handle of the *WolfeSelle* and staggered slightly under its weight. She held it while the pack circled restlessly. Apparently unwilling to attack.

They watched snarling and sullen as Tycho took the red bullet and dropped it into the muzzle of Alexa's gun, hammering it down with a spike. A flick of the pan cover revealed priming.

The one he thought was Frederick backed away.

As Tycho lifted the pistol the beast retreated further. He checked the *krieghund* on either side, wondering if he was falling into a trap. But they stood as irresolute as their leader. The bullet or the *WolfeSelle* unnerved them.

Perhaps both.

"Shoot him," Rosalyn growled.

Torn between attacking or not, their leader flexed his brutal claws. Somewhere behind those burning eyes was a human soul fighting an animal on the edge of refusing to listen. Tycho knew what that was like. Though he doubted the animal knew what the bullet did, it sensed the bullet's power.

The *krieghund* stood there, a perfect target.

"This?" said Tycho, lifting the gun. "Or that?" He pointed to the sword Rosalyn held above them. "Which scares you the most?"

The beast glanced at the sword.

"Even though my gun is pointing at you?"

Kill the *krieghund* leader, find Giulietta and Andronikos, kill him, too. Add Nikolaos to the dead list. There had to be a quicker way to get her back. Tycho thought about that and wondered how stupid he was prepared to be. This stupid?

"I saved your life once. Remember? In the dining hall? I did that for Leopold's sake." Slowly, Tycho tipped out the priming powder, lowered the wheel lock's pan cover and dropped the gun to the dirt.

"You want Leopold's sword?"

The *krieghund* that was Frederick nodded.

Tycho could remember his own transformation to whatever he'd been that night on the *San Marco*. Not *krieghund*. He'd been beyond *krieghund*. Something darker and older. Something brooding and brutal. A shadow that lorded it over his soul watched and waited. It wanted blood but not this blood.

"Give me the *WolfeSelle* back," Tycho ordered.

Rosalyn did as she was told.

As they watched, the *krieghund* leader began to change. His silver fur sinking into his skin, his flesh ripping bloodily, suddenly visible bones splintering as glistening fragments slid against each other. For a split second, Prince Frederick's entire ribcage was visible as his chest snapped and remade itself.

Fingers shortened and nails receded. His jaw crushed under the weight of an unseen blow and his forehead lifted as his skull reshaped. He stood sex erect for one instant; skinless, teeth bared and howling in pain. Then a young man with narrower shoulders and Leopold's eyes sank to his knees.

Utterly defenceless.

Around him other *krieghund* began changing.

Whimpers of agony sounding from beasts that had howled in fury only a minute before. Some soiled themselves, others sobbed as the transformation reached its end. It was as brutal a misuse of flesh as anything a torturer could do. Unhooking his cloak, Tycho wrapped it round the shoulders of their leader.

"Hell," Tycho said, "is empty and the devils are here."

"Indeed," said Frederick. "Not all of us forbidden from Noah's ark had the manners to drown." He had his half-brother's rueful smile.

Sweeping Tycho's cloak around him to perform an elegant bow, Frederick said, "Frederick zum Bas Friedland. You have me at a disadvantage . . ." It took Rosalyn a moment to realise he meant he wanted her name.

"I'm Rosalyn."

"Delighted."

"You know my master."

"Lady Giulietta's friend . . .?"

"And Leopold's," Tycho said shortly. "The man who stood by your brother in his final battle. And lover to his widow."

Frederick's eyes widened. "You admit it?"

"We intend to marry. That will make me Leo's guardian. I'm sure you've been told Giulietta's son is Leopold's heir in all things." Yes, he thought that would hit home. Frederick didn't know.

"*He's* krieghund?"

"Yes. Leopold's acknowledged son. Sworn before King Janus and Prior Ignatius in front of a church full of Crucifer knights. The king gave his permission. The Prior gave his blessing."

"Then the sword is Leo's."

"Giulietta asked me to look after it. The weapon reminds her too much of the man she lost." That wasn't strictly true but it would do. "She loved your brother in a way she'll never love another man."

That was true, and he would have to live with it.

Taking the sword from Rosalyn, Tycho rested the blade across his forearm and offered the handle to Leopold's brother.

"You mean it?"

"Until Leo is old enough to wield it."

"I swear it," Frederick said. "I will give him the sword at sixteen. When he comes of age. I swear this on my soul."

Both men knew Frederick was pinning himself down. Just as

both knew that in surrendering the Wolf Soul Tycho had given Frederick undisputed leadership of all *krieghund* for fifteen years.

Quickly, with the Wolf Brothers drawing closer as they realised they were allowed to listen, Tycho unfolded his problem.

"Andronikos has Leo?"

"And his mother."

"I doubt he knows what he has."

"I doubt he knows what he has in either of them," said Tycho, and Prince Frederick looked at him.

"You love her?"

"From the first moment we met."

"Leopold wrote saying you were dangerous. I said I'd heard you looked like a girl. He replied only a fool would underestimate you." Frederick stared pointedly at his enemy's braided hair and black silk doublet, then looked at the dead in the dirt. "I'm not a fool. Nor was my half-brother."

"You'll fight?"

"*He who dies this night is quit the next.*"

For a moment, he could have been Leopold, his bravado as big as his heart. Snapping out an order, Frederick began to change and those around him did the same. Their transformation so swift, hard and brutal that even Rosalyn, eyes still dark with fury at Lady Eleanor's death, looked away.

59

The islands forming Giudecca were not quite part of central Venice, and the people who lived there liked it that way. As well as fishing huts, it had monasteries, nunneries, warehouses and whorehouses, a cluster of squares and several small farms. Like everywhere in Venice it had churches.

Rich *cittadini* owned cottages here. Red-tiled houses fringed with tiny skirts of carefully tended land. The patriarch kept a sheep garden. Unlike central Venice, from which it was separated by a wide sound, Giudecca had fields and orchards, fir trees and graveyards.

Its name came either from the Jews who lived there, the *Giudei*, or from *Giudicati*, nobles too important to execute and too dangerous not to exile. The islanders considered themselves *giudecchini* first and Venetians second; many of the older ones refused to consider themselves Venetian at all.

The Schiavoni, Jews and Greeks – being varieties of heathen – had graveyards on Giudecca's southern edge. Out of sight of the main city and far enough away for their foreignness not to offend. It was towards these that the remaining *krieghund* war pack flowed with such certainty that Tycho let them run.

They raced the edge of darkness with the threatened promise of dawn on one side and the safety of black-hearted night on the other. Tycho ran with them, aware that he too occupied the shifting boundary between human and not.

The *WolfeSelle* looked grotesque slung across Frederick's back, and he wondered if the prince could even wield it in his *krieghund* form. Maybe he carried it as a totem or a battle honour. Tycho would ask some other time.

Like him, like Rosalyn, the war pack moved through the fog inhumanly fast, shadows and blurs to anyone watching. Not that there was anyone watching. People were hiding in their houses behind locked doors, shutters bolted and lights out, listening to cannon fire roar like distant thunder.

Leaves twisted in the wind as the *krieghund* crossed another orchard, entered a tiny square and flowed around the squat stump of its wellhead before filling narrow streets that became mud lanes and fields shortly after. In a handful of seconds, they reached and half crossed the biggest island, swept round the walls of a farmhouse and down a slight slope towards the gates of a fog-shrouded graveyard. The southern shore of Giudecca was somewhere beyond.

The stink of resin rose from surrounding pines, the smell of urine strong from the fermenting needles crackling under their feet. The mist flowed around them like smoke. It concealed what was up ahead. And hid them in their turn.

"Let the *krieghund* attack first . . ."

Rosalyn nodded.

The Wolf Brothers were Sigismund's shock troops and shock troops were disposable. Foot soldiers and shock troops always were. The second might be trained and the first not but both existed to do one thing: die. To that list of the disposable could be added slaves.

They were the first to bear any attack during Tycho's childhood. He'd seen the man he thought his father driven beyond the palisade, armed with a crude sword and left to die in his own time. Even if a slave turned and ran for Bjornvin's locked gates, chasing and killing him would tire the Skaelingar, making the red-painted savages less able to face warriors who fought later with real weapons.

Ahead of them fog swirled and Rosalyn stumbled.

She swung at Tycho blindly when he grabbed her before she could fall; swung at him, missed and cursed him by the wrong name as he dragged her on. Her face was wretched, her words passing through fury into despair. Josh had been her pimp, her protector, her lover . . . Tycho wasn't quite sure what he'd been.

"*Run*," Tycho demanded.

Nursing her wrists as if they'd been bruised, Rosalyn's fingers found Eleanor's bracelet, wretchedness leaving her face.

"*Demons*," she said shakily.

The fog in front of Tycho grew solid.

It formed into the shape of Bjornvin's gates. A row of sharpened stakes framed by fat gateposts that became more solid as he looked, the wooden palisades on either side wisping away to mist. As he stared, the gates swung open.

He ran, but they remained out of reach.

In the gap, a Skaelingar chief gripped the arm of a naked girl, his fingers digging into her flesh. The chief yanked back her head and cut.

Tycho howled.

Afrior, his half-sister, non-sister, first love . . .

Whatever she was, Afrior was dead. The girl he'd first loved. The only person he thought he'd ever love. Down in the dirt of Bjornvin's gates. Shuddering and gasping and bleeding out fourteen years of brutal life.

"*Tycho* . . ."

His head snapped round.

"In my head, too. Bad memories."

Rosalyn vomited without breaking her stride and spat to one

side. Untroubled by visions, Frederick shot Tycho a wolfish grin. And through the fading fog of Bjornvin's gate Tycho saw the real world intrude.

A shield wall of Byzantine soldiers.

Menavlatoi, the empire's elite infantry. Drawn up in front of a bridge, each Byzantine soldier held a seven-foot spear topped by a fifteen-inch blade. The points of their spears were raised to catch leaping *krieghund*, the shafts dug securely into the pine-needle-strewn dirt behind them.

Frederick's war pack could face the *menavlatoi* and their spears, or scramble down one bank, wade a small creek and climb another, leaving themselves vulnerable to side attack. "Follow me," Tycho told Rosalyn.

"You said . . ."

Yeah. Let the krieghund *go first.*

"I've changed my mind." As a hard-faced *menavlatoi* steadied his spear, confident in his superiority, Tycho gripped the spear below its blade, ground the shaft even harder into the dirt and vaulted halfway over the shield wall, releasing the spear to drop behind its owner. He broke the Byzantine soldier's neck before he could defend himself.

Two soldiers away Rosalyn copied him.

An upward jab of Tycho's dagger caught the soldier between them just behind his chinstrap, the blade skewering the man's soft palate to enter his brain. Whipping the blade free, Tycho let him drop, and the *krieghund* swept through the suddenly broken wall, killing as they hit.

Had they kept going they could have taken the bridge.

But the *krieghund* fought singly, ferociously, without any obvious plan until a snarl from Frederick made them fall back to regroup for another attack. The Byzantines used the time to remake their shield wall.

It was only then that Tycho realised how terrified Rosalyn must have been the night she watched Leopold's war pack break the Blade. Giulietta even more so. All those circling beasts. All those *assassini* dying to keep her alive.

"This time we wait," Tycho said.

Rosalyn nodded.

As a Byzantine soldier jabbed his spear at a *krieghund* the beast caught it, yanked hard and tumbled a *menavlatoi* from the line. Screaming meat became silence. Another *krieghund* took a spear through the shoulder, broke the spear's shaft and ripped out his enemy's throat with vicious claws. It was cruel and would quickly have become final if a robed figure hadn't abandoned the fir trees on the far side of the bridge and ordered the *menavlatoi* to stand aside.

His voice could be heard by all.

Although it was quieter than the snarls of the *krieghund* and a dying spearman's screams, it carried perfectly. Two people walked behind the man. A smirking blond youth Tycho imagined was Nikolaos, and Lady Giulietta, her wrist firmly in Nikolaos's grip. The princeling glanced at the baby in her arms. Whatever he said made Giulietta pale.

Andronikos stared at the ground.

A second later, he raised his gaze to the sky.

"Down," Tycho said.

When Rosalyn didn't move he kicked her feet from under her, rolled himself on top of her, and, holding her tight, rolled for a newly dug ditch on the far side of a gravel path. Something to be grateful for.

"What . . .?"

"Andronikos."

The ditch hid them from the words tumbling from Andronikos's mouth. Although Tycho saw their impact when a charging *krieghund* stumbled a dozen paces backwards, caught his heel on a root and fell. Fur flowed to reveal skin, bones twisted, the wolf mask receded, revealing the face of a boy of Tycho's age. His flesh was ripped, his eyes ruined, as if slashed by splintered glass.

"Stay down," Tycho told him.

Sliding his dagger from its sheath, Tycho crawled to where the boy gasped and begged for help in a language Tycho didn't understand. His dagger took the boy through his ribs, stilling his heart. Breath was leaving his body as Tycho closed his eyes. The boy looked as if he'd been tortured.

"Say a prayer," Tycho ordered Rosalyn.

She stared at him, not understanding.

"I don't know any. You say a prayer while I load this."

She said the one even whores and street children knew. The one they had reason more than anyone else to hope true. A prayer that didn't even belong to her people. And while Tycho listened to Rosalyn say the paternoster and wondered if she believed it, he tapped out the bullet he'd loaded earlier, letting the silk-wrapped charge remain.

Then he wrapped the scarlet bullet in a scrap of leather and tapped it into place. Filling the pan, he closed the lid and lowered the flint. He would get one shot. The bullet would harm Andronikos wherever it hit, but an injured Andronikos might prove more dangerous than an uninjured one.

Alexa had been clear about that.

"Wait," said Tycho, when Rosalyn tried to look over the edge.

The mage spoke again and animal shrieks filled the night air. If they were animal, it was because his words reduced the already re-human *krieghund* to that state. Climbing to his knees, Tycho saw that all of Frederick's war pack were now human. Some were dead, others dying. Frederick and a companion, badly wounded from the look of it, hugged the dirt behind a rotting stump.

The prince's ribs were lacerated and his face ripped along one cheek. His body looked as if scourged by thorns. He half raised the *WolfeSelle* for a second, offering it to Tycho, and then lowered it again. He lacked the strength to do more.

Tycho lifted his gun in reply.

On the bridge itself stood Lady Giulietta with Leo in her arms.

Prince Nikolaos stood beside her staring in Tycho's direction. He shouted something to his tutor. Andronikos nodded. At his snapped command the remaining *menavlatoi* – less than a quarter of his original force – headed for where Tycho crouched.

Three in all. Without Andronikos there would be none. One look at the men's faces told Tycho they knew this. That if they feared attacking him, they feared Andronikos more. Rising, Tycho put his dagger into the throat of the nearest. "Two left . . . I need you to protect Giulietta."

Rosalyn glared at him.

"I know you hate her."

She didn't bother to deny it. "What do you want me to do?"

"Die if necessary."

"For her?" Rosalyn's mouth twisted.

"Do it for me then."

"I'm not sure people like us can die." Rosalyn tried to smile but her eyes were bleak and he knew that, whether or not she believed the words of the paternoster were true, she doubted they applied to people like her, if she was *people*, which she also doubted. The pain in her eyes was almost physical.

"See that man over there?"

She glanced at Prince Nikolaos.

"He sent the archer who murdered Eleanor."

"You swear it?"

"On my soul." That was a form of words used by people who believed them. Until he'd come to Venice Tycho hadn't even heard of souls. He doubted anyone from Bjornvin had them.

60

For Eleanor . . .

Rosalyn would kill him for Eleanor. The scar under her breast was a simple stab wound. All that blow did was take her life. The prince's archer destroyed what made her heart beat; gave her ice for a heart where Eleanor should be.

"*Rosalyn . . .*"

Tycho obviously knew her other thought.

War was unpredictable, brutal. People died in battle all the time. If Lady Giulietta was killed in the next few seconds would Rosalyn really be to blame?

She watched Tycho pull back the cobra-headed hammer on his wheel lock and steel himself to face the thin man who stood so confidently in front of the bridge.

"On my count of three," Tycho said.

Always three. Something Atilo had taught him.

When Tycho began to back away, using the ditch for cover, Rosalyn understood what was intended. He would distract Andronikos to let her slip past him to the Byzantine prince waiting beyond.

She nodded and he began his count.

"Two . . ."

"Three."

Andronikos glanced between Tycho and her as they stood, noticed Tycho's strange weapon and hesitated. All the time she needed to reach a *menavlatoi*, kill him in passing, avoid Andronikos and head for the princeling. Nikolaos let go Giulietta's arm to scrabble for his sword.

"Run," Rosalyn howled at her. Only a fool wouldn't run.

But Lady Giulietta simply stood here, staring towards Tycho and for a second Rosalyn felt tempted to kill her anyway. And then she stopped caring about Giulietta, banished Andronikos from her mind and hit Prince Nikolaos full-on, knocking him backwards on to the bridge.

The princeling swore, bared his teeth and looked down.

Suddenly he was grinning as if seeing the funniest thing in his life. Following his gaze Rosalyn saw what amused him and recognised the coldness in her gut. His sword pierced her, protruding at the back. Black blood oozed from the wound.

"What a silly little bitch."

She recognised in his tone the contempt of all those who never bothered to understand how hard it was for people like her to live on the streets. How staying even half human as a street girl was a victory in itself. Still grinning, he began to twist his blade. And agony lit the sky scarlet around her.

"No," she said. "You don't."

His eyes widened as she gripped his wrist, returning the sword to its original position.

"You shouldn't have killed Eleanor."

"Not me. Now, if you'd said Theodora . . . You wouldn't believe how cross her father was about that."

"Enough."

Keeping her grip on his wrist, Rosalyn reached for his black and gold breastplate to drag him close, feeling his blade push through her. Then she walked him backwards so she no longer stood over water.

"Look away," she ordered Giulietta.

Sinking her teeth into his neck, Rosalyn gulped mouthfuls of vile memories, because she needed his strength to heal and fight, until their squalor appalled her so horridly she eased herself off the blade and let his body drop.

"Now we're all even," Rosalyn told him. "You're dead. And Tycho's woman has been repaid for taking me to Alta Mofacon."

"Thank you," Giulietta said unsteadily.

"I don't want your thanks."

"You didn't have to save me."

"No." Rosalyn's voice caught. "I could have killed you instead."

The last of the spearmen must be dead. The proof was that Tycho held all of Andronikos's attention; and that gave Rosalyn time to back Giulietta against a fir tree and reach out to grip her face with unforgiving fingers.

"Your child would have died within a month."

"*What?*"

Rosalyn made herself let go.

"He intended to kill it. You wouldn't have been that lucky. He planned to keep you locked away while you produced a brat for him. If you were lucky he might have killed you after that."

Giulietta vomited.

At which of that night's particular horrors Rosalyn didn't much care.

61

Tycho stood armed with a spear in his left hand, and Alexa's handgun primed and loaded hanging on its lanyard from his shoulder. The mage had backed himself to the middle of the bridge. At first Tycho had thought it retreat. Now he realised Andronikos wanted to put himself above water.

"So. Alexa's pet."

The mage must know Giulietta vomiting meant something had happened behind him. The stolen spear in Tycho's hand prevented him from turning to discover what. So long as Tycho held it ready to hurl he had the man's attention.

Andronikos needed to gather focus.

But the moment he stilled to draw strength from the water lapping beneath him, Tycho would throw. Each knew this and tried to outwait the other. *I should be closer*, Tycho realised. The handgun was untested and he didn't trust himself to hit Andronikos's heart from this distance.

"Venice chooses Sigismund, then?"

Tycho looked at him.

"At least I assume it does. Since you're protecting that." Andronikos jerked his chin contemptuously towards where

Frederick and his one remaining follower hid behind a rotten tree stump. "Strange. Given his brother destroyed the Blade."

"I have orders to kill him."

"And you dare disobey?" Andronikos asked.

"I usually disobey Alexa's orders."

"Believe me, you wouldn't dare disobey mine."

"I wouldn't take yours in the first place."

The mage's eyes narrowed and Tycho knew the conversation was at an end. He imagined it had served only to let Andronikos see if he could be swayed.

Tycho threw the spear so hard an ordinary man would have said it vanished. And with it thrown he began to follow, only for Andronikos to brush the spear aside. Tycho's boots cut scars in dead pine needles as he skidded to a halt. And discovered he'd given Andronikos the time he needed.

Lowering his gaze from the sky, the mage stared at the creek for a split second and raised his eyes. Smiling when he saw Tycho realise what was about to happen. The word Andronikos shouted was *SLAVE*.

Everything it contained hit Tycho.

The night he almost died in a snowdrift. The whippings and worse. Days chained by Bjornvin's main gate, naked and wearing a spiked collar.

Glass-sharp memories blasted Tycho's body and the shock of their pain locked his muscles tight, freezing the scream that tried to force its way from his mouth. Blood oozed from a hundred cuts and for a second he staggered under the weight of all the things about that time he'd tried to forget.

Blood slowed and his cuts began to heal.

You can stand this, he told himself. But Andronikos had already drawn power. He was simply waiting until he had his victim's attention. There was no smile this time. The alchemist's face was inscrutable. His silhouette in the almost-cleared fog as thin and black as the firs behind him. He'd thrown whole sentences at the *krieghund*. Howled Germanic phrases that left them blinded and staggering.

He barely raised his voice for the next word.

"*Bjornvin.*"

And the nightmare in the mist filled Tycho's head.

He whimpered as fresh wounds opened across his chest and flesh showed glistening and moist through the silk doublet that was meant to hide his sins, its cloth as ripped by the memory as his body. He tried and failed to raise the pistol.

So much guilt at what he'd done.

Once Bjornvin fell there were no Vikings in Vineland, only Skaelingar with their oil and ochre bodies and their bows and stone knives. Thorns now grew where the settlement stood. He had delivered the last Viking town to its enemy. As the wave of guilt receded so his wounds knitted, skin closing over veins and sinews.

Somewhere Giulietta was shouting.

Tycho caught a flash of black as Rosalyn launched herself at the mage and saw her hurled back to lie in a bloody heap. When she tried to rise, the man turned to her. "No," Tycho croaked. "Your fight is with me."

Andronikos laughed.

And Tycho's gut knotted in anger.

Night had given way to the dark-thread moment.

The precursor tints that heralded daylight threatened the horizon. Tycho saw what Giulietta could not. A thousand subtle shades of light in what she saw as darkness. All Andronikos had to do was hold him here.

Sunlight would race from the sandbanks at the lagoon's mouth, across the beaten lead waters of the lagoon to where he stood, and Tycho would die without having saved Giulietta. To save the woman he loved he would have to become what he became on the deck of the *San Marco*.

Then she would see him for what he really was.

Focusing on the man in front of him, Tycho realised Andronikos was waiting for Tycho's full attention, that arrogance was unexpected, a weakness.

Tycho knew the next word before it was whispered.

Memories of Afrior began ripping his flesh apart like a thousand glass knives, cutting him to the bone. Battered, abused, betrayed. Her eyes on his as the Skaelingar chief drew his stone knife across her throat. Afrior's body, the body he'd betrayed his family for, flopping in the dirt as she bled out.

Hell had entered Bjornvin.

"*Tycho . . .*"

Hearing Giulietta's scream, he found himself several paces behind where he should be standing. Blood oozed from wounds that in others would be gushing blood. His left arm was broken, splintered bone jutting from his wrist. Loops of entrail showed through a hole in his stomach.

His power to heal would keep him alive. It was his ability to withstand the pain Tycho doubted.

"Sweet Gods," he whispered. "Help me."

Only silence answered. There had only ever been silence for him. Looking up, he saw Andronikos, face triumphant. This time the mage merely mouthed, *She was your sister.*

Skin peeled from Tycho's face as he fought to reply. He felt flesh shred away until only his skull remained. He would happily embrace death if only it could find him. "She was *never* my sister," he said between breaking teeth. "I was not *them*. They were not *me*. I was *Fallen*. I was always *Fallen*."

Time's flow stuttered, dammed upstream.

Until only Tycho and Andronikos were awake. The others a tableau in the earliest of very early morning light. It stuttered again and Tycho saw shock etched on Andronikos's face as he failed to fight whatever magic entangled him.

"Alexa?" Tycho asked.

The voice snorted.

"You came to my city," the *genius loci* said. "Now I come to you."

Venice's mouth found his in a carrion kiss.

His gut hurt, his throat was sour. Tycho wasn't sure what had happened but he'd always suspected the island city of Venice was alive. It was too strange, too other not to be inhabited by an ancient spirit of place. Although the very adult version of A'rial that rose to greet him was older than he imagined.

Far older than history claimed.

Venice felt strange because it was strange.

A maze of death and sex, blood, love and hate. Bound by water that locked in ghosts and history until every street and alley, every canal and basin piled thick with overlaying memories from the city's earlier inhabitants. The words A'rial left him with were raw in his mind. *I was young when you were.*

"Me?" he'd asked.

Your kind. The originals.

And Tycho remembered Leopold's words the night Tycho defeated him, and he gave Giulietta Leopold's life because he didn't know how to refuse her, condemning himself to torture as a galley slave. *You're meant to be dead.*

"I'm alive," he'd said then.

As he'd said it tonight. Unseen hands had clapped. Perhaps mockingly, perhaps in real admiration. "Become yourself," the city said.

"I am myself."

"Then become better . . ."

As time began its flow and A'rial's carrion presence sank through the water and mud, pilings and gravel to wherever Venice's mother spirit usually slept, Tycho watched the world return to something approaching normal, or as normal as it would ever be in this strangest of cities.

He saw Andronikos blink.

Watched him turn to where Giulietta crouched, Leo in her arms, Rosalyn standing guard over both. He saw the mage's gaze flick to Prince Frederick and the wounded Wolf Brother crouching behind their rotten stump.

The man was wondering what had changed.

Only what had changed was standing in front of him.

Andronikos looked at Tycho and seemed surprised to find him standing. This, Tycho realised, was a war of words as much as of strength. What you love makes you stronger than the worst damage inflicted by what you fear.

He knew that now.

He had Alexa's pistol on its lanyard, Frederick still gripped the *WolfeSelle*, but the weapon Tycho needed was already on his tongue. He knew suddenly what he needed to do. Putting his hand to the tattered ribbon circling his wrist . . .

Tycho spoke a word of his own.

"*Giulietta.*"

The alchemist grinned.

He spread his hands to show that he was unhurt, that Tycho's words had done nothing to harm him, and was about to raise his gaze to the pre-dawn sky to draw power when his grin faded.

And Tycho felt the word consume him.

His mouth opened in a silent scream as flames flowed up his body, and snapped back having varnished him in light. Shadows flung themselves in all directions, streaming from trees and grave markers in wide circles around him. It was not the change he expected. Inside his chest he could feel a heart.

Burning white like light in the darkness.

Flame pumped through his veins, savage wings of fire flared from his shoulders to shrivel needles on the nearest pine trees. He could smell resin burning as he raised Alexa's pistol, flipped open the pan cover and exposed the primer. Tycho didn't even bother with the trigger, simply touched his thumb to the primer powder and watched it flare.

Too late Andronikos strained for a word, his counter-attack lost in the shock of watching Tycho transform. As the bullet entered his heart scarlet and gold script licked across the mage's skin. The body that crumpled to the ground was that of an old man, nothing more.

Having inspected the body, Tycho knelt to unclip the mage's cloak and crossed the bridge to where Rosalyn stood, draping the cloak around her as protection against the coming sun. "Alexa's soldiers will be here shortly."

Giulietta nodded. Her face slightly awed.

"This isn't me," Tycho said. "The me you can ignore will be back soon."

She wanted to say she could ignore this version of him, too, but they both knew that was untrue. She could no more ignore it than he could. The monstrous creature on the *San Marco* had not been what he would become. Simply halfway to whatever he had been until a moment ago.

"Leo is safe?"

Giulietta nodded.

"Good," he said. "Take Leo to the first house you find. Tell them you need shelter until soldiers arrive. Wait there."

"Yes, master." Her voice was more mocking than Rosalyn would ever dare. She walked away without looking back.

Tycho grinned.

"Don't let Lady Giulietta see me like this," Prince Frederick begged.

In her hand, Rosalyn held the cloak Nikolaos had worn in life. After helping the *krieghund* princeling to his feet, she wrapped it carefully around his bruised and naked body. "Why not?"

"She'll never want to marry me."

"She's not going to marry you," Rosalyn said. "She's going to marry him." A jerk of her head indicated Tycho. "And she's gone anyway. If I were you I'd go home."

"My father . . ."

"Will be impressed," said Tycho, "that you return with the Wolf Soul. You can also point out that you are alive while a competing Byzantine prince and a Byzantine mage are dead. Leo is your brother's heir. The odds are on your father's side. He can afford to wait."

Prince Frederick nodded slowly.

Day was coming and the graveyard around Tycho had blurred to a harsh whiteness that grew brighter until he had to squint to see anything and even that was agony. Rosalyn at his side was hiding her face in her hands.

"Your eyes . . ." Prince Frederick said.

"They hurt."

"Huge," the prince agreed.

The clarity Tycho's sight brought to the darkest night was torture in any light this close to dawn. His head ached and he felt a nausea that made him want to hide. The last vestiges of the being he became had withered, without the flamboyant pain changing back usually brought.

Tycho was simply himself again.

"I need your help."

"You have it," Frederick said. "What do I do?"

"There's a half-dug grave over the rise," Tycho said. "Cover us with earth and pine needles and tell no one. Say we simply vanished. Do it swiftly."

62

A week had passed since the bombardment of Venice's lagoon and the sun was settling over the western horizon when the Byzantine Empire's commander took his leave of the Ten. The meeting had been formal, scrupulously polite.

At the Council's orders, the bodies of Lord Andronikos and Emperor John V Palaiologos's youngest son had been returned. So they could be sent to their homeland for burial as was proper.

Prince Alonzo had objected publicly.

Until, in private, Duchess Alexa pointed out the obvious. What looked like kindness was really a warning. *See*, it said, *attack us and you get your greatest mage and an imperial prince back in a barrel, gutted and steeped in brandy for the journey.*

Alonzo was quiet after that.

He would be quieter still after tomorrow's conversation, which would be very private indeed. It was the one where Alexa told him what Giulietta had told her. That Tycho had originally been shipped to Venice to kill her and, possibly, Marco and Giulietta herself. Seljuk hunters might have captured him, and Mamluk mages prepared him, but it was Alonzo who funded the scheme.

He would bluster that she had no proof. And she would show

him an order, undated and signed in one of Marco's increasingly common moments of clarity, ordering Alonzo's arrest and trial for treason. Alexa hoped her brother-in-law would be grateful for the exile she offered. Not least because any trial for treason would reopen the investigation into the explosion at San Lazar, the attempt to poison Marco and the attack on Giulietta's life.

The penalty for the poisoning would be death.

But first she had the problem of Giulietta. Who had turned up in the early morning a week before, silent and filthy, clutching Leo and firmly refusing to say what had happened on Giudecca the night before.

She slept in her new room at Ca' Ducale, and had left the palace only once for the burial of Lady Eleanor. And she spent most of that watching the basilica doors as if waiting for someone to join her. Sir Tycho, probably. Unless she looked for the ragged girl who became Eleanor's friend.

Neither one came.

So now Lady Giulietta glided through Ca' Ducale's marble corridors as silent as a ghost, her quiet politeness to guard and servants as unnerving as her arrogance had ever been. She ate little, slept less.

The dragonet was currently out looking for Sir Tycho, Alexa's bat flew over the streets in all directions every night. Orders for information had been issued to spies. Rewards had discreetly been offered.

Prince Frederick had known something, Alexa was sure of that. He came in person to thank her for returning the bodies of his men. A quiet, subdued young man, shocked by the loss of his friends and whatever else happened. He'd asked permission to say farewell to her niece. Giulietta had refused to see him.

"My lady . . ." A maid stood in the doorway.

"What?"

"News of Sir Tycho."

Putting down her cup, Alexa stood. It was hard to know which would be worse. The boy alive or dead; still in Venice or in someone else's employ. She had, she hated to admit, become fond of him in her way.

And then there was Marco.

Her son always asked, specifically and clearly, where Tycho was, if he was all right, whether he was happy. *My grievous angel* her son called him.

"Send the messenger in."

A ragged-looking fisherman entered, instantly shocked to find himself in the presence of the Mongol duchess. After a stammering start he found his voice. His wife's family lived on Giudecca; the Nicoletto shrugged as if to say he liked her for all that. A baby was due soon so she'd returned to her mother.

One night last week he'd been offered money by a grey-haired young man to sail him and a ragged girl direct from Giudecca to Dalmatia. The girl had remained there and the young man had returned.

The fisherman hadn't realised . . . If he had . . .

"When did you return?"

"An hour ago, my lady."

"And where is this man now?"

"He told me he was going to change. That he had a girl to see. He thanked me for making the trip to Dalmatia and paid me."

"What did he pay you?"

The Nicoletto hesitated. "Twice what he offered."

"And what was odd about the way he wanted your boat prepared?" At her question, the fisherman stared at Alexa and his eyes widened as he obviously decided that everything he'd heard about the duchess being a witch was true. She smiled sourly. "Well?"

"I had to fill my boat with earth."

Alexa rang a small glass bell and told a servant to give the fisherman five silver grosso, take him to the kitchens and make sure he was well fed, then find him a clean blanket for his wife. The baby would need it in the winter to come.

The man left, stammering his gratitude.

Fear and favour, and an uncertainty as to which would be found – Alexa had built her reputation on that mix. A second later, her study door burst open and Giulietta was there. Her black dress replaced by crimson velvet and her hair up as befitted a woman once married, but with so many flaming strands escaping in all directions it seemed her hair at least was uncertain of her exact status.

"Someone said Tycho was here."

"He landed an hour ago."

"Then why isn't he here?"

"*Giulietta* . . ."

"He should be here." She looked around, as if expecting to find him hiding in the study somewhere.

"He went home to change."

"Then he's on his way . . ."

You don't know that, Alexa thought; but Giulietta obviously thought she did, because she abandoned the doorway and hurried along the upper colonnade oblivious to guards coming to attention around her.

There was a commotion in the Cortile del Palazzo, and a young man in black pushed his way through a crowd of outraged senators in scarlet robes leaving an evening meeting of the Greater Council.

His wolf-grey hair shone in the light of torches set around the courtyard. Ignoring the senators' outrage, he scanned the upper corridor already knowing where to look. His eyes found the person he wanted and he waved.

Marble stairs existed to allow a stately progress from the upper galleries to the courtyard floor for the duke and his retinue. The finest architects in Italy had drawn up the plans between them.

At no little argument on their part, and no little expense on the part of the late duke.

Duchess Alexa – Mongol princess and widow of that duke – watched her niece, the daughter of a Millioni princess and a Byzantine prince, launch herself from the top of the stairs and run their entire length into the arms of the young man below, who swept her off her feet and swung her round like a child.

Alexa could hear Giulietta's laughter from where she watched, hear her laughter and see the senators' shock. Then the whole departing Senate and the servants and guards in the courtyard and the open corridors saw the young man wrap his fingers into Giulietta's hair and raise her face so they could kiss.

And every one of them saw Alexa's niece throw her arms around his neck as if clinging on for dear life.

Moving away from the window, Alexa sighed.

Epilogue

"The silver one makes me fall in love with you and the gold one makes you fall in love with me?" Grinning, Giulietta folded Tycho's hand around the two pills in his palm and kissed his fingers.

"Save them," she said.

"For what?"

"For when I fall out of love with you . . . That was a joke," she added, seeing his expression. "I don't need them. I never will."

Slipping Dr Crow's final creations back into a leather pouch, Tycho dropped it on the pile of clothes beside her bed. His clothes, discarded in a hurry.

"Do you think my aunt knows you're here?"

"The whole palace knows."

Giulietta blushed sweetly in the candlelight. Their love-making had been noisy and frantic and then noisy and slow. She couldn't help it. He did things she hadn't imagined possible.

"By tomorrow," Tycho said, "the whole city will know. And then the world beyond. Does that matter to you?"

"This is Venice," she said. "The world will expect no less."

Tycho lost his grin at her next comment. "You realise," Giulietta said, "Aunt Alexa intends to offer you the Blade?"

"I failed my apprenticeship."

"You killed Iacopo, who was the previous master. You led the *krieghund* into a trap on Giudecca that damaged them as badly as they damaged us the year before. You sent Frederick home with his tail between his legs . . ."

Giulietta put a finger to his lips to still his protest, yelping when he bit it. "That's how Aunt Alexa sees thing. You'd be wise to leave her thinking that."

"She doesn't know about giving Frederick the *WolfeSelle*?"

"The what . . .? She plans to make you a baron. Give you Atilo's house to go with your own. Both of which the Ten will confirm. I swear she'd make you a member of the Ten if you weren't so young."

"I haven't agreed to be Blade."

"You will."

When the candle burnt out, they lay in the darkness, covered by a single sheet that apparently left her chilly. Because she huddled closer and Tycho wrapped one arm around her to hold her tight.

"Can I ask something?" Giulietta said.

Tycho nodded, expecting a question about being Blade, or killing Andronikos. Neither he nor Giulietta had yet talked about what he became that night. He was uncertain what she had seen. How what had happened to him looked from the outside.

"Did you know about Rosalyn's friendship with Eleanor?"

"No. Did you?"

Giulietta shook her head.

"Is that why Rosalyn left?"

"I imagine so . . ." Tycho sucked his teeth, cross with himself for not telling the whole truth. "At least in part. Also, Venice holds bad memories. I gave her money. She has her . . . abilities. I imagine we'll hear of her one day."

"Rosalyn is in love with you."

Tycho froze. The girl in his arms seemed untroubled by what she'd just said. With Giulietta you could never be sure.

"I doubt it."

Smiling, Giulietta kissed his brow. "A good man but oft-times a fool. Of course she's in love with you. Having been friends with Eleanor doesn't mean she can't be in love with you as well . . ." Giulietta sighed.

"I wasn't in love with her."

"That's why she left. No Eleanor and no you. My mother had estates in Carpathia. Towns and villages I've never seen."

"I'm not sure . . ."

"They won't come from me," Giulietta said firmly. "They'll come from Alexa, signed by Marco. A reward for her services to Venice. You understand I'm serious? About marrying you and making Venice a republic again?"

Tycho smiled.

Acknowledgements

There's a misbegotten, misplaced belief that cats are independent creatures that might deign to eat your food and sleep in your bed but will vanish come morning, prefer to walk alone and do not need and can barely tolerate your company. When, in fact, they're much like other pets but with better PR. Working writers are much the same. We survive because there's a support network of lovers and friends, agents and publishing people ready to catch us when we get trapped up trees of our own making or walk out on branches too thin to take our weight.

My thanks go to them.

extras

www.orbitbooks.net

about the author

Jon Courtenay Grimwood was born in Malta and christened in the upturned bell of a ship. He grew up in the Far East, Britain and Scandinavia. For five years he wrote a monthly review column for the *Guardian*. He has also written for *The Times*, the *Telegraph* and the *Independent*.

Shortlisted for the Aruther C. Clarke Award twice and the BSFA seven times, he won the BSFA Award for best novel with *Felaheen* featuring Asraf Bey, his half-Berber detective. He won it again with *End of the World Blues*, about a British ex-sniper running an Irish bar in Tokyo.

His work is published in French, German, Spanish, Polish, Czech, Hungarian, Russian, Turkish, Japanese, Finnish and American among others. He is married to the journalist and novelist Sam Baker, currently editor-in-chief of *Red* magazine. They divide their time between London and Winchester.

Find out more about Jon Courtenay Grimwood and other Orbit authors by registering for the free monthly newslettter at www.orbitbooks.net

if you enjoyed
THE FALLEN BLADE

look out for

THE FOLLY OF
THE WORLD

by

Jesse Bullington

Feast of the Annunciation 1422

"The Topsy-Turvy World"

The little boat slowed, both rowers setting their oars and kicking up amber water as they came to the willow wood bordering the village of Oudeland. In all directions the meer stretched flat and cold, but here at last the smooth expanse yielded to what lurked beneath it. The craft brushed the treetops, the few dead willow shoots that broke the filmy surface snapping like old rushes as the boat drifted through them. The two men peered over their respective sides, murmuring to each other where larger boughs threatened the belly of their vessel. Gray bream huddled in the rotting nests of their former hunters, eels festooned through the branches like Carnival ribbons.

The boat slid between the last fence posts of dead limbs, and then the town itself was beneath them. It was a shadow village, without thatch for its roofs to keep out the wet and the cold, without paint or color for its disintegrating shutters and doors, without any sun at all, only a vague, shimmering moon, never waxing, never warming. The mill had kept its blades but the great fan felt no wind in the ever-gloaming depths, yet all clotheslines and carts and even the well house had long since blown away. The boat scudded over Oudeland, quiet as thieves in a church or leaves on a lake, and there at last rose the old elm, what had once been the tallest tree in thirty leagues now only a tangled, naked bush pushing out of the water like a mean clump of blackthorn on the edge of a canal.

It had been a grand tree for climbing, if one could get a leg up to the lower branches, and one of the two men recalled the feel of rough bark against rough palm, the sound of laughter above and below, as close to flying as any could come in this life. Yet here they came, like unquiet spirits returning through the air, and with wonder they saw a figure balanced there in the boughs of the elm, waiting. They coasted past the bell tower of the church, a wide mooring post with a thorny crown where four herons had recently come of egg and age, and then the nose of the boat nuzzled the branches of the elm, the men staring at its keeper.

Much of the ram's hide had come away in greedy beakfuls, but enough had hardened in the sun to lash it to the boughs, a sunbleached and waterworn puppet tangled in the treetop. Its bare, eyeless skull was tilted upward with jaw agape, like a child catching snow or rain, and its forelegs were spread and caught amongst the branches, as if it were falling into flight or rising to crucifixion. The two men in the boat stared in silence at the ram, the vessel motionless upon the face of the deep, the moment seeming to stretch on and on, longer than all the roads and rivers in the world, and behind them, beneath them, the wheel of the mill mutely turned, kicking up silt as a great shadow slid past its mossy blades.

All Saints Day 1422

"Shitting Upon the Gallows"

Heaven bled when they took Sander from his cell, the condemned man scowling into the East as if offended by dawn's decision to attend his execution. In Dordrecht the harbors would be turning to molten gold, the walls of the city transforming into the gossamer white robes of angels, but here in Sneek the first light of morning shone only on shit, and all the alchemists in the witch-riddled West couldn't turn a turd into more than what it was. These were the thoughts Sander harbored as the cart he stood in squelched through the muddy square to the gallows-tree, and not even the rotten apples and clods of filth the mob hurled at him could detract from the thrill of anticipation. They were going to hang him, and Sander grinned as he spied the thick hempen rope. A ball of horse dung struck him on the teeth, the thankfully dry clump leaving an earthy taste in his mouth as he spit into the cheers of the crowd. He focused on the noose, trying to secure the burgeoning erection already firming up in his breeches—he was going to enjoy this.

Sander assumed that most people in his circumstance dreamed of escape, reprieve, *something*, but he would not allow himself the indulgence. Nor did he dwell on the life that had led him to this doomed place as surely as if he had followed a path without fork or intersection, much as men in his place are thought to. Were he to hang, the vast conspiracy he had carefully navigated, like a man creeping over an uncertain fen, would never be fully understood; the countless secret enemies who had orchestrated this farcical display would go unpunished...but he did not deign to give them his ruminations. No, Sander thought only of rope, coils of it wrapping around his ankles and thighs and balls and waist and chest and arms and elbows and wrists and, especially, his neck. Itchy, tight, sinuous rope constricting him until there was nothing left but braided, bloody knots.

That thought was what helped him fall asleep on nights when the dream-countries proved elusive, but now was not the time to linger on such fantasies, and he knew it. His heart beat faster as he looked around the town square, saw the hundred contorted faces of the crowd, lit for a moment on the desperate thought of *Escape*! like a horsefly flirting with a butcher's apron, and then settled back on rope. Cord was what bound his hands behind his back—also hemp, thick as his thumb, tied in his cell before they led him to the wagon. Sander flexed his hands, confirming the make of the knot he could not see and smiling all the wider. He let his fingertips curl up to stroke the knot a single time and then spread his hands again; a gull's wings taking flight, an over-bloomed rose falling apart.

A pair of guards with crude pikes waited at the stairs of the gibbet. As the wagon jerked to a stop, each hopped into the bed and grabbed one of Sander's elbows. He thought he recognized them as militiamen from some other town, some other setup, but quickly calmed himself. Bland, halfwit boys like these were a pfennig a bushel, and so odds were they were local muscle, which would legitimize it all as far as Sneek was concerned. Fools. A priest and the hangman waited on the platform, and the guards brought Sander forward, their tugging on his arms causing the binding cord to cut into his wrists. His cock throbbed from the sensation.

There was no trapdoor awaiting the convict, only a shove off the edge of the cramped platform, and the guards stayed on the final step as they delivered Sander to his death. The hangman wore no hood, only a stupid-looking feathered cap, and the edge of the priest's habit was powdered with dry dust instead of wet muck—he must have raised it like a noblewoman careful of her skirts when he left his church. A man in the crowd swallowed from his bottle too quickly and choked on it. The things Sander noticed as the hangman slipped the noose around his broad neck and yanked it tight.

"Sander Himbrecht," the priest said without raising his voice, and it took several moments for the tide of elbows and hisses to work its way back through the crowd until the morning was as quiet as it should have been had men never learned to speak. Sander couldn't properly converse in the garbled garbage-tongue of the Frisian, but like many people of the South, he usually got the thrust of what was barked at him by the stiffheads. The priest said something like, "Sander Himbrecht, you stand here a dead man, but need not fall a damned one. It is established you shall serve as an example to what wages a blackguard and killer is paid in Sneek, but here at last is a chance to also demonstrate the power of repentance, of salvation at the cusp of ruin."

Something like that, only like as not less pretty-sounding— priest or no, Frisians were not known for their eloquence.

"Hang the dicksucker!" said a straw-haired, wheat-mustachioed man at the front of the crowd. Sander understood that bit perfectly. "Don't let 'em off, Father!"

Sander licked his lips, the man's outburst a confirmation that they knew much more than they should, each and all of them. That this was inevitable as sin, that he was flat-out lucky they weren't having him quartered instead. Sander rubbed his wrists against the rope, eyes flicking to the blond heckler and back to the priest, breathing deep to better feel the noose against his throat, his cock positively aching up against his breeches like a drowning man kicking his last to break the surface of the water. He knew the priest was waiting for him, but he also knew the hangman had an unobstructed view of his back, and so he turned a bit to better put the clergyman between himself and the executioner as he stalled. The old boy had a strip of red cloth in his shaky hands, and Sander smiled at the realization that in Sneek they must have the priest do the blindfolding after the last rites and all—funny, that, and a far cry from the communion he was expecting.

"It's like this," Sander said quietly, not even trying to ape the stiffhead dialect. "I would if I could, but I'm not, so I can't, yeah?"

"Not what?" said the priest in proper-talk, evidently a learned man who knew a real language when he heard it.

"Look." Sander nodded down. Behind him, he relaxed his aching wrists from the strained position he had held them in all morning, before they had even bound him. If they had used baling twine or something thinner, he might have been in real trouble, but—

"What is it?" The priest blinked at the condemned man's damp, diaphanous tunic, as if Sander were trying to point out an especially interesting stain. Then Sander knew the older man had found it, his eyes opening wide as silver double-groots, his lips pursing tighter than the strings on his purse. To seal the deal, Sander bore down a little, making his cock nod upward at the priest through his thin breeches and thinner tunic. There was a moment of silence on the platform as the ancient stared at Sander's unmistakable bulge and Sander grinned over the priest's shoulder at the hangman.

"He's getting loose!" someone in the crowd with a vantage of Sander's back shouted.

In response, Sander bit the priest on the face.

Brown teeth met brown stubble and were proved the victor, bumpy cheek yielding to smooth enamel, and Sander tasted blood. His left hand came free of the amateur knot, loosing its twin in the process, but before he could properly grab hold of the priest, the hangman lunged forward and shoved Sander. A lesser executioner might not have dislodged him from the priest, but the hangman had a smith's arm, and Sander came away with but a flap of skin and meat as he pitched from the platform.

Sander's left hand caught the rope as he fell, and an instant before it went taut, he flexed all his muscle, saving himself a snapped neck at the cost of a dislocated elbow. His arm immediately dropped limp and the noose clamped tight around his throat. Sander did not let the glorious distraction of being hanged consume him, and as he was strangled, he kicked his legs in the air to spin around. It worked, and he twirled in the air almost too quickly.

Almost, but not quite. As the chest-level platform swung into his tear-blurring vision, he saw the feet and hands of the sprawled-out priest. More importantly, he saw the hangman's heel coming down to stomp his shoulder and affect what the drop should have, had he not caught the rope in time. With his right arm Sander snatched the hangman's boot and jerked him downward, which tightened the noose even more. The startled lummox tumbled from the platform, lamely slapping the air as he fell past the still-spinning Sander. The familiar black wheels were spinning larger and faster in Sander's vision, and though it pained him, he reflexively heaved his injured left arm to his crotch and rubbed himself as the platform came back around.

Slapping his right arm down beside the half-prone priest and focusing all his strength, Sander arrested his spin. Clawing his arm forward, he dug his fingernails into the platform until he could verily taste the oak splinters through his quick. His right elbow set beside that of the doubled-over priest, Sander heaved himself onto the platform. The hangman knew his business well, however, and so the noose did not relax even as Sander scrambled to his feet on the wooden deck. Before he could get his fingers under the rope to save himself, the two guards on the stair shook off their shock and rushed forward, jabbing at him with their pikes. Sander hooked the elbow of his good arm under the now-wailing priest, hoisting him upright in the nick of time. The clergyman accepted both spear points in his chest as easily as he accepted the more exciting confessions from the young women of Sneek. One pike became entangled in the priest's ribs, but the other broke clean through the man, nicking Sander's left shoulder.

Even without the dying priest grinding against him from the

impact Sander would have come then, the noose too tight, the hemp too coarse. Delicious. Even as he grunted his satisfaction, he got his fingers under the rope collar and jerked it loose, gasping like a landed herring from more than the release in his breeches. He had dropped the priest, but the guards still held the man aloft with their weapons, neither sure what to do given the circumstances.

The tunnel of Sander's consciousness expanded to take in exactly what had happened, and he tried to laugh but gagged instead. Pulling a face as he widened the noose, he slipped it over his head just as several crossbow bolts whizzed past him and the fallen hangman regained the platform behind the horrified guards. Sander kicked the priest in the back, driving him deeper onto the pikes and managing an actual laugh through his dry retching fit. He had known it would be a grand day but could never have anticipated such a glorious fiasco.

That said, getting out of the ropes was the easy part; getting out of town was where things got tricky. What kind of savages held their executions in the main square, instead of outside the village walls like civilized folk? *Stiffheads*. Going on the wave of furious peasants crashing below him at the edge of the platform, his killing of their priest was not liable to make his escape any easier—even those who hadn't been actively involved in the plot to hang him would certainly want him dead now. There were only a few streets leading out of the thronged square, and even the one behind the gibbet was a good fifty paces off. Tempting though it suddenly was to simply give up, Sander knew they probably wouldn't still be satisfied with a hanging given the recent turn of events, and he would be damned before he went to his maker in any other fashion.

Well, then, he had to do something. Sander jumped from the platform, landing feetfirst on a fat man. They both hit the ground hard, but Sander rolled forward and onto his feet as his human cushion spit blood and teeth.

They were on him then, the edge of the mob washing over

him, but Sander was a dirty son of a bitch's bastard's whore, and what's more, he knew it. The citizens of Sneek should have suspected that a man willing to bite a priest would not shirk from snatching a scrotum or poking out an eye if he could, but in their fury to catch him they failed to consider this. Thus, the first man to lay hands on Sander had his testicles crushed and twisted by thick fingers, and the second had his left eyeball hooked viciously with a thumb, the entire orb popping loose of its socket and bouncing against the poor fellow's cheek.

Three fists and a knife connected with Sander. The knuckles bounced off his leathery skin, but as he twisted away, the knife carved a neat little flap in his already bloodied, dangling left arm. Then he saw it. Saw *her*. The pommel of his beloved had appeared just beside him, and he caught a glimpse of brown hair and brown eyes, a handsome face he loved more than jellied herring or fresh beer materializing from the mob—

—But then the weapon was in hand and her hooded deliverer swallowed back up by the crowd, and Sander howled with joy to once again wield Glory's End.

Her blade had been recently whetted, and in bringing the sword up to put her between himself and the crowd he clipped off three of a man's fingers. Before Sander could get a proper swing across, the crowd had already fallen back, and he used the moment to catch his breath. He had a clean break to the side street he had been making for, but then he saw three militiamen with crossbows atop the platform, their weapons leveled at him. Before he could blink, the bows fired.

And, incredibly, all missed. One quarrel whipped through his long, manky hair, the other two splashing into the muck at his feet. Sander stared at them for a moment, grinned, and ran away. The crowd recovered its courage at the sight of his back and followed after.

Sander gained the side street…and ran directly into four more militiamen, likely shirkers late to the execution. Their pikes were not leveled, praise to the appropriate saints, sparing Sander an end similar to that of the priest. Glory's End flashed in the shadows of the alley, and before the first man realized he was disemboweled, the second was hacked to the collarbone, both falling in a welter of gore and blood as their stunned compatriots stumbled back. Sander kept moving, tagging another on the knee as he fled down the street. The man shifted his weight the slightest bit and immediately pitched forward, gasping as the thin red slit in his beige leggings split into a yawning fissure of wet muscle and exposed bone, and the fourth militiaman stared aghast after the demon who had butchered his friends.

The alley opened onto a lane between rows of squat, tightly packed houses, and glancing back over his shoulder, Sander saw the mob only half a block behind him, the hangman now leading them. Sander turned left, booking it for all he was worth down the narrow street. Left turned out to be a rather poor decision, as another group of militiamen rounded a bend before him, but he only ran faster, making it to another alley just before the new crew reached him. This avenue was clogged with low-hanging laundry, the lines of which Sander cut as he ran to bring the drying clothes down on his pursuers. Sander laughed to hear the shouts behind him become angrier still, and then burst through the last row of dangling sheets and toppled into the canal into which the alley terminated, Glory's End flying from his hand as he struck the gray water and sank like a millstone.

VISIT THE ORBIT BLOG AT

www.orbitbooks.net

FEATURING

**BREAKING NEWS
FORTHCOMING RELEASES
LINKS TO AUTHOR SITES
EXCLUSIVE INTERVIEWS
EARLY EXTRACTS**

AND COMMENTARY FROM
OUR EDITORS

With regular updates from our team,
orbitbooks.net is your source
for all things orbital

•

While you're there, join our email list
to receive information on special offers,
giveaways, and more

•

Find us on Facebook at www.facebook.com/orbitbooksUK
Follow us on Twitter @orbitbooks

imagine. explore. engage.

orbit

www.orbitbooks.net